WITHIN THIS FRAME

FROM USA TODAY BESTSELLING AUTHOR
LINDY ZART

Within This Frame
Lindy Zart
Published 2015 by Lindy Zart
Copyright 2015 Lindy Zart

ISBN-13: 978–1517572488
ISBN-10: 1517572487

Cover by:
Cover to Cover Designs

Cover Photography Credit:
Kelley C. Hanson

Formatted by:
Perfectly Publishable

Edited by:
Wendi Stitzer

This book is a work of fiction.

Names, characters, places, and incidents either are products of the author's imagination or are used fictitiously. Any resemblance to actual events or locales or persons, living or dead, is entirely coincidental.

All rights reserved. Printed in the United States of America. No part of this book may be used or reproduced in any manner whatsoever without written permission except in the case of brief quotations embodied in critical articles and reviews.

To my grandmothers Betha and Mary—with love.

From Jamie, a reader:

I judge the way I look, the way I talk, how unorganized I am and how my anxiety issues make me boring or seem crazy. I could go on and on. I am 28 and I still struggle regularly, probably more than I did as a teen or young adult. I know what it is like to not like yourself and to constantly tear yourself down. I'm the queen of self-deprecation. Anyway I think everyone has issues with themselves to some degree, and I hope others out there realize that the only one who even cares enough to judge you as harshly as you think people do is you. Everyone else is in their own little world full of their own issues and too busy worrying about themselves to really care about the shortcomings we beat ourselves up over every day.

MAGGIE—2010

SHE DIDN'T UNDERSTAND how something so pretty could be lethal. The card was cream vellum with words tinged in gold abounding from it. Appealing to look at, deadly to read. Each word pulled her farther into despair the further she read. It was a joke. It had to be a joke.

It wasn't a joke.

Maggie realized she had the invitation crumpled between her fingers and let it fall from her limp hand to rest upon the kitchen table. Her eyes unseeingly grazed each surface of the spacious, cheery salmon and butter yellow room until they came back to the small piece of paper. She stared at it as though it was a venomous snake, poised to strike. Strangely enough, she'd already felt the piercing of it, right into her being.

She checked the date on the invitation. September 5th was roughly four months away. Maggie took a deep breath and crossed the room to get to the foyer. Once there, she stopped before the mirror to examine herself. Could she do it? A frown of displeasure was glued to her face.

A list of names swept through her mind: Benton Jamison. Tabitha Volden. Judith Fletcher. Steven Stephens.

Lance Denton.

That last one dug in like a blade to the heart and she swallowed around the painful pulse of it.

They weren't the only names that had ever held importance to her, but they were the ones she'd never forgotten. Each name elicited a mixture of determination and hopelessness. Could she face them all again? There was no doubt in her mind that most, if not all, of the aforementioned would be there.

She had varying reasons for not wanting to see them—some because she loathed them and others because she adored them.

With trepidation, Maggie opened the purple robe and cringed at the sight that met her reflection. She tried to avoid her image as much as she could because it depressed her. There were bulges where there shouldn't be, more hips than she cared to see, and flesh that sagged. Four months. How could she possibly shed the extra thirty pounds she'd gained over years in months?

There was one person Maggie knew could help her and she really didn't want to contact her. That would give Nora a reason to raise her perfectly arched eyebrows and smile her triumphant smile. Unease slithered down Maggie's back like talons of dread. She retrieved her cell phone from the antique desk in the foyer and headed toward the back of the house. She opened the kitchen patio doors and stepped outside onto the sunlit deck.

Maggie took a deep breath and hit her sister's number.

All her good intentions flew away as soon as Nora answered with, "Bacon! I haven't talked to you in months. Since Easter, yes? When you took a nosedive into the chocolate pudding pie."

"Hello, Nora." She ground her teeth together before she could stop herself.

Maggie glared at the copse of maple trees that shaded her from the sun, their branches reaching down like leafy arms. The longer she stared at the foliage surrounding her yard, the calmer she became. She sat down and focused on the therapeutic sound of trickling water from the manmade pond located directly beneath those bountiful trees. Agitation began to seep from her limbs.

"We should do lunch, play catch up. When and where? I'm pretty busy, but I can fit you in next Tuesday. You're my sister, after all."

Tension prickled her skin like angry gnat bites and she shifted uncomfortably on the wrought iron bench. "Actually, I wanted to ask you something."

"Oh? What is it?"

She gnawed on the inside of her lower lip until she tasted blood. "Is there a personal trainer from your gym you would recommend to work with me?"

The pause on the other end of the line was profound, and nerve-wracking.

"For?" Nora finally asked.

"I have an event coming up and want to get in shape before it," Maggie said in a rush.

Nora squealed and Maggie briefly pulled the cell phone away from her ear. "It's about time! You have no idea how happy hearing that makes me." Some of her enthusiasm diminished when she continued. "We're short-staffed at the moment, but I could come over after seven every night to work with you."

"No! I mean, I couldn't. That would be taking advantage of you and your business. Also, I thought . . . I thought I might listen better to a guy," she lied. It was bad enough asking Nora for help, there was no way she would survive dealing with her on a daily basis.

"Oh." Disappointment flooded the word and guilt washed over Maggie. "I'll ask around. Like I said, we're short-staffed right now, but we do work with private trainers once in a while. I'll look through the list and set something up.

"How soon do you want to start? I recommend tomorrow, at least to talk to them anyway. You'll also want them to make up a meal plan for you. I'd toss out the bacon you got stockpiled before they show up." Nora laughed.

Maggie wanted to say she didn't even eat bacon anymore, but that would be a lie.

"Yeah. Right. Thanks."

"Do you have a scale? If not, I know some good ones you can purchase. You need—"

"I have to go now. Cake in the oven," she interrupted and ended the call to the sound of her sister's gasp.

Maggie set down the phone and the itchy, irritated feeling faded once more. Warm wind rustled her shoulder length auburn waves. She shifted on the bench and squinted against the sunlight as it rayed her skin and heated up her scalp.

The more she thought about it, the more determined she became. She just needed a little push in the right direction, someone to help her make better food decisions and motivate her to exercise. Excitement stamped her face with a bright smile.

Realizing she hadn't had lunch yet, Maggie made her way back inside and perused the refrigerator contents. Leftover pizza beckoned from the top shelf. It was topped with a rainbow of vegetables in the form of green and black olives, tomatoes, red onions, mushrooms, and green peppers. Fingers tight around the refrigerator door, she told herself it couldn't be that unhealthy for her.

Move along.

There was expired yogurt, wilted lettuce, and crabmeat to choose from in place of the pizza.

She applauded herself on her show of willpower as she reached for the crabmeat instead of the pizza, but it soon left her as she melted butter for it.

"It's healthy . . . ish," Maggie muttered as she sat at the white table and popped a butter-laden morsel in her mouth.

LANCE—1996

SHE WAS LOOKING at him in that way again—the expression on her face one he couldn't put into words, but to which he was simultaneously pulled and repelled. He'd been the recipient of similar looks since he was twelve. Lance offered a small smile from where he stood across the room and immediately looked away. Let her wonder if that smile was intended for her or someone else.

"All right, people!" Herman Lyle clapped his hands. His vocal volume was set for 'headache inducing loud' at all times. "It's almost time to film the first scene of 'Easier Said'. I'm so excited I could shit myself."

Some laughter followed that, but there were more rolled eyes and humoring looks than anything. Herman Lyle was a schmuck. It was by pure chance that he'd been hired to direct 'Easier Said', and they'd soon enough find out if that was a good thing.

The show was primarily set in an oversized cottage with blue siding, a red door, and brown shingles. Lance liked the neutral tones found inside and the plain brown furniture. He'd pick it over the interior of his dad's house any day. The central air was on, but with the dozen or so people cramped into the downstairs of the house, it didn't feel like it.

"Let's do one more read-through before initial filming begins! Derek, Cecilia, take your places."

Herman's bald head turned in a shiny circle as he searched for his main characters. He found Maggie, timid and silent, near Judith Fletcher, the actress hired to play her mom on the show. Judith offered Maggie one of her sparkly smiles and a pat on the head, like she was a pet. Herman pointed at Maggie and jerked his thumb back to where he wanted her.

"Derek! Get out here!" Herman bellowed as he dabbed a stained red handkerchief against the sweat dripping from his fleshy, overheated face.

"It's Lance," Lance said as he disengaged from the wall and moved toward the director.

"It's Derek in about two seconds."

Lance offered a smile, but it wasn't a friendly one.

Maggie hesitantly made her way to him, hands clasped together and head tilted down. Lance usually liked skinny girls, but his body liked her curves well enough. Sixteen years old and recently initiated into the world of sex, he was eager to experiment with any and all kinds of the female population.

Stop thinking about sex before you embarrass yourself.

Her looks were unoriginal until she lifted those eyes, as she did then. He hated her eyes. They weren't really brown—almost red in certain lighting, too big for her face, and framed with thick, long eyelashes that should be creepy but were instead pretty. Her eyes sank into him like they could see all of him. It made him uncomfortable.

Maggie offered a shy smile as she stopped beside him and he nodded before turning his gaze away. He caught the fall of her smile, felt guilty about it, and told himself to quit being a wimp.

"Where are you two supposed to be? Not where you are," Herman answered himself, motioning for them to move. "Outside. Let's take this outside."

The first scene was to take place at Cecilia Monroe's house. Due to his parents divorcing, Derek Ryan recently moved to the area and was her neighbor. In a twist on the customary guardianship placement, he lived with his dad instead of his mom. Used to being popular and well-known in a small town, he was relocated to a city where no one knew him.

Cecilia befriended him over the summer and Derek thought she was cool, until school started and he realized how uncool she was. The basis of the show was forged in an unlikely friendship that transformed into love as the years went on, if the show made it that long. Each episode had a conflict and resolution, most of them cheesy to Lance, but like the show writers cared about his opinion. Maggie Smiley also was not his first choice as love interest for the show—not even second or third.

He walked toward the front door and out it. Lance's skin was instantly saturated with sweat, the humidity in the air making it hard to breathe. Virginia in the summer was unbearable at times. He squinted against the sun, wishing he had the day off. He'd be at the beach playing volleyball and hanging out with his friends, checking out chicks—what any normal teenage guy would be doing on a hot summer day. Any normal teenage guy that wasn't an actor, he corrected.

"Makeup girl! You! Yes, you. Freshen up the kiddies. They have sweat. Remove the sweat," the director hollered.

The faint scent of oranges reached him and Lance glanced over his shoulder. Maggie, dressed in a turquoise sundress, stood behind him. Her skin was as pale as snow, lips kissed with pink. She looked like a summer picture, nothing about her needing a touchup. Jackie Miller, in her early twenties and hot for him, blotted Maggie's skin anyway.

With a coy smile, she did the same to him, but slower. Jackie winked at him when their gazes clashed. She wasn't the first older woman to hit on him. He'd lost his virginity to a nineteen-year-old close to a year ago. Because of his body, muscle tone, and deep voice, people thought he was older than he was. And when they found out his real age, it didn't make a difference.

"Stop fondling the minor, Jackie," Herman said dryly. One thing could be said for Herman Lyle—he said what he wanted and didn't care what anyone thought. That might have something to do with his two disorderly conduct misdemeanors and six-month stint on probation.

With a droop to her shoulders and a blush on her cheeks, Jackie hurried back toward the masses of people necessary to put a television show together. They were faces instead of people to Lance. A few of them stood out to him—like Jackie—but most of them did their jobs and held no interest for him, unless he directly had to interact with them.

"Positions!"

Maggie swept by him, close enough that her citrus scent messed with his senses for a second and a long strand of reddish-brown hair caressed his arm. His body tightened and he blew out a noisy breath, shaking his head. Lance avoided looking at her as he took his spot near the crew workers.

An excited buzz started, bringing with it a hum of tension, but when Herman shot his beady brown eyes at the ones conversing, it got quiet quick.

Herman knelt before Maggie, probably talking in what he thought was a quiet, reassuring voice that was actually loud and commanding. "Remember, Cecilia, this is a leisure day for you. Think peaceful. You're happy it's summer, you're enjoying the sun. The book you're reading is poetic and captivating. You're not simpleminded, but you're easily pleased. You see Lance and you want to extend that to him, especially with how troubled he looks. Got all that?"

He waited until she nodded before standing with a groan as his back popped.

A hush fell, even traffic on the street seemed to pause, and with a frown, Lance lifted his head to gaze at Maggie. He went still and silent as well. It was aweing to watch the transformation take place. Maggie's expression softened, her eyes widened, and a faint slackness of her mouth turned her small lips fuller, but also gave her a young, innocent look.

Looking at her was like looking at a picture out of focus. Surreal.

When Maggie lifted her head, she wasn't Maggie Smiley anymore. She was Cecilia Monroe. He was enthralled by her talent, how she could change her whole demeanor with a few small changes to her facial expression and stance. In that moment, Lance fell a little in love with her.

Herman wordlessly motioned Lance forward when he forgot to move.

Derek Ryan was easy for Lance to portray because he was a lot like him, even down to living with his dad instead of his mom. Lance's parents had never been married and his mom died from a drug overdose when he was two, but there were other similarities. Derek was popular and good at sports. So was Lance. Derek was cocky. Lance had been called that, and worse, a time or two. "Little shit" was usually added to the "cocky" part. Derek was good-looking. Lance winked at Maggie as he strode toward her. He'd never been called anything less.

Her eyes dipped to the pages of the book she held, but he saw her chest rise and fall faster than it had before the wink. Luckily no one else noticed or he'd get chewed out for messing with her before a final read-through. Judith Fletcher was especially protective of the Iowa native staying in Virginia.

"Hey." He stopped by her feet, noting the peach shade of polish on her toenails.

Lost in the book, she didn't respond.

Lance looked up and down the street before returning his gaze to her. Irritation lining his features, he repeated, "Hey!"

Maggie's character was supposed to be surprised and she pulled it off beautifully when she jolted to her feet, dropping the book in the process. Her skin turned pink. Flustered, she reached down for the book and swooped it into her arms to hold against her chest like a talisman to ward off impure advances.

"Hey. Hi. Hello." She chewed on her lower lip and tried to smile. "Who are you?"

"Who are you?" he shot back. Lance's character was angry at the world, but especially at his father for relocating them. He decided to be angry at the unknown girl too, just because she was near him and seemed easy to intimidate.

"Cecilia Monroe. I live here."

"I gathered that. Derek Ryan. My dad and I are moving in next door." He jerked his head in the direction of their pretend house. "He says you have the key."

Her mouth pursed. "No. I don't have a key."

Lance rubbed the back of his neck. "Are your parents home?"

Looking confused, she answered, "Yes. But I won't have the key whether they're home or not."

A few chuckles rang out at how well Maggie played the clueless girl.

Exasperation interlaced his words as he said, "Look, we have a U-Haul out back full of stuff and my dad's waiting for me to bring him the key. The landlord said someone at this house is supposed to know where it is. Can you see if either of your parents have it?"

"Sure." Maggie turned and walked up to the door.

Once there, she whirled around to face him, the bottom of her dress slowly following the motion of her hips. The look on her face grabbed Lance's throat and squeezed. Hope was etched into her raised eyebrows, shyness reddened her cheeks, and the way her eyes sparkled with friendliness made it hard for him to swallow.

It's not real. It's just an act. This girl is a character. Cecilia Monroe does not exist.

"Would you like to come in? I made cookies and lemonade this morning. There's nothing better than cookies and lemonade on a day like today."

Lance's eyes dropped. In his interpretation of Derek, his mom used to make cookies every Sunday and he'd have a tall glass of milk with the treat. His dad would steal a few and go back to work on his novel in the den. It was also a frequent scene Lance imagined in his version of a perfect world. The unnecessary kindness a stranger showed a jaded boy unraveled something tight inside Derek.

He looked up and offered a small smile. "I'd like that."

"Acceptable!" was the immediate shout from Herman. He hurried to Lance and clapped his shoulder, bringing the scent of onions and garlic with him. "Not bad, Denton. Maggie, you were brilliant." He divided his gaze between the teenagers. "Think you can do it again, but better, and with the camera rolling? Of course you can! Let's go!"

Maggie caught his eye roll and smiled. "He's ferocious, isn't he?"

"Like a pit bull," Lance agreed.

MAGGIE—2010

THE DOORBELL RANG in three quick successions.

Maggie sprang into a sitting position and wildly eyed her surroundings before she realized what was going on: she had been asleep, in her bed, until some jerk decided to wake her up. She put a hand to her matted hair, brushing wayward strands from her eyes, and heaved herself from the bed. Grabbing the robe from the settee, she slid her arms through the sleeves and knotted the tie at her waist.

A glance at the clock on the wall told her it was seven in the morning. With a groan, she clomped down the stairs to the foyer. A normal day got her out of bed around eight, sometimes nine. Seven in the morning was a number she rarely saw on the clock.

"This better be important," Maggie mumbled to herself as she swung open the door.

She met dark blue eyes and a taunting smile, felt her heart explode in her chest, and immediately slammed the door shut. Maggie then spun around to rest her back against it so she didn't crumple to the floor. She knew those eyes, that mouth. She'd been intimately acquainted with the man to whom they belonged. It had been years since she'd seen him in person, but he hadn't changed that much. If anything, he looked better, which was unfair.

Maggie splayed her palms against the cool wood of the door and counted to thirty as she told herself to not freak out. She hallucinated him. He wasn't really there. Too much late night sugar was getting to not only her body, but her head as well.

It was time to stop that shit.

The doorbell rang again. Maggie covered her face and groaned. He was really there. Her chest was tight and each lungful of air she sucked in was painful. Lifting a hand, Maggie stared at the way it trembled. She had on no makeup, her hair was a nest. She weighed a lot more than the last time she'd seen him and she had on a pink and yellow cat-print robe.

When she didn't budge, the knocks began. Firm, consistent thumps that sounded every ten seconds.

Why is he here? He has no reason to be here. Ever.

Just get it over with. Let him laugh and say whatever it is he has to say, and then he'll go away.

Fear bunched her stomach in knots, told her she was deluding herself. Well, why not? She was good at it.

Maggie took the doorknob within her hand and carefully turned it, hoping he would magically be gone once the door was fully opened. She could deal with insanity, but Lance Denton, not so much. She looked up and deflated against the doorframe. He was still there, still smiling, still too good-looking. His gaze was piercing, locked on her in a way that made her insides twist.

"Why are you here?" Maggie considered herself a nice person, normally, but if anyone could change that with their presence, it was the guy who stood on her doorstep.

"You asked for me."

She snorted. "Pretty sure you're the last person I would ask for."

"Wasn't I?" His tone went quietly seductive, laser eyes zapping her with their heat.

Maggie tried to swallow and found that function no longer available to her. His eyes traveled up and down her frame, mockery clear in them as they stopped on hers. Lance's facial features were sharper than she recalled, and the stubble along his jaw was new as well. She knew he was judging her appearance, him with his super fit body and her with her unfit one. Well, she was judging too. Sadly, she couldn't come up with any needed improvements on his end.

"Why are you here? Remember that time, long, long ago, when we decided we wouldn't see each other again?"

He cocked his dark head and looked deep in thought. "Was that what we decided? I thought it was you deciding you despised the very air I breathed, and couldn't stand the thought of sharing such a thing with me anymore."

"Well, I couldn't maim you, so the logical alternative was to never see you again," she said sweetly. Fire scorched her veins and heated her skin. The last time Maggie had seen Lance, she'd told him she hated him and never wanted to speak to him again.

"Oh, but you did," Lance whispered, seeming closer and yet not moving an inch.

"Did . . . what?" she choked, reeling from the fact that Lance Denton stood before her, looking at her, talking to her. Being.

"Maim me—right here, right where it counts the most." He patted his chest, expression mocking even as his eyes were indecipherable.

Maggie's eyes narrowed. "I doubt it."

The somberness cleared from his face and amusement simultaneously put stars in his eyes and lightened them. "You would."

"Fun time is over. You came, you saw, you laughed. Now go." She pointed a finger over his shoulder and hoped he'd move in the direction it faced.

"Don't you want to know why I'm here?"

"Not really."

Instead of leaving, he straightened and posed in a way that showed off his toned upper half through the yellow shirt he wore. "You probably already know this, but along with being superbly talented as an actor and model, I'm a trained fitness expert, personal trainer, and nutritionist."

He flexed a bicep and looked from it to her face. He rotated his shoulders, showed her his profile, and winked. "Your sister's gym called me yesterday and told me you were in need of someone of my expertise."

Maggie's throat went dry, and then her mouth, and then her eyes.

"Obviously I can't refuse a cry for help from Cecilia Monroe. What would fans think of Derek Ryan if I did?" He stopped preening long enough to look at her in a way that meant she should understand what he was saying.

"The same thing they thought before—that you're a selfish, egotistical, narcissistic ass."

"Ouch." With a sigh, Lance dropped his arms. "You do know I'm a fitness expert, right?" At her dubious look, he said, "Oh, come on, you had to have seen some of my promotional stuff on TV."

"Whenever I have the misfortune to catch a glimpse of your face on

TV, I change the channel."

"Must do a lot of channel surfing then."

"I'm closing the door now. There is no way I'm working with you. I'd rather work with my sister." Maggie shuddered and moved to push the door shut, but Lance quickly put up his hand to stop it. She met his eyes. "Let go."

"No," he said cheerfully.

A scowl took over her mouth and she shoved harder, but Lance was an unmovable wall, and the door merely inched forward. His expression said it all: See? You're a pudgy wimp. You need me to make you strong, and hopefully get you slimmed down as well, if we can keep the doughnuts out of your hands. With an angry exhalation of air, Maggie stepped back quickly and Lance stumbled into the entryway. He shot upright and gave her a look, smoothing black locks that didn't need it.

He looked around the space. "You go for the old look, huh?"

"It's not old. It's antiquated," she corrected, crossing her arms when she remembered she didn't have on a bra and his eyes liked to wander.

"Whatever you say." He paused. "Show me around."

"No!" The word was loud and violently executed, and the look he aimed her way hinted that he wondered at her mental stability.

Maggie sucked in a sharp breath that was meant to be calming, and blew it out with excessive force. It didn't calm her down. "I'm not showing you my house. I'm not hiring you. I'll find someone else."

"There is no one else. That's why I was called. I'm sort of all you got."

"Now, wouldn't that be a horrible, horrible predicament in which to find oneself, having to rely on you for anything of importance."

Lance rubbed his jaw. "I don't remember you being this feisty when we were younger."

"That's because I didn't know enough to stay away from you."

He didn't move, but the way he looked at her took all the space between them and crushed it. "You knew."

Maggie swallowed. She couldn't refute that. She had known what Lance Denton was like, from the very first day of their acquaintance, but it hadn't mattered enough to keep her away. She couldn't stay away—he was ablaze with life and danger and rawness and she was pulled to him, wanting to dance along the shadows of his presence.

"And if you didn't, I warned you."

Another truth. It was time to move on.

"What do you get out of this, other than my humiliation?"

"Money?"

She snorted. "You have to have loads of that lying around. I'm sure you wash your body and brush your teeth with it. Wipe your butt . . ."

Lance didn't answer, giving her a look.

Maggie glanced down at his bare ring finger. "Aren't you supposed to be in England or Australia or whatever foreign country you inhabit with your wife and daughter during the winter and spring months?"

His smile evaporated. It was interesting how dark his face went. "Recently divorced."

She'd known that. "Oh. Is that why you're here? I thought you lived in Florida part of the time."

"I did."

Lance's abrupt tone let Maggie know she'd hit a nerve. She decided to torture it a little bit. "Why are you in Iowa then?"

"Don't you know, Maggie?" he whispered, voice and eyes beseeching. He lifted a finger and trailed it along her jaw, tingles following his touch. "You."

She swallowed, struck speechless. Shaking her head, she got her wits back in order and glared at him. "You're good," she said grudgingly.

Lance flashed a sinister smile. "I'm better than good, and you know it." His eyes dared her to say otherwise.

"You didn't answer me—why are you in Iowa?"

"I did answer you." He glanced at her as he walked farther into the room. "You."

As she tried to steady a pulse that was presently erratic, Lance moved for the alabaster and wood staircase. He took one step and something snapped inside her. It didn't even make sense—she just knew he could not go upstairs. That was her home, her life, and he was not allowed to enter it as he pleased and make it a mess by putting his Lance Denton figurative lips all over it.

Maggie lunged for him, tackling him around the waist and swinging him around with her weight. They both landed on the hard floor, but he was gentlemanly enough to spin them so he took the brunt of it. He hit the wood with his back. Maggie was draped over him, still as stone as air forcefully left him in a painful rush.

They lay like that for some time, neither feeling the need to move. Maggie, because she was appalled by her behavior and their current physicality, and Lance, she assumed, because he was having a hard time breathing. As the seconds turned into minutes, it started to get awkward—or more awkward.

Lance's tone was conversational as he asked, "You're not wearing a bra, are you?"

Maggie began to take note of things. The hardness of his chest, the boniness of his hip as it dug into her abdomen, how close her face was to his neck—how well her breasts molded to his shoulder and arm, and the fact that she was feeling a draft in a place she rather would not be feeling one.

"Shit!" She scrambled back and spun away as she tucked a boob back within the confines of the tank top she wore under the robe. Then, brave person that she was, she sprinted up the stairs, dove into her room, and flipped the lock on the door.

Chest heaving, blood burned through her veins as her heart thundered out a fast beat. Maggie took quick, shallow breaths, but all that did was make her need more air. She would stay in her room, wait him out. They had too much history, too much pain between the two of them, to be anything but strangers. He would leave eventually. He'd get bored, or hungry, or realize it was futile to think she'd ever hire him on as her personal trainer.

Maggie nodded to herself. Right. That was exactly how things would go.

That settled, she sat on the bed and listened for the front door to shut, a clear signal that he had left the premises. Instead she cocked her head as a faint, scratching sound met her ears. Not owning a pet of any kind, that puzzled her. She moved for the door, reaching for the doorknob just as it powerfully swung open and smacked against her forehead.

"Ow!" Maggie stumbled back and careened to the left, hand held to her stinging flesh.

"Oh. Whoops." Lance stood with his hand raised, bobby pin within it. He tossed it over his shoulder and stepped inside. "Nice room."

Maggie's voice sounded like gravel as she said, "First of all, why are you carrying around a bobby pin?"

Lance blinked at her. "How else was I going to open the door you so rudely locked?"

"It's my bedroom," she shouted, a slice of sanity sliding away. "I could have been naked!"

His eyes went up and down the length of her, lingering on her breasts as a smile skipped along his lips. "Don't tease. It's unkind."

Palm to her head, she seethed at the man standing in her bedroom. "Get . . . out . . . of . . . my . . . house."

He moved to sit on the bed, bouncing up and down a few times before looking at her. "You need me."

"I need you like I need—"

"Watch it. You might regret what you say and then you can't take it back." He reclined on the bed with his hands behind his head.

"I doubt I'd want to take it back."

"I like your bed. It's comfy." Lance jumped to his feet like a spring and clapped his hands together once. "So . . . where's my room?"

Maggie gaped at him, hand falling limply to her side.

"Downstairs, down the hall? Guest house? I see my physical perfection has you speechless." Shrugging, he said, "That's okay, I'll find it."

When Lance reached her, her hand shot out and slammed against his chest.

He looked down. "If you want excuses to fondle me, I could think of better ways to go about it."

She snatched her hand back. "You're not staying here, you're not working for me. And if you don't leave now, I'm calling the police."

His eyes narrowed. "You would do that?"

Maggie's resolution wavered. "Yes."

"What about the scandal it would cause?"

"No one would have to find out." They could find out, easily.

"Well, they would, with me telling them and all."

"Are you . . . are you . . . blackmailing me?" Anger had her sputtering.

"Of course not. Not unless I have to," he added.

"Why are you so adamant about this?"

"You need a trainer, I need a job. I don't see the problem."

"Except we used to date and I would rather scratch out my own eyes than have you as a personal trainer."

"Such harsh words, Maggie." Lance's expression turned serious. "Okay, look at it this way—do you want me to help you or do you want your sister? Because there isn't anyone else. I'm it. She was ready to call you and tell you when I got back to her and said I'd take the job. I know you two don't get along," he continued. "I remember."

"That was years ago," she hissed. "She's changed. I've changed." Lies. All of it.

"Sure." Lance didn't sound convinced.

Maggie thought of her food and exercise obsessed, self-absorbed, judgmental sister, and then she turned her gaze to Lance Denton. The man who had once been the boy who had her heart and didn't want it enough. Neither was ideal. He was slightly better—very slightly.

She eyed him. "Why do you have to stay here?"

"You have the space, and I am temporarily without a permanent residence."

"Why?"

"Why what?"

"Why do you not have a home?"

Shadows shifted through his eyes. "It's personal. Besides, hands-on is always better. Less cheating that way."

"You would know about that."

"About hands-on?" The curve of his lips was sensual.

"About cheating," she corrected.

He placed a hand to his heart, even as his eyes flashed dangerously. "You got me, right here."

"How long will it take to get me in shape?"

"That depends on you. Your eating habits, your exercise routine, your dedication. I always say it takes three weeks to notice a change, and three months to make it stick."

He actually sounded like he knew what he was talking about. *Probably read that in a book.*

"If you stay here, you get paid less." She raised her eyebrows as she waited for his response. Maggie hoped he'd refuse. The thought of being within such close proximity to him for months had her palms sweaty and her stomach swirling.

Lance hesitated, then nodded. "Deal."

"What do you usually charge?"

"One hundred dollars an hour."

"And how often do you see your clients?"

"Three to five times a week, one to two hours each time."

Maggie's mouth dropped open. "You're insane."

He shrugged. "I'm worth it."

His tone lacked its usual arrogance, which told her he wasn't exaggerating.

Eyeing him, she said, "I'll pay you half what you usually make, and you get to stay here and eat my food. We'll have a two-week trial run. If I can't stand you, you're gone."

"At least make it fair to me."

"Fine," Maggie ground out. "If I can find a single good thing about you being here, you can stay."

Lance grinned. "That I can do."

"We'll see," she muttered. "How are you able to devote the next three months to me? Don't you have other clients you need to be working with?"

"I do, but for now, Maggie, I'm yours," Lance said, his eyes dark and smoldering.

Apparently her body liked his tone, jerking at his words as though brought back to life from a somber reality. She slowly inhaled. "I need to put on clothes."

He didn't move.

"Leave."

"You're no fun."

"I know. Wasn't that one of the reasons you didn't want to be with me anymore? I wasn't exciting enough for you."

A shadow of something swept across his features. Lance's jaw tightened, and then his expression was clear once more. "I'll be in the kitchen."

"You don't know where it is."

"I'm sure I can find it," he called over his shoulder as he sauntered from the room. In the hallway, he turned to face her. "How many bedrooms are in this place anyway?"

Maggie strode for the door. "Oh, you know." She slammed the door shut, smiling as she imagined it hitting his face.

LANE GYM, OWNED and operated by Nora Lane, was one of the most reputable workout centers in Dubuque, Iowa. The city was close to, if not over, sixty-thousand strong, which said something. Nora was a controlling and high strung perfectionist, which worked well for being successful.

As Maggie stepped inside the white building with matching walls and flooring, she was besieged by the appearance of muscled, sweaty beings working out with weights or exercise equipment, and the sound of upbeat music. The air was cool, high-powered ceiling fans propelling it around. Beyond the main room, there were two smaller rooms where classes were given. Maggie looked at the windowed wall that faced the parking lot, wondering how people could be okay with others staring at them as they worked out.

She preferred to mortify herself within the privacy of her own home.

Maggie stopped at the front desk, smiling at the receptionist. "Is Nora in?"

Julie, a college student with a tiny body and a huge smile, looked up. Her straight brown hair was pulled back in a tight ponytail and a pink top and shorts that looked more fitting for a doll graced her body.

Smile brightening her brown eyes, she said, "Hey, Maggie! She's doing a yoga class right now, but it should be done in about five minutes, if you want to wait."

"Sure. I'll wait."

"Your parents are here." Julie pointed a finger.

Maggie faced the rows of treadmills, elliptical machines, exercise bikes, and weight machines, catching sight of her mom and dad. Both retired Math teachers, they spent an hour each weekday at Lane Gym, followed by lunch with a fellow retired couple, book reading, and relaxing at their home. Maggie was the only family member who struggled with her weight, to her eternal exasperation. Of course, she was also the least physically active—and she enjoyed her desserts, carbohydrates, and fried foods more than the other Smileys.

"Thanks. I'll say hello."

She walked over to them, stopping near her father as he was closest.

"Hey, Dad," she greeted, waving at her mom on the treadmill. Jennifer Smiley waved back and faced forward.

Gray-haired and sporting wire-rimmed glasses, at five feet six, Leon Smiley wasn't much taller than Maggie. He picked up a set of free weights and did chest curls.

"Maggie, what brings you here? Did you decide to conform to your sister's ways like the rest of us?" A smile trailed his words. Perspiration lined his craggy face and dampened his black shirt.

"That would make Nora much too happy."

"I'm not sure anything could make her *too* happy," he halfway joked, one bushy eyebrow lifted.

Maggie nodded, biting her lower lip to keep all news of Lance Denton from passing them. It was obvious her father and mother didn't know, or they would have contacted her about it. They would ultimately keep their opinions to themselves, but Maggie wouldn't have to hear them to know they wouldn't be in Lance's favor.

Cautious with the idea of Lance and Maggie dating as teenagers, they'd been friendly but somewhat reserved with Lance anytime they were around him. When everything fell apart, they were there to helplessly witness her shattered pieces lying among the debris of her heart. As much as they wanted to help her, they couldn't.

No one could mend a broken heart—no one but the one who'd broken it.

Her mom walked over. "That color looks great on you. You should wear it more often." She warmly squeezed Maggie's bicep. Short and compact, the blue top and black shorts she wore molded to her trim figure in a flattering way. Jennifer Smiley had short brown hair laced with gray and an unlined face that allowed her to pass for being much younger in years than she was. She was routinely mistaken for Nora's sister, much to Nora's annoyance.

Maggie looked down at her rainbow shirt and blinked. "Which

one?"

"What? Oh. All of them. It's a happy shirt." With a twinkle in her amber-colored eyes, Maggie's mom turned away and drank from her water bottle.

She laughed. Her mother made sure to compliment her every time she saw her, whether it was valid or not. Maggie had self-esteem issues, and that was her way of trying to make her feel good. Maggie appreciated the effort.

"Bacon!"

The smile was wiped from her face and her shoulders stiffened. Her sister, on the other hand, seemed to enjoy her insecurities. She caught the chastising look her dad gave Nora as she turned to face her sister.

"Nora, don't you think it's time to come up with a new nickname? Something not quite so juvenile, possibly?" Jennifer said, lips pressed together to show her displeasure.

"Why?" Nora blinked. "I've always called her that. Maggie likes bacon. It fits. Besides, she knows I don't mean anything by it." In Nora's mind, if she didn't mean to offend someone, then they shouldn't be, regardless of whether or not her words were actually offensive.

With strawberry blond hair that rested on her shoulders, large green eyes, and a smattering of freckles along the bridge of her nose and cheeks, Nora was slender with defined muscles and overflowing confidence. Not that Maggie ever wanted to be like her, but to have that self-assuredness would be nice.

If someone told Nora she couldn't do something, she told them to watch her.

"Hi, Nora," she said in a strained voice.

"You wanted to see me? How's the personal trainer working out? I bet you were surprised, huh?" She smiled her straight smile, hands on hips. In the white t-back top and short shorts, her muscular physique was displayed to be readily admired.

"You hired a personal trainer?" Leon asked.

"When did this happen?" her mother added.

"Uh . . ." Maggie stared at her sister. "Just today, actually. We haven't started yet."

"Good for you." Her dad set down the free weights and patted her arm. "I'm going to hit the elliptical machine. How about we get some coffee later this week, go for a walk along the river?"

"Sure, Dad. That sounds great," Maggie said, tilting her head to the side to better allow him to press a chaste kiss to her temple.

"Maggie," her mother said, touching her hand. Concern floated in the depths of her dark eyes. "It's wonderful that you want to get in shape, but don't overdo it, okay? It isn't worth getting skinny if it's harmful to you. Remember that. And . . . if you need to talk to someone, do you still have Dr. Morgan's phone number?"

Her stomach clenched, but all she did was smile and nod. "I know, Mom, and yes, I do. Don't worry. I'll do it the right way."

"But if you need someone to talk to . . ." Her mother gave her a pointed look.

"I'll call him. I promise. I've talked to him off and on throughout the years. Everything is good, and it will remain that way."

With a satisfied nod, she turned to her older daughter and waggled a finger at her. "Be nice."

"Mom," Nora whined. "I'm always nice."

"Be nicer. See you later, girls."

Nora rolled her eyes and turned to Maggie. "She acts like I'm the meanest sister ever." She eyed Maggie. "I have, like, two minutes before my next class. What's up?"

Maggie tucked a lock of hair behind her ears, watching her mother bend and stretch on a mat. "Why him?" When Nora didn't say anything, Maggie focused on her sister. "Why Lance Denton? Out of anyone you could have sent, why was it him?"

Nora shifted uncomfortably. "All the other trainers are booked for months. And . . . he's freelance, so he can work with anyone."

"He isn't the only trainer like that."

"No. But he was the first one I thought of, the one I know—"

"And he doesn't even live in Iowa!" Maggie interrupted, frustrated with her sister, and Lance, and herself. "He lives in, I don't know, Florida, or Italy, or something. The whole thing makes no sense."

"He lives in Ohio. He moved there after the divorce was finalized a few months ago."

Maggie frowned. Lance let her think he didn't have a home, or that the home was in Florida, or—he let her think all kinds of things. He wasn't obligated to correct what she did or did not choose to believe. He didn't owe her explanations.

"How do you know all this?"

Nora rolled her eyes. "Come on, Maggie. You've kept tabs on him. I guess I just kept better ones."

Maggie studied Nora. There was more to the situation than what she was being told, but she decided to leave it alone for the time being.

"He flew in early this morning to see you." She locked her eyes on Maggie. "You're right, I could have asked someone else, but I know he'll get you to work, if for no other reason than to prove to him you can. You don't have the motivation to do this on your own."

Maggie opened her mouth to argue that.

"You don't, or you wouldn't look like you do. You're either too thin or overweight. There is no happy medium for you. Lance can help you find it."

"Thanks a lot," she mumbled, knowing it was true.

Nora shrugged. "He'll get you in shape, and that's what you want, right? So go get in shape—the right way. I have to start my next class. We'll talk soon." She spun on her heel and flounced away, hair bouncing as she moved.

Maggie waved to her parents with a weak smile on her face and headed out the door. It was a sunny day, the periodic breeze cool and nice. She walked to her car, not expecting to see Lance posed against the side of the Camry, relaxed and confident. With a glance at the building to see if her parents were aware of her visitor, she continued the steps it took to reach him. He'd changed into a shirt the same blue as his eyes, sleeves cut out to better show off his muscled arms, and loose gray shorts with neon yellow tennis shoes—the shoes especially were a cry for attention.

"What are you doing here?" she demanded. "And how did you know this was my car?"

"You know, after all this time, you still smell like oranges. How is that possible?" he said in a low voice. The expression on his face was closed, but the heat in his eyes was alive with unspoken emotions.

Mouth going dry, she swallowed, and swallowed again, tearing her eyes from his.

He reached out a hand, taking the car keys clutched inside her palm, and traced a finger over the faded glittery pink 'M' keychain. Her face burned, but Lance never said anything, the past vibrating around them like an undeniable heartbeat. Lance's dark head didn't raise until he slowly gave the keys back.

"I thought you got rid of everything."

"I didn't realize I still had this until after I moved back to Iowa." And then she'd kept the keychain anyway.

A thoughtful look passed over his features, one she didn't care to dissect. Lance smiled. "The license plate of this white Camry matches the one on the white Camry that was in your driveway this morning. It wasn't that hard to figure out."

"Oh." Maggie looked down the street. Lane Gym was located in a strip mall four miles from her house, shoppers going in and out of the stores on either side of it at a nonstop pace. "And why are you here?"

"I have to talk to your sister about some things." His tone said that was all he was going to say on the subject.

Maggie frowned. "How did you get here?"

He lifted his eyebrows and pointed to his shoes. "Most fascinating thing—I walked. You have that ability too, you know."

Her frown turned into a scowl when Lance laughed.

"How did you get to my house this morning?" she asked suspiciously.

"Did you know Dubuque has a taxi service? Oddest thing." Half of his mouth lifted mockingly.

"Well, I'm going now," Maggie said lamely, waiting for him to move away from the car before getting inside.

"See you soon," he taunted, waving with exaggerated cheerfulness.

She drove off, sure he was laughing at her when she glanced in the rearview mirror.

LANCE—1996

LANCE KNOCKED ON the apartment door and waited for it to open, restless energy not letting him stand still. He knew she was home—he'd watched her walk inside the apartment about fifteen minutes ago from where he sat in the sand. He also knew Judith, her designated guardian while filming in Virginia Beach, was not.

He heard movement on the other side of the door, imagined her checking the peephole, and then the door slowly opened. Lance put on a fake smile, but when he focused on her, it became real. She looked nervous, cheeks red and eyes shifting to him and away. Reddish-brown hair waving around her face and shoulders, dressed in the white sundress as she was, Maggie looked sweet. Pretty.

"Hi, Maggie."

"Hi."

He'd been warned to stay away from her. By Judith, by Herman. By just about everyone who knew him and Maggie. That only made him want to be near her more.

She bit her lower lip, causing an embarrassing reaction in him, and asked, "What are you doing here, Lance?"

"I . . ." He swiped a hand through his hair, unsure why his pulse thrummed so fast. "I thought maybe we could hang out? Practice some lines for next week's episode?" Lance held up the papers he'd brought along to make his visit seem authentic. He didn't need to go over his lines. He'd had them memorized since the day they got them.

Maggie's eyes flew to his face. "Why?"

It wasn't a demand. She sounded like she genuinely wanted to know why he sought her out. He understood the basis of her question. They'd been working on the show for over a month and that was the first time he'd initiated interaction with her outside of the set. He wasn't really sure why, but the more he was around her, the more interesting she became.

Lance shrugged and turned to face the beach. It was getting dark, the sky painted in tones of purple, red, and blue, but there were still people in the sand and water. Facing her, he said, "My dad is out of the state for the month, and Mitch, the guy I'm rooming with? He's gone for the night. It's . . . really quiet in the apartment."

She heard something in his voice or words that caused her expression to soften. The door opened wider. "Come on in. I've actually been having trouble with some of my lines. Judith's been trying to help me, but it might be better to hear your lines from your voice instead of hers."

He caught her smile as he stepped inside, the sweet scent of oranges teasing his senses. Lance stopped beside her. She was looking at him, eyes alight with innocent warmth. He could kiss her. She'd let him. Maybe she'd let him, he corrected, continuing into the living room.

"How do you like staying here?" Lance looked around the room, noting the lack of electronics. He dropped the papers on an end table near a recliner.

The room was decorated in whites and grays with a wall of windows facing the beach. He had the same view, one floor up. The furniture was light gray, the carpet white. Maggie's clean scent was faint, whereas Judith's floral one was overpowering the space. He preferred Maggie's.

"Here, or in Virginia Beach?" Maggie stood near the opening to the small kitchen area.

"Both."

She shrugged, disappearing around the corner. "It's different from Iowa. Faster-paced, warmer, obviously. The apartment's . . . nice, but it isn't home."

"I noticed you have no television."

Maggie peeked around the wall to wrinkle her nose at him. "Judith doesn't like the looks of gadgets. That's what she calls televisions and radios—gadgets. She thinks they mess up the natural calmness of environments."

"If you ever want to watch television or listen to music, you can come to my apartment. Mitch has a sick entertainment center."

"Oh. Thanks. I actually have a small television and radio in my room. Want something to drink? I'm making lemonade."

A smile caught his lips and he walked up behind her, liking how she jumped and blushed at his nearness. The kitchen followed the white and gray theme. He suspected all of the apartment did. "Did you make cookies too?"

"No." Maggie tucked a rebellious curl behind her ear, moving away. "I don't eat cookies."

Lance frowned. "What's wrong with you? Everyone likes cookies."

"I didn't say I didn't like them. I said I don't eat them." Maggie handed him a glass of lemonade.

"What?"

"Nothing." She sipped from her glass, careful to avoid his eyes. "Ready to work?"

Studying her frame, his eyes lingered on her full breasts, rounded stomach, and hips. Was she worried about her body? She wasn't fat, by any means, although she did have a more defined figure than other girls her age.

"Yeah. Sure." Lance cleared his throat and dragged his gaze away. "Lead the way."

Maggie set her glass of lemonade on the counter. "I'll be right back. My lines are in the bedroom."

She walked down the short hallway, entering a room on the left. Lance smiled. His bedroom was in the same exact spot. She slept beneath him every night, a thought that his body enjoyed much more than he wanted.

He followed her into the room, surprised by the bursts of vibrancy in an otherwise colorless setting. The room made him think of a heart, or lips, maybe love, shades of reds and pinks prominent in the bedding and decorative pieces. Even the dresser and lamp were pale pink, though the bedframe and nightstand were white.

"I like your room." Lance picked up a book from a white chair by the door and studied the cover. It looked like a horror novel, the letters of the title red and bubbled up like dripping blood. He set it back down.

Whirling around from the closet she was peering in, Maggie's skin went pink. She clutched a sheaf of papers to her chest, eyes wide. "You shouldn't be in here."

Eyebrows lifting, he walked to the bed with a pink and red-striped comforter on it. "Why not?"

"Because it's my . . . my bedroom and . . . you're a guy."

"Thanks for noticing. I was worried." Lance kicked off his sandals and hopped on the bed. It smelled like her and he rolled to his stomach to hide the evidence of what that knowledge did to him. He seriously needed to get laid, or things were going to become embarrassing.

"Lance, you—I . . ."

He lifted his head to look at her. "Yes?"

"I promised my dad I would be good," she said pitifully.

Her tone of voice taunted his conscience. Lance turned and sat up. "How is this being bad? We're co-workers, working."

"Only we haven't actually done any work yet—and we're in my bedroom." She smiled weakly.

"So we will." He patted the mattress. "Come on, let's do something productive." He could think of better ways to spend time in a bed.

Moving slowly, like she was approaching an unpredictable beast, Maggie made her way to him. "Don't you need yours?" She shook the papers in hand.

"Nah. I think I'll be okay." He waited until she sat down, aware that she was careful to keep a good amount of distance between them. "What scene is giving you trouble?"

"The first day of school, when we're—they're—arguing. I couldn't get into character with Judith. I kept laughing instead of crying every time she yelled at me. I could tell she was getting annoyed with me."

"How could you tell?"

Maggie laughed. "She told me."

Lance jumped from the bed and offered a hand to Maggie. "Come on, we need to stand for this. We're by the lockers, in between classes, right?"

She placed her hand in his. He tried not to think about how soft it was, how well it fit within his larger, darker one, and pulled her up from the bed.

"Yes. The popular kids wanted you to sit with them at lunch, and when you said something to me about it, I acted funny."

"Ready?"

Taking a deep breath, she nodded. The transformation was merely seconds long, but he was hypnotized watching it take place.

Anger roughening his voice, Lance said, "I don't get it. Those are the people I want to hang around. I'm new here, and I need to make friends. What's your problem? Why are you trying to ruin that for me?"

"I'm not trying to ruin anything for you," she whispered, voice higher as Cecilia.

"Really? Then why don't you want to sit with them at lunch?"

Grabbing the book from the chair near the door, she hugged it as she met his eyes. "They want you to sit with them, not me. And you should, you should sit with them. You belong with them, and I don't. We had a good summer, but summer's over now."

"I don't understand."

Her wine-colored eyes were sad. "You will. I have to go to class."

When Cecilia turned to leave, Derek was supposed to grab her arm, halting her. Lance did, the proximity of her body to his messing with his head. She stared up at him like he was everything. He forgot his lines, all of him tight with need and something else. Longing. Swallowing, Lance blinked and dropped his hand, stepping back. He clenched his fists, hiding the tremor in them.

"What's wrong?" she asked, the dewy look gone from her eyes.

He tried to smile, but it wouldn't come. "Guess I need my lines after all. I'll be right back."

Maggie looked down at the paper she held. "'What aren't you telling me?'" She looked up. "That's the line."

"Right." Lance rubbed his forehead. "I'm not really feeling it right now. How about a break and we get back to it in a bit?"

"Sure." She shrugged. "What do you want to do?"

"What do I want to do, or what do I think we should do?"

"Um . . . I don't know? Aren't they the same thing?"

"No. Not at all." Lance inhaled deeply, a choked laugh leaving him. "Let's go for a walk on the beach. How about that?"

It was full dark out, the ocean painted black with night. Earlier packed, the beach was empty except for them and a few people farther in the distance. The warm air smelled of salt, damp with humidity as it touched the skin not covered by his tee shirt and shorts. The white sand glowed beneath their feet as they walked barefoot along the shoreline. The sound of crashing waves was relentless.

"It's like walking on sugar," Maggie commented.

Born and raised in Virginia Beach, Lance never thought too much about what his surroundings felt, smelled, or looked like, but it was fun watching Maggie's reaction.

"It doesn't feel like sugar when the sun's on it. It feels like you're walking on gritty fire." He glanced at her, watching how the breeze lifted and parted her hair, baring her pale neck. "Have you been on the beach much?"

Maggie glanced at him and shook her head. "No. I've wanted to, but didn't want to go by myself. I don't have any friends here, other than Judith, and she refuses to be outside for more than a few minutes at a time. She says the sun gives you horrible tan lines and wrinkles."

Lance had never thought about how it must be for Maggie, staying in a place where she didn't know anyone other than those she worked with. She had to be lonely.

"There's a beach party tomorrow night. One of my friends is throwing it. Swimming, drinking, dancing. Good times. You should come. I can introduce you to people our age so you don't have to hang out with the old folks."

"Oh. Okay. Maybe."

He stopped walking, touching her wrist to get her attention. "I'll come over at eight. We'll go together."

A smile lifted her lips, and it was like the sun deciding to obliterate the night. Lance inhaled sharply, quickly looking away from it.

"That sounds fun. Thank you, Lance."

He nodded, throat tight. "Sure. No problem. It's not a big deal. Just trying to help out the new girl." He made sure his tone conveyed how little her acceptance meant to him. It was fake, but she didn't know that.

Her smile fell. "Right. Of course. I appreciate it." Maggie's gaze dropped to her feet. "Thanks for walking with me. I should go back."

Without thinking about what he was doing, Lance touched her chin. She lifted her eyes to his, and he studied her features, looking for one simple thing to make him understand her appeal. He couldn't find it, and yet, it was there. Lance leaned close, a breath and nothing more between their lips. He wanted to kiss her, was desperate for it. Maggie gently turned her face away, stepping back. She wouldn't meet his eyes, crossing her arms to look out into the endless sea.

Self-deprecating smile in place, he shrugged and slid his hands in the front pockets of his shorts. "I'll walk you back."

She nodded.

No words were spoken as they made their way to the apartment complex.

At Maggie's door, Lance said, "See you tomorrow."

Time paused as she looked at him. As he'd searched for something in her face moments ago, she seemed to do the same. "Okay. Good night, Lance."

"Good night, Maggie."

THE NEXT DAY, he was at her place at five to eight. He'd styled his hair, something he only did for special occasions, and put on cologne. Dressed in khaki shorts and a white buttoned-down shirt, he felt overdressed for a beach party, and still not dressed up enough for Maggie. Lance knew it wasn't a date, but his nerves acted like it was.

Her dress was purple and flowing, fitted perfectly against her breasts, and his mouth went dry at the sight of her. Maggie's smile was hesitant, her wavy hair piled on top of her head with strands framing her face. Impulsively, stupidly, Lance reached for her and kissed her. A sound of surprise left her. She tasted good, like the oranges of which she habitually smelled.

Part of the thrill was wondering if she'd kiss him back or shove him away. Taut with need, he didn't even care which it was. Maggie's mouth slowly formed to his. Her hands rested on his shoulders as though to push him away, but she didn't. Lance's lips curved around the kiss, he deepened it, felt her respond. He wanted to take her to the nearest bedroom and ditch the party completely.

"Get your paws off her, Lance Denton." The voice was sharp, powerful, and felt like ice on his skin.

Lance flinched and tore his mouth from Maggie's, looking over her head to meet Judith Fletcher's piercing gray gaze. Established as a talented actress at the age of nine, presently in her early forties, the blond had an aura of poise and no-nonsense. She wanted to protect Maggie. And she didn't like Lance. More specifically, she didn't like his father, and that dislike trickled down to him.

"Hey, Judith." He gave her his most charming smile.

She narrowed her eyes at him before turning to Maggie. "Remember what I said."

Cheeks red, Maggie nodded without looking at her.

Judith pointed a long finger at his face. "Treat her with respect. She isn't one of your toys. And if you hurt her, you'll answer to me."

The door shut, causing Maggie to jump.

He waited for her to look up before saying, "I'm not going to apologize for kissing you."

She blinked at him. "What do you mean?"

"I don't regret it. Do you?"

"I'm not sure," Maggie answered carefully.

Lance frowned. "You're not sure? Didn't you like it?"

"Well, yes, I did, but . . ." She shrugged.

"But what?" he pressed.

Maggie stepped off the sidewalk and onto the sand, her back to him. Her voice was soft as she said, "I expected something different for my first kiss."

Two things simultaneously hit him: joy that he was the first guy to kiss Maggie Smiley, and guilt that he'd selfishly taken that from her.

Clearing his throat, he walked up to her. "Ready?"

"Yes."

"You look pretty, by the way," Lance told her after they'd walked in silence for a few minutes.

She gave him a sideways glance, facing forward to ask, "Is that why you kissed me?"

Uncomfortable with the direct question, Lance rubbed the side of his neck. "Yeah. I guess."

He'd felt compelled, spellbound, as if kissing her was the only thing he knew how to do, and not doing so would be detrimental.

Maggie smiled at him. "You look pretty too."

"Pretty?" he scoffed. "Guys don't look pretty."

"No?" One eyebrow lifted. "What do they look like then?"

"I don't know. Manly. Sexy. Irresistible."

"I see." She looked at him thoughtfully. "I suppose you could pass for sexy."

He grinned. "Irresistible is pushing it, huh?"

"Yes. Just a bit."

Lance grabbed her hand and tugged her toward a group of teenagers. Chances were, the party would be broken up before too long, and if anyone was caught by the police, there would be fines to pay. No one seemed worried about that, including Lance. He'd had tickets before. He paid them and continued on.

"I will bet you five dollars that by the end of the night, you find me irresistible."

Maggie laughed. "Really? And how would you know, either way?"

"Oh, I'll know."

"Okay. Deal."

Greetings were called out to him as they approached the party. Green Day played from a CD player in the sand. Girls and boys occupied chairs, or stood in small groups, while others sat or lay on the sand. There was heavy making out, talking, and laughter. A few kids argued. Most hands held alcohol of some kind. The mass of twenty or so bodies were a colorful mix of clothing and skin and hair tones. Maggie's hand stiffened inside his and he unconsciously squeezed it in reassurance.

"It'll be okay. They're just people, like you and me," he quietly told her.

She inhaled slowly and nodded, giving him a smile.

"Lance!" a blond squealed, jumping on him and causing him to stagger back. Arms threaded around his neck, and the girl pressed her lips to his, tasting of beer and cigarettes.

His stomach twisted in revulsion and he set Brittany Sanders away from him, swiping an arm across his mouth. "Give it a rest. Enough is enough."

She'd been after him for months, ever since he'd drunkenly made out with her. He hated to think how she'd be acting if he hadn't passed out. She was skinny with big boobs, but she wasn't too smart, and that dumb blond thing she had going was only cute for so long.

"That's not what you said last time."

"Last time?" he scoffed. "There was only one time, and that's all there'll ever be. Stay away from me."

Lips pursing in a pout, she called him an asshole and sauntered away, bee-lining for one of his friends. He shook his head and turned away. Realizing Maggie was no longer beside him, Lance spun around in a circle, searching for a purple dress and a reddish-brown head of hair. Panic began to set in when he couldn't find her.

He shoved his way through the crowd, spotting her near the edge of the party. Rick Jerry, a twenty-year-old who liked to hang out with younger kids and make advances on naive girls, offered her a cup of something as he watched. Lance's jaw hardened and he saw himself ripping Rick apart. He would enjoy that, a lot. Sprinting toward them, he knocked the cup from Rick's hand as he gave it to Maggie.

"Don't drink anything unless I get it for you, and especially don't take anything from this guy," he said harshly, eyes on Rick's smug face.

"Whoa there, Lance, no need to overreact." Rick held up his hands. "It was only water."

"Sure it was."

"It really was. I saw him open the bottle," Maggie told him quietly.

He tore his gaze from Rick, taking in her confused expression. "It doesn't matter. Stay away from him. He's bad news, Maggie."

"You're one to talk," Rick sneered. His long black hair was pulled back in a low ponytail, his lean frame clothed in a blue shirt and black shorts. "You think just because you're famous, people don't know or care about what you're really like. They do, and they talk."

"Shut up," he warned, hands clenched at his sides.

"What's he talking about?" Maggie asked.

"Nothing. Let's go." He grabbed her hand and pulled.

"I know about Lacey McCall! Everyone knows about her. And the others—"

Spinning around, he slammed his fist into Rick's long nose and heard a crack. Rick fell to his knees, moaning. Lance towered over him, rage shouting at him to do more, hit him more. "And I know about how you lure girls into trusting you, and then you take advantage of that trust, and use it to make them do things they don't want. At least everyone I've been with has been because they wanted it, not because they felt like they had no choice." He spit on the ground and stalked away, not caring if Maggie followed or not.

The setting sun was red, reflecting his present mood. Lance's hands opened and closed as he moved, stiff with the need to hit something else. He was halfway to the apartments when he heard her voice. Lance wasn't aware if she'd just called his name, or had been the whole time. Whatever the case, it registered then, when it hadn't before. She called it two more times before he slowed down, stopped, and finally turned around.

Maggie stared at him, hair fallen from the clips that held it up. The display was erotically at odds with the innocence stamped upon her face as a brand to keep him away. Chest lifting and lowering with each fast intake of air she took, she gasped, "Why did you run off?"

"Because if I hadn't, I would have beaten the shit out of that guy."

"What was he talking about? Who's—who's Lacey? What happened with her?"

Lance's jaw shifted. "Just a girl I knew."

Hands clasped before her, she bowed her head. "Okay." Maggie looked up and to the side. "And the girl that kissed you? Just another girl you know?"

"Yes," he said roughly.

She nodded, the determined cast of her profile saying she'd come to some kind of decision. "I'm going to go home now."

Maggie got in a dozen steps before he was running after her. He caught her wrist and swung her around. Lance looked down at her, remorse squeezing his heart at the words he was about to say. He didn't want her to know the kind of person he was, not yet.

"We went on a date or two, messed around. It meant more to her than it did me, and when I told her, she . . . she got upset. Really upset. She drove off. There was a car accident, and . . . she didn't make it."

He went silent, swallowing thickly. Waiting. Waiting for the judgement. The coldness. The blame. The rejection. He didn't get them. Instead Maggie lifted a hand to his cheek and held it there. It was a kind gesture, comforting. Empathetic.

Unwanted.

Needed.

Lance blinked his eyes and averted his head, embarrassed by the prick of tears.

"How long ago did it happen?"

He shrugged. "Five months."

"Thank you for telling me."

Looking at Maggie, seeing the sincerity on her face, Lance's chest compressed more. That time, she kissed him. Other than their lips, no part of them touched. It was slow and deep. He'd kissed a lot of girls, had a lot of them kiss him. Passionate kisses. Hard kisses. Kisses that made him mad with need and out of control. He'd never been kissed like that before.

That was a true first kiss. Shared with Maggie Smiley. It should have felt wrong. It didn't. It felt like it meant something.

When she pulled away, he opened his eyes, mesmerized by the fan of eyelashes on her cheeks. He wanted to kiss those as well. She looked at him and touched trembling fingers to her puffy lips. Lance ached for her.

"That's the kind of first kiss I wanted," she told him shyly.

Lance grinned. "Are you going to make me work for the five dollars, or are you going to concede? I can play the wounded soul if that helps."

"Are you playing?" she wondered, head tipped to the side.

"Of course," he replied coolly.

Maggie narrowed her eyes. "Hmm. I'm not sure." Grin stretching her lips as her expression cleared, she skipped backward, eyes on him. "I think you need to work for it a little more."

"Oh yeah? We'll see about that." Lance chased after her, grinning as her eyes widened. "Get moving, or you're mine."

Maggie laughed as she spun around, sprinting along the beach, kicking off her sandals to move faster. Lance did the same, water folding over his feet as he ran. It was cool against his skin, but he was on fire. She whooped, hands above her head, jumping and dancing farther down the beach. Lance stilled, mesmerized by her graceful movements and carefree spontaneity. She turned into the water, became a part of the ocean instead of a person separate from it.

He blinked, shook his head, and jogged the remaining distance.

When he reached her, Maggie grabbed his hands. They spun in a circle, faster and faster, kicking up sand as they moved. Laughing into each other's eyes. Lance felt like a kid. He was only sixteen, but he felt so much older most of the time. Not with Maggie. With Maggie, he felt free and invincible.

"Tell me a secret," she called, grinning mischievously.

Lance shook his head, heart pounding, pulse racing. It was silly, but he wondered, if they kept spinning, would they twirl into non-existence, like a time-traveling machine? If he could go back in time, where would he go? And in that question, there was a secret, one he'd never admitted to himself, let alone anyone else. He focused on Maggie's face, the two of them moving so fast they seemed to not be moving at all.

"I wish I could have known my mom better."

Her expression changed, and they slowly came to a stop. He was dizzy, awkwardly trying to keep his balance, and then Lance released her hands and let himself fall to the lumpy sand. Maggie plopped down beside him, face lifted to the moon, chest moving up and down as she breathed. A hand, small and cool, clamped over his, squeezing it. Lance shifted his position and stared at the star-filled sky, wondering if his mom was watching him. He closed his eyes against the thought.

Maggie didn't offer condolences, or try to make him feel better, and he appreciated that. He'd heard it all through the years, good and bad, and none of it changed what was.

You're better off without her.

She couldn't be what you needed.

She loved you, in her own way.

Think of what things would be like, if she were still around. Think of how much more messed up you'd be.

"I hate spaghetti."

He turned his head and met her odd-colored eyes.

"That's my secret," she elaborated. "I hate spaghetti. The noodles make me think of worms, and with the red sauce, it's like bloody worms." She shuddered, a small smile on her face. "I don't tell people that, though, because then they make fun of me."

"What would you do if someone cooked you spaghetti and expected you to eat it?"

Maggie's smile grew as she showed him her profile. "Suddenly feel ill."

"What about Ramen noodles?"

"Same. And have you ever actually tried to eat them? It's impossible to chew them. They just sort of slide down your throat, like slippery, thin, malnourished worms."

Lance laughed, tugging his hand from hers to place his arms behind his head. It was peaceful, lying there, talking with Maggie, nothing directly around them but the ocean and sky.

"I live off Ramen noodles most days," he confessed.

"Gross! That's so sad. You shouldn't have to live like that."

"I like them."

Maggie placed her head on a hand and stared down at him.

"What?" Uncomfortable with the straightforwardness of her gaze, he averted his eyes.

"What's your favorite food, and if you say Ramen noodles, we can no longer be friends."

Friends. He tested the word out in his head, and determined whether or not he liked it. For the moment, it would do, but he wasn't satisfied with that term defining them.

Lance smiled up at Maggie. "Lasagna. Is that acceptable?"

She nodded thoughtfully. "Yes. This is the plan." Hopping to her feet, she wiped sand from her body and looked down at him, waiting to speak until he stood before her. "I'll cook you dinner this Tuesday. Lasagna. Wednesday we work from noon to ten, so we don't have to get up early. Judith will be gone Tuesday night too, so she won't be there breathing disapprovingly down your neck."

"Caught that, did you?"

"She doesn't like you."

Lance laughed. "No, but more importantly, she doesn't like my dad."

They began to walk.

Maggie glanced at him. "Why is that?"

"She dated my dad before he got involved with my mom, who was one of her friends. It was a big deal back in the day, I guess. Lots of gossip, tabloids, embarrassing incidents. Name-calling, public fights, anything you can think of that would draw negative attention to celebrities, really." Lance shrugged and faced the apartments as they came into view.

"That's not your fault."

His cheek lifted with the pull of a half-smile. "Isn't it? I am my father's son, after all."

"That's stupid," she huffed.

Lance stopped fighting the grin, letting it take over his mouth. "So dinner every Tuesday?"

Maggie paused. "Every Tuesday? I only committed to one."

"What if I cook the next time?"

"You know how to cook?" The surprise in her voice would have offended him, had anyone else been the one to show it.

"I do. I make a mean spaghetti," he said evilly, wiggling his eyebrows up and down.

Maggie scowled at him, but it quickly faded as she laughed. "Then I pass."

"What about chicken with broccoli? Would that be acceptable?"

"Yes," she said, looking at him out of the corner of her eye. "It would."

They reached the sidewalk that led to their separate apartments.

Lance put out a hand, palm up. "Pay up, Maggie."

"Who said I find you irresistible?" she teased.

"The fact that you offered to cook for me."

"That could have been pity."

"I doubt it," he derided.

When she continued to watch him, smirk in place, Lance stepped closer. "I'm willing to make a trade. Five kisses in place of the five dollars—one kiss for each dollar."

Her expression said she had reservations about committing to that.

"What's the matter?" he taunted. "Afraid you'll end up falling in love with me? I can't say there isn't a good chance of that."

Determination sparking to life in her eyes, Maggie grabbed his shoulders, closed her eyes, and tilted her face with pursed lips. Lance moved his head back, waiting for her to open her eyes. The seconds ticked by, spent with her posed for a kiss and Lance studying her pale face.

With a sigh, she finally looked at him. "What are you waiting for?"

"I didn't say when I was going to collect them. I'll decide when each kiss is to be given. And right now isn't when."

"You're cocky, you know that?"

"Yes. I am." Lance winked at her, moving away from the door of her apartment when the living room curtains parted to reveal a displeased Judith. He waved and turned to Maggie as the curtains snapped shut. "What are you doing tomorrow?"

"I don't know." Maggie sounded irritated. "Practicing lines, probably."

"That sounds boring. How about I teach you to surf with a boogie board instead?"

"That sounds dangerous," she retorted.

"Maggie," he chastised softly. "It isn't worth doing if it isn't. I'll be right there, at eleven tomorrow." He pointed near the shoreline. "If you show, you show. If you don't . . . have fun practicing your lines."

The mockery was plain, and she caught it, a frown marring her face. "Thank you for the memorable evening. Good night," she told him with polite reservation.

Lance blinked.

That wouldn't do, not at all. He'd turned her off with his arrogant attitude. Maggie wasn't intrigued enough to continue to spend time with him. She'd cook him dinner once, out of obligation, and then she would move on. He needed her to want to be with him. He didn't understand why, only that it was necessary. Maggie could not give up on him, not before she knew all there was to know about him. Then, he would accept it. He expected it even. But not yet, not before she gave him a chance.

Desperate to keep her tethered to him, he blurted, "It was my mom's idea to have me act. I was a baby, what did I know about it? My dad seemed to agree, since both of them dabbled in the business themselves—before my mom became a cokehead and my dad a lawyer.

"I was taught at a young age that, for me, it was the only acceptable means of having a career, and it's all I know. Sometimes, though, I wonder what it would be like . . . to be something else. To have a choice in the matter. Do you ever feel like that?"

Maggie's mouth pulled down. She pushed hair from her eyes and directed her face toward the sea. "How can you talk so cruelly about your mother?"

"I didn't know her. I mean, I don't remember her. She died a few days after I turned two. Some say it was the best birthday present she could have given me."

Maggie glanced at him, a second of shattered eyes combined with a heartbroken expression filleting his heart. He didn't want her to look at him like that. He was about ready to say forget about it, it was nice knowing her for about two seconds, and go to his apartment. He didn't need anyone feeling sorry for him.

But then she spoke, and he couldn't leave.

"This is what I want to do. This is the only thing I want to do." She looked at Lance. "I was told I couldn't do it, it was hinted around that I would never be anything special, and that's why I am determined to prove them wrong. All of them."

He tilted his head as he studied her. "Then are you doing it for you, or for someone else?"

"Does it matter?"

"Yes."

"Are you doing it for you?"

"No." Lance smiled cynically.

Maggie looked down, wiggling toes with pink-painted toenails. "My sandals are on the beach," she mused.

"Mine are too. I'll get them." Lance would hold them for ransom if he had to, all in the quest to get her to hang out with him again.

"I'll go with you."

He put out a hand to stop her. "Nope. I'll have them waiting for you, tomorrow, at eleven. Wear a comfortable swimsuit. The waves are strong."

Thoughts clear as they shifted across her face, Maggie finally laughed, shaking her head. "Okay. Fine. You win. I'll see you tomorrow at eleven."

Pleased with himself, Lance waited until she'd gone inside before patrolling the sand in search of their shoes. The wind picked up, pushing and pulling at him as he walked. He looked up at one point, toward her bedroom window. The light was on, and he pictured Maggie lying on her bed, soft and warm. Inviting. Instantly, painfully, stiff, he held still until he had control over his body. Walking around with a boner wasn't something he felt the need to do.

It took a few times of walking up and down the beach, but he finally found the two pairs of shoes. Maggie's sandals were small and black with silver shining on the parts that went over the top of her feet. He stared down at them, bemused by everything that had anything to do with her.

Restless and agitated, he dropped them off in his bedroom and left the building, heading toward the sound of music and voices. He took an offered cup of beer, slammed it, and went in search of a refill. If he drank enough, he could forget about Maggie, pretend his nerves weren't spastic around her.

He found a girl that was more than happy to keep him company, and with her draped across his lap as he sat in the sand, he commenced to get plastered. If he got enough beers in him, he could obliterate Maggie from his mind. If he got enough beers in him, he might even believe that.

MAGGIE—2010

THE POUNDING ON the door at six in the morning was not appreciated. Maggie let Lance know by grabbing a hardcover book off the nightstand and hurling it at the door. It made impact, and even she winced at how hard it hit. The door was probably gouged, which, of course, was Lance's fault as well. She'd spent the remainder of yesterday avoiding him, and he'd allowed it, both of them knowing the next day would be a different case.

"Go away!"

"Rise and shine, Maggie. It's the first day of a new you."

"Suck it, Lance Denton!"

Maggie burrowed deeper under the blankets. Just as she was about to doze off, the door crashed open. She sprung upright and stared at the doorway through a tangled web of hair. She should have known he'd unlock it with his damn handy-dandy bobby pin. She needed to find his supply and dispose of them. And then get a deadbolt.

Light from the hallway surrounded him as he advanced, but his features were hidden by darkness. He was purposeful, determined, stalking toward her like she was his prey, and Maggie's insides responded in kind. She didn't want to find anything about him attractive, but unfortunately for her, she did.

After all those years, after everything . . . it was loathsome to admit.

"I like the old doors, easy to unlock," he supplied with a thumbs-up sign. "I approve."

That made her want to modernize every inch of the house, stat.

"Get out," she said nastily.

"You say that a lot."

"And yet, here you remain."

Lance propped his hands on either side of her, leaned down so that his face was close to hers and the scent of freshly shampooed hair hit her, and said quietly, "If you are not up and out of bed by six in the morning, every morning, this is not going to work. You hired me to do a job." He straightened. "Let me do it."

Her pulse thrummed, more from his words than his proximity, which was odd. It was the way he'd spoken them, confident and without any bullshit. Maggie let her head fall back onto the pillow and looked up at a black ceiling. "Okay. You're right. Okay. But why can't it be at seven?"

"I'm sorry, what did you say? I didn't quite catch that. Did you say you were sorry? And it's six. I have other things to do with the rest of my day."

Maggie propped herself up on her elbows and glared at his head. Lance stood with his legs apart and arms crossed over his expansive chest. She couldn't see his face, but she didn't need to, to know that it was smug.

She raised a hand, one particular finger lifted. "Let me know if you catch—"

"I'll meet you downstairs," he hastily interjected.

Deciding it was too much effort, and a wasted one, to make herself presentable, Maggie tugged on a sports bra that mashed her D-cup breasts into one, huge uni-boob. She finished off the ensemble with a yellow tank top that had seen its share of grease and dirt, and red shorts. She didn't brush her hair, and she didn't brush her teeth. If Lance saw her at her worst, his expectations would be low, so when she actually tried to look decent, he would be impressed.

Not that she cared what he thought.

The bottom of the stairs seemed unreachable as she made her zombie-trek down them—a slow, disjointed, swaying amble with the purpose to remain upright and mobile. Lance leaned against the kitchen counter and watched her advance, sipping from her favorite mug. It was pink with a heart on either side. She wanted to snatch it away from him. He should have been embarrassed to use such a cup, but as with all things concerning Lance, he looked good holding it, totally natural. Annoyingly so.

"That's my cup."

"Aren't they all?"

She gave him a slit-eyed look and took a different, boring, non-favorite mug from the cupboard overhead. Stepping into the colorful kitchen usually had the ability to make her happy, but Lance's presence had sucked all the joy right out of her. "That one's my favorite."

He offered it to her and Maggie almost hissed at him. With a shrug, he retracted his hand.

"What are you doing?" he asked when she reached for the coffeepot.

"Getting a cup of coffee."

"Yours is over there."

She followed his nod and laughed at the bottle of water standing on the counter. "No. I don't think so."

"How many cups of coffee do you drink a day?"

"I don't know, one."

"You drink one cup of coffee a day?"

"No, one pot of coffee."

Lance straightened. "You drink twelve cups of coffee a day?"

"You don't have to sound so stunned," she muttered, pouring black, liquid stamina into her cup.

It was immediately removed from her hand.

"There's no other way to sound, since I am thoroughly, one hundred percent, without a doubt, stunned. Drink this instead." He set the bottle of water before her.

"No." She crossed her arms.

Lance raised his eyebrows. "Yes."

"You are out of your mind if you think I'm giving up coffee," Maggie ground out, glaring into his blue eyes.

"I'm not saying you have to give it up, but limit it, yes, and drinking it first thing in the morning? No."

"You're drinking it." She realized she was being childish, but Maggie really didn't care. She was tired, and crabby, and she wanted her coffee.

"I've been up since four. I drank my water already, and I also already got my workout in for the day. You can join me then, if you like."

Maggie snatched the bottle of water from the counter.

Amusement flickered in his eyes. "Those are yours as well." He nodded to a square packet.

Maggie stared at it. "Are you trying to kill me, or get me in shape?"

"You need energy to work out. These will give you that, and also tide you over until you can have a proper meal."

Grumbling, she opened the package of unsalted almonds, chewing the bland nuts as her face twisted with displeasure.

Lance smirked. "What was that?"

"I said, what is a proper meal to you? A piece of lettuce slathered in nothing?"

He laughed. "No. Not quite."

"You're enjoying this," she accused, swallowing the nut and slowly placing another in her mouth. They tasted like cardboard.

He shrugged, not denying it. "I've always enjoyed your personality."

"Don't . . . bring up the past," she warned. If he did, she would remember the bad things, sure, but then she'd also be forced to remember the good, and she didn't want that.

It had taken years to get over him, and the thought of doing it all over again was reprehensible. Lance was the one guy she'd loved more than anyone else. She'd loved other men, of course, but none like him. Him, she'd loved without reservation, with her whole heart, with every bit of her.

And he'd given her heart back—torn, bloody, wounded, aching. Scarred. Jaded.

"It's all we got, Maggie." His tone was somber, but then he grinned and winked, and she was transported back into that life they'd temporarily shared. Everything was brighter then, better, new. They loved under a haze of youth and misplaced dreams, and it crashed all around them—or her, more specifically.

"How was the couch?" she asked sweetly, needing to get control of the conversation.

Maggie wouldn't be surprised to find that he peacefully slept, oblivious to his surroundings and anyone near. Maggie, on the other hand, spent the night tossing and turning, dreaming of blue eyes and firm lips. When she woke up, memories took place of the dreams—the sweet, masculine scent of his skin, the heat of his body. The strength of his hands when they unconsciously dug into her skin. The night tormented her.

Lance grabbed an apple from a bowl on the counter and tossed it back and forth between his hands as he talked. "It's a nice couch, lumps in all the right places." He sank his teeth into the apple. Frozen, he mouthed around the fruit, "This isn't a real apple, is it?"

Maggie snorted and looked away to hide her smile.

Lance spit out the wax fruit and grabbed a paper towel from the holder and rubbed his mouth. He tossed the paper towel in the garbage and said, "You need real fruit, not fake."

"Real is always better than fake," she agreed, giving him a pointed look.

"Oh, Maggie," he purred, moving closer. "Everything about me has always been real."

Her breath hiccupped. "Oh, Lance. I know." She was glad that her voice didn't shake.

Time froze, turned heavy as Lance stared at her with enough intensity to tear the air from her lungs. Looking at him made her dizzy, and when he studied her like he was looking into her, seeing through the present and into the past, seeing her in the way only Lance ever could, it made her weak in the knees.

He narrowed his eyes, and then his expression cleared. "I noticed a bunch of doors. Would any of them happen to lead to spare bedrooms?"

"Nope."

"What are they then?"

"Doors."

"Doors," he repeated doubtfully.

"Yep. Just doors. Nothing behind them but walls."

"Interesting," he mused, rubbing his jaw. "Because I opened one, and lo and behold, it led to a room. With a bed."

Maggie scowled. "If you make it past two weeks, which I sincerely doubt, then you can pick out a room."

Lance offered his hand.

She gingerly took it.

"I look forward to it," he said, shaking her hand.

Maggie tugged her hand from his, the limb tingling from the feel of his strong, calloused grip.

"We need to go over some things, like how you should be eating five to six small meals a day. No skipping meals." The expression on Lance's face was severe. "We'll set up a meal plan for you later. First things first, though." He eyed her critically, lingering a touch too long on her chest before meeting her gaze. "Show me your underwear."

She choked on the nut she was in the process of swallowing, coughing as it scraped her throat on the way down. "No," she rasped.

Lance shook his head, already heading toward the stairs. "Get your mind out of the gutter."

She ran after him, not in eagerness to reveal her undergarments, but to keep him away from them. "Don't you dare go through my dresser drawers!"

He paused halfway up the stairwell, looking over his broad shoulder at her. "Why would I do that when you're simply going to show me?"

She sputtered, charging up the stairs after him with more exuberance than she'd shown in a long time. The bedroom walls were painted lavender and decorated with watercolor artwork that usually had a calming effect. The room seemed to shrink with Lance inside it. He stood near her dresser, eyebrows raised expectantly.

When she didn't move any closer, he sighed. Tone blunt, Lance said, "There are key elements to getting healthy—what and how much you eat, of course, and how often you exercise, along with the kind of exercise you're doing. Getting enough water, and cutting out sugary drinks, is also necessary.

"What a lot of people don't realize, is that what you wear while you exercise is just as important. You have to be comfortable, but also have proper support. That thing you're passing off as a bra needs to be burned."

Maggie's face flamed and she protectively crossed her arms.

Lance slowly walked around her, sending prickles of awareness down her spine with his nearness, and stopped in front of her. "Take off your shirt," he ordered.

The command sent desire coursing through her, and she gritted her teeth against it. She would not be wooed by him, intentionally or otherwise. Maggie refused to find him attractive and she would remain firm in the face of his animal magnetism—all while secretly lusting after him.

"Are you crazy?" she demanded in a tight voice.

He fingered the hem of her top, a thoughtful frown on his lush mouth. "Not at the moment." He looked up, features hardening. "Do it."

"I will not."

"Do it or I will." Menace was woven through his words and reflected in the shards of blue glass that passed for eyes.

Heart thundering in her chest, Maggie tried to breathe, only a gasp of pitiful air leaving her. "Try it and die."

The sensual mouth turned inflexible, and instead of intimidating her, she remembered the feel of it against her mouth, her body. He'd turned her inside out with that mouth. She shouldn't be able to recall such a thing, but there it was. Maggie fought to swallow, her lips and mouth dry. All of her was rigid with longing for a man she told herself she loathed. The body was quick to call one a liar, when needed.

"Gladly."

And just like that, her arms were over her head, the material of the shirt twisted around her before it was dragged up and off, and she stood before Lance in nothing but her uni-boob bra. To say that she was mortified would be a drastic under-exaggeration. She was beyond that. He was seeing the top half of her body in a way he hadn't in close to a dozen years. Oh, how it had changed within that time span. Pudgy, fleshy, pale skin. Maggie wanted to hang her head in shame, so she instead lifted her chin defiantly and met his gaze.

Half of his mouth curved at the silent challenge. He didn't move or look away. Lance placed a hand over his mouth as he studied her chest with avid interest. She saw no revulsion in his expression, but then, she wouldn't, if he didn't want her to. Lance was a talented actor.

Lance touched one of the straps, his fingers drawing across the sensitive flesh of her shoulder. She closed her eyes, pulse picking up, and dug her nails into the palms of her hands. His hand lingered, and Maggie stood still, wanting him to move away and wanting him to move closer. When she couldn't stand the paused moment any longer, she opened her eyes. Lance watched her, face bleeding emotion like raindrops of sorrow and pain. She blinked, and it was gone, his expression closed.

He went behind her, near enough that she sensed the heat of his body, felt his words as well as heard them. "This should be outlawed. What do you call this, a form of torture under the guise of a sports bra? How can you stand it? I hurt just looking at it."

Lance stopped before her, movements brisk as he touched and prodded along the bottom of the bra, inches away from her breasts. He snapped and tugged, shaking his head as he examined the garment. The material was flimsy enough that it was obvious that she was cold, and she was. Cold. Nothing else.

He looked at her. "Are all of your sports bras this nipple death trap?"

An unintelligible sound left her. "Nipple . . . death . . . trap?"

Impatiently gesturing to her chest, he said, "Yes. Look at them. They're crying out to be released. Poor things. And your breasts—why are you being so cruel to them? They need to breathe, Maggie. Be kind to your body. More importantly, be kind to your boobs."

Mouth hanging open, feeling oddly, properly chastised, Maggie blinked and straightened. "Well . . . well . . . I don't wear this that much." Why was she defending herself? Why was he making her feel it was necessary to defend herself?

"Even once is too much," he said concernedly. "I think, for the benefit of future you, you should remove it. Now. Immediately." The teasing light flared to life in his eyes as he met her gaze, and he smiled unabashedly, unable to keep up the act.

"You ass," she muttered, smacking his arm.

"Seriously, you can't wear this anymore." Not seeing the tongue she stuck out at him, Lance tapped his mouth with a finger as he turned toward the dresser. "I think before we do anything else, we need to go shopping. What kind of workout clothes do you have? And underwear—what does your underwear look like?" His tone was innocent, but again, when he caught her eye, she saw the amusement he couldn't contain.

"Socks too," he continued. "Shoes. All of those things matter. Do you have clothes specifically for working out?"

"I wear tee shirts and shorts."

He was shaking his head before she stopped talking. "No. If you can't afford workout clothes, those will do, but you can."

"How do you know what I can or can't afford?" she asked suspiciously.

"Do you experience chaffing?" His gaze was aimed at her crotch.

Maggie nervously crossed her legs. Why, she didn't know. He still had a perfect view of her clothed nether regions. "I'm not telling you."

"I'll take that as a yes. So." He clapped his hands once and focused on her crimson face. "Today we'll walk to the sports store near Lane Gym. Not much in the way of hardcore exercising, but we need to start out slow. Less chance of injury that way. And please, for the love of all things holy, get rid of that bra before we do. I'll wait downstairs."

"The sports store doesn't even open for over three hours," she called after him.

He paused near the doorway. "You're right. Good time to get a physical assessment while we wait. See you in the basement." His voice was sinisterly as he said that.

"How do you know there's a basement, or where it is?" she demanded.

"I am a man without limits—and I snooped around the house last night after you went to bed."

Lance closed the door after him, leaving a sputtering Maggie in his wake. She wasn't surprised that he'd snooped through her house last night. She was sure he'd even used the gym located in the basement that morning. At least someone did, she grudgingly acknowledged.

With a sigh, she rifled through the dresser drawers, deciding on what to keep, and what to toss. She had no suitable underwear for working out; most of them were thin and miniscule, and the majority of her bras weren't supportive enough.

It was a struggle to get out of the bra she'd squeezed into, arms bent at odd angles and grunts leaving her as she fought with the apparel. It got stuck somewhere between her armpits and the top of her breasts, and with a cry of fury, she pulled it over her head, causing her arms to ache in the process. Out of breath and sweating, she heaved the sports bra to the floor and put on a slightly better one that didn't make her look like she had one boob instead of two.

Clothed in her customary exercise shirt and shorts, shoes on feet and hair up in a ponytail, Maggie stopped in the upstairs bathroom to brush and floss her teeth and wash her face before meeting Lance in the basement.

Maggie had the makings of a workout room in the semi-finished basement. So far the area had a treadmill, elliptical machine, and a punching bag. She'd had most of the equipment for over three years and had used a combination of it less than a dozen times. She stood in the middle of the cream-toned room and stared at her reflection in the mirrored wall. The mirrors were supposed to work as a motivator, but they worked as the opposite most days. A television and DVD player were set up in a corner of the room with a yoga mat, free weights, and resistance bands.

It came as somewhat of a surprise that there weren't cobwebs covering the majority of the contraptions.

Lance had a set of pink ten-pound free weights in hand, back to the mirror as he lifted and lowered, muscles forming and releasing as he moved. She was surprised that he wasn't staring at his reflection, preening at his physical perfection, although it wasn't like everywhere he went, he wasn't reminded. Women had always fawned over him. Maggie doubted that had changed.

He set the weights down, not in the least bit winded, and wiped his hands on the gray athletic shorts gracing his muscular legs. A band of black material showed beneath the hem of the shorts, which had to be compression shorts. Lance was a runner. That didn't surprise her.

"What is your activity level?" he asked, picking up a notepad and pen from the floor.

Maggie frowned. "Are you taking notes?"

"Yes."

She squinted at his hands. "That's the notebook I use to make my grocery lists!"

"Is it? Nice. Very sturdy."

"You went through my desk too?" she growled, sounding disturbingly like a bear, or some other large, rabid beast.

There was important, private material in that desk. She could clearly picture him rummaging through her things in the dark of night, thoroughly amused with any information pertaining to her that he could get his grubby hands on. Suddenly it made sense how he would know whether or not she could afford workout clothes—her financial papers and checkbook were in a drawer of the desk.

The glare intensified, to the point that her face was grooved in discontent, all of it aimed at Lance.

"Good thing too, or I wouldn't have found these." He lifted the pen and paper with a disarming grin.

There was no positive outcome from getting too upset with him. He wouldn't notice, or care.

"If you were an average person, you wouldn't get away with nearly as much as you do," she commented, more of an afterthought than a direct one.

"Alas, I am so much more than merely average." Lance held a hand to his chest and closed his eyes.

"In all areas," Maggie muttered, thinking of the conceited gene he seemed to have in ample supply.

Back to business, he asked, "How active are you, on a daily basis?"

"I don't know." She avoided his eyes.

Maggie wasn't active at all. She wandered around the house during the day, and sometimes sat outside. Once in a great while she'd go for a short walk, but mostly, she led a solitary, sedentary existence. It sounded bad when spoken out loud. Sure, she had her hobbies, but those were done either standing or sitting. All in all, she was a couch potato.

"Tell me how a usual day goes for you," he pressed, eyes on her.

"Um . . ." Maggie played with her ponytail, careful to keep her gaze trained to the left of him. "I get up, eat, ya know, do stuff . . ." she trailed off, swallowing thickly.

The silence grew, full of unsaid observations and awkward tension.

"Can you elaborate?"

"No," Maggie snapped. "I can't." Instantly remorseful for being snippy, she supplied, "Okay. So. I don't do much. Okay? Like, anything, really. Judge away."

"Maggie."

She finally looked at him, fighting the urge to run from the room and out of the house, even if it was hers. She wanted to get away from him, especially when she saw the understanding on his face.

"I'm not judging you. I'm here to help you. I have to know your history to know where to start, that's all."

Nodding, she took a deep breath. "All right. I don't get much physical activity. I go for walks, occasionally, but nothing routine. I never use any of the stuff in this room. Well, maybe, like, once every six months."

Lance blinked, but quickly hid his expression by focusing on the paper he held. "What are your fitness goals?"

That one she knew.

"I don't want to be skinny—I want to be strong."

He nodded in approval, and it was sad how pleased she was by that.

"With your history as it is, you have to be careful," he remarked, blazing her with the intensity of his eyes. "There's a line between healthy and unhealthy, and you don't want to cross it." *Not again*, remained silent.

"Don't lecture me."

"I'm not. I said my piece, and I won't mention it again. Fair enough?"

She rubbed her forehead. "Yeah. Fair enough."

"Height?"

"Five feet three inches."

"Weight?"

Maggie hedged, not wanting him to know the fatal number on the scale.

Lance sighed and placed his hands on the back of his head. He leveled his gaze on her. "Did you know," he began conversationally. "That muscle is denser than fat? You can weigh the same as someone else, but look bigger or smaller, depending on the amount of muscle you have. Muscle is good. Your weight is a number. It has no bearing on your fitness level."

"Except my fitness level is non-existent."

"Not for long." He dropped his hands and resumed his brisk manner. "Weight?"

"One hundred and fifty-two pounds," she mumbled, crossing her arms and dropping her gaze to her blue and white shoes.

He paused, seeming undecided, and then said, "Technically speaking, you're not that overweight for your height and age. A solid ten to fifteen pounds off and better eating and exercising habits and you'll be set."

"If what you weigh doesn't matter, why do you keep acting like it does?"

"It matters, of course, but not as much as people think. People also think it's all about the cardio. Cardio is important, but strength training is more important. Cardio burns calories, but strength training burns fat and builds muscle. Make sense?"

"No."

"Okay, let's measure you," he said, acting like she hadn't spoken.

"Lance."

"Yes?"

"This is not my idea of fun." She moved over to where he stood.

A faint smile brightened his face. "I know, Maggie, but you'll thank me later—or not," he added at the dubious look she sent his way. "Trust me, once you get into the routine of it, you'll miss it if you don't do it. You'll feel empowered, invincible, and you'll want to do it every day."

"In other words, I'll feel just like you on any given day," she mocked.

"Exactly." He roughly spun her around. "Lift your arms above your head."

She did, staring at their reflection in the mirror. It was like looking at the two of them, fast-forwarded and aged from when they were teens. Maggie never thought she'd be standing so close to him again, let alone have him in her house. He'd gotten taller since the show. Where he'd once had four or five inches on her, it was closer to seven or eight. It wasn't like she hadn't somewhat kept track of him through the years, but seeing someone on television was different from seeing them in person.

Lance tugged her top up once more.

"Why do you insist on seeing my stomach?" she grumbled, hands holding up the shirt.

He ignored her, arms going around her torso to meet above her bellybutton. Maggie froze. Lance looked up, meeting her gaze in the mirror. If not for the horrified look on her face, it would be easy to believe they were intimate, with the way he was wrapped around her. Something cold touched her skin and she jumped. Lance smiled and his head disappeared from view. Holding the body measuring tape to her frame, he walked to the front of her, the bendable plastic gliding along her skin with him.

"This is the proper spot to measure. At the juncture of your natural waist," he said quietly.

She was imagining the faint roughness to his deep voice, not to mention the way his fingers lingered on her skin. It was all in her head, obviously.

Lance bent down to read the tape, putting his dark head disturbingly close to her breasts. Her fingers curled, wanting to touch his silky hair. She didn't trust herself around him. Next thing she knew, she'd be begging him to seduce her. They'd run through that scenario before. His hair brushed her skin as he straightened and she swallowed. He wrote a number on the paper and told her to remove her shirt.

"Again?" she whined, but obliged when his blank expression didn't change. "Is this essential?"

"Lift your arms," Lance directed.

Maggie raised her arms above her head.

"That's too high. Like this." He adjusted her arms so that they hovered at shoulder-length.

Lance took another measurement, this one around her breasts. She sucked in a sharp breath when one of his fingers grazed the slope of her breast as he stepped away. He was quick to avert his face, but she caught the smile.

"You're having way too much fun with this."

"Yes, I am," he agreed.

He went on to measure her biceps, neck, hips, and each thigh, his face directly in front of a place that would remain unnamed. She held perfectly still during that, not even wanting to breathe. Then she began to wonder why he didn't move for so long. When he abruptly stood and turned away, she thought she understood, although the thought was implausible. Him, turned on by her, in her present state? Not likely. It was more probable that he got a cramp in his leg.

The next hour was spent going through her cupboards and refrigerator. Maggie wanted to weep as the pile of food to donate grew and grew, and the pile of food to keep remained abysmally small.

"There are good fats and bad fats. This—" Lance shook a bag of potato chips in front of her face. Maggie swiped at it with her hand, but he pulled it out of reach. "—is a bad fat." He tossed it into the pile of food that she was no longer allowed to eat whenever she felt like it.

"What are good fats?" Her tone was snarky. She didn't care.

Lance trained his gaze on her. "Nuts and seeds, avocados, salmon, olives, peanut butter, and most oils."

"So all the things I don't like. Wonderful."

"You know what?" Lance looked at the counter laden with all the delicious food. "Let's take your car and drop this stuff off at the church. We'll make a stop at the sports store before the grocery store and then come back to start your training. You can walk on the treadmill today."

It all sounded like too much work, and not in the least bit desirable. "I am regretting this more and more."

He slammed a hand on the countertop, causing Maggie to jump. Lance put his face at eyelevel with hers and stared into her soul with dark, malicious eyes. "Enough with the comments. I don't want to waste my time on someone who isn't serious about getting healthy. I don't need your money that bad. Either you're in this, or you aren't. Which is it?"

Maggie stared back, startled by the outburst. The longer she looked into his unflappable gaze, the more she realized he was right. It was her idea, and although Lance wasn't her first choice as a personal trainer, she had to cut him some slack and let him do his job. Moaning and carrying on wasn't helping anyone—not her, not him.

"You're right. I'm sorry," she said, the words thick and bitter in her mouth. "I'll stop complaining."

A smile took over the stony expression, and he straightened. "Well, you are allowed to complain a little."

As they walked out the front door, both with a box of food in their arms, Lance looked at her and said, "This isn't something minor. You need to be in it one hundred percent, or it isn't worth it. Every time you go to eat or drink something, you have to think about what you're about to put in your body. It's a lifestyle change, and you should be ready for that. All right?"

"All right, Coach," she joked, bumping her shoulder to his when his eyebrows lowered.

"Coach," he said softly, testing out the word. "I like it." Lance puffed out his chest and jabbed his thumb at it. "That's right. I'm in charge."

"As long as I continue to pay you, you're in charge, you mean," she said with a lifted eyebrow.

Lance tugged at her ponytail with his free hand, causing shivers to cascade down her arms. "You'll pay me, one way or another."

That sounded erotically threatening, and she wondered if he would demand payment in kisses, a thought that would usually make her scowl at a memory, but that time, made her smile.

LANCE USHERED HER into the first sports store they came across in the strip mall. The store was warmer than necessary and smelled like feet. Rows and rows of clothing were set up throughout, shoes lining one wall. Hard rock music played, making Maggie twitch with the need to angrily storm around the place.

He grabbed random articles of clothing, throwing them her way. "Let me see these when you have them on."

"You don't even know what size I am," she said, putting back the clothes.

"Oh, but I do," he said near her ear. "You're a size sexy."

Maggie stepped back with a frown on her face, divided between laughing and hitting him. "Why would I need to show you anyway? I know what fits me and what doesn't."

"It's part of the job."

"Really?" A thought came to her. "How many of your clients are women?"

"About sixty percent."

She nodded. "And how many of them have to go clothes shopping with you?"

Lance's eyes narrowed. "I know what you're getting at."

"Think so?"

"You're implying that I have unprofessional relationships with my female clients."

"Do you?" She lifted an eyebrow.

"Only with you." He winked.

Maggie snorted. "I wouldn't doubt your idea of doing your job is seeing how many of your clients you can sleep with."

"Does this include all one hundred percent of them, or just the sixty percent that are actually women?"

"Whatever floats your boat."

"Bad choice of words. Brings up a horrible visual," he added in a mutter at her look, tossing more pants and tops at her. "Try these on and then come out."

Maggie caught them against her chest. "Why can't I have one of the workers let me know if they fit? Why does it have to be you?"

"Like that worker?" He nodded to a tall, gangly blond who was picking his nose. As they watched, he wiped his hand on his shorts and went in for another dig.

Maggie cringed.

Lance turned to her. "You really want that horny, nose-picking teenager to be groping you?"

"As opposed to you?"

"I'll only grope a little." At her look, he grinned. "I'll make sure you like it too."

Maggie turned on her heel and stomped for the fitting rooms. She took off her shirt and shorts, then grabbed the first top. It was a size extra-small. She made a sound of disbelief.

"Everything okay in there?" Lance called, sounding thoroughly happy with himself.

Maggie checked another top. It was an extra-extra-large. Scowling, she hurriedly went through the rest of the clothes. Out of the ten garments, two tops and one pair of exercise shorts were actually her size.

"Need some help?"

"I do, actually."

"Open the door and I'll gladly assist."

"I bet you would," she muttered, swooping up all the outfits into her arms. Maggie said in a louder voice, "Can you stand by the door so I can give you something that doesn't fit?"

"Okay. I'm here. What do you n—"

She threw all the clothes over the top of the door, hoping they all landed on his head. Through the space between the bottom of the door and the floor, she watched with satisfaction as a rainbow of clothes formed around his tennis shoes.

"I guess they don't fit," he said calmly.

"No. I guess they don't. If you'd actually looked at the sizes, you would have known that."

"Are you naked right now?"

"Tell you what," she purred from inside the small clothing room as she looked with displeasure at her image in the mirror. "I'll get naked, when you get naked."

"Don't tempt me."

With irritation burning through her, Maggie grabbed a shirt that actually fit and chucked it over the top of the door.

"Are we getting naked then?" he asked after a pause.

Maggie tugged on her shirt and shorts, unlocked the door, and slammed a palm against it, smiling slightly when the door hit Lance in the shoulder. "Why are you standing so close to the door?"

"I thought maybe I'd acquire x-ray vision if I stared at the door long enough," he said, rubbing his shoulder.

"Did it work?"

"The results are inconclusive. I was still working on it when you hit me with the door."

"Lance," Maggie said, looking out the window of the store. The parking lot was filling up with people and their vehicles. "I think I can manage to pick out clothes that properly fit me."

Eyeing her chest, Lance shook his head. "I'm having doubts about that. Remember the nipple death trap you were trying to pawn off as a bra?"

Maggie walked to the nearest rack of shirts, rifling through them before choosing one in her size. With Lance following, she found a pair of shorts, and a sports bra. Lifting her eyebrows at him, she stepped back into the fitting room, unclothed, put on the athletic garb, and swung the door open. Exercise clothes were great for giving the appearance of being slimmer in certain areas of the physique, but that fat had to go somewhere. Maggie's stomach and hips were overly rounded at the moment.

She strode out, met his eyes as she struck a pose, turned around, and did the same before facing him again. "Well?"

He rubbed his jaw as he walked a circle around her, Maggie rolling her eyes when his met hers. Laughter danced within the blue depths of them. The Lance before her seemed more carefree than the one of younger years—or he'd become a better actor. Everyone changed as they got older, but did they really change that much? She wondered in what ways Lance had, and in what ways he hadn't.

"I think I need to see one more before I can give a definitive answer." At her scowl, he laughed and held up his hands, palms out. "I'm kidding. They look good. How's the bra?" He reached out a hand and she slapped it away.

"It fits just fine. It's tight enough to be supportive but also comfortable."

"Even if you're running? Maybe you should try it out, jog in place a bit, jump up and down. I'll watch, give my qualified opinion." Lance gave her a cheeky grin.

Maggie picked out two more outfits, bras, socks, and a pair of tennis shoes. At a department store next door, she got basic, sturdy underwear. Once she had the appropriate apparel, and a heart monitor calorie tracker thing Lance insisted she needed that she was sure she didn't, they left the strip mall and headed toward the grocery store down the road.

Lance drove her Camry like it was his, pulling the vehicle into the parking lot of 'Gramp's', a local, privately owned grocery store. They spent an hour in the store, and Maggie spent a load of money as well.

More than once she complained, "Why is healthy food so expensive?" It was like the world wanted everyone to be fat. Three apples cost more than a meal at a fast food restaurant. He gave her a pat on the head as she pushed the cart stocked with food out of the store, his attention elsewhere. When he stiffened next to her, then just as quickly relaxed, she looked in the direction he was.

"What is it?" Maggie demanded, even as she noticed the two women. Both brunette, seeming to be in their early forties, they stood near a car in the parking lot, first gawking at them—or more specifically, Lance—and then talking to one another. Their expressions were equally excited and fearful, which was a common look for fans.

She gestured to them. "Better get to it. You know you'll make their day if you sign something."

"Day?" He glanced over his broad shoulder at her as he strode for them. "More like infinite days, or even their whole existence."

She couldn't deny that, and with a much slower pace than Lance, Maggie pushed the cart in their direction. She watched as Lance hugged them both quickly, their squeals and chatter reaching her as she closed the distance. He'd always been more comfortable around fans than Maggie. She felt weird even saying she had them. It didn't seem natural to idolize another person, flawed and mortal as they were.

One of them said something to Lance. He went still, then shook his head. The woman's face fell and she looked behind him to Maggie. Her steps slowed, and she knew she wasn't going to like whatever awaited her. They all turned their attention to her.

"Hello," Maggie greeted softly.

Her hands were taken by one of the ladies and tightly squeezed. "Maggie Smiley," she breathed. "It's so great to meet you. I—we're—both huge fans of 'Easier Said'. I watch reruns of it all the time."

"Thank you so much." Sincere though the words were, Maggie always felt they were lacking somehow. If not for fans, the show wouldn't have gone anywhere.

She hugged the woman, asking her name. Her name was Beth, and the lady beside her was her sister Rachel. Maggie hugged her as well, again thanking them for their love of the show.

"I was so upset when the show was cancelled. I moped around the house for weeks."

Maggie shifted her eyes down, the ghost of guilt creeping along her spine. She didn't look at Lance, not wanting to see whatever expression he wore.

"She really did," Rachel supplied, tucking a lock of brown hair behind her ear. "I had to force her to watch 'Black as Sin' to get over it."

Beth placed a hand on Maggie's arm. "Not that it was even close to being as good as 'Easier Said', but the murders on the series did take my mind off things."

Lance murmured, "I imagine it did."

Maggie looked at him, found his eyes on her. A faint smile lined his mouth.

"Can we—would it be okay to get some pictures with you two? I'm sure you get asked all the time, but . . . and I didn't realize you were talking to one another! That's so great. Any plans for future co-projects? It would be great to see you together again on television." Beth paused and sucked in a lungful of air.

"She rambles when she's nervous," Rachel told them.

"We actually have to get going, lots of food that needs to be refrigerated," Maggie said, avoiding the questions.

Beth's eyes dimmed. "Oh. Okay. Of course. Thanks for talking with us." She turned to her sister. "Let's make sure we pick up some pie for

Greg. Blueberry, if they have it."

"I think we can manage one picture," Lance said to Beth as the sisters started to walk away, but his words were for Maggie.

Maggie's shoulders stiffened, but she pasted on a smile when the sisters turned their gazes to her.

"Really?" Beth went still. As quickly as the joy was wiped out of the woman by Maggie's comment, Lance's put it back in place. He had an uncanny ability to make anyone feel special.

"Really. Got a camera or your phone handy?" he asked.

"Yes! Hold this." Shoving her purse at her sister, Beth opened the car door and rummaged around inside the car before triumphantly waving a camera in the air. "Got it! Rachel, take our picture."

Rachel obliged, and with a widely smiling fan between them, Maggie and Lance had their first picture taken together in over ten years.

"Was that so hard?" he asked as they left the women.

"I didn't want my picture taken with you," she fumed as she angrily pushed the cart toward the car.

"Why? You made a fan happy. It wasn't that much of a sacrifice."

Maggie stopped walking and glared at him. "I realize your ignorance and insensitivity are things you can't seem to control, but even you should comprehend what that photograph could mean."

"I'm not following."

She tossed up her hands. The cart rolled down the pavement until Lance dove for it and halted it.

"First of all, you look great. I, on the other hand, do not." Maggie sliced a hand through the air when he opened his mouth. "Second of all, where do you think that picture is going to show up? Everywhere," she bit out.

"All social media platforms on the internet, possibly in magazines. And there will be talk, and speculation, and I'm so tired of the gossip. It's been years. Why can't people get over things and move on? We had a show, we don't anymore. It's over."

She wasn't only talking about 'Easier Said'—she was talking about them. When they broke up, the world seemed as heartbroken as she was. It had been hard enough on her without having the media involved in it. Their love life was outlined, and so was their split, and every hurtful thing they did to one another afterward. She'd cut him from her life, but he never really left it.

Lance stared at her. "It's just a picture."

Shaking her head, she turned away. "It's not just a picture, not with us."

They quietly loaded the groceries in the back of the car, neither speaking until Maggie asked, "What did Beth ask you when I was walking over?"

Lance shot her a look, immediately redirecting his attention to the grocery bags. "She asked if we were together again, as a couple."

Briefly closing her eyes, she took the empty cart and put it in the drop-off area. Maggie could already see the headline: Is reconciliation in the future for former sweethearts and co-stars of the hit show 'Easier Said'?

LANCE—1996

LANCE FIXED HIS hair, checked his jaw for any missed stubble, and left the bathroom.

Mitch whistled from the doorway where he was pulling on a pair of boots. "Who are you all dressed up for?"

Mitch Hermsen was a grease ball, a guy in his twenties with the sole ambition to drink and have sex with as many women as possible. He was on the setup staff for 'Easier Said' and spent his days leering at the female cast and crew more than he worked. The only reason Lance shared an apartment with him was so he wasn't obligated by his father to share one with someone he'd want to be shacked up with even less. And Mitch was hardly ever around, so the place felt like Lance's instead of theirs.

"No one," he said coolly, glancing at the clock on the wall above the couch. It was almost five and Maggie was due any minute. He wanted Mitch gone before she showed up.

Pushing brown hair behind his ears, Mitch grinned at him. "Come on, man, who's the latest chick?"

Ignoring him, Lance went to the kitchen and surveyed his attempt at dinner. It was their second Tuesday meal together, Maggie having cooked the first. That lasagna had been the best he'd ever had, and he'd told her. Her face had lit up like stars lived beneath her skin. He'd decided then that Maggie needed as many compliments as he was able to think up, just so he could see that look on her face and know he put it there.

The chicken was pink in spots and slimy with an unpleasant aroma. The broccoli looked wilted and mushy. And the rice was hard—he'd tried it.

A faint knock at the door had Lance barreling from the kitchen, only to have Mitch block him with his body draped across the door.

"Uh-uh-uh. Not yet, lover boy. Tell me who it is first, and I'll let her in."

Lance met taunting brown eyes, and his jaw shifted forward. He ground out, "Don't you have somewhere to be?"

"I do." He nodded. "Hot date with Simone from lighting. Know her?"

He glared at him.

Mitch shrugged, rubbing at a stain on his green shirt. "Anyway, she'll wait." His grin was tainted with brutish intent. "Tell me who it is, and I'll open the door."

"I could hit you," Lance said evenly.

"You could. But then your dad would make you move out, and you don't want that. You like your freedom." Mitch crossed his arms and gave Lance a thoughtful look. "I know, I'll guess her name."

"Mitch! Come on. She's going to leave!" Anxiety pumped through his veins instead of blood.

"Your call."

"Fuck you, asshole," he growled.

"Let's see . . . Rachel? No? Hmm. Megan? What about Lisa?" Mitch snapped his fingers together, halting in his list before naming off a fraction of the girls Lance had had in the apartment at one time or another. He remembered their names better than Lance. "I know! Denise. Yes? No. This is so difficult. I mean, there've been so many." He laughed.

He said her name to shut up Mitch, but also in hopes that she heard him and didn't leave. He walked a thin line with her, he knew. One wrong move too many and Maggie was gone.

"Now open the door," Lance seethed. "Before I decide I don't care if I have to find a new place to live."

Smiling, Mitch kept his eyes on Lance's as he reached around him and turned the doorknob. He stood inside the door, allowing just enough room for someone to squeeze around him and enter. No one walked into the apartment. Lance stepped around him, seeing a blank spot where Maggie should have been. With an angry expletive, he shoved Mitch out of his way and ran onto the porch that led to the stairwell.

"Don't be like that, Lance! Uncle Mitch was only having a little fun. We'll kiss and make up later," Mitch called after him, laughing.

He was going to punch him in the face yet.

Lance looked over the railing, saw Maggie's copper and bronze hair as she headed toward the beach, and vaulted over the ledge. His knees popped as he landed, and a sharp pain shot up his left leg. He hobbled until it wore off, then sprinted through the sand, calling her name.

She spun around, hair following her like a waterfall of sunset.

Out of breath, Lance lifted a hand and bent over at the waist, trying to steady his thrumming pulse while simultaneously making her stay. He wasn't doing very well at either one. "Mag—Maggie . . . just wait. Okay? Give me a second."

Arms crossed, she watched him. Then she nodded and turned away, her feet moving fast in the opposite direction. "You had your second."

She wasn't talking about then. What Maggie was really saying was that he'd had his chance with her and he'd blown it.

"Maggie! Damn it, Maggie, wait!"

Maggie faced him, a scowl set into her features. "Don't you swear at me!"

"Don't walk away from me!"

"Don't tell me what to do!"

Desperate, Lance grabbed her hands. "Don't give up on me." She froze, and he added, "Please."

Maggie swallowed and pulled her hands away. "You and I can be friends. That's it."

He didn't think it was the proper time to bring up the three kisses she still owed him, so he nodded. "Okay. Fine. Deal." *No*, his brain screamed. *Not fine. No deal.*

"No more impromptu kisses," she continued.

"That's a big word," he said wryly. "Okay. No more kisses." Lance promised not to kiss her, but if she wanted to kiss him, that was her doing, and he would be more than happy to help her out. That's what friends did.

"I'm sorry about not answering the door. My roommate—"

"I heard," she interrupted.

Maggie went quiet, giving him a sidelong glance.

"What is it?" Lance asked, unable to take the silence any longer.

"Did you really date all of those girls he named?"

He swallowed. "I don't know if *date* is the right word."

Shadows pirouetted across her features. "You just had sex with them?"

"No!" he denied, and then amended, "Well, not all of them, but a lot of them."

Maggie looked down the beach, still as stone. "Is that what you plan on doing with me?" When her eyes came back to his, he was struck speechless by their intensity. "You'll be nice to me until you get something out of it, and then you'll forget about me? I'll be some name on a list?"

Lance blew out a breath. Lies didn't work with Maggie. If he wanted to get anywhere with her, he had to be as honest as he could be, even if he upset her. She respected the truth. She disliked liars.

"I don't know," he said straightforwardly. "I hadn't thought that far ahead. I just—I just like being around you. I don't understand it, I don't even like it all that much, but . . . that's how it is. And if things did go a certain way, I wouldn't be upset about that, but is that my plan? No. My plan is to be around you until I'm sick of you and can move on." He smiled wanly.

Maggie shrugged. "Okay."

"Okay?" That was way easier than he'd expected.

"Yep. Okay. You were honest with me, even if it showed me you're sort of a slime ball. Where's my dinner?"

"Slime ball?" he repeated faintly.

The look Maggie gave him challenged him to claim otherwise. He didn't.

They turned back to the apartment building.

Lance winced. "I have something else to tell you."

She took one look at his face and laughed. "You can't cook, can you?"

"I guess not. But I did try. Points for effort, right?"

"Or negative points for lying."

"I didn't—" he began to protest, but snapped his mouth shut at her knowing look. "I may have stretched the truth," he said cautiously.

She hid a smile as she ducked her head. "Now what?"

"I can make popcorn," he offered. "And we could watch a movie?"

Maggie studied him for a moment, and then nodded. "Okay. But again, we're friends. That's it."

Lance stepped back, hands up and palms out. "I know. That's why I was wondering why you were standing so close to me. I didn't want to say anything, but now that you mentioned it, keep your distance. You're giving me mixed signals."

Her mouth dropped open and she shoved his arm. "You're standing in my personal space, I'll have you know. Remove yourself, at once."

"I was just trying to keep you warm."

A smile teased Maggie's lips as she turned and headed for the apartments. "Because it's so cold out."

"Frigid." He wrapped his arms around himself and shivered.

Maggie laughed softly.

Lance reached for her hand as they got to the stairwell. She stiffened, curling her fingers as she started to pull away. He firmed his grip, looking from their hands to her face. Maggie watched him with a frown line between her eyebrows.

"Friends can hold hands," he said quietly.

She gave him a dubious look.

"The ground is treacherous and the stairs are wobbly. It's what friends do, Maggie. They help each other out," he said mockingly.

She slid her hand from his, shaking her head as she climbed the stairs. He opened the door for her, and her nose crinkled up at the aroma permeating the area. It was pretty bad. Half-cooked chicken and overcooked broccoli did not smell the greatest after sitting out for a time.

Lance raced around the kitchen, throwing all the ruined food in the wastebasket, dousing it with air freshener spray, and washing the dishes. Maggie watched him from where she sat at the dinette, chin rested on her fist. Washcloth in hand, he cleaned up the countertops and tossed it in the sink.

He leaned his hips against the counter ledge, crossed his arms and ankles, and nodded at her with half-lidded eyes and pursed lips. "How's that for cleanup?"

"Impressive," she murmured, eyes trained on him.

Lance straightened, nervous with the intensity of her strange-colored eyes on him. "What?" His tone was clipped.

He wasn't used to people staring at him like that. He was used to dopey-eyed, dreamy looks, and now that he'd been a recipient of each, he had to say, he preferred the dazed ones to her intelligent one. It felt like she was looking into his soul when she did that, and found him deficient.

"It's just . . . I've watched you grow up on television. You were this, I don't know, untouchable star. Someone I would never know, but grew up with, just the same. I even had a poster of you in my bedroom." Maggie's face went red and she averted her eyes.

A grin slowly spread across his face, and when she looked up and frowned at him, it deepened.

"I never thought I'd meet you, let alone be on the same television show as you. I especially never thought I'd play your love interest on it," she mumbled. "I was so nervous around you at first, and, well, I still am, at times, but . . ." Maggie shrugged. "I thought you were one way, and now that I've met you, you're not entirely the way I thought you were."

"I'm better looking, right?"

She shook her head, but she was smiling. "You're more down to earth than I thought you'd be, but then, you're just as arrogant as I thought you'd be too."

Lance straightened and walked toward her. He stopped when his shoes bumped against her sandaled feet. "I'm confused—are you complimenting me or insulting me?"

"Neither. You're in my space again."

He backed up and Maggie got to her feet. She gave him a questioning look, and he remembered they were supposed to watch a movie. And popcorn. He was supposed to make popcorn. Lance blinked and turned, wondering how his mind got off track so effortlessly with her. He made two bags of buttered popcorn, one after the other. The scent of cooked kernels replaced that of his disastrous attempt at dinner, the sound of them popping taking the place of conversation.

"Do you like salt and butter?" he asked as he poured the second bag into the large bowl with the first. He popped his head around the kitchen wall and saw her knelt before the entertainment center.

"Sure, whatever," Maggie answered distractedly, searching through his collection of videotapes.

"You like scary movies?" Lance walked into the living room, arms wrapped around the warm bowl of popcorn. He set it on the coffee table and sat down beside her.

"I do. How'd you know that?"

"You had a horror novel in your bedroom." Lance opened a glass door on the entertainment center and pulled out a stack of movies. "I have every collection of horror movies made, from the seventies to now."

"You do not." Her voice was doubtful, but excitement shone in her eyes.

"I do. What are you in the mood for? Halloween? Freddie or Jason? There's Damien as well, Poltergeist . . . Chucky. The Exorcist. Candyman. Name your pleasure. If you want it, I got it. What sounds good to you?" Lance knew what sounded good to him—Maggie, naked.

Hormones and instincts slammed forth like an unknown enemy, and it was a strain not to lunge for her. He shot to his feet, startling her, and moved to the couch, where he didn't have a clear view of her breasts beneath the flimsy pink top she wore, and he couldn't be tortured by the way she smelled. She smelled good, too good. And she was warm, and soft, and right there.

"Do you bathe in oranges or something?" Lance's voice was harsh, irritable.

Maggie slowly stood, confusion pulling down her mouth. She touched a lock of hair. "It's my shampoo."

"Do you have to use so much of it?" He knew he sounded ridiculous.

The frown grew. "I . . . don't. Is something wrong?"

"Yeah, something's wrong." Lance gestured to his crotch. "I've had a boner since I started hanging out with you, and if I don't get rid of it soon, I'm going to go out of my mind, that's what's wrong. And you act like you have no idea. You just—torment me with your scent, and your body, and your voice. And . . ." Lance groaned and let his head fall back, briefly closing his eyes before glaring his ire at her. He was insane, he knew he was being insane. He felt insane. That didn't make his erection go away.

She stared at him, disbelief frozen on her face. Maggie glanced down, toward his crotch. A small sound left her and she twitched, like she wasn't sure if she should flee or remain still.

He yanked a pillow from the couch and held it before him. "I'm not going to do anything, don't worry."

"With—" She stopped, licked her lips, which dragged another groan from him, and started over. "With me, you mean."

"What?"

"You're not going to do anything . . . with me. But you will, with someone else." Her eyes locked on his, challenging him to tell the truth.

"Yes," he admitted.

Maggie nodded, looking down. "I think . . . I'll go read or something. I'm not sure I'm up to watching a movie."

"No!" he shouted, causing her to flinch. Lowering his voice, struggling to control it, Lance said, "No. Please stay. I'll . . . I'll be okay, I promise."

She looked at the pillow he had clutched to his groin. A faint smile touched her eyes as she met his. "I don't think you will be. That would be mean of me, wouldn't it? To continue to torment you?"

"Well, seeing as you're the only one here, and I'm not looking to go anywhere just now, what other choice do I have?" he asked dryly.

Maggie bit her lip. "Does it hurt a lot?"

Lance laughed, but it was strained. "Yeah. It'll be fine. Can we—can we talk about something else? Or put in a movie? Something? I won't attack you or anything, don't worry," he added when she hesitated.

They decided on 'Nightmare on Elm Street', and with a pillow on his lap and a bowl of popcorn between them—and the two of them seated as far from one another as they could get while remaining on the couch—they watched the movie. It didn't help his current affliction that Maggie glanced at him throughout the movie when she didn't think he was paying attention. If he hadn't already seen the movie a dozen times, he wouldn't remember a single thing about it.

But Maggie—he remembered everything about her.

Her sharp intake of breath at certain scenes, how she covered her eyes and peeked between her fingers when she couldn't stand to watch but also couldn't not. The nervous tapping of her fingers along the arm of the couch. The way she played with a lock of hair as she concentrated. When she shifted to get comfortable and finally tucked her feet under her legs. The yawn she tried to hide. How she studied his profile when she thought he didn't notice. Her soft smile when he turned his head and looked at her.

Night came, and with only the faint glow of the television for light, Lance and Maggie sat, not touching, not talking. At the end of the movie, she said a quiet goodbye, and left. Lance dropped his head against the couch and closed his eyes. He was painfully tense, alert and aching in a way only sex would alleviate.

Grimly determined to do just that, he left the darkened apartment and headed for his Jeep. It wasn't supposed to feel like a chore, but as Lance drove toward Donovan Randolph's house, the place where a night never went by without a party, it felt exactly like that. Lance wondered if he'd even enjoy it. Snorting to himself, he entered the house. Music pounded in his ears and he got lost in a mass of bodies.

MAGGIE—2010

"WHAT ARE YOU doing?"

Maggie jumped and dropped the wooden spoon she was using to ladle soap into the molds. She snatched it off the floor and spun around to face Lance. He stood in the doorway, arms raised and fingers gripping the doorframe above his head. The pose was nonchalant, but also sensual, each line of his arm muscles visible. The purple shirt and khaki shorts counterbalanced his messy black hair and dark, unshaven jaw. She swallowed and went back to filling the soap molds.

"Making soap," she muttered.

"Is that the same stuff that's in the bathroom?" His voice was closer, his body heat rolling from him to singe her.

"Yes."

Sweat forming on her forehead, she swiped an arm across her face, wincing as her bicep uncomfortably pulled. Her muscles were sore from the last four days of training—arm muscles, leg muscles, abdomen muscles, even her butt muscles. So far, they'd rotated free weights and yoga with jogging and walking. Maggie knew Lance was taking it easy on her. She hated to think how she'd feel when he pushed her harder.

She finished filling the last of the twelve racks. The room was tucked away in a corner of the basement. Windowless and cool, it was a perfect environment for the soap to cure, but the constant movement and bustling around always heated up Maggie. Other than basic necessities, the workshop was unfinished, the walls and floor cement, the lighting dim.

"I didn't know you made your own soap. How often do you make it?"

"I don't know, probably every other month."

"Maybe you can teach me sometime." Lance stood across the worktable, faint admiration in his tone and eyes. He dropped his gaze to the table. A grin spread across his face and he nodded to one of the molds. "I like that."

Maggie looked at the mold he referenced, biting back her own grin. It was in the form of an alien head. "The kids do too—which makes sense," she commented, looking at him.

He narrowed his eyes at her, but only said, "The kids? What kids? What do you do with the soap after you make it?"

She shrugged. "I use it myself, donate it, give it away for gifts."

"How long have you been making it?"

"I don't know," Maggie mumbled, moving the trays to a large shelf that took up one whole wall of the basement room. "Half a dozen years, maybe. Why?"

Lance carefully picked up the tray of alien head molds and set it beside a tray of snowflakes. "It's interesting." He walked by her as she took another tray over. "You made it sound like you sit around all day and vegetate, but you don't. You're doing things. That's good. What made you decide to learn how to make soap?"

It had been a form of therapy for her. She'd seen a craft show on soap making and taken a class. The mindless work calmed Maggie, and gave her purpose when she needed it most. She liked mixing scents and trying new combinations, and she enjoyed giving the soaps to people who appreciated them, or needed them. Plus it was healthier than buying soap from a store. But she wouldn't tell Lance any of that.

Maggie set the last of the trays on the shelf and faced him. "Why all the questions?"

Lance stared at her. "Why not?"

"It isn't necessary."

"It isn't forbidden," he rejoined.

"You're supposed to train me, right? Our training's done for the day. You don't need to hang around and chitchat with me. In fact, I'd prefer it if you didn't."

She took the dirty supplies to the washtub and set them inside, turning on the hot water. The sound of rushing water hitting something solid was the only noise in the room. Maggie could not get too friendly with Lance, because if she did, there was every possibility that she'd fall for him again. It could happen, so effortlessly. His charm was lethal.

The less time they spent around one another outside of her training, the better.

"You're dressed like you have somewhere to go. You should go," she said when Lance remained quiet.

"Do you still hate me?"

She flinched at the softly spoken words, back to him as she said, "I never hated you."

"Are you sure? Because you told me you did, quite forcefully, and multiple times."

"Maybe a little bit," she admitted, finally turning to face him.

Humor clashed with remorse, turned his face into a twisted canvas. "Well, if you don't hate me anymore, maybe we can try to get along, get to know us now instead of remembering what we were like then. I'm an adult. So are you."

Maggie's eyes drifted over his features in the way her fingers used to. "You make it sound easy."

He lowered his gaze to his hand. "I'm not trying to minimize what happened. Things didn't end well—for the show or us. I hurt you, and I wish I could go back and change things, but it's in the past. Let's leave it there." Lance looked up, a hopeful look on his handsome face as memories danced across his features like light and dark. "It would be nice if we could be friends."

Her eyes dropped to the floor. There was a time when being friends wasn't enough for him, and he was asking to be exactly that.

"If you have to fight to keep someone away, it usually means you should stop," Lance continued.

"Think so?" she questioned, head tilted. Maggie saw their past in almost every conversation they had. It was eerie.

"Yeah. I do."

She took a deep breath. "I did fight to keep you away, once, and then I stopped." She didn't need to elaborate. The result of that had been catastrophic, as Lance knew.

"And I kept fighting—myself, you, how I felt," he confessed, eyes dark and steady on her face. "Ten years, Maggie. That's a long time to think about things. It's also enough time to forgive."

"I have forgiven you. I had to, if I wanted to get better." Maggie picked at a chunk of unhardened soap on her shirt. She didn't blame Lance for what happened to her, but their breakup seemed to be the catalyst for each of their spirals into a dark place.

The magazine articles chronicled each girl Lance slept with, each time he publicly drank, every incident that ended up with him either in jail or paying a fine. The court appearances. The pictures of him where he was clearly on something. They also posted each mental relapse Maggie had, each time she was in and out of a hospital, every new doctor or therapist she went to see. Pictures of her pale, haunted eyes and her too-thin body. Being under the media spotlight was a gift, and more than that, a curse.

He stepped toward her and she stepped back, warily eyeing him.

Lance paused, a faint, sad smile on his mouth. It took over his eyes, burned them midnight blue. "Are you scared of me?"

"Yes," she choked out, pressing her lips together.

"Don't be."

Maggie stared at Lance, seeing behind the face and into the man. One time he'd warned her away, told her she should be scared of him. He was so at odds from the Lance she remembered, but the same, where it mattered.

The silence drew out, grew more and more awkward.

Lance broke it, clearing his throat as he looked away. "I'm going to the gym to meet with a potential client. I'll be back in time to help with supper. We can try out a new recipe from the healthy eating cookbook. You pick whatever sounds good. In the meantime, have a *healthy* snack."

"No pizza or chocolate," she gathered.

"No."

"You're no fun," Maggie joked weakly, wanting the seriousness of the moment to dissipate.

"We both know I'm *too* much fun. See you later."

Maggie wordlessly saluted him, not looking at him as he left.

After getting everything cleaned up and the workroom back in order, Maggie showered and dressed in a pair of teal shorts and a black tee shirt. Hair up in a loose ponytail, she perused the cupboards for a snack, settling on a handful of walnuts. Her natural sweet tooth was not impressed. Sighing dejectedly, she grabbed the cookbook Lance mentioned, and with her elbows resting on the counter, looked at the contents.

Lip curled with distaste, she flipped through pages of foods she either didn't know, or didn't like. Settling on lemon garlic tilapia with a tomato chickpea salad and brown rice, Maggie checked to make sure they had all the appropriate ingredients. That done, she made a pot of coffee. She loved coffee, but she especially loved it with flavored creamer. Lance told her to start enjoying it black.

Maggie had been regulated to a limited carb, sugar, and dairy diet. It was hell, although, to be fair, she was able to eat more frequently, even if the portions were smaller. The idea was to eat a lot of protein, whole grains, vegetables, and fruit. Maggie felt better and had more energy. She wasn't as hungry either. She knew there were healthy and unhealthy ways to be thin—she'd personally gone through them all at one point or another. Then she'd given up, letting herself completely go. It was the cravings that would be her downfall, if she chose to give in to them.

She didn't have to be hungry to want to eat.

She remembered watching a television show once. Well, she'd watched a lot of those over the years, but one in particular stuck out to her. There was some dramatic scene—the male lead could have even been Tom Selleck—and all she could think about was the carrot. The lady sat at a table eating a cooked carrot for dinner. That was it—that was her meal. That baffled Maggie. Did people really live on a meal of a single carrot? And if so, were they happy that way?

Maggie had pondered the oddity of that while eating a bag of chocolate, her meal for the night. The irony of her dinner and how she looked compared to what the actress ate and how she looked was not lost on her. She got it. She just didn't understand it. Chocolate was delicious. Carrots—not so much.

Freshly brewed coffee in hand, sans creamer of any kind, Maggie made her way to the backyard. It was a nice day, with summer nearby. The fenced-in nook was alive with varying trees and bushes. She stepped down from the deck and found her spot on the bench near the curved pond. The slow moving water flowed down the rocks, soothing her. Closing her eyes, she relaxed into the seat, hands clasped around the warm mug of coffee, sun on her face.

It didn't immediately sink in that she was being watched, but when it did, she wondered how long she'd unknowingly been under scrutiny. Maggie slowly opened her eyes and looked toward the deck. Lance hadn't made a sound as he'd opened and closed the patio door. He leaned over the railing, arms resting on the side of the deck, hands clasped together. The sun blocked out his expression, his stillness making her nervous.

"Why now?" he asked softly.

Maggie jerked as the sound of his deep voice broke the silence. "What?"

"You've been overweight for a while, right? Why are you just now doing something about it? What happened to make you decide to get in shape?"

"Nothing." She lowered her eyes, knowing he had to have received the same invitation she did. Among other television show actors, it had been addressed specifically to the cast of 'Easier Said'.

It seemed vain to confess that that was why she'd decided to get in shape, even if it was true. Maggie had been unhappy with her appearance for a long time, but she'd needed gumption to make a change. The invitation, and then Lance, provided that.

"Really? You just woke up one day and decided it was time?"

"Yes? Are you saying I can't do that?" Maggie's fingers tightened around the cup.

"I'm not saying that. I'm just saying there's usually a reason people make life-altering changes." Lance straightened and jumped down the steps, moving to the pond.

"Maybe I got tired of seeing my fat ass in the mirror every day."

Lance gave her a look.

"What? What are you thinking?" Maggie shot to her feet, setting the mug on the uneven ground. Her fingers trembled and she crossed her arms to hide it. "You're agreeing with me, aren't you? I know. I got fat. I used to be skinny and now I'm fat. Nothing I don't already know."

His mouth twisted to the left. "It's not that at all." He sighed and shoved fingers through his hair, messing it up in a way that complemented his looks—naturally. Slamming his hands on his hips, he locked eyes with her. "You're not fat."

She snorted. "I don't think deluding me is part of the job. But thanks." She patted his shoulder as she passed by.

Lance grabbed her arm, halting her. "You're not fat."

Maggie faced him, her throat closing.

"I mean, yeah, you have some extra weight, but you don't look bad." He dropped his hand. "You still look good. You're still you, the same person you were when you were fifteen, or seventeen, or even twenty-five. And you're beautiful. You always have been, no matter your size. Don't be so hard on yourself. You look better now than you did when you were underweight."

Her heart was ripped apart at his words. She couldn't believe them. If she thought Lance really thought that of her, she wouldn't be able to distance herself from him. Maggie fought to hide the crack in her exterior with harsh words. It was the only ammunition she had, so she used it.

"This, from the guy who's never had to try too hard at anything. You just be and everything is easy for you. Try out for a role, it's yours. Smile at a girl, she's yours. Exist, everything is yours. Breathe, and you're perfect."

He stiffened. "You think you know me so well, don't you?"

As she took in his angry stance, Maggie realized she didn't know him that well. She knew a version of him—a younger, arrogant, insensitive version of Lance Denton that didn't appear to fit him anymore. It had been a long time since she'd been privy to his life and a lot could happen to a person over the years. She swallowed, feeling like a jerk. The cameras only showed one version of reality. Maggie knew that better than anyone.

"It's because of the fundraiser, isn't it?"

Maggie spun away, her silence affirmation.

"Damn it, Maggie," he quietly chided.

"I don't want to show up looking like—like I do now. You know there will be all kinds of pictures, part of it, if not the whole thing, will be televised. I know it seems . . . stupid, but . . ."

"It is stupid. Why do you care what any of them think or say anyway? It isn't like the cast of 'Easier Said' has been living perfect lives these past ten years. Judith Fletcher is so focused on her career that she's missing out on actually living. She works, that's all she does. Have you seen pictures of her? I can't recall the last picture I've seen of her with an actual smile on her face. She isn't happy."

She faced him.

He ticked off fingers as he spoke. "Benton Jamison is an alcoholic and recently married his fourth wife, who happens to be thirty years younger than him. Tabitha Volden can't even get a job anywhere because she's a selfish, demanding bitch who thinks she has way more talent than she does. Sure, she looks good, but that's the only thing she has going for her. Steven Stephens—well, he's actually doing well. He's one of the main characters in a drama that's getting a lot of notice. Herman Lyle moved to Europe and no one's seen or heard from him in years, so I can't say how he's doing."

Lance paused, a sardonic light entering his eyes. "And then we have Lance Denton. He got in so much trouble during his early twenties that he's a liability and pretty much no one will touch him. The few shows he did get hired for never had the greatest reviews. Apparently he was only good at one role, with one co-star."

Maggie's stomach dropped.

"He went through women like they were candy, and when he did finally settle down, the marriage lasted all of three years. He was forced to earn money on his looks, not talent, which, as so many magazines deemed, he does not have."

"That's not true," she rasped. "You're an exceptional actor, Lance. You just—you stopped trying."

A faint smile tipped one corner of his mouth. "I was only at my best with you."

She swallowed. Her heart pounded, fast and hard.

"You shouldn't be doing this for anyone but you." He leaned his face down until he was at eyelevel with her, blue gems simultaneously blinding and transfixing her. "You always gave everyone else too much of you and didn't leave enough of yourself for you."

Lance showed her his profile, his jaw tight. "It shouldn't matter what everyone else thinks. When 'Easier Said' ran, you wanted to please them all, the whole world, me, and look where it got you." He looked at her, the conviction in his eyes strong enough to force her back a step. "Do it for you. Do everything for you. If you don't, none of it means anything, all right?"

"Did you . . ." Maggie paused, eyebrows furrowing. "Did you have to do something for you?"

The smile grew, tipped his eyes in sadness. Lance trailed an index finger down the side of her face, a caress that barely touched her skin but was felt all the way into her bones. "I did. I had to learn to like myself, flaws and all." He straightened, took a step toward the deck, and the moment was gone. Maggie still felt it, though, living through her. "I'm starving. What did you pick out?"

Maggie picked up the mug of cooling coffee and followed him into the kitchen. Her throat felt like sandpaper and when she spoke, her voice came off gruff. "Some fish thing."

Lance glanced over his shoulder at her, a grin in place. "Some fish thing? Sounds delicious."

She set the mug on the counter. Maggie could continue to push him away, or she could enjoy Lance's company while she had the chance. Keeping up her emotional walls was draining, and she didn't want to do it anymore. She wanted to know the older Lance. He was open in a way the younger one hadn't been permitted.

Maggie smiled, her chest tight, but the rest of her was light with relief. "It sounds about as delicious as every other thing in the cookbook."

"Be adventurous."

"Trust me, I am." It wasn't that Maggie didn't like healthy food—she ate various fruits and vegetables—but she liked basic, simple meals. The stuff listed in the cookbook was beyond her. If she couldn't pronounce something, she wasn't sure she should be eating it.

After checking the recipe page of the cookbook Maggie left open, Lance rummaged through the white cupboards, finding garlic and lemon seasoning in the pantry. He raised them up for her inspection and Maggie gave him a thumbs-up sign. She got the thawed fish from the refrigerator and retrieved a bag of brown rice. Lance brushed by, setting her skin on fire, and grabbed two tomatoes from the bowl of real vegetables and fruit on the counter that was in place of the fake ones previously there.

"We need garlic, lemon juice, fresh parsley, olive oil, and salt and pepper for the salad. Can you find all that?"

"I would hope so, it's my kitchen."

He pointed a tomato at her. "No lip."

Maggie crinkled up her nose at him and collected the items he'd called off.

"You know what else we need?" he said, using a can opener on chickpeas.

"What?"

"Music." Lance looked up. "Music is a must for cooking."

Turning on the small, vintage radio near the refrigerator as a Sara Bareilles song came on, Maggie remarked, "Remember how bad of a cook you used to be? You've improved." He'd wowed her taste buds a few days ago with honey garlic chicken, forcing her to grudgingly compliment him.

"I remember," he commented, giving her a look. "I've had a lot of years of practice to make up for the chicken and broccoli debacle. I made most of the meals when . . . when I was home with Olivia and Ivy."

A dark cloud washed the joy from Lance's eyes and he turned away. Olivia was his ex-wife and Ivy was their baby. Maggie wondered why he was working in another state instead of spending as much time as he could with his daughter, but it wasn't her place to ask. He had to miss her, and maybe he even missed his ex-wife. She directed her attention to the tomatoes, slicing them up to dump in a medium-sized bowl.

Lance handed her a red onion and she went to work on that, eyes stinging and tears streaming down her face. The onion was potent, taking over her senses to the point that that was all she smelled. Maggie sniffled, nose running, as she cut the vegetable as quickly as she could.

"Don't cry," Lance said from behind, his body close enough that she felt the warmth of it against her backside. "It'll make you seem clingy and we can't have that."

Maggie partially turned and tossed an onion chunk at him, laughing when it hit his chin. Lance blinked, and then a mischievous glint entered his eyes and he shoved a hand into the can of garbanzo beans and flung a handful at her. They rained on her like pellets, hitting her hair, face, and front. Maggie stood frozen, mouth open.

When the sound of Lance's laughter filled the area, loud and warm, determination sparked through her, heating her blood. Maggie went on a fruit and vegetable rampage, throwing whatever was accessible at him. Lance ducked, arms raised to block his head, and then he found his own edible ammunition.

"You throw like a girl," she taunted, her feet skating along various food matter that covered the floor.

"Good. Girls throw better than boys."

Maggie paused at that, and Lance took advantage of her momentary befuddlement to grab her around the waist, pull the top of her shirt away from her body, and drop tomatoes down the front of it. She shrieked, reaching for the bowl of chopped onions as she clung to him, their feet imbalanced on the slippery floor. They swayed back and forth as Maggie rubbed the onions onto his cheek, eyes tearing up at the close proximity to the strong-smelling vegetable. Lance's blue eyes filled as he stared at her, chunks of onion hanging from his face.

"Don't cry, Lance," she teased, tossing his words back at him with what she knew to be a devilish smile on her face. "We had a good run, but now it's time to move on. Wouldn't want to seem clingy, would we?"

His eyes narrowed even as a sexy grin claimed his mouth. With his gaze locked on hers, he bit his lower lip and grazed his upper teeth along its fullness. Maggie fought to breathe, fingers digging into his biceps. Aware that his hands held her waist, his body inches from hers, she closed her eyes and counted to herself, trying to steady her crazy pulse.

"Not even a week," he said with derision, dropping his hands and moving away.

Maggie opened her eyes to find him studying her.

"Not even a week around you and it's like no time at all has passed."

She crossed her arms. Maggie felt it too—that unquestionable force that had her gravitating toward a person that should have remained a part of her history, not standing in her kitchen in the present.

"I wonder why that is."

Lance's mouth quirked as he looked her over. "I have phenomenal sex appeal."

Face on fire, she averted her gaze to her chest, dismayed to find gobs of mashed tomatoes coating the tops of her breasts and shirt. "We should probably start over on the salad."

Smirking as he walked past, Lance said, "Only if there isn't a chance of a rematch."

"You started it," she lied.

A lone chickpea flew through the air to smack her shoulder. "I did not, and you know it. Chickpea and tomato salad, round two, here we come," he muttered, grabbing another tomato.

Frowning at the remains of the onion lying on the counter, Maggie grabbed the knife and chopped up the rest of it.

"My face is burning," Lance commented a few minutes later, rubbing his cheek against his shoulder as he worked.

So was hers, but not because an onion had been mashed against it. It was the guy in the room with her—the sound of his voice, the way he looked at her, the power he exuded merely by being. Even as Maggie smiled at him, she knew she was in trouble.

LANCE—1996

SINCE THE NIGHT of his embarrassing erection and the viewing of 'Nightmare on Elm Street' some months back, he and Maggie had fallen into a friendly, if somewhat reserved, association. Lance fought it at first, but it soon became clear that Maggie would not be anything other than a friend to him. She distanced herself, having excuses any time he asked her to do something, and he finally allowed it. He found a diversion in the form of Anne York, an eighteen-year-old model who was visiting relatives in Virginia for the fall.

'Easier Said' debuted in August and ratings for the show were promising. The show was picked up by a prominent network and if ratings continued to climb, a second season was guaranteed. It was nearing the middle of October and things were looking good for the cast and crew of the show.

Grin in place, Lance climbed the stairs to reach the bedroom used as Cecilia's in the show, knowing Maggie was inside. He knocked on the door, and at the sound of her voice, opened it and entered the girlish space. The interior of it was all wrong for Maggie—frills and lace and colors of cream and white. It worked for Cecilia, but it was too soft for the girl who played her.

Maggie fiddled with her hair as she stared at her reflection in the mirror. She scowled and dropped her hands, turning to face him. "I hate wavy hair," she mumbled.

Over the months he'd known her, she'd transformed from a soft, awkward girl into a slim, graceful young woman. She'd had her sixteenth birthday, bringing her to the same age as him for a brief three weeks before he had his own and was once again a year older than Maggie. She didn't have her driver's license yet, waiting to take the test when she was home again.

Lance had given her an 'M' keychain in pink sparkles for when she passed her driver's test and got her first set of car keys. Maggie had given him a shirt that said 'Legend Status'.

"I like your hair."

Maggie shot him a look full of doubt, and he shrugged.

"What's up?" She turned to stack what looked like hundreds of pieces of papers in order. They were show scripts, he knew.

Lance sprawled out his long body on the bed and let his head drop back as he closed his eyes. In spite of his speeding pulse, he kept his tone neutral as he said, "Herman insists we do the kissing scene before the end of the week."

When there was no response, he lifted his head and opened one eye. Maggie had gone pale, throat bobbing as she tried to swallow. She shifted her eyes to him and away, skin flushing. Lance looked her over. The peach and white dress she wore complemented her coloring. She was radiant, like a damn sunshine walking around.

He got to his feet, resentful that he still wanted her, still thought of her more times than he should. He'd been looking forward to the kissing scene way too much since he found out about it a month ago. The scene was part of a New Year's Eve special, scheduled to air Christmas week.

Anne was tall and slender with golden skin, emerald green eyes, and wavy blond hair that ended at the small of her back. She was sexy and sensual. Perfect. She was a model, for crying out loud. And she didn't make his heart pound or his palms go sweaty like Maggie. It was incomprehensible.

"It's Thursday," she said.

"It sure is," Lance said cheerfully. "Look at you, remembering your days of the week."

Maggie wadded up a piece of paper and chucked it at him. It hit his shoulder and fell to the floor.

"Why are you always throwing stuff at me?"

She crossed her arms. "Name the last thing I threw at you."

"You."

Maggie opened her mouth, but no sound came out. She shook her head as soft laughter fell from her lips. "You're incorrigible."

"Don't say words I don't understand."

She narrowed her eyes and pointed a finger at his face. "Don't act dumb when you aren't."

Shrugging, Lance touched a lacy curtain and gave her a slanted look. "We can practice, if you need it."

"If . . . I . . . need . . . it," she repeated slowly.

He nodded. "It's been a while since we kissed. I'm sure you're rusty. Don't worry, I've been working my lip muscles on a daily basis."

"Kissing people's asses?" she inquired politely. "Maybe talking out of yours?"

Lance glared at her. "You know I only kiss the asses I want to—and they're all female."

Maggie lifted one shoulder and averted her face as she said, "Just because I haven't kissed you in months doesn't mean I haven't kissed anyone."

Lance went motionless, his expression devoid of emotion. Inside, though, his blood blazed with jealousy, his heart thundering with it. He felt cold and hot and sick and furious, all from the thought of another guy's lips on hers. Maggie didn't notice, thankfully, turning her back on him as his hands curled into tight fists.

"When does he want us to do the scene?"

"Now," he bit out.

She looked at him, one eyebrow lifted at his harsh tone, and nodded. "Okay. I'll be ready in two minutes."

Lance couldn't think of any logical reason to hang around, and with a bitter taste in his mouth, he swung toward the door. The door shut with satisfactory brute force, and with evil intent in his blue eyes, Lance headed down the carpeted stairs.

He grabbed a bottle of water from an assistant, noted the cute body and features, a smile creeping over his face when he winked and she turned a brilliant shade of red. Why the hell didn't Maggie Smiley fawn over him like all the other women? Shrugging his shoulders in irritation, Lance met up with the first group of guys he found. Most were stagehands, but there were a few show extras.

"Hey," Lance said, leaning close. "You guys know my co-host, Maggie Smiley?"

The six men went quiet, all shifting their eyes and feet. It was obvious they did, but they were leery of Lance. He didn't blame them. He was moody—one minute friendly and the next vicious.

A cautious, yet brave one asked, "Yeah, what about her?"

His name was Jeff Mitchell. He was one of the stagehands, possibly in his early twenties, and decent enough looking. He wanted to professionally act, but was working for now until he got a permanent gig. Lance knew all that because Jeff had tried out for the role of Derek Ryan. He kept tabs on competition. Lance wondered if he was the guy who'd placed his filthy mouth on Maggie's. Too old for Maggie, he decided.

Feigning nonchalance, Lance leaned against the kitchen wall, directing his gaze toward the windows that showed a backyard of trees. "Well," he began slowly. Acting hesitant, he met Jeff's brown eyes. "I shouldn't say anything, but . . ."

All eyes were on him, breaths held in anticipation. Lance was younger than every one of them, and yet, because of his status as an actor on the show, they treated him with deference.

"We're supposed to do this kissing scene today—"

A few snickers sounded, even more faces showed glimpses of envy. Lance paused at that, wondering if Maggie was just as appealing to other guys as she was to him. The thought made him want to tear each and every one of their heads from their bodies so they were unable to look at her ever again. He knew it wasn't rational, and swallowing thickly, he put an awkward smile upon his lips and continued the charade.

"I was told Maggie has horrible breath—an onion, garlic mixture of rancidness. Any of you able to confirm that?" Lance wasn't completely sure what he was going to do with the news if one of those guys had kissed Maggie, but he had to know. And if none had, his words would assuredly keep it that way.

Jeff opened his mouth, and Lance went tense, staring at him with all the deadly calmness of a snake before it struck its victim with its poisonous bite, but then Jeff's eyes shifted away from his face to beyond him. Even though he hadn't done a damn thing wrong, Jeff's face went red and he took a step back.

Lance briefly closed his eyes before turning around, having a good idea who stood behind him.

Maggie glared at him, her face pinched like she'd unknowingly bitten into a lemon—stunned, horrified, and disgusted.

"I knew you were behind me," he lied.

Her eyes narrowed.

"It was a joke. Really."

When she inhaled a sharp breath, but remained mute, Lance shrugged. "I'm sorry?"

She spun on her heel and stomped away. Lance watched her go, finding it hard to breathe normal. He kept his eyes on her until she disappeared from view, lost behind the bodies that were required to properly put a television show together. Then he looked at the half dozen guys near him. One shook his head, another smirked. They quickly departed, like Lance was a disease they didn't want to catch.

Jeff stayed back, eyeing him.

"What?" Lance snapped.

"That was low," he informed him.

As if he didn't already know that.

Lance shoved by him, finding Maggie near Herman. Herman gestured with his hands, red in the face as he talked. Maggie bowed her head, nodding now and then. Herman patted her on the back and Maggie lifted her head. She looked miserable, face pale and eyes wide with disharmony. Her gaze found his and Lance went still, not knowing what to do. Apologizing didn't seem good enough—because it wasn't. Lance's temper and impulsiveness got the best of him again and again. The paleness of Maggie's skin morphed with color and she quickly turned away.

He moved for her, but Judith was suddenly there, pressing a restraining hand to his chest. Her blond hair was side-parted and flipped up at the ends, black dress and jacket formed to her slim frame. With gray chips of ice for eyes, and an equally frigid expression on her face, she said in a clipped tone, "What did you do to her?"

Lance shook off her hand and tried to step around her. "Nothing."

Judith stepped with him, close to his height in her black heels. "If you didn't do anything to her, she wouldn't be trying to get out of the New Year's Eve scene. That girl would work sick rather than delay production of the show."

He looked away from Judith's cold gaze, searching for Maggie.

"How many times and by how many people do you have to be told to leave her alone? This is her job, and she is the star of the show. Don't screw it up for her."

Lance focused on the actress. "Come on, Judith, I didn't mean to upset her. And she's the co-star." He gave her one of his most charming grins. If anything, the glacial look of her deepened.

"That's Miss Fletcher to you," she said through lips that didn't move.

Rubbing a hand over his face, Lance mumbled, "I tried apologizing."

"Don't do anything that requires an apology. Any time you are outside of work, make sure you keep your hands to yourself and your mouth shut. Her parents entrusted Maggie into my care, and I'm going to make sure no harm comes to her, especially from you." She slapped a manicured hand against Lance's shoulder and walked away, head high, shoulders back.

"Thank you, *Miss Fletcher*," he called after her.

Judith's back went rigid, but she kept walking.

"Derek! Why aren't you in Cecilia's bedroom? We're waiting! Some of us would like to go home and drink ourselves into a coma yet today!" Herman shouted from a few feet away. Lance didn't bother correcting him on the names.

Lance walked to the stairwell, eyes locked on Maggie. He willed her to look at him, but she didn't.

"What the hell is this?" Herman demanded, rushing over to them.

The director's garlic-onion smelled permeated the area as he stepped between them, and Lance shot Maggie a guilty look. She glared back, arms crossed. He mouthed that he was sorry, but her expression never changed.

"Why is there this tense, cold feeling? This won't do at all. Where are the shy, adoring looks? Or even the smug ones?" Herman looked pointedly at Lance as he said that. "Come here." He motioned for them both to get closer. When they were inches from him, Herman stared each of them in the eye, one at a time. "As soon as you get close to one another, you're Cecilia and Derek, got it?" He waited until they nodded before continuing.

"I don't care if you're sick." He looked at Maggie. "And I don't care what your daily problem is." That to Lance. "Get your shit together and be professional. Let's go! Upstairs!" Herman clapped his hands and walked toward the camera crew.

Lance followed Maggie up the stairs, eyes locked on the stiffness of her back. People clopped up the stairs behind them, but all he cared about was the person before him.

Maggie sat on the bed, head lowered. Lance took a deep breath, and when cued, knelt before her. Everyone went quiet. It happened every time they had a scene. The onlookers felt the magic too—the chemistry that sparked to life between Lance and Maggie when they were together. Anything that stood beyond them faded from existence. It was only Lance and Maggie in their pretend world.

Her small hands were gripped tightly together in her lap. Only he was close enough to see that they were held to stop their shaking, and that they shook anyway.

It wasn't in the script for Lance to touch her hands, but improvising was allowed, so he did. He wasn't doing it for the show anyway—Lance placed his hand over hers because what he'd done was wrong, even if he hadn't meant to hurt Maggie. He had.

"Hey," Lance said in a soft voice. The trembling picked up and he squeezed her cool hand. "I'm sorry for what I said earlier at the party. It wasn't fair for me to act like that to Liam. A lot of the time I say things before I think about how they make people feel." Ironic that his character was apologizing, just as Lance was. They were so alike that Derek could have been written after him.

Maggie raised her head, those amber eyes staring through him with all the heat of her being.

Faced away from their audience, Lance offered a sheepish smile. "Please," he mouthed.

Snatching her hand from his grasp, Maggie hopped onto the bed and stood as far away from him as the bed would permit.

Head tilted, Lance studied her. "What are you doing?" he asked in bemusement. That wasn't in the script either.

"Liam was my date. You were rude to him," she said through clenched teeth.

"How was I rude?" he scoffed.

A twitch formed under her left eye and Lance wondered if that was intentional. "I am allowed to date. You do not get to choose my boyfriends for me. You're my friend. That's it."

Lance raised an eyebrow and launched himself onto the bed, steadying himself on the imbalanced terrain. "He's not your boyfriend."

"He could be," she insisted.

Glare in place, Lance said, "Liam is a jerk-face. Find a better guy to be your boyfriend."

"What, like you?" Maggie narrowed her eyes. "And you're calling Liam a jerk-face? You would know." She tossed her hair over her shoulder. "Anyway, what about Sylvie Stallone?" she sneered.

Lance jumped once and Maggie went into the air, eyes wide as she propelled her arms until she got her balance and landed on her feet. "What about her?"

"She was your date. And she's an airhead." She jumped, sinister smile in place.

Lance bounced on his feet and returned the motion. They formed an angry rhythm, back and forth like an unattached seesaw. Maggie's hair lifted and fell as she moved, arms out at her sides to remain upright.

"Aren't you supposed to be the nice one out of us?" he wondered.

Maggie blinked. "I am nice—until I'm mad."

Lance grinned and leapt closer to her.

"What are you doing?" she asked warily.

"Jumping on the bed with my friend." Hands outstretched, he grabbed her wrists and they sprang up and down together.

"I'm still mad at you." Her voice turned breathless, the pulse at the base of her throat fluttering like the wings of a butterfly.

"I know you are, and that's okay. You're still my friend."

Resentment and sorrow chased one another across her features. Maggie stopped bouncing. They stood in the middle of the bed, Lance's hands loosely gripping her wrists, and looked into each other's eyes.

"Sometimes, it's really hard to like you," she said unevenly.

Lance lowered his gaze, knowing that was Maggie talking to him. His chest clenched and released. He nodded. "I know." He looked up, found her eyes on him. Lance wondered what she thought, when she studied him with such concentration.

"You insulted my date to the point that he left. I was stranded at the party."

"All I told him was that you hated tulips, which you do. If a guy's going to bring a girl flowers, he should at least know what kind she likes. Anyway, he shouldn't have left you, no matter what I said. That was wrong on his part. And you weren't stranded," he added. "I was there."

"You implied that he didn't know how to dress. You also tried to find out if we'd kissed," she accused, mouth a straight line with displeasure.

Lance swallowed. She'd known what he was up to then. "I was looking out for you."

Maggie pulled her hands from his. "No. You were looking out for you. It doesn't matter if you want something or not—you're just selfish and don't want anyone else to have it either."

"That's not true." It was true, to a point. Lance needed constant attention. It went along with his profession, but it probably also had something to do with the way he grew up. No mother, distant father, homeschooled, never really having a permanent home of any kind.

"It is true!" She jumped down from the bed and walked over to the dresser, her back to him. "Tell me why you were so mean to Liam then."

"Because." Lance got down from the bed and took two steps toward her.

"Because why?"

"Because—because he isn't good enough for you, okay? No one is, but he definitely is not. He doesn't even know what kind of flowers you like!"

Maggie turned to face him. "And I suppose you do?"

His jaw shifted. "I do."

"Well, let's hear it. What kind of flowers do I like, if not tulips?"

Lance walked closer. "You don't like flowers," he said faintly. "They make you sneeze." He lifted a hand to touch her face and Maggie jerked back. He let his hand fall to his side.

"I don't—" He worked his throat to swallow. "I don't want other guys around you. They're all losers that won't treat you right."

She laughed, but it was sharp and unpleasant. "Other guys? Meaning you're excluded from the losers that won't treat me right?"

"No," he mumbled. "You should stay away from me too."

When he looked up, something in his eyes made her go still. Maggie didn't look like she took a breath, all of her motionless.

"You're my friend," she whispered. "I can't stay away from you."

Voice low, Lance spoke fast to get out all the words before he never said them. It was a masked confession, a weak apology to explain his actions. "Ever since I met you, I've felt half mad. I want you, I don't want you. I try to be your friend, but being your friend isn't enough. I tell myself to stay away, but then the thought of you with anyone else makes me want to find any guy that's ever looked at you and pound them into nothing.

"And I know—I know I'll just keep screwing up things with you, and it isn't fair for me to ask, but I need you in my life. And more than anything, I want to kiss you. How's that for being a friend?"

Maggie inhaled slowly. "I think, right now . . . this is the truest friend you've been."

Lance closed the distance between them, staring down at her lowered head. "I didn't mean what I said. I was jealous, thinking of him kissing you. I don't want anyone to kiss you."

She raised her head. "It isn't up to you to decide who I do or do not kiss."

He touched the side of her face, his fingers curling in at the feel of her soft skin. Maggie didn't pull away that time. "I want it to be."

Maggie's eyes shifted from him to the wall behind him, and she whispered, "It's midnight."

"Happy New Year," he replied.

Lance dipped his head, not giving her a chance to move away. His lips brushed across hers, gentle as air, and his body went painfully tight. She tasted like mint, his conscience calling him an ass for saying otherwise. Maggie tipped back her chin, allowing him better access. Lance put one hand around the nape of her neck, and the other cupped her jaw.

Tingles broke out along his lips as they met hers once more. He'd missed the feel of Maggie's mouth on his, the way his brain shut off and he got lost in her. Maggie kissed him like it was the same for her. Her hands moved up his back, pressing him to her.

"And that's a wrap!" Herman shouted from the darkness that was reality. It danced along the seams of his consciousness as he was regrettably pulled back into the present.

A sharp pain registered in his muddled head, and he tasted blood.

Lance drew back, touching his lower lip. Tiny drops of red coated his fingers. "You bit me!"

Maggie schooled her features to innocence, but the gleam in her eyes countered it. "My teeth must have slipped."

"Teeth don't slip."

She shrugged one shoulder and stepped back. "Maybe it was the onion and garlic breath comment then."

Lance stared at her, knowing he deserved whatever he got, and resenting her present attitude anyway.

"All right, people! That's it for today. See you all bright-eyed and bushy-tailed tomorrow at seven in the evening for the boat party scene. Not you! You stay," Herman hollered, pointing to Maggie. "You stay too," he said to Lance.

They exchanged a look and faced the director.

"I want you to tell me," he said slowly, dividing a livid look between them. "What parts of that scene were in the script?"

"Uh . . ." Lance searched his brain. "Liam?"

"The flowers," Maggie helpfully added.

Lance said, "The kiss."

"Barely! Neither one of you stuck to the script! Who put you two in charge of the show? You think you can just say and do whatever the hell you want, with total disregard to the writers? This isn't your show! You don't ad-lib a whole scene," he roared, spittle flying from his mouth.

Herman ranted for a good solid four minutes about minors and punks thinking they could run the world and there not being enough booze in it to deal with them before falling silent. His chest heaved with each breath he took, and he put a hand to his shiny bald head. He dropped his hand and glared at them with brown eyes darkened to black in anger.

"All of that aside," he said smoothly, like he didn't just have a tantrum. "You both were exceptional. Such passion, such angst! It felt real, and that's what we want. No more biting!" He jabbed a finger at Maggie's face and she flinched.

"Before I forget, you two have a magazine photo shoot and interview the Sunday after next. Be at this address by six in the morning." Herman shoved a business card at each of them. They were damp with sweat from being in his back pocket. "They want to do some sunrise shots. God knows why. Wear white."

He waved a hand at them, a look of disgust on his face. "Now get out of here—lock up before you go. I need a drink." He marched from the room, the heavy footfalls of his shoes on the stairs the only sound until they went silent.

Lance shifted his feet and looked toward the door. "Can I give you a ride home?" he asked carefully. His lip throbbed as it rubbed against his upper one.

Maggie kept her face turned away. "Why did you say it?"

"I said why." Lance pressed his lips together, refusing to repeat words he had to initially tear from himself.

"Not really. You specifically said something you knew would hurt me, if I heard it. And I did."

"I didn't know you were going to hear it! In fact, I was hoping you didn't."

"Right. You just wanted to talk bad about me in front of everyone."

"It wasn't everyone," he argued.

"It might as well have been! Because of your infantilism, you decided to make me look bad. Thanks a lot."

"You don't understand," Lance tried, words escaping him. He didn't have any good reasons for why he said what he did, and if he was honest with her—well, that wasn't going to happen.

"I don't understand most things with you," she agreed, averting her eyes from his. "You act like . . ." Maggie swallowed. "You act like, just because you know me, I'm your possession or something. That's not how friendships work."

"Did you kiss Jeff Mitchell?" he demanded, barely hearing her.

Maggie's lips thinned in anger, her amber eyes flashing like liquid toxin. "That is none of your business. Do I ask you who you've kissed?"

"No, because you know there would be no point in it."

"Only because you've kissed so many girls you can't even remember who they are," she retorted icily.

Lance stepped closer and lowered his voice as he said, "I remember kissing you."

She eyed him. "Don't play your games with me. You should know by now they don't work." Maggie walked toward the door. "Thanks, but I don't need a ride home."

Lance rubbed his face and stared at the doorway as Maggie passed through it. He never got far with her. That was probably a good thing. She'd chew him up and spit him out if he made her too mad. She had fire for blood and ice for veins.

He slowly left the house, turning to stone as he watched Maggie climb in Jeff Mitchell's car. She didn't see him, but Jeff did. He stared at Lance, and then he faced forward and drove off. Angry and full of guilt, Lance flipped the lock on the door and stormed to his Jeep Wrangler, kicked the tire, and then climbed inside.

It was a fifteen-minute drive to the beachside apartments, and he kept Jeff's silver Cavalier within view the whole way. With the cover off the Jeep, the wind destroyed his hairstyle. He didn't know what he was going to do if Jeff didn't take Maggie home and instead went somewhere else. He didn't logically have any reason to pursue them, other than possessiveness. Lance talked himself down as he drove, knowing that being a dick to Maggie was the wrong way to go about things. If he wanted to get along with her, he had to be nicer than he customarily was. It sounded like a lot of work, maybe too much, but he'd try.

For Maggie, he'd try.

He parked the Jeep in the parking lot on the backside of the apartment complex, averting his gaze from Maggie when she looked his way. *Keep it cool. Act natural.* Strolling past them like everything was normal and he and Maggie hadn't just fought and he didn't want to punch in Jeff's face, he went around the white structure to the beach. Near the stairs that went up to his apartment, Lance kicked off his tennis shoes, removed his socks, and with his jeans rolled up to his calves, headed for the water.

Voices and music flooded his eardrums, but he tuned it all out, focusing on the water. It was the color of blue and green with white tips. The crashing waves soothed him, and without consciously being aware of it, his shoulders loosened. Lance stopped on the wet sand, his toes sinking into the smooth grit, the ocean water gently lapping over his bare feet where he stood. The sun burned his skin, heating him to the point that he felt chilled. He lowered his head and clasped the back of his neck with threaded fingers, closed his eyes, and breathed in the salty air.

Never close with his father and used to being on his own more times than not, Lance wasn't one to miss people or feel lonely, but since he'd met Maggie, he'd felt both.

"Lance." The voice was soft, hesitant.

He swung around, surprised to find Maggie behind him. He frowned, wondering what she was going to say, and also sure it would be warranted, whatever it was.

The wind picked up, lifting her hair and tossing it to the side. Her eyes shone like fire under the sunlight. There was no judgement on her face, none of the recrimination he'd expected to find.

She motioned to his face. "I'm sorry about biting you. That was childish."

"I'm sorry about saying you had onion and garlic breath. You don't," he added when her face turned red.

Maggie nodded, turning her face toward the sun.

She smiled, but it quickly faded as she focused on him. "You're dating someone now, right? I heard that you were. A model? She must be really pretty to be a model."

Lance squinted at the blue sky, uncomfortable with her questioning. It seemed wrong to talk about his girlfriend with the girl he really wanted.

"Yeah," he muttered.

"Jeff asked me out this weekend. He wants to go out for supper Saturday night, and maybe bowling."

His head shot up and anger scorched his retinas. He was surprised Maggie didn't burn up from the heat of his gaze. "Why are you telling me this?"

"Maybe you could ask your girlfriend if she wanted to double date with us. If you want to, I mean. I don't know Jeff that well, and . . ." Maggie focused on the sand beneath their feet. "I'd feel more comfortable if you were there too, even though I'm not sure why," she said wryly.

"I'll be there," he said in a rough voice.

Maggie met his eyes, frowning. "And your girlfriend. What's her name?"

Lance stared at her, his mind blank.

"Lance? What's your girlfriend's name? You have to bring your girlfriend for it to be a double date," she teased.

"Uh . . . Anne." He actually forgot her name. They'd been dating for close to a month and he'd forgotten her name. He shook his head and focused on Maggie. "Jeff's too old for you."

"He's nineteen. He's not too old for me," she countered.

"He drives a Cavalier."

Maggie looked at his serious expression and laughed. "I'll see you later. I have schoolwork to do."

She waved and walked to the apartments. Lance watched her go, feeling the lonely clench of solitude on his being once more.

MAGGIE—2010

WHEN SHE ENTERED the workout area, Lance held up a finger. "Go back out, count to ten, and then walk in again."

She frowned. "What?"

"Just do it."

"You're crazy."

He straightened from where he was fiddling with the stereo system. "You're right, I am. Now do it."

Grumbling about fanatical personal trainers, Maggie left the room, counted to seven, and came back in the room to the song 'Eye of the Tiger' playing.

"You have got to be kidding me," she muttered, fighting not to laugh as Lance went into a Rocky impersonation of air punches.

"You didn't count to ten," he yelled over the music.

She shrugged.

"Are you ready to do this?" he asked, turning down the volume.

"Yes." No. Lance wanted her to try lifting heavier free weights.

They were on their second week of working together, and she could already notice a change. She'd lost pounds and inches and that was enough to motivate her to keep going. Maggie had more drive, and just the fact that she was making an effort to improve herself had risen her self-confidence. It was her fault she was overweight when she didn't exercise and ate junk—it wasn't if she was eating healthy and exercising. That outlook was the difference between self-respect and self-loathing.

"Take the ten-pound ones," he directed, nodding at the pink weights.

Maggie took the weights, eyeing Lance with apprehension.

"You got this," he told her convincingly.

"Yes." She swallowed. "I got this."

"Bend your knees slightly. Good. Just like that." Lance walked around her, briefly pressing a hand to her hip. "Tuck in your butt."

"I can't. It's too big."

"Tuck in your butt," he commanded, eyebrows raised.

Maggie tucked in her butt.

"Stomach in, back straight. Beautiful. Let's work the triceps. Lift both hands above your head, but don't completely straighten your arms. Leave them a little loose. Excellent. Put the weights together. Now lower them behind your neck. Great. Lift them back up. Steady and slow. You're doing great." Lance's voice was authoritative, but soothing, and Maggie found herself enjoying his encouragement.

Her sister was right. If anyone could get Maggie to listen, it was Lance.

Maggie did various lift positions, three reps of ten each time, before Lance told her to move on.

"What . . . made you . . . decide to . . . do this?" she gasped, her leg and arm muscles burning from the elliptical machine. Maggie had only been on it for a total of ten minutes, but it felt like a hundred. She wanted to stop, but she'd tried that last week, and Lance had made the resistance harder on the machine.

"You don't give up. You don't stop. Ever. Not until it's time," was what he'd told her, his face a grim thunderstorm of relentlessness.

Maggie wouldn't stop. Even if her legs and arms became noodles, she wouldn't stop.

"I enjoy watching you work out. I find your gasping breaths a mega turn on and the sweat that drips from your body enough to make me cross-eyed with desire. Smelly, perspiring Maggie is hot."

She shot him an annoyed look and he laughed, landing a round of uppercuts to the punching bag. Her pace picked up as she watched him—not because she enjoyed the sweat that clung to his dark locks, or the way his muscles bunched and pulled as he moved, or the confident power he showed.

"I didn't mean making me . . . do . . . the elliptical machine. I meant . . . you . . . becoming a personal trainer." Water. She needed water. And a brownie. Maybe some pizza. Maggie would take a plain piece of bread at that point.

Lance grinned at her through the reflection in the mirror. "I know."

In two days, it was officially the fourteenth day of their current association, and out of the three bedrooms available, minus hers, of course, Lance got to choose which one he'd like for the rest of his stay.

He grabbed a set of free weights and did bicep curls. "I modeled a lot after 'Easier Said', which was fine, for a while. I made decent enough money, but I felt cheapened by it. Being known for your looks is all right, I guess, but it wasn't enough for me, especially after the success of 'Easier Said'. I was drinking a lot, eating junk, and I was making money off my image. I felt like a fraud."

Lance paused and said, "I decided to use my handsomeness for good instead of evil."

Maggie blew out a loud breath and rolled her eyes, checking the time on the elliptical. Fifteen minutes to go.

"I got into healthy eating and fitness, joined the gym, and took classes. I won't lie, my previous celebrity status helped make my name as a professional fitness expert and personal trainer. I've done a lot of shows, ads, infomercials, talk shows. I have a couple videos out. You name it, I've done it. I know you've seen me on television."

"Yes," she admitted. She'd seen a lot of Lance on television over the years—a lot of it bad, some of it good. Each time his image appeared, it was a stab to her heart. Thoughts plagued her of what was, what wasn't, and could never be.

"Is that what you want to do for the rest of your life?" she asked, curious. What dreams did Lance have?

He eyed her, not answering. Then he asked, "What about you? What do you want to do? I don't imagine hanging out at your house for the rest of your life is at the top of your list."

She shook her head, damp hair sticking to her cheeks. "I asked first."

"I know. But I want you to answer first."

Maggie focused on the floor. "I want to show the world, one last time, that I'm not a washed up actress, that I still have it in me to do something spectacular. And then I'll go back to hanging out in my house for the rest of my life." She smiled faintly, catching his eyes on her as she looked up.

She was lucky enough that she could remain unemployed and live comfortably. Frugal with her money and never one to get too excited over expensive items, Maggie was careful and smart with her income from 'Easier Said'. She knew Lance was not. He'd lived in the moment and she'd lived in the future. That was the way it had always been with them.

"I have an idea for a show," he said casually, avoiding her eyes. "Donovan Randolph—remember him? He's my agent. Anyway, he thinks it could be good with the right people."

"Oh?" Maggie tried to look uninterested, but the way he wouldn't meet her gaze had paranoia clutching her insides with dread. "What is it?"

He dropped the weights and rotated his shoulders. "A celebrity fitness show."

She went still, the machine slowly following.

"Keep moving," he commanded.

"Who do you have in mind to be on this celebrity fitness show?" Her voice was cold, like Lance's heart.

"Me, obviously. I'd be the host-ess with the most-ess." He smiled widely.

"Mmm-hmm." Eyes narrowed on his cheekily grinning face, Maggie stood on the elliptical machine and waited for the rest of his wounding words to bomb her. Regrettably, she knew where the conversation was going.

"Stephie Watson came to mind. Dean Silvers. Henry Baxton. Have you seen him? He's about one hundred pounds heavier than he was five years ago. Some others . . . there are a lot of notable people out of shape. I mean, a little extra weight isn't a bad thing, but obesity is a major problem, and not enough people are doing something about it. That's when someone needs help, because it's gotten to the point where they can't control their eating habits on their own.

"Blame is put on people for gaining weight, like it's their fault. Some of it is, of course, but there are times when they can't control it. I think if everyone could, no one would choose to be heavy. People with eating disorders are not only those that starve themselves or make themselves vomit after eating. People who overeat, or are emotional eaters, or eat out of boredom, also have an eating disorder. That tends to get overlooked by society."

Lance didn't look at her as he said the words, but they were directed at her, regardless.

"What if you just like to eat because things taste good?" she joked.

He squinted his eyes and continued. "I am aware that the premise is unoriginal, but with me, it'll be better than all the other shows out there like it. I want it heartfelt, motivating, but also funny. I want the people on the show to inspire others, and to be inspired by others. And . . . maybe you would want to be on it. That would make it appeal to a lot of people it might not otherwise." Lance glanced at her, gauging her reaction.

"No," she bit out. He said exactly what she hoped he wouldn't.

"Hear me out before you say no."

"No."

"I'll give you time to think about it."

"No."

"Maggie," he said with a sigh.

"No."

They stared at one another, her with potent distaste in her gaze and Lance with disappointed wariness.

"Okay," he finally said, severing eye contact. "Fine. But if you decide you want to know what the show is about, let me know. You're not done yet," he said, pushing her arm to get the machine started again.

Lance left, and once he was gone, Maggie dropped her head forward. She finished the last of the designated thirty minutes, her skin clammy from emotions, but sweaty and hot from physical exertion. She should have known his reasons for showing up would be more about him and less about her. He was a selfish man, thinking of himself above all others. He probably thought coming to help her under the guise of his profession was the perfect setup to get her to agree to be on his possible show. He probably laughed as soon as he ended the phone call with her sister, and the whole flight there.

Scowling, she jumped down and moved to the mat to stretch. Maggie was no longer a silly, lovesick girl who chose to see the small glimpses of good in a boy who had more bad.

"WHAT'S NEW?" HER father asked it too nonchalantly, letting Maggie know he knew what was new.

Maggie and her dad met up for coffee once a week, and sometimes her mom joined them, but generally, she invited Maggie over for meals to play catch up. Maggie hadn't mentioned Lance yet. It was a good assumption her sister had since she'd last seen her dad.

She took a sip of her black coffee, the Styrofoam cup doing little to save her fingers from the hotness of the liquid inside, and directed her gaze to the choppy brown waters of the Mississippi. It was so different from the ocean—dirtier, smaller. The smell of fish and watery plants wafted up to them. She missed the ocean. The spicy tang in the air, the sound of crashing waves, the merging and fading colors, the way she'd felt while near it.

"Lance Denton is staying with me." Saying the words made her pulse pick up. They were impossible to believe, and they were true.

They walked along the Mississippi, periodic bursts of wind pushing against them like they were inconsequential. Maggie shivered in her lightweight jacket, wishing she'd worn something thicker. Birds sang as they flew around them. The walkway was miles long and designed with multi-colored cement. The path was set up hundreds of feet higher than the river, with grass and rocks between it and the water below.

Dubuque, Iowa was one of the few larger cities in Iowa to have hills. The river and architecture around and in it brought tourists to the city. The downtown part housed many historical buildings, adding to its appeal. As far as cities went, it was a decent one—large enough to have any store needed but small enough to be able to maneuver through.

Leon pushed his glasses up his short nose and nodded. "Nora was only too thrilled to tell your mom, especially when she realized you hadn't mentioned it yet. She never learned tact. I'm not sure if the blame falls on your mom or me for that one."

Maggie smiled slightly. "I think Nora has her own ideas about things, Dad. She always has."

"Hmm. Yes. He's the one helping you?" He motioned to her frame.

"Yes. He's actually really good at what he does," she said carefully, glancing at her father and away.

It was early yet, just past eight, and overcast. Maggie loved the sunshine days, but there was something about the dreary ones that made her content as well. They were days for baking, and watching television, and snuggling under covers, without feeling as guilty as on nice days—they were acceptable lazy days.

"I see that. You look great." He paused, taking her hand and squeezing it before letting it go. "I hope you know, Maggie, that no matter what size you are, you're good enough exactly as you are."

She brushed hair from her eyes and smiled at her dad. "That's a nice thought. I wish I believed it. But . . . I haven't been happy for a long time. I haven't exactly been miserable, but I wasn't waking up excited to start a new day. Since I've been working with Lance, I already feel better."

"Don't you think part of that might have been because of your insistence to avoid the past, and not necessarily how you looked?"

Maggie came to a stop, facing the water. On the other side of the river was a world of sand, grass, trees, and hills. "Well, even if it was, that's not possible anymore, is it? The past knocked on my door two weeks ago and wouldn't go away, even when I told it to."

"Lance always was a determined one."

"Yes. He was," she said softly. "Pushy too."

"I never told you this, but your first Christmas together, when the two of you spent a few days with us?"

She nodded that she remembered.

Leon hesitated, rubbing a hand over his thick gray hair. "I told him if he hurt you, I'd hunt him down and shoot him."

"Dad!"

He shrugged, his cheeks faintly pink. "You know I wouldn't have—I don't even own a gun. But I was looking out for my daughter. There was this perfect-looking kid offering her the world and it worried me. Want to know what he said back?" He didn't give her time to answer. "He said that if he did hurt you, he hoped I would. What guy says that to the father of the girl he's dating?"

Maggie's throat closed and she took a shaky breath.

"One that cares a great deal," he finished quietly.

"You obviously didn't hunt him down and shoot him." Drollness dripped from her words.

"No." Leon sat down on a bench and Maggie did the same. "I visited him a few weeks after you were out of the hospital. He hurt you, there is no doubt of that. But you hurt him just as much."

A needle jabbed her conscience, told her brain what her heart already knew. In their quest to love, they'd broken one another. She liked to blame Lance, because it was easy. It was also wrong. He hadn't understood love, hadn't known how to properly love someone. And she'd pushed him to show something he didn't know how. She was as much at fault as him.

Her dad said, "He was a mess, Maggie, an absolute mess. Hadn't showered in what looked like days, eyes so bloodshot it was obvious he'd been crying a great deal. I showed up angry. I was concerned over you, and I took it out on him. He asked me to put him out of his misery. Not that I would have ever seriously shot him, but it wouldn't have been right of me to wound a man already in anguish, not even with words or fists."

"What did you . . . what did you do then?" she whispered, blinking eyes that stung with unshed tears.

"I bought him a meal, told him to take care of himself, and I left."

The love she'd shared with Lance had been amazing—not perfect—but amazing. And then it was ripped away, without warning, without Maggie having time to prepare.

Face forward, she reached for her dad's cool hand and tightly gripped it. "I love you, Dad."

"I love you too. Be careful, all right? I don't just mean with Lance. I mean with you and what you're doing."

"I know."

She took a drink of the coffee. She had a few people she occasionally hung out with and considered friends, but no one with whom she would discuss anything of consequence. Her father was the closest thing to a best friend she had.

"Dad?" Maggie felt his eyes on her without looking. "Why do you think Nora called him? And why did he say yes?"

He didn't speak, and when Maggie turned to him, he had a thoughtful look on his intelligent face. He was a thinker; one who thought of all possibilities before coming to a decision, and when he didn't know something, he was truthful about that as well. They'd spent many nights over her adolescence discussing the improbable, playing board games, or sitting on the couch, each of them with a book in hand.

Shaking his head, he said, "I don't know. You'll have to ask them."

"I feel like I'm missing something," she mused. "And it involves the two of them."

Her dad patted her knee. "Let's walk some more."

They were almost to their cars when Maggie blurted, "He brought up an idea he has for a celebrity fitness show, and he wants me on it."

He paused near her car. "How do you feel about that?"

"I feel like he wants to use me, like the only reason he agreed to help me was because he had it in his head that he could get something out of it," she said in a rush, her heart pounding in beat with her words.

"Then don't do it."

"I said no."

Removing his glasses, he rubbed the lenses on the sleeve of his black jacket. He resituated them and said, "And what did he say to that?"

Maggie shifted her feet. "Nothing. He's been acting normal, like nothing was ever said about it."

"Then you know he's not using you, or he would have been gone by now."

"Or he just really needs my money."

Amusement flickered in his green eyes. "Your money works just as well in the stores as anyone else's."

She blinked. "I guess so."

"What if you're wrong? What if he doesn't want to use you? What if he wants you on that show because he knows he needs you to make it great? That's a compliment. And if that's so, and you aren't completely against it, why don't you negotiate terms?"

"I never thought of it that way."

He hesitated, and then asked, "Have you ever wondered why he chose that career path?"

Maggie shrugged. "He said he wanted to use his handsomeness for good or something lame like that."

A smile tipped his mouth. "I bet he did. I find it interesting, though, that given everything that went on with you when you were younger, that he chose to work in a field that directly correlates with it."

"I'm sure it's a coincidence," she mumbled, eyes downcast.

"I'm not."

She looked up.

He rubbed a circle onto her back. "Whatever you decide to think or do, the choice is yours. Something to ponder. Have a good day."

"Thanks. You too."

Inside their cars, they waved and went their separate ways. Sundays were rest days, meaning Lance didn't drag her out of bed at six in the morning, all sickeningly chipper and devastatingly beautiful. They were also cheat days, which had her taste buds salivating, because she could eat whatever she wanted and however much of it she wanted. Maggie figured if she balanced her food, it wouldn't be so horrible—mix the good with the bad. She made a quick stop at the grocery store, thoughts on Lance and his proposition as she drove to the house.

The most time they spent together was the one to two hours she exercised under his supervision and when they made meals. Other than that, Lance did his own thing and she did hers. Her daily life was more interesting with him around, and as exasperating as he was, he did make her laugh.

Grocery bags in hand, she stepped into the kitchen, the quietness of the house surreal, even as a few short weeks ago it was natural. It was temporary. She knew it was temporary. Don't get attached, she told herself, fearing she already was.

Maggie quickly put away the food, tucking the box of cookies behind a row of canned goods, and went in search of her personal trainer. She found him in her bedroom on the bed, clad in black lounge pants and a long-sleeved white shirt, asleep with his hands clasped over his stomach. She couldn't be upset about finding him there, the peacefulness that emanated from him aweing. She hadn't realized how tense he was until she witnessed the absence of it.

She tiptoed closer, admiring the sculpted features of his face, eyes lingering on his lips and jaw. When she was to the bed, she stared down at the man she'd loved as a girl, as a young woman, maybe even yet.

"I know what you're thinking—it's a sin for a mortal man to be this good-looking," he murmured, eyes closed.

She jumped, her thoughts eerily similar to that.

A hand snaked around her waist, tugged, and she was partially lying on top of Lance and staring into blue eyes. He smiled up at her. "I picked my bedroom."

Maggie twisted her body to get away, but his grip around her only tightened. Letting out an irritated huff of air, she told him, "You're insane if you think you're sleeping in my bed."

"Who said anything about sleeping?" His eyelids dropped, giving him a sensual, drowsy look.

"Lance," she warned as his hands settled on her bottom and slowly made their way up the sides of her body, turning her hot, and dizzy, and aroused. "Stop," Maggie gasped.

"What if I don't want to?" he taunted.

Lifting her head, she glared at him. Maggie moved again, but all that resulted in was Lance shifting so that she lay full on him, making her aware of all the hard edges of his body—and other things. She closed her eyes, face burning, and tried not to think about what was perfectly lined up with her lower half.

"Nine months."

"What?" she choked out.

"It's been nine months." He rotated his hips against her, one slow circle around that had her forgetting all logic.

"That's . . . not my . . . problem." Maggie moaned, dropping her head forward. It had been over two years for her, since her last boyfriend, and her body ached for the touch of Lance, whether she wanted it to or not.

"You're right." Lance sat up, effectively dumping her off him.

Maggie landed on her back, struggling to breathe, all of her coiled tight and ready for a man she wanted to hate. She closed her eyes as she willed her heart to steady. She tried to think of fruit to get her mind off things, but all that did was make it worse—plums and bananas decided to morph into other images and torture her.

"I actually like the room across the hallway," he said conversationally. "That way, if you decide you want to participate in any extracurricular activities—bonus points for exercise, Maggie—you'll have easy access to yours truly. I am your coach, after all. I have to be there for you, at all hours, any time, for any situation . . . any need you may have. I'm being a good friend, really. Going above and beyond. It is my—"

Maggie grabbed a pillow and slammed it against his head. "Shut up,

Lance."

He grabbed the pillow from her and threw it across the room, eyes locked on hers. The space between them closed as he brought his face inches away from hers. "There's no point in pretending I don't want you. You know I do."

"You don't want me. You just want someone," she whispered hoarsely.

Lance argued her words with a simple chastising look. "That's a lie. I could have anyone—you know I'm not exaggerating, but I want you."

"But I'm . . ." She gestured to her curvy body.

"You're perfect," he said, voice harsh. "Quit saying otherwise. Quit thinking otherwise. Start believing it."

She enfolded his words into her arms and heart. Maggie dropped her eyes from his, faintly nodding. He was right.

"And you?" she questioned.

"What about me?"

Maggie lifted her gaze to his, the blueness of it as lovely as any sky. "You never wanted anyone to know what you struggled with, how you felt unloved and unlovable, but I did. In the end, it was one of the reasons you pushed me away."

"I've learned a lot since I was a teenager." He got up from the bed, his back to her. "I know you'll find this hard to believe, but I don't get involved with my clients."

Maggie pressed her lips together to remain mute.

Lance looked over his shoulder at her, correctly assessing her expression. "It's true. I'm not the kid you remember me as."

She slowly stood up. "You're not. I know that. I can tell."

Relief smoothed his features. "I won't touch you. Much," he added when she narrowed her eyes. "But as soon as the last day of our contract is up, Maggie, either submit, or run."

He walked out of the room like he hadn't just taken the air from her lungs or the willpower to stand from her legs. Maggie collapsed on the bed and closed her eyes, deciding to hide in her bedroom for a while. It was either that or hunt down Lance and ravish him.

LANCE—1996

THINGS WERE BAD from the start.

Jeff wanted to take his Cavalier and Lance insisted on taking the Jeep. Maggie stood between the two of them, looking from one to the other. The lavender top and white pleated skirt she wore looked good on her, and she had her hair up with loose waves around her face. He'd wanted to kiss her as soon as he'd seen her. It was hard to remember he had a girlfriend when he was around Maggie.

"If it's that big of a deal, we could walk," Maggie suggested. "It's not that far."

"It's at least a mile away," Jeff complained.

"We have to pick up Anne yet anyway." Lance checked the watch on his left wrist. "And we need to get going or she'll be wondering where we are."

"Well, you can take the Jeep and get Anne. Jeff and I will meet you guys at the restaurant."

Jeff put an arm around Maggie's shoulders and ushered her toward his car. "Fabulous idea."

Lance grabbed Maggie's wrist, halting them. "Except it makes more sense to take one car."

With a tight jaw, Jeff eyed the place where Lance's hand touched Maggie. "It isn't far enough to make a difference one way or another."

"It might be, depending on what all we do tonight," Lance said pleasantly.

"Can we just get in a stupid vehicle already and go?" Maggie shook off Jeff's arm and pulled her wrist from Lance's grasp.

"My car is safer," Jeff said, scowling.

"Mine is cooler."

Jeff's brown eyes narrowed.

Maggie sighed and tucked a piece of hair behind her ear. "Each of you pick a number between one and ten. We'll take the car of whoever guesses closest to the number I'm thinking. Lance, pick a number."

He rubbed his jaw as he studied Maggie's exasperated face. "Eight."

She looked at Jeff. "Pick a number, Jeff."

"Three."

"It was nine. Get in the Jeep." Maggie turned from them and marched toward the black Jeep.

Lance gave Jeff a smug look. He stared back, not speaking. Shrugging, Lance followed Maggie to the Jeep. She was already seated in the back. He paused, wanting her up front instead of Jeff, but one look at her face made him think better of mentioning it. She did not look happy. He wouldn't be happy either, if the guy he was going on a date with drove a Cavalier.

Top down, radio blaring, Lance drove to Anne's aunt and uncle's house. He put the vehicle in park and waited for Anne to come out, ignoring the sigh of relief Jeff let out when the Jeep was no longer moving. He'd grumbled about his driving the whole way. Asshole. Jeff got out and climbed in back with Maggie. Lance scowled at the street.

Maggie cleared her throat and he met her gaze in the rearview mirror. Lance lifted his eyebrows when she didn't say anything.

She shook her head and finally said, "Aren't you going to go to the door?"

"What for?"

"To pick her up and say hello to her relatives?"

"Why would I want to do that?"

Jeff snickered. "Because that's what gentlemen do."

"Gentlemen?" Lance rolled his eyes. "I'm not a gentleman."

"We know," Jeff said all too cheerfully.

Lance shifted his jaw and angled a glare over his shoulder. "I suppose you walked to Maggie's door and greeted Judith before you met me outside?"

"Yes. I did," he said, unashamedly gloating.

Cursing, Lance opened the door and jumped out, jogging up the curved sidewalk that led to the brick-sided house. Lance glanced back at the car as he waited for the door to open, wondering what Jeff and

Maggie were doing inside the Jeep. Hands fisted, he thrust his jaw forward and stared at the brown door.

He felt like a jerk, mostly because, out of all the times he'd come to pick up Anne for anything, he'd never come to the door. It wasn't his thing. And yet, there he stood, all because he had to compete with Jeff. The surprise on Rory York's face confirmed the rarity of Lance's present position.

"Hello, Lance. Come in."

A short and stocky computer genius in his mid-forties, Anne's uncle was soft spoken and pleasant. He had caterpillar eyebrows and squinty blue eyes with a long, wide nose and a small mouth. Anne clearly got her good looks from her mother's side.

Lance returned the greeting and followed him inside, clenching and unclenching his hands as his eyes swept over the modern decorating the York family favored. Bold colors, shiny electronics, and geometric shapes took over every room of the high-ceilinged and spacious house. Anytime he'd come to the York house, there was a heavy floral scent present that made him think of old people and funerals.

"Got big plans for the night, Mr. York?" Lance set his expression for casual interest. He felt trapped, like coming to the door meant some kind of commitment he wasn't ready for, and never would, not with Anne.

Rory York went red in the face, clearing his throat as he looked at the stairwell. "Oh, well. Jessie and I thought we'd stay in, watch a movie. The kids are all at friends' houses tonight. Anyway, you and Anne have a good time. Anne's in her room." He cleared his throat again and glanced at Lance quickly before speed-walking from the room.

So. Mr. and Mrs. York were in for a little kid-less entertainment. Lance watched his retreating form, a smirk lifting his lips. He tapped his fingers on the banister, and with a sigh, vaulted up them. Patience was not his thing either.

Anne's bedroom was the first door on the right. Lance knocked on the closed door, the sound of music pulsing through it. In three weeks she would travel to Hawaii for a two-week long photo shoot, and then it was back home to California. They'd both been aware of the temporariness of their relationship when it started.

Lance didn't do long term relationships, and he didn't do long distance ones either. In fact, he didn't really do relationships too much at all. He and Anne weren't even to the one-month mark, and it was the longest he'd stayed with one girl. Already, he was cagey.

The door swung open, he was hit with the scent of apples, and a squeal sounded in his ears as arms wrapped around his neck and a warm mouth latched onto his. Instincts kicked in and he kissed her back, fingers gripping her bony hips. Anne was only two inches shorter than Lance, all of her long and sleek. She didn't kiss like Maggie, an assessment firmly solidified in his mind with how recently he'd kissed the other. Anne wasn't a bad kisser, but it felt different. Lukewarm where intensity should be.

"Hi, baby," she said softly against his mouth.

Lance disengaged her arms from him. He hated being called that, and had told her enough times that she should remember. "Hey. Ready?"

Anne flipped her long blond hair over her shoulder. "I sure am. I haven't had anything to eat all day. And I worked out for three hours. I've been saving up for tonight." She flashed a blinding white smile.

She had glittery purple stuff around her eyes and her lips were unnaturally pink, like cotton candy. Lance noted the skimpy yellow top that showed a good deal of her midriff and the short ripped shorts that barely covered her butt cheeks. White cowboy boots completed the ensemble. Physically, everything about her was perfect, and for the first time that he could remember, it bothered him.

He mentally compared what she wore to what Maggie did, and turned away. "Great. Maggie and Jeff are waiting in the Jeep."

Fingers wrapped around his bicep as they walked, Anne gushed, "I can't believe I get to meet Maggie Smiley! I *love* her. She is so great on the show."

A faint smile touched his lips. "You are dating her co-star, you know."

Anne briefly rested her head against his as they descended the stairs, dropping her hand from his arm. Her voice was dreamy as she said, "I know, and I love him too."

Lance froze, and when Anne kept walking like she hadn't just said words she had no right saying, he swallowed thickly and followed her out the door. He heard Maggie's laughter as they got in the Jeep. The sound of it made him want to smile, but then he remembered it was because of Jeff, and not him, and he slammed the Jeep door.

Maggie, Jeff, and Anne kept the conversation going as he drove. He felt the heat of Maggie's inquisitive eyes on the back of his head, but refused to meet her gaze in the rearview mirror. Maybe Anne hadn't meant it like that. She said she loved Maggie too, and until a few minutes ago, she hadn't known her. He was paranoid, that was all. Overthinking things. People didn't say they loved each other that early into a relationship. Relationship. The word sounded vile, full of rules and expectations.

The restaurant, 'Early Bird', specialized in breakfast foods in uncommon, but amazing combinations. Locally owned and operated for over twenty years, it had been featured in countless magazines and won multiple prizes for its cuisine. Lance ate there at least every other week.

A blackbird with 'Early Bird' above it in red cursive lettering was plastered on the side of the pale yellow building, with another on top of the roof. The parking lot was full, which was to be expected on a Saturday night. The air was warm, but not overly humid, and the scents of fried food wafted from the building as they approached.

Hand interlocked with Anne's, his eyes were on Maggie as they walked toward the door. Jeff walked on the other side of Maggie, shooting Lance irritated looks that he continually ignored. Lance wanted the date to be his and Maggie's, and forget Jeff and Anne.

Maggie smiled when she caught him watching her, and Lance smiled back.

"I've never been here before," she told him.

"I know."

"Lance has brought me here a few times," Anne said. "They have great food."

"We'll have to come again, on our own," Jeff said to Maggie.

Maggie gave a noncommittal reply, which made Lance's smile widen and Jeff's frown deepen.

They were seated immediately in a corner booth of the loud, bustling establishment, the hostess blushing and stuttering over her words as she stared first at Lance, then at Maggie. Lance sat directly across from Maggie, with Anne next to him and Jeff across the table from her.

Not yet used to fame, even of a small degree, Maggie looked as nervous at the hostess as she continued to gawk. There was a smile on her face, but it was forced.

"You must be a fan of the show," Lance said to the brunette, offering a wide grin as she redirected her attention to him.

"Oh my God! I thought it was you two! I mean, the reservation says Lance Denton, but, and then, here you are, and so, yeah, I love 'Easier Said'! You two are amazing on it. I mean, I've watched everything you've ever been in, even the commercials, but . . . wow. My name's Emily, by the way." She blushed and pushed hair from her face, eyes on Lance.

"Thanks for being a fan, Emily," he replied. "Maggie and I appreciate all our viewers."

"Can I . . ." She stared at Maggie and then Lance, hesitating. "I'm not supposed to ask this, but can I get your autographs?"

"Sure," he said, taking the pen and napkin presented.

Lance scrawled his name onto the napkin and pushed it across the table to Maggie. Her hand trembled as she gripped the pen, and he didn't release it until she looked at him. Lance winked, and with a shaky laugh, Maggie took the pen and signed her name.

He stared at their names, liking how close they were, paired together like that. Lance Denton and Maggie Smiley. The hostess took the autographed napkin, gushed some more, and disappeared, saying their waitress would be over soon.

"You're from Iowa, right, Maggie?" Anne asked, eyes sparkling with friendly interest.

Maggie smiled, taking a sip of water. "I am, yes. Are you from the area?"

"Oh, no, I'm from California, way across the country. I'm just staying with my aunt and uncle while I do some modeling work. I'm leaving in a few weeks."

"Oh." Maggie shot Lance a look, as if gauging his reaction to the imminent departure of his girlfriend.

He stared back, no expression on his face.

"I've been to California before. My grandparents live there," Jeff said. His arm was around the back of the booth, hovering above Maggie's shoulders.

"Really?" Anne cried excitedly. "What part?"

"Near San Francisco. I'm going to stay with them over Christmas this year."

"No way! That's where I'm from! We should totally get together when you're there. I could be your tour guide, show you all the cool places."

Jeff looked at Maggie, his face going red. "Oh. Yeah. Maybe."

She tilted her head questioningly. "You should. It sounds fun," Maggie told him reassuringly.

The color on his face deepened and he leaned toward her. He opened his mouth, paused, and then said in a low voice, "Well. It's just that . . . do you . . . I mean . . . I was going to—"

"Maggie, isn't there a ski trip planned over Christmas for the cast? Near where you live. Somewhere in Minnesota," Lance said, effectively talking over and silencing Jeff. No way was Maggie getting on a plane and going out of state for two weeks with that guy.

He returned the glare Jeff aimed at him, only he was sure his was more poisonous.

"Um . . . yes. There is." Maggie gave Lance a relieved look. "I'm going. Are you?"

"Wouldn't miss it," he murmured, eyes locked on her.

Maggie turned to Jeff. "You're not going on the ski trip?"

"He's not a cast member," Lance stated, even though the three of them already knew it.

Jeff's features went from irritated to deadly. "It's for crew members too," he said in a toneless voice.

Lance shrugged.

"But no," he said to Maggie. "I promised my grandparents I'd visit them. I was going to ask you to come along, but it looks like you already have plans."

Maggie blanched.

Lance sat back. It appeared he didn't need to do anything—Jeff was well on his way to sabotaging things with Maggie without any help from him. They were on their first date, and he was asking her to go on vacation with him. Classic.

"I was hoping you'd come visit me over Christmas," Anne said to Lance with a pretty pout on her face.

It was Jeff's turn to smirk as Lance went still and silent. He didn't answer Anne. Things were supposed to be simple between them—they dated while she was in Virginia, and then it was done when she left. They needed to have a talk, but at the restaurant was not the place.

Maggie, noticing the tension, drew Anne into conversation. She put the focus on Anne's modeling career, a subject Anne was happy to talk about, excessively. Amidst the female chatter, Lance studied Jeff as they waited for the waitress. He was shorter and bulkier than Lance, with short brown hair and eyes. There was nothing about him that was better than Lance.

Safe came to mind. Jeff was safe. Safe was dull. He looked at Maggie as she chatted with Anne. Safe would not work for long with Maggie.

The food showed up. Lance frowned at Maggie as she pushed her meal around on her plate without eating much of it. Anne ate all of a salad, minus the dressing, and a roll, and acted like she overindulged. Well, for her, maybe she had.

Anne and Maggie continued to carry the conversation throughout the meal, and when the bill was paid—Maggie insisting she could pay for her own food instead of allowing Jeff—it was obvious the night was close to an end. From Jeff and Maggie's expressions, bowling looked like it wouldn't be happening. Good. Because Lance wanted to ditch Anne and Jeff and have Maggie all to himself.

"What now?" Anne wondered, trailing fingers up and down his arm.

"I'm, um, actually really tired," Maggie said, not meeting anyone's eyes. "I think I'll pass on bowling, if that's okay."

"Me too," Lance said happily. "Really tired."

Leaning close, Anne pressed her small breasts against his arm and said, "Want to cuddle and take a nap?"

Lance stepped away. "Not tonight." His tone was cooler than he planned, and when her face fell, he knew their needed discussion was not going to be fun.

"I'm ready to go home too," Jeff said, staring at Maggie with anger and sadness on his face.

"Well, this was a great double date. We'll have to do it again," Lance said with a touch too much enthusiasm. "Shall we?"

The ride was quiet, and when he parked the Jeep outside of Anne's relatives' house, he got out at the same time as Anne. Guilt and purpose knifed his skin in short, methodical stabs as he walked her to the door. She was a sweet person. Sure, she was obsessive over her body image, but as a model, that was warranted. He knew she was going to cry. He hated it when they cried.

"Anne," he began, and she burst into tears. Already? Lance briefly closed his eyes. "Anne," he tried again.

"You're breaking up with me," she wailed, hands over her eyes.

Lying would be pointless, and cruel. Lance said evenly, "Yes."

She dropped to her bottom on the cement steps and cried. "It's because . . . I said . . . I love you, isn't it?" Her voice was muffled, hair glowing silvery blond in the dark.

Lance sighed and sat down beside her, careful to not touch her. "That was part of it, yeah." He clasped his hands and stared at the darkened Jeep. "When we started this, we agreed that it would end when you left."

"That's in t-three weeks!"

"Right. And you want me to visit you over Christmas," he reminded her.

Anne dropped her hands, revealing smudged eyes and tear-stained cheeks. "Because I love you."

"Anne, you don't love me," he told her, voice hardening.

Her lower lip quivered. "But I do."

"You don't know me well enough to love me."

"Lance—" She reached for his face and he got to his feet.

"No." The word was coldly delivered, and inarguable. Lance stared down at her. "You don't love me. I don't want you to, and I don't love you. I'm sorry."

He left her crying on the doorstep, feeling like an ass, but also relieved. No one spoke when he got inside, Jeff stiffly seated in the front. At the apartments, Jeff left without saying a word, tires squealing as the Cavalier raced from the parking lot.

"That was fun," he said to Maggie.

Face expressionless, Maggie slapped him.

His cheek instantly stung, her handprint branded upon his skin. "What the hell was that for?" he demanded, staring into angry eyes.

"That was for Jeff, and Anne."

"What are you talking about?" he demanded.

"Jeff doesn't want to see me again," Maggie supplied. "Because of you."

"And that's bad why?"

"He's a nice guy."

"Nice, and boring," he agreed.

"And you broke up with Anne, all because she cares about you more than you do her."

"So?"

"You're an ass." Mouth twisted with distaste, Maggie stomped away.

"Did I somehow, at some point, give you the impression that I wasn't?" he called, striding after her.

Maggie headed toward the sand, kicking off her sandals and storming along the gritty path like each step she took was on Lance's face. He chucked off his shoes and socks and went in pursuit. He felt like he spent a lot of his time chasing Maggie. Being a Saturday night, the beach was covered in people, and a live band played 'Runnin' Down a Dream' as people danced. The song was much too appropriate—each time he reached her, she ran. When he fell behind, she walked.

She kept going, past the people, past the structures, until all that was around her was air, and sea. Out of breath and pulse thrumming, Lance caught up to her, but then he paused, not sure what to do or say. Her back was to him, arms crossed over her like a hug. She looked into the black and blue water, a bruise upon the earth, and went motionless. He wondered what she thought as she stared into the ocean.

And then he asked her.

It took her a long time to answer, and when she did, her voice was uneven and soft. "I used to be fat."

He blinked at the unexpected words, taking a careful step closer.

"I wasn't always fat, and my parents say I was never that, that I was chubby, like that's better. When I was six, I went from skinny to overweight. My older sister, who's always been thin, used to make fun of me, telling me I had enough rolls to start a bakery, calling me a cow and mooing when I was around. When I was eleven, I got taller, slimmed down, and was no longer fat. I still had curves—I think I always will."

She didn't speak again until Lance was beside her, looking out at the choppy waters with her, not wanting to breathe in case the sound of it would hide her words from his ears.

"I still see her, when I look in the mirror." Maggie glanced at him, a slice of eyes that scalded his skin. "I still see that fat little girl. Then I came here, and I met you, and . . . I feel like I can't be as unattractive as I think, not with how interested in me you seem to be, but then, the next second, I feel uglier than I ever have before. Because of you, and your games. You're not good for me. You're destructive and—and rude."

He took a painful inhalation of air, unable to refute her words, but there was something about her he had to say. Lance moved for her hand but she shifted out of reach. "You're not fat. You're not unattractive. There's nothing wrong with you. You shouldn't base your worth on how you think others see you, not even me. Tell the world to screw off."

She was silent for a long time, not looking at him, the pulse fluttering at the base of her neck. Maggie swallowed and said, "Tell you to screw off?"

Lance shrugged.

"Right." She shook her head. "Everything I feel for you, or around you, is equal parts good and bad. I think I hate you at times. I want to stay away from you."

"That might be hard, since we're on the same television show and everything," he mocked softly, eyes trained on the gray horizon.

"You terrify me."

Lance looked at her. Maggie watched him, her face open in a way that made his insides clench and his body tense. He understood the confusing, conflicting emotions she had for him, because he had them as well. Denial and acceptance—he constantly fought between the two.

"I should terrify you," he told her. "I use people. I don't care about anyone more than I care about myself. I've never loved anyone, but I've told tons of girls I did. I break hearts, and it doesn't bother me. I'll break yours, if you let me."

Maggie sucked in a sharp breath, eyes wide and bright on his face. They glowed in the dark like a lighthouse, beckoning him forth from the treachery of his own existence to the safety of hers.

"Maggie," he ground out, fingers curling with the need to touch her.

She backed up a step, closer to the water.

Lance followed, feeling like a monster tracking its most prized victim. "Why do you keep fighting it?"

"Fighting what?" she whispered, lips barely moving.

"Me. This. You feel it too. You feel it when we kiss. You know there's something between us. Everyone knows. Everyone sees it. Even Jeff saw it." Lance took another step closer, and she took another back. "Staying away from you is driving me insane. I'm tired of it. I want you so much."

"If we—if we get involved . . . it'll end badly."

"Yes." He knew it would. He wanted to get lost in her anyway.

"I'll get hurt."

Lance inclined his head. "So will I."

"You just broke up with your girlfriend," she pointed out, frustration tightening her features. It was for him, and for her response to him.

"I did, and I don't even care, because the whole time I was with her, I wanted to be with you."

"Do you realize how bad that sounds?" she demanded, her voice high with incredulity. Maggie was in the water up to her ankles.

"Maggie. I don't care," he said slowly and clearly.

"I'll just end up like her, like all the other girls you go through. Unwanted and discarded for someone new."

Lance stared at her, his eyes drifting over her eyes, nose, and lips. She would never be like all the other girls. "I don't think so, but I don't know how things will end," was the most honest answer he could give her.

"And you don't care," she whispered.

Lance stood there, unapologetic, as Maggie looked into his eyes, into his being, and saw him for what he was. It was humbling, knowing someone could see all the flaws in him, and not turn away.

"I tried. I tried to be your friend. I can't. I can be more, and maybe nothing, but I can't be that." Lance inhaled raggedly, closing the distance between them. He touched her cheek, fingertips tingling at the feel of her soft skin. "You're like the pretty flower my dirty hands should never touch."

"But you're going to anyway," she said shakily.

Water moved around them, but they remained motionless. It was cool, and gently lapped against their legs. The moon silhouetted Maggie like sunshine and clouds at odds with one another. Lance faded to nothing as he looked into her expressive eyes, seeing his reflection. Seeing Maggie.

"Only if you let me." Lance moved his hand to her lips, brushing his fingertips across them. They felt like silk, and he repressed a shudder. "But then you're mine, and no one else's."

She didn't say anything, but she didn't move away, and when her eyes closed and her head fell back, exposing her neck to the moonlight, Lance knew her answer. He threaded his fingers through her hair, dislodging the ponytail holder to fall into the ocean, and brought his mouth to hers. Maggie's eyes flew open, her hands gripped his forearms, and then she swayed toward him, falling into him as he fell into her.

Kissing Maggie was comparable to finding air, and losing it, just as quickly. He was full of life, he was without it. Her lips tasted like candy, her tongue like velvet, and she consumed him. All he wanted, all he knew, was her. Maggie was his. The thought made him tremble with fear, because if she was his, that meant she could be taken away. Lance kissed her harder, wanting to wipe out the doubts, and the need, but all kissing her did was make him want her more.

A high wave hit them, plastering them with cold water, and she pulled back with a small shriek. Lance laughed, and the surprise in her eyes turned to delight as she laughed with him. Her dress was soaked, clinging to the curves and hollows of her frame. His body tightened, his nostrils flared, and Lance gripped her shoulders to keep his hands from more intimate parts.

He felt dazed in her presence, knowing she was his, for however long he was given—or took.

"What now?" she asked, breathless.

Her eyes sparkled. He put that light in her eyes.

"Hmm," Lance murmured, bringing her fisted hand to his mouth. It was cold and wet, and tasted like salt. "How about we find our shoes and go for a ride?"

"But we—our clothes are wet," she said, shivering.

"We could always take them off," Lance offered.

She laughed, shaking her head. "You're insane."

"Not yet, Maggie," he promised. "But I could see myself going there, real fast. You make me crazy, wanting you like I do."

Her lips parted and her eyes became unfocused. "Lance, you can't say things like that."

"I can." He tugged at her hand. "Come on, let's go. I'll be good." He glanced at her as they walked. "I know a place where you can practice driving."

"I haven't practiced driving in months. I'm sure I've forgotten all the important things I need to know by now. I'll probably wreck or something."

They left the water, the air cool as it slowly worked at changing their clothes from wet to damp messes. Chilled and yet somehow feverish, Lance fit his hand around Maggie's, the simplicity of their joined hands monumental to him. Her small hand shook inside his.

"I won't let you wreck—not unless you want to." He paused on the beach to look at her, the sky above them a kaleidoscope of clouds and stars.

"Why would I want to wreck?" she questioned softly, looking at him like she didn't understand him.

Lance smiled, the blackness of it reflecting his thoughts. "Sometimes crashing is the only way to deal with things."

She frowned, doubts flitting across her face. "You worry me."

"Good." He nodded. "I should. When I stop worrying you, you know you should get away from me as fast as you can."

"Why would you say that? What do you mean?" She took a step back, caution stiffening her shoulders. She looked posed to run, should he say or do one wrong thing.

Lance gripped her face between his hands, staring at a face that should have been plain but wasn't. It was her eyes, and her innocence, and her *goodness*—she was stunning.

Breaths shallow and fast, he said thickly, "When you stop worrying, Maggie, it means it's too late for you. It means you've given me your heart. It means you'll get hurt."

"You act like you're some monster. You keep warning me away and then you keep pulling me back. You're just a boy. A messed up one, but still a boy," Maggie said, voice shaking.

A twisted smile tried to form to his lips and he bit his lower lip hard to keep it at bay, tasting blood. "Maggie, I've never been just a boy. I was never allowed that. I was born with expectations and responsibilities."

"Poor Lance," she taunted, crossing her arms.

He shrugged, looking down at the sand. However it sounded, what he said was true. His dead mother wanted him to be an actor. Out of guilt or love for a woman he couldn't save, his father pushed it. Lance spent his childhood being told the most important thing in his life was something that wasn't even real. Acting wasn't a career—it was a life, an unrealistic one, and one decided for him.

Maggie brushed the back of her hand across his cheek.

Lance jerked from her touch, eyes downcast.

"You're not lying."

He met her gaze, saw the sorrow and wonder in the rise of her eyebrows and the frown on her face. "Of course I am. It's what I do."

Lance took off at a fast pace, shaking away the gloomy thoughts. He found their discarded shoes and carried them as he strode for the Jeep. *What would you be, if you could pick?* Hell if he knew. Lance was to the Jeep and had been for a few minutes before Maggie got there. He handed Maggie her shoes. Part of him had wondered if she'd follow or ditch him entirely and go home, maybe call up safe and dull Jeff. His jaw clenched at the thought.

Lance needed a distraction. Knowing his preferred method of going about it would most likely result in him getting slapped again, he decided on a more acceptable one. She would drive his Jeep, and maybe, if he was lucky, she would kiss him again. It was better than nothing.

He removed his car keys from the pocket of his jeans and dangled them in front of her face, a disarming grin in place. "Ready?"

"Lance, I'm serious," Maggie hedged even as she walked closer, a worried expression on her face. "I don't think I should drive."

"You finished Driver's Ed, right?"

"Yes."

"And you passed, right?"

"Yes," she said with a sigh.

"Get in."

He opened the passenger door for her and smiled as she climbed inside. Maggie rolled her eyes and faced forward. The drive was ten minutes long, and when they reached the parking lot of an old, abandoned cheese factory, Lance put the Jeep in park. The building rested on the edge of the pavement, glowing gray and eerie under the moonlight.

Lance watched it a moment, wondering what memories haunted the place. Structures were funny that way—they took on the life of those once inside them, the past echoing through the walls. His dad's house was like that. Even though he didn't have a single recollection of his mother, she was still there, in that house Max Denton refused to sell.

"Why do you have that look on your face?" Maggie asked quietly, touching his shoulder and causing him to jump.

"What look?" he asked, keeping his eyes lowered from hers.

Her hand fell away. "I don't know. Sad, or maybe hurt."

He looked at Maggie, refusing to address that. She already knew more about him than most people. "Ready?"

She chewed on her lower lip, eyes wide as she stared at him. "No."

"It'll be fun. Don't be a wimp, Maggie. Show me your wild side."

Anger took the place of unease on Maggie's face, and Lance's breaths picked up in response to the heat that flared to life in her eyes. "Why are you pushing this?"

"Because I want to see you out of control and reckless. It turns me on."

Maggie choked as she inhaled, coughing until she caught her breath. "I thought that was my shampoo," she said unevenly.

"Your shampoo, your voice, your words. Everything about you, actually. Even the thought of you." Lance admitted, "You've turned me into a hormonal mess."

Shaking her head, she stepped out of the vehicle and moved to his side. Maggie leaned down and said, "I'm sure that was the case long before I came along."

Lance got out, waited for her to get in, and shut the door. "I'm sure my condition's worsened since I met you." He jogged around to the passenger side and got in, tapping his palms against the dash. "Let's go. Show me what you got. You trust me, right?"

She nodded jerkily.

"Let me trust you."

Lower lip between her teeth, Maggie held still with her hand around the keys. Then, with a quick look at Lance, she started the Jeep.

"Look at you, starting the Jeep. What will you do next?" he softly mocked. "I dare you to put it in drive."

Eyes narrowing, she did, pushing her foot down hard on the accelerator. The Jeep took off, Maggie's gaze set forward and her face a mask of determination and fear. Lance studied her profile as they raced toward nothing. That was the perfect analogy for his life. He was always running, always heading for something, and it was never what he wanted, because he didn't know what he wanted.

Her.

He wanted her.

Lance glanced at the pavement, seeing the end of the parking lot approaching. After that, it was a line of grass and then a street inhabited by parked and moving vehicles, with houses beyond that. They didn't want to head that way.

"What do I do?" Panic sharpened Maggie's voice. "What do I do, Lance?"

"Maybe you should try turning."

Maggie jerked the wheel to the left and the car swerved.

"Slowing down first is always a good idea," he said calmly, his pulse tripping. Lance noticed his hands were fisted and he relaxed them.

She hit the brake and they lurched to a stop before she took her foot off again and the Jeep inched forward.

Lance laughed and she shot him an apologetic glance.

"Keep going," he urged.

Maggie released the brake and the vehicle crept forward. She turned the wheel to the right and it took a good minute for the actual turn to come to fruition.

"I'm horrible at this," she said with a sigh.

"Give it more gas."

Maggie complied and the Jeep picked up speed, then stalled when Maggie thought it was going too fast, then picked up speed again, only to slow down. Lance's body jerked forward and back as he fought not to laugh. She took a deep breath and turned the wheel to the left, then to the right, and they swerved across the parking lot like a large, slithering worm.

"What are you doing?" he asked conversationally.

"I don't know. I suck at this," she cried, flinging up her hands.

"Hands on the wheel."

A glower tightened her features, and Maggie listened.

Construing his expression to nothingness to keep from smiling, Lance said, "I think we need to try different scenery. Driving in circles isn't teaching you anything. We should be on an actual road."

"No. No way. This—that's illegal. I'm done. No more driving for me. It isn't safe. You can't make me." Maggie shook her head, fumbling with the gearshift. She put it in park and jumped from the Jeep.

The beams of the headlights illuminated her as she stood in front of them, hands on her hips. With the tangled mass of her damp hair and the unrestricted view of her body the lights allowed, Lance went motionless. She looked ethereal, and wrathful. Every curve was visible, every dip or hollow dry clothes hid was right there for him to see. He wanted to rip her clothes from her body and kiss the salt from it, and then he wanted to be inside her. Craved it. Ached for it. Needed it. Knew it wasn't going to happen. Everything was too new, barely there, tenuous.

Lance swallowed once, twice, three times, before he could get his body to cooperate with his head. Namely, to tame itself down, and then, to get out of the vehicle. Stalking toward her, Lance loomed over her with a menacing look on his face. He didn't speak, his silence loud. Lance knew he shouldn't push Maggie to do something she didn't want, and that made him want to do it more. He wanted to see her wild, and he didn't care how it happened.

Maggie needed to show him she felt like he felt. Reckless. Partially mad. He couldn't be the only one that wondered if he could be driven out of his mind by the emotions plaguing him. It was mean and immature and Lance relished the thought of wholesome Maggie giving in to her bad side.

Everyone had one—they only had to realize it.

Face tilted up as she met his gaze and held it, she finally demanded, "Are you trying to intimidate me?"

"Is it working?" Lance's voice was low, and edged with barbs.

Her eyes, in that indescribable shade, and glowing when the light hit them, glared into him, into his jaded being. "I want to go home."

"Okay." He stepped back and motioned to the Jeep. The engine thrummed, waiting for someone to have a little fun with it. "Drive us home."

Making a sound of frustration, Maggie kicked at a piece of gravel. "Forget anything nice I've ever said about you. I take it back."

"Have you said nice things about me?" he wondered, grinning.

"You'll never know, because I just took it all back."

Lance shrugged. "Your choice: drive home, or take some back roads."

"How about I just walk?" Haughty and angry, Maggie crossed her arms and aimed her feet in the wrong direction of the apartment buildings.

He watched her, waiting until she was clear across the parking lot to call out, "You're going the wrong way!"

"Lance Denton," she screamed as she whirled around, her face hidden by night but the rage clear in her tone. "You are an awful person!"

Maggie then proceeded to have a temper tantrum, punching the air with her fists and having a kick-out as she shouted unintelligible words Lance was glad he couldn't make out. He watched her, entranced by her rage. She ranted away, gesturing wildly above her head as she marched one way, stopped, chose another path, and continued on. It was comical to watch, and even more than that, breathtaking. Lance decided it was best Maggie didn't realize how entertaining he found her, hanging back in the shadows as her meltdown reached its peak.

"You want me to drive?" she shouted, striding toward him. "All right! I'll drive."

Maggie reached him, her face red and eyes alight with deadly intent. Lance swallowed, wanting her to use that passion on him any way she deemed, even as a trickle of unease slid down his spine.

She pointed at him and he flinched. "Get in the car."

Damn. Lance's pulse picked up and he inhaled sharply, liking her present bossy, domineering attitude. He practically ran to the Jeep and dove onto his seat, snapping the buckle of the seatbelt with large doses of enthusiasm. It was hard to keep the glee from his face when Maggie got in, slamming the door and attacking the gearshift after buckling her own seatbelt.

Once in drive, she wrapped her fingers around the steering wheel and squeezed—Lance was sure she was imagining it was his neck she gripped so tightly. He fantasized it was something else and his mouth went dry.

"I'll drive this stupid car," she muttered, jabbing a finger against the radio buttons and finding a hard rock station. She turned the dial and the small space was filled with head banging mayhem.

Lance's trepidation grew and he rubbed the back of his neck, pressing his lips together to keep from talking—or shouting. His eardrums throbbed from the guitar and drums pounding out of the speakers.

Maggie's foot slammed against the pedal and the car shot forward. As she sharply twisted the wheel to make a left hand turn, a car slowly drove by in the other direction.

"Don't hit the car!" Lance braced himself as the Jeep went in the other car's lane.

"I'll drive how I want to drive," she yelled over the music, shooting him a glower with eyes that shone with an unholy light. "You told me to drive, I'm driving."

Lance groaned and slunk down in his seat, placing a hand over his eyes. *Great plan, really great plan. Idiot.*

Maggie punched the radio off a minute later.

"Thank you," he mumbled, ears ringing.

"That car turned around, and is following us."

"What?" Lance shot up in the seat and twisted around to view the white car steadily gaining on them. Cursing, he looked from the car to Maggie, swallowing a mouthful of dread. "It's a cop."

Her eyes flew to his.

"Watch the road!"

"What do I do? Tell me what to do!" The car rode too close to the curb. "I'm pulling over."

"The hell you are! Get back in the lane." Trying to think, Lance stared at the road and said, "Take the next left."

"I'm pulling over, Lance," she insisted, voice high.

"Maggie," he said roughly, clapping a hard hand to her wrist to keep the wheel straight. "If we get pulled over, you will not get your license, understand? And mine will be taken away. Keep driving—and in a straight line, please."

"Whatever happens, I blame you."

Lance glanced over his shoulder. "You can blame me all you want, just drive the damn car like you think you know what you're doing. Blinker," he hollered when she started to turn. "A blinker would be nice here!"

Maggie's lip wobbled as she flipped on the blinker. "This is all your fault. And mine. I let you get to me. Why did I do that? I'm going to hell. I'm going to get sent back home. I'll never act again. My parents will lock me in my bedroom until I'm twenty. My life is over."

Lance stared at Maggie. "Don't be melodramatic. Take the next right."

"Where are you taking us?" she yelled, eyes riveted to the road.

He thumped the back of his head against the seat. "You're going fifteen miles an hour. Speed up." Lance's leg bounced in agitation and he looked behind them. The police vehicle was closer. "Speed up now."

"Why?"

"Because I think we're about to be pulled over."

"So I pull over, right? Don't I pull over? Why am I not pulling over?"

"Maggie," he said in a calm voice. "I don't want to worry you, but if we don't lose the cop in about two seconds, things are going to get real bad. The next right goes out of town. Take it fast and then you drive like the wind."

"You have the worst ideas. The worst," she snapped, taking the turn and progressively accelerating.

"Shut up and do as you're told," he warned, his face and voice cold.

It was necessary for him to keep her composed, no matter how rude he had to be about it. He was on edge, and Maggie was making it worse, for both of them. One more ticket of any kind and Lance was in serious shit. His dad had threatened to make him move back home if he got in any more trouble.

Lance would rather chew off his own foot than live in the house that was a shrine to his mom. Maybe if his dad was ever around, it would be tolerable, but business kept him gone half the week, and even when he wasn't flying around dealing with clients, he was either in his office or court. It was the price they both paid for his father's success as an influential celebrity lawyer.

Jaw taut, Maggie listened as Lance told her what turns to take, when to speed up, when to slow down. With the moon above them and the cop car finally turning off and heading back to town, he led her up a winding path to a small mountain, more a hill than anything.

Lance let out a deep sigh and told Maggie to pull over.

When they reached the lookout point, she killed the engine, fumbled with the door as she angrily mumbled to herself, and stormed from the car—after banging shut the door.

Lance was slower to remove himself from the Jeep. Maggie was furious with him, and yeah, rightly so. He shoved his hands in the pockets of his jeans and ambled over to her, careful to keep a good amount of distance between them. Back stiff, Maggie stood near the fence that separated visitors from the roughened terrain below. She stared into a blackened night with the concentration of one who hoped if they ignored something for long enough—namely Lance—it would disappear.

"You did a good job driving," he offered as a compromise.

The moon haloed her as she spun around, face slashed with shadows and light. "You purposely pushed me to do that. You knew I didn't want to, and you wouldn't stop until I did. You're a-a bully," Maggie told him.

It would be pointless to contest that, and his reasoning wouldn't make it justified either. Lance looked at the trees surrounding them, their appearance that of dead, black-stained creatures, spindly branches reaching out like ghoulish arms. An owl hooted and he listened to the sound, finding it eerily beautiful. Peaceful. He looked at Maggie. Unlike her.

"I want to hit you," Maggie announced, fingers pointed out like her control on them was slipping and she was about to gash out his eyes.

He cocked his head, turning to train his gaze on her. "Twice in one night? Could be a record."

"Only, I think, that if I start, I might not stop."

"Hmm. It was a nice thought anyway, right?"

"I hate you," she vowed in a wavering voice. Maggie's words should have flayed him.

"No, you don't." Lance's voice was quiet. "You wish you did, but you don't."

"How do you know?" Her eyes were large with pain, her heart-shaped mouth tipped down with it.

"Because it's the same for me."

Her face fell. "You wish . . . you hated me?"

"Yeah." He showed her his back as he watched the wind pick up dead leaves and swirl them around on the ground. "Couldn't you tell? The first month or so I had myself convinced I did hate you. And then . . . then I couldn't keep pretending." Lance turned back to face her.

"Why would you want to hate me?" Maggie's eyes shone with hurt, and it was sad and lovely.

"Because I can't—I don't know how to . . ." Lance swallowed and shook his head.

Maggie clasped her hands together and waited. When he failed to elaborate because he couldn't explain what he didn't understand, she said, "My favorite season is fall. For a lot of people in Iowa, it's winter. I do find winter to be beautiful, with the snow and all the decorations and lights, but fall is my favorite."

Her smile was sweet and faraway. "There are so many different colors in the leaves. Maybe it should make me sad that the falling of them symbolizes a death of sorts, but I'm not. Even if it means the end for a single leaf, it also means the tree will have regrowth in the spring, something to replace the fallen leaves. I used to walk around town, just counting how many different colors I could find within the leaves of the trees."

Maggie focused on him. "What's your favorite time of the year?"

It had to be the stupidest, most random thing she could say, and Lance's eyes pricked with gratefulness. He took a deep breath, trying to smile around a hurting heart. "I don't have one. I have a least favorite, though, if you really want to know."

After a brief pause, she nodded. "Yes. Tell me."

"Summer. I hate summer."

She walked closer. "Why?"

"It's when my mom died. Sort of puts a dark taint on the whole thing, you know? Especially my birthday. My dad gets depressed every summer. It used to be a real bummer, celebrating my birthday with a guy who could barely be around me without thinking of the woman I looked so much like. He's better now, but . . . ." He shrugged and looked at his shoes. "It helps that I'm not around him that much."

When he lifted his head, Maggie was before him. Eyes dark with an unreadable emotion, she shook her head when he opened his mouth to ask her what she was doing, and then her mouth locked with his. Instant heat scorched him, inside and out. He reached around her and palmed her back, pushing his lower half against hers. The taste of her mouth, the scent of her skin—one touch and Maggie owned him.

Maggie would be a virgin. Hell, she hadn't even been kissed before a few months ago. Her first—Lance would be her first everything. He would be her first love, the one she would never forget, not even when she wished she could. The knowledge of that had his fingers digging hard into her hips, his mouth making promises he would keep and destroy.

Lance moved back, but she followed, her small but strong fingers holding his jaw on either side. Maggie's body demanded what she didn't know how to say, or couldn't. He had to take things slow with her. His body screamed its disapproval of that, but it was irrelevant. She pushed against him, her breasts pressed against his chest, and he moaned low in his throat.

Before he knew what was happening, they were alongside the hood of the Jeep, Maggie's bottom wedged against it with Lance between her legs. Even with their clothes on, he felt the heat of her desire, her body a furnace of want. While his mouth trailed across the features of her face, his hands learned the contours of her back, the dips of her shoulders, the curve of her neck. Lance felt Maggie in a way he'd never cared to know a girl before.

"I want to make summer your favorite," she gasped when they paused to catch their breath.

"This past one was," he confessed.

Maggie cupped Lance's face, their mouths close but not touching. Her fingertips were little pulses of sensation against his skin, and he placed his hand over her heart as their eyes met, needing to know its erratic beat was for him, and what he made her feel.

"You don't understand," Maggie said softly. "I want to . . . to . . ." She twisted away and Lance stepped back. Maggie got to her feet, tugging at her skirt to straighten it. Her hair waved in disarrayed locks around her face and shoulders.

She wouldn't look at him as she said, "I want to find every broken thing inside of you, and I want to heal them all."

Time paused, the only sound registering in his brain that of his wildly beating heart. Unsteadiness hit him and he closed his eyes against it. Without acknowledging her or her words, Lance strode for the Jeep.

"Let's go," he commanded shortly, his gaze locked on the ground. A piece of glass glinted when the moon caught it and he focused on that, forcing his breaths to stay level as he listened to Maggie get into the Jeep and shut the door.

The ride back was tense, Lance purposely driving like an ass. He went too fast, took corners too sharp, wanting a reaction out of Maggie, and getting none. She quietly sat, fingers locked together in her lap, her head bowed. She couldn't say things like that to him. She couldn't think them. He didn't want that from her. Lance's jaw tightened. No—he did want that from her. That was the problem.

When they reached the apartments, he got out and headed toward his, not bothering to wait for her, or open her door, or any of the chivalrous things a nice guy would do. He wasn't a nice guy. Eyes burning with anger and something else, hands fisted to the point they ached, Lance ground his teeth together and swung around, backtracking to Maggie. She stared at him as he approached, eyes guarded, sparks of anger in hers just as he knew there were in his.

"You don't get to say things like that to me," he growled, pointing a finger at her.

Maggie slapped his finger away, giving him a small shove. He staggered back as she told him, "You don't get to boss me around. I'll say whatever I want. You don't own me."

Lance opened his mouth, then closed it. He threw up his hands in frustration. "This was a stupid idea. I'm going to bed."

He was halfway to his apartment when her tremulous voice broke the air. "What was a stupid idea? I was a stupid idea? Kissing me was a stupid idea? Getting me to like you was a stupid idea? What was a stupid idea?"

Lance halted his footsteps, not turning around. "I don't need anyone to fix me, all right?"

"I didn't say you needed it! That isn't what it's about. It's about . . . it's about . . ."

Unable to keep his gaze from her any longer, Lance turned in a slow half-circle.

Chin up, eyes steady on his, Maggie said a sentence that crushed him, and built him back up. "That I care enough for you to want to, that's all."

He left her there, racing toward his apartment like he could escape her words. His chest throbbed at hearing them. Lance put a hand to it as he vaulted up the stairs, half expecting a bruise to appear on his flesh. *Coward. You're a coward.* Lance burst through the door, startling Mitch and his latest conquest in the middle of making out on the couch. Mouth twisted with disgust, he flew past them to reach his bedroom.

Slamming shut the door, he immediately flipped the lock. Lance snorted. As if that could keep him from replaying her words in his head, as if a door had the power to block her from his heart. He climbed onto his bed in the dark and held his head. He was scared, proof of that in the trembling of his hands where they were pressed to his temples. Lance laughed, the sound unusually loud in the blackness and silence of his room.

Lance Denton, hiding from a girl.

That was rich.

MAGGIE—2010

"WHAT ARE YOU doing?" he demanded as he entered the kitchen. Perspiration glinted off his tanned skin and he rubbed a hand towel against his damp black locks.

Maggie quickly swallowed the food in her mouth. "How many times a day do you work out?"

Lance gave her plate of food a pointed look.

"Are you crabby? You seem crabby."

"Maggie. Answer the damn question!"

"You can see what I'm doing!" Her face was hot, and she fought the urge to grab her plate and hide.

Lance eyed the plate and then scowled at her.

"It's my cheat day," she grumbled like a petulant child.

"Maggie, love, yesterday was your cheat day," Lance said evenly.

She tried not to react to the endearment said with sarcasm, but her heart pounded an extra beat anyway. "Maybe it should be on a calendar then, so I don't forget."

Without removing his eyes from hers, he tapped the calendar on the refrigerator. "Busted," he whispered.

"You're not my parent, you know." Maggie inwardly rolled her eyes at her juvenile behavior. The plan was to be out of the kitchen with all evidence of her meal disposed of before Lance decided to make an appearance. She should have known that wouldn't happen.

"Yes. I am aware of that. I'm your personal trainer . . . that you hired . . . to train you to make better food and exercise choices."

Sighing, she constructed her features to guiltlessness. "I'm only eating a salad."

"Really? With chocolate?"

Maggie froze. "What?"

"You have chocolate on your face." Laughter twinkled in his eyes even as a frown marred his face. Lance reached out and brushed a thumb across her mouth, making her lips itch.

"Oh, um, how did that get there?" Lame. That was lame. She tried another tactic. "Why can't I have a salad and a candy bar? Isn't that balancing? Right? I mean, I eat something not so healthy, and then I eat something healthy, so really, it's like I didn't eat anything, because they cancel each other out," she said in a rush.

He stared at her for a long time, and then he shook his head as though to clear it. "Maggie," he chided. "For one thing, you drowned your salad in dressing." He put his head next to the plate and looked up at her. "Do you hear that?"

Maggie blinked, wondering if Lance was mentally sound. Maybe the lack of sex was messing with his head. "Hear what? I don't hear anything."

"That's the sound of your lettuce dying. You don't hear anything because it's dead. Are you taking notes?" He straightened. "Don't kill the lettuce." Each word was punctuated with a finger jab to the air.

"You're being slightly melodramatic."

"There is no slightly about it."

"Okay," she said slowly, wondering if he realized he'd agreed with her. "It's only dressing."

"Only—let me show you something." Lance opened the refrigerator door and grabbed the ranch dressing Maggie purchased yesterday, along with her cookies and chocolate and other various foods that Lance didn't know about. The vinaigrettes he'd been forcing her to use were getting redundant. She needed substance, fat, calories.

He shoved the bottle in front of her face. "Read the back. Tell me what you see that's good in this bottle."

She crossed her arms, refusing to look. "I know what's on the back."

"Then you know you shouldn't be using it." He dropped the full bottle of ranch salad dressing in the wastebasket, and Maggie's stomach went with it. "Where is it?" Lance searched the cupboards and drawers, the sound of them opening and closing the only noise in the room.

"Where is what?" Maggie averted her eyes when he spun around to glare at her.

"You can't keep junk food in the house. If you want to have a treat, that's fine, you go out and get a single serving of something, because if you keep the stuff here, you're going to eat it."

"You're being rude."

Lance closed his eyes and took deep breaths. Eyes opened once more, he said, "I'm not trying to be rude. I'm trying to make you see why hoarding junk food is not a good idea. Case in point: two cheat days in a row. You don't get two cheat days in a row. No one does. Now . . ." He crossed the floor to her. "Where is the junk food?"

"Is this because of yesterday?" She really didn't want him to find her stash, but he was overreacting.

He went still, slowly tilted his head to the side, and stared, daring her to say it.

"With the bed . . . and the . . . and you . . ." She trailed off, unable to say the words.

"Oh, you're wondering if I'm sexually frustrated and taking it out on you." His tone of voice was scarily cheerful.

Maggie took a step back.

His features went hard. "If that was the case, I'd be in a much better mood, wouldn't I?"

"What?"

Lance closed the distance between them and cupped the back of her neck, holding her in place so that she had no choice but to look into his lethal gaze, lips a mere inch from hers. "If I was taking my sexual frustration out on you . . . I'd be in a much better mood, wouldn't I?" His words seduced her as well as any touch could. Sweat fought with the clean scent of his deodorant, a rich aroma that made her head spin.

She *wanted* him to kiss her, to do more, to do anything he desired.

"In the cupboard to the left of the fridge," she gasped, needing space. "There are cookies behind the canned goods."

He held her a moment longer, looking into her soul with hunger while smugness adorned his features. Lance moved away, taking the air she needed to breathe with him, and found the cookies. He opened the package and let the cookies fall into the garbage can. Luckily for the cookies, she'd eaten most of them by then. Only a few would endure the tragic death of being tossed away instead of consumed.

"What else?"

Head bowed in shame, Maggie told him where the chocolate was, and the chips, and the ice cream—that one she'd hidden in the freezer downstairs.

He pushed everything into the wastebasket, removed the bag, and tied it. "I'll take this out." He paused on his way to the door that led to the attached garage. "Do you need a moment to say your goodbyes?"

Maggie crossed her arms, lips pressed firmly together.

Lance chuckled as he walked from the room.

No longer hungry, Maggie dumped her partially eaten salad down the garbage disposal and turned it on. It sounded like needles being shredded, and she found it oddly soothing.

When Lance came back, Maggie surprised him by asking, "How are you really doing? With everything."

He gave her a suspicious look and pulled out a chair from the table, contorting his tall frame into a sitting position. "What do you mean, with everything?"

"Olivia, Ivy, life." She shrugged.

"Why?"

Maggie leaned her hips against the counter near the sink and eyed him. "You're keeping things from me. I want to know what they are."

"You sound like you care." His gaze was a slice of dark disdain.

Maggie swallowed, not responding.

"You want the truth?"

She waited.

"I need this show, and I need it to have a phenomenal debut, or I'm screwed. The divorce did not end well for me financially. Half of everything I own is gone." Lance looked at her. "I'm struggling."

"Is that the real reason you wanted to help me? So you could wiggle your way back into my life to use me again?"

"No, and I never used you," he answered harshly. "You know I didn't."

"Then why did you agree to help me?" Maggie wanted him to tell her all kinds of lies, even if they were exactly what she wanted to hear. He couldn't stand to be away, he thought of her all the time, he cried himself to sleep every night at the guilt he felt from hurting her the way he had . . . she was brilliant and he was a jackass. Stuff like that.

Shaking his head, he said, "Being on my show could be the comeback you mentioned, the chance to let everyone know you are not done until you decide to be."

"Being on your show is not acting, that's just me being me."

"Exactly. It's better than acting. It's you proving to the world that you're strong, mentally and physically. You dictate how your life is going to be, and it could be the best opportunity for you to show that. You'll inspire people."

"Routinely being in the public eye didn't work out well for me the last time I tried it."

Lance tapped his fingers against the tabletop. "I know. I went to see you at the hospital the night you were admitted." The smile he offered was black and bled with regret. "They wouldn't let me in."

"I know." She swallowed. "I told them not to."

He nodded, eyes trained down. "Did you hear me outside the door to your room before I was told to leave?"

Maggie closed her eyes, taking a slow breath. She'd never forgotten the sound of his voice, beseeching, broken, panicked, and terrified, as he called out to her from the other side of a door that would not open.

"No," she choked out, the lie pulled from her without conscious consent.

Lance's expression told her he didn't believe her, but all he said was, "It's just as well. I embarrassed myself big time that night."

Desperately needing to talk about something else, Maggie said, "I'm sorry you're having money problems right now."

Lance didn't look up, but she caught the wince and tightening of his jaw. "Yeah. Not exactly something I like to admit."

When he stood, pride had his shoulders back. His stance said it was time to end that particular line of conversation.

"So . . . um . . . you know how when you put your arms up over your head, like this?" Maggie demonstrated, watching as interest came to life in Lance's eyes.

"Mmm-hmm," he murmured.

"It would be nice if my stomach could be like it is now at all times, when my arms are raised up."

Lance shook his head, a faint grin taking over the gloom. "I suppose you could walk around like that all the time. Sounds like an awful lot of work to make your stomach look smaller."

"It could work," she insisted, dropping her arms.

"Okay." His tone said Maggie was delusional.

"Or when you lie down on your back, and all the fat goes to the sides, so your stomach looks skinny, even though it isn't," she continued.

"You've put a lot of thought into this. Why don't you lie down and lift up your shirt and show me?" he offered, the shadows all but gone from his visage.

"And serving sizes. What's this *about* stuff?"

Lance lifted his eyebrows.

"On some things it says a serving size is *about* this or that. That's just asking for trouble, because you know what I do?"

"Please." He gestured with a hand. "Fill me in."

"If it says five or six or whatever of something is about a serving, I add about three or four more, because it doesn't specify, so that means it's up for interpretation, right?"

A grin took over his lips. "I suppose you could argue that."

"I used to think a whole package was the serving portion. I didn't understand the nutrition facts on the packages. I just thought, you know, what you got was what you were supposed to eat. And hey, if I ate less than the serving size, being the whole container of doughnuts or whatever, then I was winning, because I consumed hardly any calories. When I figured out what the nutritional values were for, it was a really sad day for me." Maggie schooled her features into disappointment.

Lance laughed, walking across the room to her. He set a palm on her shoulder and leaned down to meet her eyes. "Thank you. I needed that."

Maggie smiled back. "I did too, oddly enough."

LANCE—1996

"HI, MAGGIE." HE felt shy, an emotion he couldn't recall experiencing prior to Maggie Smiley.

She glared at him from where she sat in a chair as a makeup artist colored and blended her face, changing it from average to exotic. Her long hair was lassoed into a side braid with fiery locks of hair left out around her face and ears, small pink flowers threaded through it. Dressed in a flowing, strappy white dress, Maggie reminded him of a fairy, or some other mystical being.

"Hi." The greeting was cold and curt.

It was the morning of their appointed sunrise photo shoot. Other than when forced to be near each other for the show, Maggie had strategically ignored him the past couple of weeks. When he went to see her at her apartment, Judith informed him she was either sleeping, not there, or busy. By the seventh time he stopped, even she seemed empathetic to his plight, firm though she remained.

When the blond told Maggie she was finished, Maggie got up from the seat and walked toward the photography crew that was set up near a boulder. Lance fell into step beside her, sand sliding between his toes as he walked. He wore a white buttoned-down shirt with the collar up and the buttons near the bottom of it left undone. White slacks straight and crisp, they'd been rolled up for him so that his ankles showed. Lance's hair was styled high and floppy, a chunk of it hanging over his forehead. He'd pushed it back once and was scolded. He hadn't touched it since.

"Can we start over?"

"Start what over?" she asked suspiciously, crossing her arms and picking up her pace. "There has to be something first, and then that something has to end, for there to be something to start over."

"Don't wrinkle your dress," the photographer barked as she glanced up from readying the lens.

Black metal contraptions were set up around them like a photography prison, people rushing around to fix or change things with the setup. It was interesting how much work it took to make something seem simple and flawless.

Maggie dropped her arms like her dress was on fire, her expression abashed.

Lance gave the photographer a glower, which she returned with a lifted eyebrow, and turned back to Maggie. "Everything. I want us to be . . . whatever we were . . . and more. I've had plenty of time to think these past weeks while you've pretended like I don't exist—"

She snorted, looking at the ocean in the distance. Lance followed her gaze. It built up, crashed down, only to rise again. He looked at Maggie, staring at her profile like his eyes had the power to make her give in to him.

"—and I realize I did and said things I shouldn't have, and . . ." Lance swallowed thickly. "I miss you. Can we start over? Please?"

They were at a privately owned part of the beach, and Lance was positive it cost the magazine company a pretty penny to be allowed to have the photo shoot there. The sky was gray, not yet ready to wake up. Lance was tired as well, his mind foggy and slow. Maggie didn't seem to have the same affliction, but he imagined she'd probably slept better than he had. He hadn't gotten a full night of sleep since the evening of the road trip, all because Maggie wouldn't talk to him—and maybe some residual guilt for the way he'd acted and talked to her.

A cool wind flared up, washing over him like an invisible wave. He hunched his shoulders against it as it drove through the thin material of his clothes to icily stab at his skin.

"Why?" Maggie demanded as she stopped moving. "Why should we? It'll just be the same thing again, like it has been every time I get too close—you push me away. You can't have it both ways, Lance. You can't want me when you want me and then treat me like dirt when you don't. I deserve better."

"You're right, you do deserve better, and I know I'm asking something I shouldn't, but . . . will you take me anyway?" Lance reached for her hand and she closed hers, refusing to let him hold her hand. He hung on to the limb anyway. He had to touch her, to feel her warmth. "I . . . Maggie . . ."

"Are you two about done? I know your conversation is more important than the whole world, but we do have pictures to take. The rest of us have a schedule."

"Give us two minutes," he snapped, glaring at the woman the popular fashion magazine had hired to photograph them.

Short and compact, but with a ferocious look on her face, Denise Zanders reminded him of a Chihuahua—especially when she bared her teeth at him. Even her short brown hair seemed to bristle as she frowned. He knew her sharp attitude wasn't personal, but it still irked.

"I'll give you one," she stated firmly, stomping off to check something with lighting.

He was running out of time, and not because of the photo session. Every day Maggie slipped farther away. He'd seen her talking to Jeff Mitchell a few days ago and he'd had to leave so he didn't deck the guy. Instead he'd slammed a fist through his bedroom wall. An uneven hole now graced the wall beside his door.

Lance spoke in a rush. "You told me you care about me. I care about you too. A lot. More than I wanted to admit. It terrified me, okay? It still does. But I'm trying to . . . accept it." He inhaled deeply, staring into her wide eyes. "I'm telling you now because I can't stand being away from you anymore. Please, please, Maggie, can we start over?"

"Yes," she whispered.

"Yes? You're sure?" He wanted to believe her, but it seemed too good to be true.

"Yes." Maggie nodded. "We can start over. But this is it, Lance. Push me away again and I'm done." Her words were firm, and when Lance looked into her eyes, he knew she meant them.

"I'm allowed into your personal space? I promise not to try to cook anymore—and I'll carry a pillow around with me at all times, should you request it. I'm pretty sure I'll be needing it anyway." Half of his mouth lifted.

She burst out laughing and Lance smiled, pressing a kiss to her neck as her arms went around his neck.

"Will you be my girlfriend?" Other than yes, there was no acceptable answer.

Maggie turned motionless. "I don't know, will I?"

"Yes," Lance responded without hesitation.

"Then I guess you'll be my boyfriend. Is that what you want?"

"Yes." Lance's pulse tripped and sputtered, but not in fear. It was with gladness.

Her arms tightened around him. "Yes. I'll be your girlfriend."

Lance's stomach swirled and he swallowed, unable to speak. It felt like he'd just proposed, or spliced his heart to hers for the rest of his life.

"Oh, for crying out loud!" Denise shouted. Exasperated resignation lined her words. "Can we just—"

He released Maggie and clasped her hand in his as they both looked at the photographer. Even her sour expression couldn't dim his mood. Joy split his face in a grin and it felt like the sun radiated through him. Lance glanced at Maggie. She smiled with her heart in her eyes.

Whatever she was going to say died on Denise's lips. She stared at them, eyes tripping over Maggie and then moving to Lance. She leaned forward and put out a hand. "Don't . . . move. That look, I have to capture that look. Don't move!"

Fingers locked around Maggie's, Lance looked at the camera as it clicked away.

"Move around, look at each other, do whatever feels natural," Denise commanded, waving her hand at them.

"She's so indecisive—move, don't move," he muttered to Maggie, who smiled and shrugged.

Lance gripped Maggie around the waist and lifted her to the large gray rock as the sun peaked on the horizon behind her. Even without being able to see her eyes, he knew she stared down at him, her palms resting on his shoulders. Light played peek-a-boo with her body, making her glow and appear to be on fire. He tipped back his head and drank in the sight of her.

"You're so pretty," he told her, meaning it.

Maggie's face went pink, a shadow of doubt darkening her eyes.

"You are," Lance stated resolutely.

The unsureness faded from her face and she smiled shyly. "Thank you."

Then he swung her around and down, smiling as she yelped in surprise. Maggie let her head fall back and lifted her arms to her sides as Lance turned and lowered her feet to the sand. The click of the camera was background noise, the people nearby only vaguely existing. Lance knew they were there, that he and Maggie posed for them, but it was as if they were alone. And the words they said to one another—those were for Lance and Maggie.

Maggie set her hands on his biceps and looked into his eyes.

"Spend New Year's with me and my dad," he invited impulsively. Lance went still at his own words, wondering at what point his mouth decided to work without his brain. New Year's was two months away. A lot could happen in two months. But as he saw her eyes light up, Lance knew he'd said the right thing.

"Are you sure?" Maggie asked, a small frown line between her eyebrows.

"Yes." And when he said it, Lance believed it.

"Okay. And you'll come to Christmas with me in Iowa—if you want." The sun rose, blanketing Maggie's face in shades of pink, purple, and orange.

Lance opened his mouth to say no, and found himself instead saying yes. He didn't commit to things unless he initiated them. Giving that control to others was loathsome, except with Maggie, it didn't feel like he was giving her power over him. It felt like he was trusting her to take care of his heart. It felt good, not bad.

"Enough lollygagging, children," Denise said brusquely, breaking into their world. "Lance, stand against the rock. Maggie, stand in front him but look off to the side. Lance, get your hands on her hips and stare down at her like she's everything and more to you. Perfect."

He found it wasn't hard to do.

MAGGIE—2010

HALF ASLEEP AND fighting to keep her eyes open against the blinding light overhead, she entered the bathroom and directed her gaze to the mirror. Maggie's brain registered what she thought was blood. A small, cutoff scream shot forth and she went still, blinking her eyes to get them to work properly. They wanted to cross with sleep and also figure out what she was looking at.

She stepped into the yellow and gray room and focused on the letters painted with red lipstick instead of what she'd thought was blood. She swallowed as she stared, unable to do anything else. The message was simple.

Every time you look in the mirror, tell yourself you're strong.

Picturing Lance perfectly in her mind saying exactly that, Maggie smiled and whispered, "I'm strong."

Doing what she went to the bathroom to do, Maggie washed and dried her hands and marched for Lance's room. The murky dark blue that shone in from the window at the end of the hallway let her know it was really late, or really early, and that he was most likely in bed. The door was cracked open, and she took only a few steps inside before she tripped on something and fell face-first into the wooden bench at the foot of the bed. Maggie's forehead smacked the corner and she groaned as she slid to the floor.

"What the hell?" a voice thick with sleep demanded.

"Why is the bed over here?" Maggie asked through clenched teeth. The place on her head she'd hit throbbed, faint but noticeable.

The lamp flipped on near the bed, and Lance was awarded a view of her sprawled out on the floor clothed in a tight blue shirt, minus a bra, and short pink shorts with hearts, clutching her head of snarled hair.

He slowly walked toward her, staring down at her. "Why? Are you trying to seduce me? If so, your aim is off. Although, you definitely get points for your outfit. Love the no-bra look on you."

"That's not where the bench or bed is supposed to be."

"I know. I was making myself more accessible to you." When her expression remained unchanged, Lance added, "The bed was too close to the wall behind it. It bothered me. If I'd known you were going to sneak in my room in the middle of the night, I would have told you."

Maggie dropped her hand from her head and glared at him. Lance jerked, eyes widening with something that resembled horror, and fell to the floor beside her. She didn't understand his inclination to be near her until she felt something wet and warm slide down the side of her face.

"You dented your forehead," he said in bafflement.

"It's fine. I'm fine."

Lance yanked his shirt over his head and pressed it against her temple. "You're bleeding. You're not fine."

His eyes met hers, hair rumpled and jaw unshaven. The warmth and smell of his skin lingered on the article of clothing and proceeded to make her dizzy. She looked down and swallowed. Lance removed the shirt and checked the wound.

"You have a perfect hole in your temple," he mused, looking torn between humor and dismay.

"Is it done bleeding?"

"Yes. I don't think stitches are required." He smiled. "If I may ask, what were you doing?"

"You left a message in the bathroom for me."

"I have no idea what you're talking about. There also is not one on the mirror in the basement, in case you decide to exercise in the middle of the night or something. Fair warning." His feigned innocence was ruined by the tipped up corners of his mouth.

Lance got to his feet, the view of his toned body making her throat parched, and left the room. He returned a minute later with a bandage.

"I just want to know, out of morbid curiosity more than anything, where you got the red lipstick? Or is that something you carry around for your nefarious dealings, like the bobby pins?"

Lance paused. "Nefarious dealings," he repeated slowly. "I like that, but alas, I cannot take credit for the lipstick. It was in your medicine cabinet."

She couldn't recall the last time she'd applied makeup, and having no idea what she did or did not have for cosmetics, what he said was probably true. "You're such a snoop."

Meeting Maggie's eyes as he crouched before her, he carefully brushed back her hair and placed it on her forehead. "There. All better."

"I appreciate the note, but I'm not cleaning up the lipstick," she told him, trying to sound firm but weakening when she looked at him. Those words were sweet, and needed.

Lance shrugged. "Okay. I just thought you could use a reminder. It's not a big deal."

They sat beside one another on the wood floor, the coolness of it seeping into her bare legs. The silence was unusually peaceful. Maggie had decorated the guest bedroom with softened masculinity in mind. The furniture was dark wood, the paintings on the walls those of forests and creeks. The bedding was chocolate brown and Lance's scent was present—expensive cologne and soap. He'd overtaken the space, but she didn't resent that, like she would have a few weeks ago.

Under the dim light of a bedside lamp, Maggie reached for his hand. She squeezed, liking the size and feel of his hand around hers, missing the touch of it over the span of countless days, months, and years.

"It is a big deal," she insisted. "I did need a reminder. Honestly, I've needed about a lifetime of them. But I'm going to try not to forget it from now on. Thank you." Maggie looked up, every good thing about her found in Lance's eyes as he stared back at her. She could see the strength he saw in her.

"I did love her," he murmured.

Her eyebrows lowered. "Who?"

"Olivia."

She tried to pull her hand away, not wanting to hear about his ex-wife, and he tightened his grip.

"Lance, I don't want—"

He lowered his gaze to their joined hands. "But it was different, not like how it was when I was with you. I've never felt that with anyone but you. I expected you to tell me to go when I showed up here. I knew it was a bad idea from the start. I was nervous about seeing you." He shook his head. "I don't get nervous, and I was nervous."

"I've seen you nervous," she whispered.

His smile was sad as he nodded. "Yeah. A time or two." Lance took a deep breath. "I've never forgotten a single detail about you, Maggie, not one. When I saw you . . . nothing was going to make me leave."

Tone dry, she said, "What about the police?"

"Maybe them." His smile grew.

The sound of chirping birds commenced, and Lance got to his feet. He took his cell phone from the nightstand and silenced the alarm. Maggie's eyes traveled along his broad back, flat stomach, and defined arms. He was more solid than she remembered, but then, she was softer. Instead of feeling bad about it, like she generally would, she accepted it with a wry smile. She was heavier than she used to be, but there wasn't a person in the world that could tell her she wasn't healthier. Maggie's smile grew. She was finally getting it. *That* was the right frame of mind.

"What are you smiling about?" he wondered.

"I used to be a lot skinnier."

Lance's expression darkened.

"Let me finish," she said, getting to her feet. "But I'm healthier now, regardless of how big or small I am. Three weeks to notice a change, you said. I thought that was only physically, but I understand now that it's mentally as well."

Eyes bright, Lance grinned. "Now you're getting it." He moved to the dresser and took out a charcoal-colored tee shirt. "You know what else you're getting?"

"No?" she asked warily.

"A run. Be ready in fifteen."

"It's five in the morning! My alarm doesn't go off for another hour." Maggie didn't think she'd be able to go back to sleep, but it was the principle of the thing.

"And yet here we are, awake and stuff. Might as well make the most of it, right?" Lance lowered his voice as he said, "Unless you have something else in mind with which to occupy ourselves until six? I admit, I would have to rush, but I think I could manage it."

"An hour wouldn't be enough for you, huh? Funny, I don't recall it taking that long." She crossed her arms, trying not to smile, and waited for his comeback.

"That's because you don't remember things accurately, with it being so long ago. The years have muddled your brain, faded unforgettable moments to allow the loss to be better accepted by you. I can remind you, if you like." Fire and mirth danced inside his eyes.

"Hmm." Doubt covered the sound like sugar on a doughnut.

"We could test it out, just to prove or disprove me." Lance winked.

She laughed. "Maybe another time. I wouldn't want to put too much pressure on you and have you fail to live up to your potential."

"I like pressure," he promised.

Maggie scowled at him, but when he lifted an eyebrow, she headed for her bedroom.

She met him in the kitchen twelve minutes later. Protein snack and water ingested, they set off for a 3-mile trail near the Port of Dubuque. It was a good mile or so to get there, the air brisk enough to make her nose cold. Maggie's house was located in a cul-de-sac, each house separated by trees on either side to offer semi-privacy. With the sun down and barely a light on in a window or a vehicle moving on the streets, it was eerie and calm.

"Do you miss acting at all?"

Maggie glanced at Lance, his expression hidden with shadows. "Not really. I guess I miss . . . the power of it, the ability to change into another person, even if they aren't real. Fictional characters, however complex they appear, are so much simpler than trying to figure out real life."

It was a few minutes before Lance spoke again. "What made you decide you wanted to act?"

She shrugged, eyes forward as they walked. "Do you remember the movie 'The Neverending Story'?"

"Yeah. Sure. Everyone our age should know about that movie."

"It was that movie. Not a single actor, or character, but all of them. They made magic. If a bunch of kids could do that, I didn't know why I couldn't. I was eleven when I decided it was something I wanted to try. I fantasized about being in the movie, any movie, actually. I had most of the lines memorized and I would act in front of my mirror. It seemed like the perfect existence—being adored by millions of people, feeling like I belonged somewhere. I wanted to be someone else."

"Let's not forget the most important detail—you fantasized about me too."

Maggie grinned. "You're right, I did. You were so cute, all arrogant and vulnerable at the same time. You always played bad-ass characters, but there was sadness in your eyes. You nailed the heartthrob role."

Lance puffed out his chest and nodded. "My biggest role, and it didn't even have anything to do with actual talent. Everyone loves a pretty face." The self-mockery was clear.

"You weren't just a pretty face," she told him, bumping her arm against his.

"I know, I had a luscious body too."

"Luscious?" Maggie snorted.

Lance shrugged, grin in place. "Let's move on. You were telling me about your acting dream."

Maggie tightened her ponytail holder as they crossed a dimly lit street. "I begged my parents to let me take acting lessons. They didn't understand why I suddenly had it in my head that that was what I wanted to do, but I wouldn't drop it. I went months where it was all I talked about. I watched television nonstop, just paying attention to facial expressions and actions, the emotions the actors put in their words. I was obsessed. They finally agreed to the acting classes after I promised not to give up halfway through and that it wouldn't affect my grades."

"Then what?"

She glanced at him. "Are you really interested in this?"

"I really am."

"After about a year of acting classes, my acting coach felt I was ready to try out for roles in school and community plays."

"And?"

Maggie smiled at the memory of the joy and shock that made her giddy as she began to get leading roles, the purpose she felt when she got up on stage and transformed herself into another being. She was made to be an actress. She'd known that at the young age of twelve. Few realized such truths about themselves then, and some never did.

"And I blew them all away, Lance." Her cheeks hurt with the force of her smile. "I got the leads in a lot of plays, won awards, and when my parents realized how serious I was about it, they got me a respectable agent. I was fourteen when I was flown to Virginia to try out for the role of Cecilia Monroe. You know the rest."

"I know some of it, not all." His expression was lined with seriousness.

"What do you want to know?" she asked softly, the start of their running trail up ahead.

"When did you become anorexic? Before or during the show?"

Even with the gentle way he asked it, the questions stole her breath and made her insides freeze.

"I don't like talking about it," she muttered.

"I know, Maggie. A lot of why we didn't work falls on me. I know that, I accept that, but . . . I wasn't the only one with things going on—seriously messed up things."

The wind brushed loose locks of hair in Maggie's eyes as she looked at Lance.

"I love acting. I always have, always will," she confessed. "But I hate the media aspect of it. Every bad review, every negative comment about me or the show or my acting ability, they all imbedded their claws in me, and I felt them. Sharp and deep. I already had self-image issues. So afraid I was going to get fat again, I already didn't eat much. And with the stress of the show, it got worse.

"I just kept thinking if I lost more weight, if I pushed myself harder, I would be good enough. I told myself I would *make* everyone love me, but no matter what I did, I could never please them all. I was punishing myself for things out of my control. It wore me down—not just physically, but mentally as well. And . . ." She swallowed. "Even though I love acting, I don't miss that feeling of never being good enough, of having to constantly prove myself. The judgment and criticism. I don't miss feeling like I'm acting for everyone but me."

The route was scenic, a good portion of it along the Mississippi river and the waterfront attractions. It looped around casinos, a museum and aquarium, and residential and business areas as well. Maggie set her hands on her hips and looked toward the water, the silence that followed her words unwelcome and uncomfortable.

Lance spoke first. "After a while, you feel like it isn't you anymore. You don't belong to you. You have this role to play, and it never ends, not even when the camera stops rolling. Because there is always someone to act for.

"One day you wake up and you don't know who you are anymore. You belong to them—the directors, the producers, the media, the fans, all of them—and it kills something inside of you. Your body isn't yours. Neither is your face. You've been told what to do for so long that now you're this thing that needs constant direction, right?"

"Right," she whispered. Maggie had wanted so badly to be pretend she was someone else, and in the end, she got what she wanted. But it was too much. Everything was taken from her. Her image, her privacy, her life.

"It meant something to you—your acting. Your success mattered, because you had to fight for it. It wasn't given to you. You wanted it, and you took it."

She nodded, bending over to stretch. Maggie was relieved that he didn't comment on her health issues, instead focusing on the acting part of the conversation.

Lance grabbed one ankle and brought his leg up to his back, then the other. "I grew up in that life, but I didn't love it. It always felt more like an obligation than a goal, which could have something to do with my lack of success. The only time I really enjoyed it or wanted it to work, was when I was on 'Easier Said' with you. Otherwise, I never cared that much."

"But you want the fitness show, don't you? That's something you want, something you'll work for. Something you believe in." Lance's quest made sense to her then, and she felt she understood him better.

He looked up at her, solemnness lining his features. "I do. I can do something amazing with it." Lance took a deep breath and sat down. "Forget I asked you to be on it. Whatever way it would benefit the show wouldn't outweigh the publicity you would get. You'd be in the spotlight again, and it would be wrong of me to ask you to do that."

Maggie stared at his lowered head as he straightened his legs, and then went to the cold, hard ground beside Lance. She did it with the perceived intention of further stretching out, but she also wanted to be near Lance. "I want to know more about it."

He glanced up, a streak of joy crossing his features with wariness to follow. "Really? Are you sure?"

She finished stretching her legs, got to her feet, and offered him a hand. "I didn't say I wanted to be on the show, but I am curious." Maggie dropped his hand as he stood.

Lance had them alternate jogging and walking. He said it was better to run only a few minutes a day than not at all, that the alternating speeds burned more fat than walking or jogging alone. Maggie liked that every few minutes she got a break from jogging, whatever the reason was for it. He'd taught her breathing techniques to make it more bearable. It was important to focus on the air as it went in and out of her lungs, to keep it even and steady. Mouth breathing was bad, unless on an exhale, but Maggie found it worked best for her to breathe in and out through her nose.

They set out at a light pace.

"Basically, the idea is to do exactly what I've done for you, and thousands of others. Change their diets and activity levels to best fit them, and see results."

"Simple," she said dryly.

Lance glanced at her. "I understand there will be hiccups, that no one is perfect. Look at you with your cookies and salad dressing."

Maggie grimaced and Lance laughed.

"You can't make them feel bad when that happens," she said earnestly. Criticism was cruel, and worked to destroy a person's self-worth. "You have to be understanding, and tell them it's natural to stumble along the way, maybe tell them about how you used to live as a way to empathize. Like, if you ever ate three candy bars in a row, let them know that."

"Have you?" he asked jokingly.

Maggie's silence was confirmation.

Lance smiled. "I'm sure I've had more than that at one time."

"They were regular-sized ones," she admitted in a mumble.

"I once ate three double cheeseburgers and two large fries. If I remember correctly, I washed it down with a thirty-two ounce soda."

They grinned at one another.

Maggie told him, "If you can connect with them, show them you're human and that you've made your own mistakes, it'll make them feel better."

"Meaning we should bond over failures?"

"Maybe. Yes," she decided. "Failures show others they're not alone."

He was quiet until it was time to walk. "I need someone with your kind of heart on the show, to remind me and the guests of that kind of stuff. I'm not saying you, but someone like you."

"A lot of things are affected by what you think you can do regardless of whether you can or can't. Even me with running—I have to talk myself into it. My body listens to what my brain tells it. When I tell myself I can do it, I do it."

Heart pounding from the first of six runs, Maggie took a breath. "And the show can't be turned into a competition. Because to the people that don't do as well as the others, that would be enough to make them want to quit. Having multiple people on the show at a time will backfire."

Excitement sparked to life inside her as she talked. "You could focus on one person every three weeks. It would be hard to work with only one person for a whole three months, like you are with me, but if you can get them started, that could work. And then, they could come back after three months of working on their own, just as a quick update, and every three months after that, as a motivator to keep them invested in their health."

The second run began.

Lance seemed to mull over her words as they jogged.

"It's going to be uncomfortable for them at first, and scary," she said when they walked once more. "Positive reinforcement every day. Don't forget."

He nodded, his gaze trained forward.

"What are you thinking?"

Lance looked at her, his expression rigid with the force of keeping it blank. "Nothing. We just—we make a really good team. Always did."

He was right, they did.

She started jogging before it was the designated time, Lance following close behind.

"So. Jeff Mitchell."

When Lance didn't elaborate, Maggie shot him a sidelong glance and picked up the pace. He smoothly caught up, not the least bit winded.

"You two dated a few years ago."

"We started dating four years ago, yes," she said, mouth tight.

"Interesting."

"Why is that interesting?"

Even with his face forward, she caught the glower on it. "Because he wanted to date you during 'Easier Said', and we dated instead."

"I would have dated him, if you'd stayed out of it."

"How long did you two date?" he asked casually, a tick forming in his jaw.

Maggie turned her gaze to the street ahead. "Two years."

"He proposed."

"I said no," she countered.

Lance stopped jogging, jerking around to face her. "You didn't date him all those years ago because you knew he was wrong for you, and I was right. That's why you dated me. And that's why you fell in love with me. And that's why we would still be together, if we both hadn't been young and dumb, but especially if *I* hadn't."

Maggie inhaled sharply, eyes wide as she felt the blood drain from her face.

"I can't believe you gave him another chance," he continued. "What did you think was going to happen the second time around?"

She narrowed her eyes. "People don't get second chances? Is that what you're saying? I gave you one, didn't I?"

Lance's ferocity wavered, and then came back full force. "Not him, not when you knew there was nothing there."

"Why do you care?" she snapped. "You got married. I wasn't allowed?"

"Not to him!"

"I didn't marry him," Maggie screamed back, her hands curled in fists.

"You were trying to prove to yourself that things would have worked for you two if I hadn't butted in, weren't you?" Lance accused, his face twisted with anger and ghosts. "You probably would have married him, just to prove to yourself that what we had was a mistake, and that you never really loved me!"

Maggie blinked and took a step back, the anger melting away as she understood what was going on. "You're talking about you, not me."

Lance's chest lifted and lowered with the force of his breathing, his expression raw and hurt. "There shouldn't have been a chance for you to date him again, or for me to marry someone else. It should have been you. There should have been one love, one woman, one marriage. I tried to forget you, I swear I did. All I did was remember you more."

His words broke her at the same time they healed. Tears fell from her eyes, and she saw the shine of them in his. Maggie sniffed and wiped a hand across her face, turning her eyes to the cracked pavement below her shoes. Lance lightly touched her hand and Maggie grabbed his when he went to move away.

"It's weird that we were hurting each other even when we weren't in each other's lives," Maggie said in a shaky voice.

"But we were, you know we were."

Maggie nodded, her head lowered. She clutched Lance's hand as if she could squeeze all of his pain away, and hers as well. "You got together with Olivia after I started dating Jeff."

"You moved on. I figured I had to as well."

A choked sound left her. "I never moved on," she whispered. "I just . . . moved."

Lance removed his hand from hers. He threaded his fingers through her hair, disrupting her ponytail, and pressed his closed mouth to the crown of her head. His lips moved against her hair when he spoke in a low rumble. "I know. I never really did either."

She lightly rested her palms on his biceps, wanting to be closer to him, knowing that would make things more difficult for them. They naturally confessed their hearts to one another, but there was a cost to that honesty. A goodbye was imminent to their current involvement, a specified date that dictated they would go their own ways. It seemed crucial to remember that.

"There are people watching us," he commented, lifting his mouth from her hair.

Maggie didn't bother looking at their spectators. "I'm sure we'll be in the papers again before too long."

"Maybe we should act like we like each other this time—or you could, you know, act like you're madly in lust with me. Follow my lead."

Lance tightened his arms and moved his mouth to hers. Maggie stiffened, the thundering of her heartbeat saying she wanted him while her brain screamed that she couldn't. She turned her head to the side, eyes down.

"What are you doing?" Her voice was breathless.

Lance pulled back. "Look at me."

Maggie wordlessly shook her head.

"Maggie."

She consented without any more protestation, turning her gaze to one of unbridled blue seas. Eyes riveted to hers, Lance brought his mouth to hers. She didn't push him away, or pretend she didn't want it. The feel of his lips on hers was like coming home. She knew him—knew the shape, texture, and taste of him. Maggie held her palms against his cool cheeks, tears stinging her eyes at the emotion that hit her like an avalanche against doubts and reservations. He was the only man she'd ever wanted to kiss, just him, always him.

He moved his mouth to her temple, his lips warm against her skin, and held her against him in a way that revered. Maggie felt his heart thrum against her, steady but fast. She let her eyes close to better feel him, to forget to think. Lance pressed a final kiss to her forehead, slowly moving away.

There was strain on his face, a hint of it in the pinched corners of his mouth, a blanket of discord dulling his pretty blue eyes. Maggie watched the pulse jump at the base of his throat, saw the way his chest lifted and lowered, his hands clenched in fists. What had that kiss taken from him? And what had it given him?

"What's wrong?" he asked. "Was the kiss too much?"

"It . . . yes, it was." Maggie's eyebrows furrowed and she stopped to peer into the dark waters of the river, hugging herself. "But . . . it was also perfect, which is why it was too much."

In a bemused voice, she said, "I never realized."

"Realized what?"

She turned her head to look at him. "That kiss hurt you, didn't it?"

His smile was tinged with cynicism, but it didn't touch his eyes. "Shallow me hurt by a little thing like a kiss?"

Maggie didn't say anything.

Lance rubbed his face, shoulders beaten down in a way that broke her heart. When he looked at her, his emotions were clearly exposed for her to accept, or deny. He opened up to her with a look so raw it had her doubting everything she'd thought she'd known about Lance Denton.

"Yeah. It hurt. It hurt a lot."

Maggie stared at the man she knew in a way she couldn't know the boy. Her heart was full with pain and longing and hope. And sadness, always the sadness. He watched her, allowing her perusal. She didn't know what she searched to find, and his once again masked face kept her from seeing anything.

"We should finish up. I have to meet with Donovan later this morning," Lance finally said, facing the path. His voice was firm, but his hands trembled.

"Right. Yes." She nodded, dizzy with the recent revelations.

They set off again, neither speaking.

LANCE—1996

MAGGIE NEVER ASKED why he didn't spend Christmas with his dad, and he never supplied an explanation. His dad was never big on holidays—to him they were another day he could use for work. Over the years, Lance was rotated from one relative to the next for holidays. Sometimes his dad was with them, but most times he was not.

He didn't realize how abnormal that was until he went to Maggie's home in Iowa.

Lance didn't realize the extent of what he was missing until then as well.

Judith drove them from Minnesota, where they'd been skiing for two days, to the Smileys' residence, with plans to visit friends in Wisconsin before coming back for them in three days. Virginia had snow and cold weather, but not that much snow, and not that cold of weather. It was presently below zero with the wind chill and when the car pulled up to a three-story olive green and burgundy house, there was at least five feet of snow piled up in the yard.

Lance stared at the house. It was half the size of his, multi-colored bulbs twinkling from along the rooftop to add life to an otherwise gray-filled evening, and was surrounded by bushes that glittered silvery white with snow. That was Maggie's house. Maggie grew up there. He swallowed.

Maggie twisted in the front seat and smiled at him. "Don't be nervous."

"I'm not nervous," Lance was quick to tell her. She was his first real girlfriend—the first girl he'd dated that he legitimately cared for—and he was about to meet her parents. Lance was a few steps away from entering her world. His stomach was in knots and his hands shook.

"The only one you should be nervous about is Nora. She's not human. But my mom and dad are normal. They're excited to meet you."

Lance gave her a weak smile and jumped from the car when Judith popped the trunk. The air was like breathing icicles and he shivered in his winter jacket. How did people stand to live there?

Dressed in a long red jacket lined with fur and black boots that went up to her knees, Judith handed him his luggage and stepped back as though the thought of accidentally touching him was abhorrent to her.

"I'm not my dad. You can stop acting like I am," he said, turning his head to meet her gaze.

Face pink from the brisk air, Judith's gray eyes darkened before softening. "I know that, Lance. You are not your father," she agreed quietly. Her tone almost seemed caring as she said, "You are much, much worse. You are your mother."

Her words froze him more thoroughly than the subzero weather. "Why would you say that? What did I ever do to you?" he demanded.

"You're too good-looking, too charming, too persuasive. No one knows how to tell you no, especially Maggie. She'd walk through fire for you if she thought it would help you in some way. You're dangerous to her, whether you intend it or not." Judith glanced up as the passenger door opened and closed. She leaned close, gloved hand tight on his shoulder. "If you care about Maggie—"

"I do care about her," he interrupted brusquely, shaking off her grip and stepping back. More than he'd thought he was capable of. Judith's words impaled him, added doubts to an already existing pile.

Judith straightened, pushing silvery blond hair from her eyes. Her expression turned sad. "Then break up with her before it's too late, before too much damage has been done."

Lance's jaw tightened. "You're warning me away from my own girlfriend? You should know by now that the more I'm told not to do something, the chances are I will do exactly that."

It was a dumb-ass thing to say, and he instantly regretted it. Not so long ago, it was true, but not with Maggie. It dirtied what Maggie was to him, put an ugly taint of wrongness on their relationship. He couldn't stay away from Maggie because he was happier around her. She made his life better.

He knew he'd effectively pulled off the asshole role when Judith's skin paled and lines formed around her mouth. "You don't care about her at all, do you? You can't. You're just a self-centered boy, thinking of your wants instead of the feelings of others."

Refusing to say another word, he watched a dark rainbow of emotions appear on the actress's face.

"It's freezing out here!" Maggie bounced on the heels of her pink snow boots, face bright as she took her bag from Lance's limp hand. A red stocking cap tramped down her waves and matching mittens cloaked her hands. In keeping with her pink and red theme, her coat was also pink.

When no one moved or spoke, she looked from Judith to Lance, the smile falling from her face. "What's going on?"

"Nothing," he muttered.

"Judith?" Maggie pressed.

"Let's go in before we all get sick. I can't believe I told the Jones' I'd visit them in Wisconsin this year. I don't know what I was thinking," she said, moving past them.

With a troubled look aimed at him, Maggie trailed her part-time guardian into the house.

Lance slowly followed.

His first thought was that the house was warm—and not the temperature of the place, although, yeah, it was—but it was something else entirely. A television was on in a different room, laughter and loud voices came from yet another. The walls were lined with framed photographs, on and on they went, down the hall until he could no longer make them out. It was loud, and busy with every inch of space filled.

The room directly before him had a full, thick tree that touched the ceiling with its glittering gold star, presents in varying kinds of wrapping paper resting beneath it. White lights shone from it, ornaments in different sizes and colors swayed along its branches. The heavy scent of pine told him it was a real tree. Christmas music played from a stereo system set back against a rust-toned wall.

Lance blinked, filled with a sense of awe, and something else—something darker, and sadder.

The house was warm with life.

"I'm not sure where he went off to. I'll find him and be right back,"

Maggie said, her voice getting louder.

Winter garments gone, Lance was afforded a view of her slim body clothed in jeans and a brown sweater as she approached. They'd officially been together almost two months, and they hadn't done anything more than make out. His heart said it was enough, but his body argued, profusely, that it wouldn't be for much longer. For someone who hadn't given the act of sex much importance, he'd done a one-eighty since Maggie. He wanted it to be special for her. First time, first guy.

First everything.

Maggie smiled, and his heartbeat took off like he'd recently run miles. "What are you doing out here by yourself?" She touched his hair and kissed his cheek, turning him into an unthinking hormone. "I thought you were right behind me."

Lance took a deep breath, not wanting to embarrass himself with having an erection the first time he met her parents. "I got sidetracked." He gestured to the tree.

She laughed. "The Smiley Christmas tree can do that. Gaudy, isn't it? I usually help decorate." Her tone was wistful as she studied the pine tree.

"I like it," Lance said truthfully.

Maggie grinned. "Everyone's in the kitchen. There's hot chocolate with peppermint candy canes and whipped topping. Nora fought with Mom over who got to make yours." Her eyes danced as she looked at him.

"Great." He rolled his eyes good-naturedly. "The madness has already begun."

"I warned you it wouldn't be pretty. What do you expect when you're a super cute actor? Even my mom has a crush on you." she teased, tugging at his coat. "Let me put this away in the closet. You can take off your boots. And I'll show you my room after you meet my family, which will be your room while we're here."

"Are you sharing it with me?" he asked, stepping close as she turned from putting his coat and gloves in the closet.

She bumped into him, her breasts brushing across his chest and sending his body into turmoil once more. It didn't take much to get him excited around Maggie. A blush stained Maggie's cheeks. She stared at

Lance, longing scorching her face. It was palpable, thick. He felt it like it was his own.

"No," she choked out. She cleared her throat and started walking away. "I'll be in Nora's room with her."

"That is the saddest news I've heard all day."

"For both of us," Maggie agreed.

When Maggie's mom hugged him without hesitation, Lance's throat tightened. She was petite with brown hair and had Maggie's reddish-brown eyes. She looked too young to have teenage daughters. Jennifer Smiley smelled like sugar cookies, exactly how he pictured his own mom in his more sentimental fantasies.

"Are you hungry?" she asked, rubbing a circle onto his back. The affectionate touch made his throat close up more. "I made meatloaf, mashed potatoes, green bean casserole, and rolls. I baked cookies too. We all ate, but we saved some for you, Maggie, and Judith."

"Lance is always hungry," Maggie told her mom.

"Oh. I can't stay, Jennifer. My friends are expecting me yet tonight, and I still have two hours to drive," Judith said from across the room. "But thank you. I appreciate the gesture."

"Are you sure?" Jennifer stepped back from Lance, silently offering him a red cup of hot cocoa even as her eyes were on Judith.

Judith smiled tightly, her gaze locked with Lance's. "I'm sure. I'll be back on the 26th. Have fun. And behave."

That was directed specifically at him. He smirked, raising his cup in a salute before tasting the drink. It was delicious, the blend of chocolate and peppermint surprisingly good.

Her eyes narrowed and she said her goodbyes to the Smileys, giving Maggie an especially long hug. "I'll see you soon. Merry Christmas, Maggie."

"Merry Christmas, Judith. Have a great time. Drive safe," Maggie told her when they pulled apart.

With a final farewell, Judith left.

"I'll get you guys some food," Maggie's mom offered again.

Lance lifted his eyebrows at Maggie. When she shrugged, he turned to Jennifer. "Thank you. That would be nice. Maggie was right—I am always hungry."

"Maggie looks like she needs to eat," a redhead muttered from where she sat at the table, a scowl making her otherwise pretty face unattractive. She continually glanced at Lance, like she didn't want to stare but couldn't help it.

"I think you look great," a man with dark brown hair peppered with gray told Maggie, hugging her to his side. He wore glasses and had a mustache, his green eyes intelligent and locked on Lance.

"Thanks, Dad. Dad, this is Lance. Lance, this is my dad, Leon Smiley." Maggie wouldn't look at anyone as she made the introductions and her shoulders were down instead of straight.

"Nice to meet you, Mr. Smiley," Lance said, shaking his hand.

"And you. I've heard a lot about you. Many times. More than was necessary," he added as Maggie groaned beside him.

"Dad!"

"What? It's true."

"That doesn't mean you have to tell everyone," she hissed in a loud whisper.

"It's family, Maggie."

Leon gave Lance's hand a hard squeeze, staring into his eyes the way Lance imagined any father would when meeting their daughter's boyfriend for the first time. There was wariness in his gaze, a warning, and indecisiveness. He wasn't sure about Lance, and Lance respected the clear protectiveness he held for Maggie.

Lance looked at the redhead, knowing Maggie's brief glumness had to do with her earlier comment. Taking his attention on her as a cue to introduce herself, she stood with a wide smile and glided toward him. Her body was long and thin, the black top and jeans she wore fitted to her frame in a way that made her clothes seem invisible.

"I'm Nora, Maggie's older sister." She stood close enough that her flowery perfume assailed his nostrils. "I'm nineteen and go to college. You're seventeen, right?"

Before Lance could answer, the doorbell rang. Nora straightened, an expectant look taking over the calculating one, and flounced from the room, calling, "That must be Hank! 'Bye!"

"Sorry about Nora. Sometimes we're not sure where she came from," Jennifer told him.

Lance looked at Maggie and her eyes slid away from his. His hands fisted with the need to touch her.

Leon cleared his throat. "There's a documentary on the moon I wanted to watch tonight. Come talk with me for a bit after you've eaten," he said to Maggie.

She nodded, trying to smile. "I will definitely do that."

"I'll warm up your food and skedaddle. I have some papers I want to finish grading before tomorrow. You know teachers, always ready with the red pen of doom," Maggie's mom said, also picking up on the tension.

Neither spoke as she bustled around the forest green room, Maggie moving to help her after a brief pause. Lance looked around as they readied their plates. The kitchen was as packed with miscellaneous items as the other room he'd seen. Pictures and artwork, sayings and furniture, all lined the walls. It should have looked tacky, but it looked homey. Lance envied their reality. Their lives were stuffed full of things while his remained empty.

It wasn't until Lance was almost done eating that he decided to say something. The food was better than any he remembered having before, but that wasn't why he kept quiet. It was obvious Maggie didn't want to talk right then.

"Maggie," he said, staring at her plate of untouched food.

She jumped, dropping her fork to the plate. "What?"

He took his gaze from her food and looked her in the eyes. "Your sister is pushy and obvious, not to mention rude. I do not find her attractive in any way."

Maggie's mouth tipped up at the corners. "Don't tell her that."

"I'm going to try to not say another word to her the whole time I'm here," he promised, meaning it. Lance reached for her hand and watched as her small fingers curled around his.

"She won't like that."

"Ask me if I care."

She laughed softly, using her free hand to tug the sweater back up when it began to fall off her shoulder, giving Lance a glimpse of her pale pink bra strap.

"Both of your parents are teachers?"

"Mmm-hmm." Maggie nodded. "Math." She wrinkled up her nose.

"You don't like Math?"

One shoulder lifted and lowered.

"Why aren't you eating?"

"Oh. Um." Maggie's face reddened. "I don't eat much. You know that."

"I do. But you haven't eaten anything."

"I'm just . . . I'm not that hungry." She wouldn't look at him.

Lance released her hand and sat back in his chair. He studied her averted face. "You barely ate anything all day."

"I ate," she argued, picking up the fork and playing with the mashed potatoes on the plate.

"What did you eat?"

She shrugged. "I don't know. I had a piece of pizza this morning."

"No. You took three bites and then gave it to me. I had the piece of pizza this morning."

"It's not a big deal, okay?" Maggie looked up, anger taking over the anxiety. "I'm not that hungry today."

"Okay," he finally said, deciding to drop it. Lance finished eating, unease telling him something wasn't right with Maggie's eating habits.

They washed and dried the dishes, and after spending an hour with her parents, Maggie showed him her room.

Lance set down his suitcase and looked around the gray and pink room. It was amazing how it smelled exactly like her, even without her being in it for months. It was half the size of his bedroom at his dad's, and showed a side of her he had yet to see. The room was Maggie, brought together with paint and pictures and CDs. Books overflowed from a case between two windows and her bed was covered in stuffed animals. He squinted his eyes and looked closer. Cats. All of the stuffed animals were cats.

"I used to be obsessed with cats," she muttered, looking embarrassed.

"I see that. Why cats?"

"I don't know. I guess because they're fluffy and soft and cute."

Lance laughed softly. "Have you ever had one for a pet?"

She shook her head. "Nora is O.C.D. and flipped out when my

mom suggested getting a pet. She complained about smells, and hair, and . . . bodily functions."

He turned to close the door and Maggie's voice stopped him. "That has to stay open when I'm in here with you. My mom and dad's one rule."

She sounded apologetic, but he smiled and shrugged. "Not a big deal."

Lance noticed the poster above her bed at the same time Maggie did. Head tilted, he stepped closer for a better look. A shriek of horror left her and she tore the image of Lance from the wall. Maggie waded it up, causing Lance to wince, and threw it behind her.

"I asked my mom to take that down and she said she did. Nora must have put it back up. She did it because she knew you'd be sleeping in here. She did it to humiliate me." Vengeance flared to life in her eyes, her whole face darkening with it. "She is so dead."

Lance reached for her, placing his palms on her back to bring her closer to him. "I think it's cute."

"You would."

"Kiss me," he demanded roughly.

He missed her all the time, even then, as he held her in his arms. Maggie's face softened as she brought her lips to his. Touching her didn't make him miss her less. Kissing her didn't help either. He needed that one connection that could never be taken away once known.

"Gross," Nora muttered loudly as she swept past the door.

Maggie smiled against his lips.

"What do we do now?"

She spun away from him, turned on a radio, and offered her hands. "Dance." 'Always' by Bon Jovi was playing. "Or lie on the bed. Or I can go, if you're tired. Or—"

Lance placed his hands on her hips and tugged her to him, resting his forehead to hers as they moved in a slow circle. Maggie slid her hands up his arms and locked them behind his neck, taking a deep breath as the song enveloped them. First slow dance as a couple. He closed his eyes and listened to the music, wondering if 'Always' by Bon Jovi was going to be their song. Lance kissed her cheek.

THE NEXT MORNING started off with a homemade breakfast of French toast, eggs, and bacon. To those that routinely shared home-cooked breakfasts with their family, it would not be a big deal. To Lance, it was. The best meals he and his dad had were takeout. The worst, microwavable.

They spent the day Christmas shopping, Maggie telling him about Dubuque as they made their way around the city. Only a few people recognized Maggie and Lance from the show, while others knew him from previous work. Lance took it in stride, helping Maggie when she stumbled with being seen as a celebrity to those she'd recently been unimportant.

"Maggie," he said when they walked from the store.

She glanced at him, eyes large with shock.

"Take a deep breath."

Maggie listened, grabbing his hand and squeezing it. "I don't... I never thought about this part of it. When—when I decided to be an actress."

"You're safe with me," Lance told her solemnly.

Maggie hugged him, nodding. "I know."

That afternoon, they had a snowball fight, Leon joining in and annihilating the both of them with frozen pucks of snow. When night came, they played board games, helped Jennifer bake more cookies, and watched Christmas movies. Nora was spending the night with her boyfriend Hank, which seemed to make Maggie inexorably chipper.

During his time there, Lance felt like he wasn't only invited to Maggie's house, but into her family, and he wanted to thank her for that. Even Nora, antagonistic as she was toward her younger sister, made it seem like a real, genuine family. They were close, they loved one another, and no matter what happened in life, they had someone to rely on. Lance wondered what his life would be like, if he had a brother or sister or two, if he had a mother, if his father paid attention to him. It would be annoying, and clustered, and brilliant. That's what it would be.

"I like your family," he told her that night.

It was after eleven, closer to Christmas Day than Christmas Eve, each of them sleepy but unwilling to part ways. They lay on her bed on top of the covers and looked at the black ceiling, the outside Christmas lights offering dim, colorful light. The slew of toy cats were on a bench at the foot of the bed.

Maggie snorted, lightly tracing a finger over his lips.

Lance took her hand and moved it away from his mouth, his lips tickled from the touch of her hand. He angled his body over hers, looking down into her eyes. Maggie wore flannel pajamas that were frumpy and sexy and Lance's tee shirt and pajama pants didn't seem like enough of a barrier between their bodies. Her eyes locked on his in a way that told him she adored him, and feared him, both at once, and equally. It was the same for him.

Judith's words ran through his head and he shoved them away. She didn't know what she was talking about.

"If you were anyone else, I would have pushed you to have sex by now," he whispered roughly, each of her wrists manacled by him.

"Why haven't you?" Maggie whispered back.

Lance dropped his head to hers, moving his face so that it was near her neck. Her pulse fluttered wildly, and he could hear her heartbeat. He breathed deeply, closing his eyes, lying there with them chest to chest.

"Because you deserve more. You deserve better. I know it sounds corny and cliché, but your first time should mean something."

Maggie stroked the back of his head, not acknowledging his words at first. Her hand paused. "Did your first time mean something?"

Lance allowed a faint smile to cross his mouth. "No, but . . . it's different for guys. I was too excited about actually having sex to worry about it being special."

"Guys are weird." She resumed caressing his hair.

"Yeah."

He relaxed into her, arms on either side of her as his cheek lightly rested on her chest. He was careful to keep their lower halves from touching. He didn't trust himself to keep his hands from her if it came to that.

Maggie nudged Lance.

He blinked and partially raised himself up.

"What if I told you I was ready?" she asked shyly.

Lance vaulted from the bed and scrambled to his feet, crossing the room to put as much space between them as he could without actually leaving it.

"Maggie, you don't know what you're saying," he said in a voice thick with yearning.

She sat up, her hair billowed around her in an untamed mass. "Yes, I do."

"It's—we've—no." He drove shaking fingers through his hair, knowing it stuck up at odd angles. "We've only been together for two months."

That was the stupidest reasoning he'd ever heard. It wasn't like he usually cared if he was dating the girl, or even if he particularly liked her. Time had no bearing on his sex life.

"So?" Maggie climbed off the bed, walking toward him.

Lance moved to the left and she followed.

"I'm weak," he pleaded. "I'll give in."

She laughed, moving her hand down his ribcage. "I know, Lance, but it's okay." Maggie went on her tiptoes and put her mouth next to his ear. "I have a Christmas present for you."

He groaned, letting his head fall back. "Maggie, if you say you're giving me your virginity for a Christmas present, I will not be responsible for my actions—and it will be nonrefundable. I want you to be aware of that."

She cupped his face, gently bringing it down so that his eyes were even with hers. "It's technically Christmas Day, and I want your first Christmas present to be from me. It's not that," she added.

Lance swallowed down his disappointment and Maggie smiled when he admitted, "I was sort of hoping it was."

"I know." She pressed her lips to his, pulling back just far enough to tell him, "I realize stuff like this scares you, and I don't want you to feel pressured to say it back, okay?"

Giving her a wary look, he said, "Okay."

"I love you."

Lance turned to stone, his lungs forgetting how to properly work. He stared at Maggie's open, expectant face, and he shut down. Panic set his pulse to overdrive and he turned his back on her. He studied the partially frosted window, tracing the designs with his eyes until his heartbeat steadied. She loved him. He'd known it. Lance loved Maggie as well, but saying it, and hearing it . . . it made him want to bolt.

Maggie put her arms around him and pressed her cheek to his back. "I don't expect you to say it back, not until you're ready, but I wanted you to know."

"You know I do?" he questioned in an uneven voice.

Her hold on him tightened. "Yes."

Lance exhaled slowly, hugging her arms to his stomach. He tipped his head back until it rested on the crown of her head. Then he spun around, grabbed her, and kissed her with need so potent he thought he could hear it sing through his veins. Maggie's hands roved up and down his front, and when she pressed her hips to his, he tensed and accidentally bit her. Lance expected her to pull away, but she only kissed him harder, fingers digging into the waistband of his pants. It would take so little to remove them, walk to her bed, and be inside her.

Except they were in her parents' house, and he didn't have any condoms, and the door was open.

Heart hammering in his chest, lightheaded with lust, Lance broke away. He took gasping breaths of air, staring at Maggie's swollen lips and eyes lit up with passion.

She touched his cheek. "Maybe I could be your first official time—with someone you love."

"My first time," he whispered, his chest feeling like a huge weight pressed against it. "You're slaying me right now. You have to stop," Lance pleaded.

"I'm sorry. I'll stop." Maggie moved to the bed and sat down. "I got you something else, but I'll give it to you later."

"I don't know if I can take any more of your gifts."

He caught her small smile in the semi-dark room.

Lance told her, "You already gave me the best gift, Maggie. Nothing can top it."

"I did?" She tilted her head. "What?"

She told him she loved him. That was the best gift, but there was also another good one, one he could say without feeling nauseous.

"You let me spend Christmas with you and your family. Thank you."

"You really do like them."

He smiled. "You sound surprised."

"I am surprised."

"Don't take your family for granted. A lot of people don't have ones like yours."

Her eyebrows lowered, but instead of replying, she stretched out and patted the bed. "Lie with me for a little longer."

"I don't know if that's a good idea."

"Please?"

Lance did as she gently commanded, careful to keep space between them. The silence was edgy, both of them wound up with emotions.

He turned his head and found Maggie's eyes on him. "Turn on your side, and face away from me."

Maggie paused. "What?"

"Do it," he said softly, looking into her trusting eyes.

The bed shifted as she moved.

Swallowing around a tight throat, he reached out a wobbly hand to her back. Lance slowly slid up her top, fingers caressing her skin. Maggie shivered, goose bumps breaking out across her flesh. He kissed the small of her back, felt her go still, and then he traced three words onto her skin. Maggie held her breath, released it, held it again, and released it once more. She reached around, found his hand, and brought it up under her arm to her neck. Lance moved closer and his body formed to the back of hers.

"What did you get me?" he asked after a while.

"I can't tell you. Then it won't be a surprise."

"I really mean it when I say I'm good without any more surprises tonight."

Maggie laughed and turned in his arms, their faces inches from one another's, their legs intertwined. "I got you a Bon Jovi CD. I think 'Always' is our song."

Lance's face split in a grin. "I got you the same thing."

"What? You did not."

"I did."

"Well, that settles it. You and I are mushy dorks."

"Mushy dorks with their own song," he corrected. He touched a lock of her hair, not wanting to say the words he was about to say. "You should go to bed before we get in trouble."

"You're right." Maggie sighed and kissed him one last time. "Merry Christmas."

"Merry Christmas."

Like she was his own personal lightbulb, Lance's world darkened when she left. He closed his eyes, repeating her words over and over in his head. She loved him. She loved him. Lance told himself not to freak out. He told himself he could handle having Maggie's love, but part of him felt sick at the thought of her trusting him with her heart. He didn't want that responsibility.

It was as if he held a bomb in his hands, and didn't know when it was going to go off—only that it would.

MAGGIE—2010

MAGGIE STARED AT the questionnaire in the magazine, muttering to herself at her answers.

Q: What do you do for hobbies?

A: ~~Eat pretzels~~ and watch Doctor Who. I used to eat pretzels. Now I eat lettuce.

Q: Where do you see yourself in twenty years?

A: ~~Eating pretzels~~ and watching Doctor Who. I really miss eating pretzels. Curse Lance Denton for taking away my pretzels!

Q: If you could meet any famous person, dead or alive, who would it be and why?

A: Matt Smith from Doctor Who. Because he's the Doctor. And maybe he'd give me a pretzel. I wouldn't share it with Lance either.

Shaking her head, she tossed the pen and magazine to the side and stared out the window, where she had a clear view of flourishing trees and an occasional glimpse of the houses across the street. When Maggie went to buy a house, she had certain requirements for the building that was to become her home. The privacy fence was a must, original woodwork inside the house was a nice bonus, and whether the house had a four-season room would either make or break the sale.

Three walls of the room at the front of the house were windowed, presently open to allow in a nice breeze. With white trim around the windows, doorway, and floor, and turquoise walls with pale yellow accent colors, the room reminded her of the ocean, and she'd decorated it accordingly. White wicker furniture, pictures of shorelines framed in seashells and plaques with beach sayings, made simply sitting in the room therapeutic. Usually.

Restlessness and something else told Maggie to leave and find Lance. There was a countdown to his last day in her employ, and each second brought it closer. She would have thought that would make her happy, or at least relieved, but she was sad that one day soon she would not be able to see Lance on a daily basis, if at all.

Due to the sudden freakish pretzel obsession, Maggie decided she must be hungry. She stopped in the kitchen and ate an apple before going in search of her trainer. Maggie heard the television from a nearby room and headed in that direction.

"Hey," she greeted as she walked into the den. "What are you doing in here?"

Lance pushed a button on the remote control and the television shut off. He sat up on the couch, his blank expression raising her suspicions. Blank generally meant guilty on Lance. "Nothing. What are you doing?"

"I was reading in the four-season room, and then I realized it was too quiet." Reading was close to the truth.

The den was a combination of dark wood and powder blue and cream. A rock-sided mantel with a functional fireplace was beneath the flat screen television, a couch and two recliners in marshmallow white were the furniture, and framed pictures of family and friends lined the walls. There were a few pictures of Lance up there with the rest of the cast of 'Easier Said', much to his arrogant delight. Upon his initial viewing of the room, it was the first thing he noticed.

"Did you miss me? I thought you liked it when I was out of sight, out of hearing distance."

"I do." She didn't. Lately whenever Maggie was alone, there was a void, a spark of life that should be there and wasn't.

"What are you doing?"

"Nothing." Lance wouldn't meet her eyes.

Maggie didn't take her gaze from him as she walked to the front of the couch. "Interesting."

"What?"

"Twice I've asked you what you were doing, and twice you responded with nothing. What is it? Were you watching porn or something?"

"Maggie," he groaned, closing his eyes.

"Don't be embarrassed. I know most guys do."

He opened his eyes, locking her where she was with their liquid heat. "Is that so?"

"Yep. It's normal, I guess. Don't feel bad." She patted his arm.

"I'm not embarrassed," he said, eyeing her hand until she removed it. "And I wouldn't feel bad about it if I was watching porn, but I wasn't."

Maggie swiped the remote from the coffee table and shook it in the air, daring him to try to take it from her.

"But I'll tell you one thing." Lance paused for dramatic effect. "I wasn't thinking about sex until you mentioned porn," he said dryly.

She went still, remote control limp in her hand. Maggie swallowed around a dry throat. "Oh?"

Lance slowly stood, closing the distance between them. Dressed in a black tee shirt and dark green athletic shorts, he looked relaxed and like he completely belonged in her house, in her life.

"Oh, yes." His tone was gruff, but the crinkles around the corners of his eyes ruined it. Lance put an arm around her, pulled her to him, and while staring into her eyes, snatched the remote control out of her hand. "Too easy."

It wasn't until he'd moved away that the double meaning of his words sank in.

"I'm too easy?" she demanded, watching him cross the room. "I know you weren't referring to me."

"Of course not." One corner of his mouth lifted. "You're more trouble than anything."

"Trouble. What? Me?" she sputtered.

"I think I spoke quite clearly."

"You're the one who's trouble," Maggie announced, pouncing for him and grabbing ahold of the remote.

She tugged, and he tugged back.

"What were you watching? Why don't you want me to see it?"

"It was dull. Tasteless. You'd regret knowing it if I told you. It was a big yawn fest."

He grunted when her elbow jabbed him in the ribs. Maggie laughed when he tickled her in the side.

"Stop it! I hate being tickled. Lance!" She lifted her foot and stomped on his.

Lance wrapped his arms around her, and with his front to her back, he went still. His mouth was next to her ear, causing a shiver of awareness to course down her body. Every part of his body was molded to hers, and she swallowed around a tight throat. He rested his forehead against the back of her head, and Maggie's breaths started coming faster. She opened her mouth to reply and nothing came out.

"Are you trying to fatally wound me?" he asked.

"Let go of the remote control and you won't have to find out," she promised huskily.

"Maggie, I am not letting go of this remote, no matter what."

"What is that?" she screamed, pointing at the floor.

"Nice try," he said, chuckling.

"You don't see it?" Frozen, with potent fear laced through her voice, Maggie stared down.

"Nope."

"What about now?"

"Maggie." His tone said he was above such childish antics.

She went limp in his arms, a sigh of defeat leaving her. "Okay. Fine. You win."

As soon as Lance relaxed his hold, she ripped the remote control from him with a cry of triumph.

"Give that back." Lance stalked her, eyes dark with intent.

"Nope. It's mine and you can't have it." She ran around the couch with him in pursuit.

"I'm the guest. I was using it. It's temporarily mine."

"Nothing is yours, not even temporarily. Want to know why? Because you're the employee, not the guest," Maggie modified, turning in the opposite direction when he tried to block her.

"Are you always going to throw that in my face?"

She snorted. "I could throw worse things."

"Like your nipple death trap bra?"

"I got rid of it," she argued.

His eyes went smoky, his expression and stance set for wooing.

"Stop it. I'm immune."

"Since when? That kiss we shared a few days ago says otherwise."

Maggie blinked, warmth flooding her veins at the reminder. "I was acting. I'm an exceptional actress."

"Mmm. Is that so?" Lance rubbed a thumb over his mouth, and her eyes were drawn to the motion. She wasn't able to look away until he dropped his hand. "Even you can't act that well."

Briefly pausing behind the couch, she pointed the remote control at the television and pressed the 'on' button. "Let's see what form of debauchery Lance Denton gets his pleasure from when he's alone."

He caught her around the waist, the force of his movement and his weight toppling them forward and over the back of the couch. It was too late—the sound of young, familiar voices filled the air. Face down on the couch cushion and legs in the air, and with Lance beside her, she lifted her head to look at the television screen.

The air stopped inside her lungs. Maggie watched for a moment, not able to talk. It was them during an episode of 'Easier Said', crazily in love with one another. Struck hard with emotion, she swallowed, striving for nonchalance when her insides were screaming with yearning. Maggie placed her chin on her fist and continued to observe the younger versions of Lance and Maggie. Lance was quiet beside her, and that was just as well. She didn't know what to say to him right then.

"This would make a great yoga pose," she said after a time, her neck and back stretched to the point that they were sore.

When Lance didn't respond, she finally turned her head to look at him. He wasn't watching the television—he was watching her. The look on his face was open and raw, like a wound always kept hidden, until one day, it could no longer remain so.

Swallowing hard, she looked down. "You watch these a lot?"

"Yes."

"Why?"

"They make me happy."

Maggie looked up in time to catch his sardonic smile as he added, "And nostalgic, and maudlin."

Unveiled as they were, she couldn't take the look in his eyes any longer, and needing somewhere else to focus, Maggie chose his lips. It was a bad idea—perfectly chiseled, hard when they should be, soft when necessary, a shade of mauve that couldn't be replicated—she wanted them on hers.

As though reading her mind, and knowing what she desired, Lance dropped his attention to her mouth. When he looked up, his eyes were midnight blue with lust. "I think, if I'm going to remain uninvolved with my clients, I must forbid you to look at me like that."

"What am I looking at you like?" she asked, breathless with the need to touch him. Maggie would take a moment of that perfect love they'd once shared, even if it meant her heart would never recover.

"Like you ache for me." Lance touched a lock of her hair, the expression on his face pained. "It wouldn't even be sex, Maggie, it would be . . ."

He sat up on the couch, helping Maggie to an upright position.

"Yes?" she pressed, legs and arms crossed protectively—not against Lance, but against herself.

"Sadly fast, and I fear, unsatisfactory for you," he said, a smile clearing the emotion from his face.

Maggie swallowed, knowing that wasn't what he'd been about to say, but thankful that that's what he decided on. They needed to take a step back, lighten the mood, and stop staring at each other with hunger in their eyes.

"Like the first time?" she teased.

Lance scowled. "I made up for it."

Maggie tried to laugh, but it sounded choked. He did. "Yes. Right. You're right. I'm going to go outside. I need some air."

She jumped to her feet and raced for the front door. Once outside, she turned to shut the door and found Lance directly behind her, a lone eyebrow lifted.

"Hey," she said breathlessly.

"Hey." Half of his mouth lifted. "I needed some air too. Can I hang out here with you?"

"Yeah. Sure. Why not?"

Maggie plopped down on the steps and studied her splayed fingers, inhalations coming too fast, her scalp hot and prickly. Lance sat beside her, silent and still. She moved her fingers up and down as though they played an invisible piano, and then she clasped them together and stared at her shirt. It didn't take long for the quiet to become too much, too heavy.

"How come you never mention your daughter?" At his sharp look, she explained. "Parents like to talk about their kids, brag about them even. You should hear my sister talk about her twins. I love Nick and Nolan, but they aren't perfect, and she acts like they are."

Maggie continued when he didn't comment. "You and I have been around each other for weeks now and you've mentioned her maybe once. I understand not talking about your ex-wife, but I don't understand how you can go without talking about your baby."

"That could be considered nosy."

"Yeah? Well, so is going through my cupboards and drawers, but you still did it." She gave him a pointed look when he remained mute.

Lance's face clouded over and he looked at the street. "She's not my daughter." He glanced at her with a sick smile on his face. "Hence the recent divorce."

Maggie swallowed. "What do you mean?"

"Olivia was having an affair for the duration of our marriage with her high school sweetheart. They broke up right before I met her. I was the rebound guy." He looked at her. "You should never marry the rebound guy. Remember that."

She rolled her eyes. "There has to be a guy first before there can be a rebound guy."

Lance studied her. "Yeah."

Uncomfortable with the intensity and directness of his gaze, Maggie looked away. "Why didn't she just divorce you? Why stay married? Did you know the baby wasn't yours?"

"I don't know why Olivia stayed. She liked the money, the fame? She was scared to hurt me? Who knows?" He picked up a leaf and twirled it between his fingertips, eyes trained on it. "I didn't know Ivy wasn't mine until I caught them. I was supposed to be out of town on a promotional shoot. I got home early, decided to surprise Olivia with dinner."

Lance's smile was wan. "What are the odds of going to the grocery store to pick up steak sauce and catching your wife and daughter with another man? And it wasn't just seeing that—it was seeing the three of them together and knowing they fit and I didn't. I was the husband, the father, and I didn't belong. He had his arm around Olivia and he was grinning down at my daughter like she was his. Seeing them together . . . there was no denying it. Ivy was his, not mine."

"What did you do?" Her voice was a croak, strung taut with sorrow for him. Lance's life was ripped away from him, and even if it had been an illusion, that didn't mean the loss of it hurt any less.

He chucked the leaf, but the wind brought it back to the ground near the steps. "I went home and waited. Confronted her, listened to her cry, died a little at her confession. I wouldn't call it a perfect marriage, but I was happy enough. The joke was on me." He tried to smile, but it fell flat.

Maggie looked away from his sad eyes. "What about the guy? He was okay with the way things were, with sharing them with you?"

"Olivia told me she planned on leaving me. She hadn't gotten the courage to do it yet. I imagine he wasn't happy about the arrangement." He shrugged. "I had my and Ivy's blood drawn, to Olivia's fury. She didn't want her baby's skin pricked. I argued that I didn't want to continue to think a baby was mine who wasn't. She finally consented. The blood test confirmed it. The legacy of Lance Denton was a fallacy and will not live on."

"Someday you'll have a wife and kids who are yours and no one else's," she told him, not sure if that was the right thing to say.

"Excuse my frankness, but I really don't want to think about kids or wives in any context at the moment."

"Right. I get it."

"I suppose you think I deserved it. You would be correct." His smile was twisted. "Guess I finally got payback for all the times I hurt people."

"No one deserves that," Maggie told him. Too much emotion leaked out of the words and made her voice tremble.

The caricature of a smile faded from Lance's face and his eyes lightened with gratitude. "Thank you."

"I mean, you could apologize for breaking my heart and maybe I'd forgive you. I thought you were the sun and nothing anyone said or did could make me think otherwise, no one except you." She looked down so he didn't catch the faint, self-deprecating smile on her face.

Maggie looked up as he slid closer. The cool cobblestone seeped into her back as she waited for an apology that may or may not come. It was so long ago that it shouldn't matter, but that hurt teenager she once was needed it just the same. Maggie as an adult needed the man that sat beside her to give that to her. She didn't understand why.

Lance's lips flirted with a smile and she wanted to blame the sun for the heat that crashed over her, but they sat in the shade. "I am sorry for how I treated you."

His face was near enough that she noted a faint scar on his jaw, one that hadn't been there years ago. Gray stars framed the pupils of his eyes and silver streaks of light filled the irises. They weren't blue eyes—they were the darkest galaxy filled with white fire.

"I didn't know what I was doing. At first, I hated how you looked at me. Because when you looked at me like I was important, I wanted to be, and I couldn't take the pressure of trying to live up to that. I couldn't be what you deserved. In the end, I loved how you looked at me and I hated that I did."

"It's okay now," she told him, meaning it. "Obviously, at first it wasn't. You were everything to me, and you shouldn't have been. But some of it was my fault too. I pushed you to tell me things you couldn't, and when it was all over, I was cruel. And I'm sorry for that."

"We're both sorry. Aces," he murmured.

They both grew quiet, lost in the past where teenagers fell in love, and summer never ended. Awkward first kisses, the strength of a hug. Where sunshine was a song and everyone danced to it. Beaches, white powder sand, waves—where kids were high on life and what it brought. First loves, last loves. The smell of campfires, the thought of being with the one person who made their heart wildly pound. The one who lit them on fire and had the power to extinguish them as quickly.

"You were messed up. But so was I." She bumped her shoulder to his before placing her elbows on the stone to recline. She looked at the street, watched a woman walk by pushing a black stroller.

He shook his head. "I was more than messed up."

"So was I," she said again, lifting an eyebrow in challenge when he looked at her.

Half of his mouth quirked, the partial smile filleting Maggie's hormones and logic. Her fingers itched to touch his face, smooth the crease from his brow. It was time to find something else to do.

She shot to her feet and wiped off her shorts. "Shouldn't we be exercising or watching a show on exercising or weighing me or . . ." She trailed off when he stood up as well.

"I miss her."

"Who?" Even as she asked it, an image of his ex-wife came to mind. Maggie had seen the photographs of Lance and Olivia Denton. Olive-toned skin, bright blue eyes and a full red mouth. She was exotically beautiful. Maggie pushed the jealousy and inept feeling away and focused on Lance.

"Ivy." He glanced at her. "Even though she isn't mine, it seemed like she was."

"Of course it did," she said softly. "She was yours. You were her father. It doesn't matter for how long."

"The first time I saw her, it was like finally everything made sense—all the bad, all the screw ups, everything—I looked at her and it was all worth it. She was my redemption, my purpose. That tiny little being had the power to wipe my slate clean," he whispered, staring at the ground.

"Have you tried to see her?"

Lance looked at her. "Honestly, I can't stand the thought of talking to or being around Olivia right now. I hope at some point I can be civil with her. I don't want to act like I'm Ivy's dad. I only want to know her, in some context." He shrugged. "It's all fresh yet. We'll see."

"Maybe you could write little notes to Ivy," Maggie suggested. "It could be cathartic to you. And someday you could give them to her."

An evil grin took over his mouth. "'Ivy, your mother is the devil. Also, remember to always eat your vegetables. Love, your fake Dad.'"

"Okay, so not those kind of notes."

Lance laughed. "Would you like to watch episodes of 'Easier Said' with me?"

"Really?" Maggie asked. "Why?"

Maggie's eyes were caught and held by his, the blueness of them exposed and genuine. "Watching us back then makes me sad and happy. Maybe it will be the same for you."

"I don't want to be sad."

"Sometimes you have to be sad for a while before you can be happy," he said quietly.

LANCE—1997

"WOW. THIS IS . . . this is like a mansion." Wonder hugged Maggie's words and the look she gave him was wide-eyed.

The long-sleeved purple and black plaid dress was loose on her frame, and the black boots added inches to her otherwise unimpressive height. Lance was dressed in black from his shirt to his boots. Maggie had teased him about his depressing outfit when he met her at her apartment. Lance hadn't replied, but damn if it didn't feel like he was going to a funeral.

It was four months later than the initial date that Maggie was to go to Lance's house. His dad ended up leaving town New Year's week and Lance spent the remainder of it at his apartment. He'd been bothered by his father's disappearance. He guessed because he knew what he was missing, while before he hadn't.

Lance tried to see the stone structure through Maggie's eyes. The rock siding and arched windows with peaked roofs made him think it looked like a mini castle. He supposed it was pretty big, but he'd seen bigger, and the size meant nothing.

"It's just a house."

She gave him a dubious look. "My house is a house. This is more than a house."

"It's just a house," Lance insisted in a harsher tone. It made him uncomfortable to think of her awestruck by what he had. It was just things. Things didn't mean anything.

Maggie smoothed hair from her cheek, eyes narrowing. She'd recently cut her hair and it hung around her face in a way that accentuated her prominent bone structure. "You're right. It's just a house. A really big, really expensive, house."

Lance stared at the building, the chilly April air sinking into him.

"It's empty. It's a big house full of emptiness." He turned to Maggie. "This was a bad idea."

"You don't want me to meet your dad?" Hurt made her words thick.

Hands around his neck, he squeezed. "It's not that. It's just—never mind. Let's go." He gave her a small smile. She'd understand soon enough.

"Okay," Maggie said slowly.

He put a hand to her arm when she moved to go up the stairs. "Maggie."

She took in his anxious expression and smiled with a hint of exasperation, touching his rumpled eyebrow. "What is it, Lance? I know you're trying to hide it, but you're freaking out over something."

Swallowing, he dropped his hand. "It's just . . . I've never brought a girl home before, and . . . you're the first girl that I've dated to meet my dad."

"You're nervous."

A frown took over his features. "I don't get nervous."

Maggie framed his face with her hands and kissed him. "Only you do, and I think it's sweet how you deny it every time it happens. I should be nervous, not you. He's not some kind of horrible monster that shouts and breaks things, is he?"

"No," he answered faintly. "He's nice. Quiet. You'll like him."

"No worries then. Everything's going to be fine. I love you."

Lance swallowed, averting his eyes. "Right. Time to meet Dad."

He pretended he didn't see the crestfallen expression on Maggie's face as they entered the house. For four months she'd patiently waited to hear him say it back. He would write it, he would trace it onto her skin, he would even squeeze her hand three times, but he couldn't say the words. He'd tried, but each time he opened his mouth to say them, they choked him.

If Lance told Maggie he loved her, that would make it real, and once it was real, it could end.

Lance knew what his mother smelled like, because his father sprayed her perfume throughout the house once a day. That day was no different. The scent of Chanel stung his nostrils as soon as he entered the house and made his stomach turn. His hand unconsciously tightened around Maggie's and she gave him a reassuring smile, but he saw the hint of apprehension in her eyes.

"You've lived here your whole life?" she questioned, looking around the entryway. He avoided looking at the pictures, but Maggie stared.

To say Max Denton was infatuated with Tammie Rose would be an understatement. Her smiling face filled the walls, the house decorated the same as she'd left it over a dozen years ago—blues and greens and grays were the theme for every room. The furniture had been replaced, but it was obvious Max had chosen what he thought Lance's mom would have wanted.

"Off and on."

Maggie moved from the foyer to the glass room directly before them, gasping at the ocean view. "It's beautiful," she murmured.

"Tammie loved the ocean," a deep, familiar voice said from the hallway.

Maggie spun around, her face red as if she'd been caught doing something wrong. Lance instinctively moved closer to her and put his arm around her, as much to comfort her as to steady him. She twisted her fingers around his and squeezed.

"As you can tell." Max Denton smiled and gestured around the room. Tall and blond with intelligent features, it was striking how much Lance didn't look like his dad. He had his height, possibly his build, but the rest of him was his mother.

"Hello, Maggie. It's good to see you, Lance." The sincerity in his voice was overshadowed by his avoidance of meeting Lance's eyes.

"You too, Dad. It's been a while." Months, it had been months. No hugs exchanged, no pat on the shoulder or handshake. Cordial and distant, that was their relationship.

Maggie unhooked her hand from his, a shy smile on her face. "Hello, Mr. Denton."

Lance's father laughed and shook his head. "Please don't call me that. I prefer Max, unless I'm in court, and let's hope I never see you there."

He entered the room, looking lawyerly in his navy blue suit, and offered a large hand.

She shook it. "I definitely hope for the same."

"I'd like to say I can take credit for the meal we're about to enjoy, but that honor belongs to Hailey. She comes in once a week to clean, and when I ask really nicely, sometimes she takes pity on me and makes food," he explained to Maggie, motioning for her to come over.

With a look at Lance, Maggie stepped into his father's awaiting arm and they started for the dining room with their arms linked. "It smells great. I'm sure it's delicious."

"You can't go wrong with spaghetti and meatballs," Max said jovially.

Lance's face cracked in a smile when Maggie's back tensed. She shot him an accusatory look over her shoulder and he raised his arms in apology. He hadn't thought to mention to his dad that Maggie didn't like spaghetti, never realizing that would be the thing Hailey, a woman in her fifties who had been an employee of his father's since Lance was a toddler, would decide to make.

Maggie ate a small salad and a buttered roll, saying she was full when it came time to eat the main course. Lance knew she probably was full—the salad and bread was the most he'd seen her eat at once in a long time. Max paused, his eyebrows lifting, but didn't comment, instead asking Maggie about her life in Iowa, and what she thought of working on a television show.

The dinner went smoothly, with most of the conversation between Maggie and Lance's dad. He could see her getting more and more confused as the night progressed. The thoughts were clear on her face: *Why doesn't he look at you? Why doesn't he talk to you?* Lance ignored her silent questions, focusing on the meal and ticking off the minutes to when they could depart.

Max excused himself, saying he needed to go to his office because he had a lot of work to complete before a court appearance Monday. "It was lovely to meet you, Maggie. I hope I see you again."

"Me too, Mr. Den—Max."

He smiled, turning to Lance, and the warmth left his brown eyes. "Things are going well for you?"

"Yes," he answered shortly, the bite of roll he'd taken lodged in his throat. Lance took a drink of water and waited.

"Good." He tapped the fingers of one hand against the tabletop. "Let me know if anything changes, or if you need anything."

"Will do," Lance muttered, looking at his plate of food.

"You two have a nice time. Hailey will clean up when she comes in the morning. Good night."

Max Denton stood, and with a final nod, left.

The purr of an engine sounded soon after that, faint but purposeful. Then it was gone.

"He's nice," Maggie said tentatively.

"Yep." He nodded. "The nicest. Best uninvolved dad I could have hoped for. Want a tour of the place? You can't get the full effect of the atmosphere unless you do." Lance's voice was hard, and he shot to his feet before Maggie could respond. He roughly stacked the dishes, the piercing clank of them against one another the only sound in the room.

"Sure," Maggie responded hesitantly, slowly getting to her feet.

"Well, this is the dining room." He waved a hand behind him, and then lifted the haphazardly stacked dinnerware into his arms. "Light blue walls, because, well, that was my mom's favorite color. Made her think of water. Ugly pictures of birds on the walls, because, yep, you guessed it, she liked birds," Lance said nastily, striding from the room.

He angrily rinsed and stacked dishes in the dishwasher. Maggie silently set dishes on the counter next to him.

"Gray walls. Made her think of an approaching storm, which, incidentally, also has to do with the ocean. You know she died in the ocean, right?" Lance swung around to glare at Maggie, his chest tight, a wildness inside him pushing to be unleashed.

Eyes large and filled with pain, Maggie shook her head.

"Yeah." He smiled darkly. "Took too many drugs, decided to go for a swim in the middle of the night. Smart lady, that Tammie. I was left alone in the house. I guess it was late and I was supposed to be sleeping, but I woke up. My dad found me in the living room, staring out the windows, screaming my head off. I don't know, maybe I watched her drown." Chills cascaded down his spine like the icy fingers of a ghost.

Lance grabbed Maggie's wrist and pulled her from the room and into another. "This is the bathroom in which she used to make herself pretty, and take her baths. There's the bottle of perfume my dad sprays every day, and restocks each time it empties, because that's not seriously messed up or creepy."

He turned to Maggie, not really seeing her, seeing his past instead. Remembering the fear, the tears. "Do you know how traumatized I was as a kid, being forced to use a bathtub my dead mother once used? I kept imagining her in the bathtub drowning, face turning blue, reaching out to a rescuer that never came. My dad couldn't understand it, because she'd died in the ocean and not in the house. I was a kid, like it had to make sense."

Maggie reached for him, her face streaked with tears, mouth trembling. Lance shook her off, needing her and denying himself.

He strode down the hall.

"I hate this house. I hate everything inside it. It's a shrine to a woman who should never have been a mother, to a kid that never should have been born. My own dad can't stand the sight of me. I look too much like her. I look like the dead woman he could never stop loving, but he can't love me enough."

Lance stopped in front of a closed door and looked at her. "How is that for irony?"

Hands over her mouth, she watched him with her pretty, shattered eyes.

Taking a shaky breath, he lowered his hand to the doorknob, head bowed, and swung open the door. Lance forced himself to enter the room, his skin crawling with unease. Her scent seemed to be the strongest in his bedroom, but he knew he imagined it.

"Lance."

Lance looked at Maggie. The pain he felt radiated in her.

"You don't have to do this. I understand now."

"I do have to do this. I do," he told her. "I'm going to give you every part of me, and you're either going to hold on tighter to me, or you're going to let me go."

She took a step toward him and he turned from her. Lance couldn't let her touch him.

The room was painted in stripes of blue and gray and housed a bed and a dresser. It was his bedroom, but it was bare of anything that marked it as such. He used to sleep in the room as little as possible, and when he was old enough, he asked to stay somewhere else, anywhere else. His father had looked appallingly relieved, and Lance felt the pain all the way to his soul. Max was glad when his son left.

"It isn't your fault—that your mom died, that your dad can't be what you need," Maggie said quietly, pleadingly. "It isn't your fault."

Instead of looking at the walls of framed photographs, he stared at Maggie. "I know that. It doesn't change how I feel. Look at the pictures. Lies. Every last one of them. Look at her holding me like she loved me, looking at me like I was her world. What a joke. I grew up looking at these bullshit pictures. My dad thought they would make me feel closer to her. All they did was remind me that a dead woman lived more in this house than me or my dad."

Lance lifted his head and studied the last picture taken of him with his mom. They were on the beach, the sun outlining them. A green toy bucket and shovel sat in the sand beside them. Her hair was dark and wild, that unruliness duplicated in the blue eyes smiling at the camera lens, her arms around a grinning toddler with matching hair and eyes.

Tears burned his eyes when he turned his gaze to Maggie. "Do you know who hugged me when I was scared, or had bad dreams, or got hurt, or just—just needed to be shown I was loved? A ghost. Not my dad. Not my mom. A ghost."

A broken sound left him and he lost the fight against tears. He went to his knees on the carpeted floor, and Maggie was there, holding him. Hugging him. His throat closed, heart tight with years of grief welling up and crashing over him. Lance's arms shook around her frame, clutching her to him, needing her. Needing Maggie's love.

She stroked his hair, and kissed his face, crying along with him, and imbedded herself more into his being. He lifted his head, staring at a face that was molded right to his heart. The face he saw when he dreamed, the face he saw when he pictured his future. He didn't know if anyone had ever cried for him before. Because of him, definitely, but for him?

Lance kissed her, his mouth hard on hers. He tasted her tears, mixed with his own. Maggie fell onto his lap as his back hit the dresser. He straightened and she straddled him, the warmth and feel of her body making him crazy. The kiss went from sweet to urgent, her hands under his shirt, his fingers gripping her hips. It wasn't enough. He craved more, ached for it, especially then, when he felt the most vulnerable.

He'd gone years without feeling loved, and Maggie gave him all of hers, and he wanted to take it, and take it, and take it. Until he was filled with it. Until it was all he knew. Until he believed he had a right to have it.

Maggie pulled back, eyes dilated, face flushed. She said one word. "*Please.*"

Lance struggled to speak. His chest and throat were tight, clenched so hard it hurt to speak or breathe. "This isn't how it should be your first time. I need you too much right now."

She tugged at his shirt, shaking her head before he finished speaking. Lance rocked forward to get ahold of his shirt, his body constricting at the sound of her moan and the feel of her pressed against him, and tore off the garment. Her palms went up and down his chest, air hissing through his teeth at Maggie's touch.

"It's going to hurt," he said in a voice like gravel, wanting to be inside her so badly.

"I don't care." Maggie moved to stand, grabbing the hem of her dress and removing it.

He got to his feet, noting the sea green bra and panties before he helped remove them. Blinded by desire, fragmented in a way nothing could heal, Lance took what he could from Maggie. The motions were fast, not enough thought put toward what they were doing. It was instinctual, and primal, and trying to fill the emptiness inside with the use of bodies. It was wrong, and right.

She was naked, then he was naked. Lance turned off the light, put on a condom, and took Maggie's virginity. She felt so good, smelled like Maggie but more intensely. Better. Her first time, his first time with someone he loved. It didn't last long, desperation and incontrollable hunger turning Lance into something that was a slave to sensation. He knew he hurt her, her sharp intake of air as he entered her evidence of that. She never pushed him away, she never told him to stop. Maggie pressed her tear-stained face against his and let him take what he needed from her.

"I'm sorry," he whispered. "I'm sorry."

When it was over, shame had him quiet and unreachable. On his back, he stared at the ceiling, pulse wild, body sated but not satisfied. Maggie shifted, intent on leaving the bed, and Lance reached for her, pulling her to his side.

"I hurt you."

She was stiff beside him, closed off to him in a way that made him ache.

"I'm sorry I hurt you."

Angrily shoving at him, Maggie twisted away to sit up on his bed. Moonlight cast her naked body under its eerie spotlight and he truly looked at her for the first time. She was beautiful, body fine-boned and slender, breasts round and full. Lance's body responded and he swallowed, feeling like the biggest of asses for being turned on again so soon after having sex—sex she didn't even enjoy.

"What is it?" Lance sat up, moving for her. "What's wrong? Are you in a lot of pain?"

Maggie shrugged off his touch and crossed her arms over her breasts. He could sense her glare through the dark. "I don't care that it hurt! I knew it was going to hurt. I knew what was happening the whole time."

"Then what are you so upset about?"

In a small voice, she asked, "Why can't you tell me you love me?"

"I . . . I do." Lance swallowed, fisting the sheet in his hands.

"Then say it!" she yelled, slapping her palms to the bed.

A roar formed in his ears as his heartbeats came faster. Sweat broke out on his skin and he swallowed, opening his mouth. "Maggie."

"Say it."

He said it, the words pulled from him with relief and regret. "I love you, Maggie," he said brokenly. "I love you so much."

"Why was that so hard to say?" she whispered, touching his face.

"Because it . . . it doesn't just scare me—it petrifies me. The people I love—they don't love me back. Or I—or I can't handle it when they do. And . . ." He drove fingers through his hair, the painful tug of it welcome. "I have this fear that you're going to go away, now that I've said it out loud."

Maggie fell on him, the warm sleekness of her figure against his side making his head fuzzy with desire. "I'm not going away. I won't go away unless I don't have a choice."

Lance held her tightly to him, playing with a lock of hair, touching her cheek. Kissing her forehead. Sweeping his fingers down her arm. He needed to constantly touch her.

"I want to do it again," he said almost timidly. "I want to do it better. Are you—is that okay?"

"Please," Maggie said immediately.

Lance laughed. "Was it that bad?"

"It . . . was how I imagined it to be, but also not."

"I won't hurt you this time. I'll take my time," he promised, and he did, loving her with reverence, loving her with all he had to give.

MAGGIE—2010

"WE'RE GOING SHOPPING. You need a dress and I need a suit."

Maggie set down the book she was reading and looked at Lance. "I have dresses. Go away."

Lance plopped down on the couch, his leg against hers, and flung his arm around her shoulders, bringing his sweet, masculine scent with him. "Maggie, I have this feeling that the dresses you own are outdated and frumpy."

Pretending her pulse didn't speed up at his nearness, she removed his arm from her. "So?"

"So my date can't wear outdated, frumpy dresses. It's bad for my image."

"Your date?" Maggie stood and narrowed her eyes at him. "Who said I was going to be your date for the fundraising dinner?"

"Well, why wouldn't you want to be?" Egotistical, as always.

"Um . . . because I already have one?"

Lance tilted his head and studied her features, eyes trailing down her previously soft but currently toned form. Instead of feeling self-conscious, she allowed his perusal. Maggie would never be perfectly proportioned or one of those people that had close to no body fat—and she found she was okay with that. She decided to love her curves, and when she saw her reflection in the mirror, she smiled instead of grimacing. Maggie hugged herself, outwardly, inwardly. That acceptance and confidence did wonders for her self-esteem.

Maggie met Lance's gaze, saw the faint smile on his mouth.

"You do not."

"I do," she retorted, her skin heating up.

"Well, you do have one, yes, but you didn't *already* have one." Lance stood, purposely brushing against her as he passed. "I'm your date, and you need a dress."

He offered his arm when she turned.

She stared at the appendage.

"I know, I'd be afraid to touch me too. It's okay, I'll let you if you promise to grope me in all the right places." Lance's eyes twinkled.

Maggie took his arm, scowling as they walked. "You can't just tell me that I'm your date, you know. That's not how it works."

He patted her arm. "It is with me."

She grabbed her purse from the entryway and unhinged her arm from his. "Which is probably why you don't have a date and have to rely on intimidation to get one."

"Oh, I had options, but I didn't want anyone else as a date," Lance said, opening the front door and stepping outside.

Maggie contemplated slamming the door in his face and locking it, but he was right—she did need a dress. And she didn't have a date. Or she guessed she did. Shaking her head, she walked out the door.

"Our clothing choices are limited on such short notice," Maggie muttered.

"I don't need anything fancy," Lance assured her.

"That's good, because I will be the least fancy version of a Lance Denton date."

It was a cool day, the colors of the houses dim and dark without the sun. Maggie zipped up her jacket and started the four-mile walk to the strip mall. Lance gave her a grin as they crossed the street.

"What?"

He shrugged. "I like that you're taking the initiative and walking. I'm proud of you, Maggie. You're going to do great on your own."

Biting back a flippant response, she said stiffly, "Thank you."

"And remember, each morning you wake up is a new chance to meet your goals, even if you slipped up the day before. Don't feel bad about that. It's going to happen. Just keep going at it. You'll do fine."

Lance prepping her for the time when he would be gone made her throat close, but Maggie nodded and pretended like she wasn't going to miss him. They had a beautiful, horrible history, and they each had come a long way since their teens. She glanced at him, wondering how he'd been able to get past the issues he'd had with his mom and dad.

A leaf fluttered across the sidewalk and Maggie focused on that. "How did you go from a damaged boy to the—for the most part—levelheaded man you are?"

"For the most part?" he repeated.

"Well, I mean, you're still conceited." She smiled sweetly.

"Years of therapy."

Maggie snorted.

Lance lifted an eyebrow at her.

Her eyes froze on his face. "Oh. You're serious." She faced forward. "Well, I had the same, so . . . yeah."

They stood at the stoplights, waiting for the crosswalk light to come on. Maggie tucked hair behind her ears and looked at the houses around them so she didn't have to look at Lance. They were all different shapes, different sizes, full of different people. All that considering them did was make her wonder more things about the man beside her, and want to look at Lance more. He had a life, a world, outside of hers, and she wondered what it was like, if he was happy.

She asked, "You live in Ohio. Why there?"

"Why not?" Their gazes clashed for a second before he turned his eyes ahead. "I was looking for houses online, and that was where I found the one I wanted."

They crossed the road.

"What was so special about a house in Ohio?" she asked.

"The house is in the country. It's . . . nice there. Peaceful."

Maggie's smile dropped to a frown. Everyone needed a place that felt like home. Lance was as human as anyone else, with the same wants, needs, losses, and fears. His outward arrogance hid a lot, but that was no excuse for her or anyone else to stop realizing everyone was as vulnerable and imperfect as the rest of them.

"Why did you say you didn't have a home?" At his blank look, she elaborated. "The first day you showed up. You said you didn't have a home."

"I wanted to be close to you."

"You're lying."

"Am I?"

She cleared her throat, eyes on the looming brown building up the hill. "The fundraiser . . . what do you know about it?"

The guests were to stay at a bed and breakfast in Missouri with the dinner held in a banquet room of the house. As far as fundraising dinners went, it was a small event, seemingly more laidback than others. The sponsors of the dinner were ones Maggie had heard of before, but didn't know a lot about.

"All of the invited guests are from family-themed shows that are no longer on the air. The money donated will be put to programs that help reinforce positive self-awareness in children."

"How do you know all that? The invitation was pretty vague."

"Lucky guess," was his deflective answer. "I heard there will be a couple guest speakers as well. Apparently one of them is an arrogant prick. I'd probably avoid him at all costs."

Maggie blinked. "Oh? Who's that?"

"We're here," he said enthusiastically, gesturing to the parking lot that led up to the shopping center. "Where should we go first?" Lance hurried his pace.

After a brief pause in which Maggie questioned his excitement to enter a clothing store, she jogged to reach him. "What's the rush?"

"Nothing. I just like to watch you run when you don't have on a sports bra."

Maggie gave him a look when he winked at her.

They entered a department store, soft piano music flowing from speakers in the walls. Rows of clothes with people rifling through them greeted Maggie and Lance. It smelled like a war on multiple perfumes was taking place.

Lance fingered a lacy white bra as they walked past the lingerie section. "Remember that night I took you to the party on the beach? The first time we really hung out?"

A flash of gray skies, warm air, the scent of salt and water, the sound of crashing waves, hit her. Piercing blue eyes that could stare through her, a velvety smooth voice that always seemed to know the right words to say to Maggie. Lance was already a mighty force to behold, even at the age of sixteen.

A small smile touched her lips. "I remember."

"That night, after I left you at your apartment, I went back to the party."

"I know. You told me the next day when we went on the boogie boards. I commented on how hungover you looked."

"I never told you, but, I went back with the intention of hooking up with someone. Anyone, really. What I felt for you was already screwing with my head, and we'd barely hung out. Plus, I was embarrassingly horny, also because of you. I figured if I drank enough, I wouldn't care who it was. I needed to prove to myself that I was in control, even if it was bullshit."

"You don't have to tell me this. It was years ago. It doesn't matter." Maggie paused, looking down. "Anyway, when I saw you the next day, I already figured you had been with someone. You were testy with me. I assumed it was because you regretted any of the interest you'd shown in me."

"That wasn't it." He laughed abruptly. "I was pissed the next day because I couldn't do it. I got shit-faced to the point where I shouldn't have cared about anything, but I still managed to think of you."

Maggie stopped by the dress shirts, one the same shade of Lance's blue eyes grabbing her attention. She touched the soft material. "I guess I should be flattered, right?"

"No, that's not why I'm telling you this," he said, shaking his head. "I kissed a girl, but that was it. I left with a cup full of beer in each hand and sat in the sand outside the apartment building, glaring at your bedroom window as I drank them. I already knew I was in trouble, and I was fighting it."

"That wasn't stalker-ish, at all," Maggie muttered, the young girl inside her rejoicing at the confession.

Lance held up two fingers. "Slightly."

"But you eventually got over your pining for me and found someone. Anne was her name, right?"

He shrugged. "If you recall, it didn't last long."

"They never lasted long."

"No. Not until you."

"And even that didn't last all that long."

His close-lipped expression combined with the feral look in his eyes dared her to argue his next words. "Some could argue the evidence that alludes to a possibility of never-ending pining for you."

Maggie sucked in a breath. "Evidence? What . . . what are you talking about?"

He abruptly left her and found a salesperson and told her his measurements, then set about finding appropriate clothing, leaving Maggie alone with her thoughts. After aimlessly strolling around the endless dress options, Maggie decided to stop dwelling on Lance and pay attention to what she was bypassing. She chose four different styled and colored dresses and went to the dressing room.

"Did you find something?" Lance asked forty minutes later, garment bag slung over his wide shoulder.

Maggie nodded, clutching closer the bag with the department store logo on it. She wasn't sure she'd made the right choice, and she was nervous about showing anyone else the dress. It fit to her form in a way she wouldn't have liked mere months ago.

"Now what?" he asked.

She shrugged. "We walk back?"

"How about some dinner first?"

"I don't . . . I don't know." Maggie swallowed. "I'm not sure that's such a good idea."

"Why?" he said softly, opening the door for her. "Afraid you'll enjoy your time with me?"

"No." That was exactly it. Maggie felt like she was being sucked back into the past, but it wasn't the same. It was more honest, more tangible.

"Then what's the problem? There's a nice diner a few blocks away. I found it one day when I was running."

Face red, Maggie said, "Okay. I guess I can tolerate your presence for a little while longer today."

"Oh, come on," Lance scoffed as he pointed in the direction they were to go. "Like you haven't been checking me out the whole time."

"You wish."

Lance grinned. "No wishing necessary."

Twenty minutes later found Maggie and Lance seated at a table in a well-known, reputable establishment. It was the kind of place in which men proposed to women and people held anniversary celebrations. The atmosphere was romantic, the lights dim in a room where small tables were coupled with candles. Instrumental music played in the background.

Maggie stared at Lance.

"What?" he asked, perusing a menu.

"This is not a diner."

"Close enough." He looked up and smiled.

"This is the kind of place you take someone you're in love with."

"We can pretend, right?"

Maggie didn't reply.

Lance set down the menu and met her gaze. "We're going to eat. That's all. Nothing else is happening here. You know that. I know that. Right?"

She swallowed. "Right."

"I've been wondering something."

Maggie raised her eyebrows and waited.

"Did you . . . think of me much?" Lance glanced at her before turning his gaze to the table.

"All the time," she admitted.

"I thought of you." He smiled. "Was it all bad?"

"No. A lot of it was good."

"Did you love Jeff Mitchell?" Lance picked up a fork and set it back down.

The waitress chose that moment to appear, taking their drink orders.

Maggie could tell by the way Lance watched her that he wasn't going to let the question go unanswered. With the waitress gone, she had no reason to delay.

She took a deep breath. "I did."

He nodded, swallowing. "He's a lawyer now, right?"

"Yes."

"How did you two get in contact again?"

Maggie took a sip from her water glass. "He was in the area for work and looked me up."

Lance smiled, but it touched his lips and nothing more. He stared at Maggie, the intensity of his gaze singeing her heart. "Why did you tell him no?"

"I loved him, but not like he deserved." Maggie took another drink, her throat dry.

"I can understand that," he said after a long pause.

"Can you?"

"You loved me, and I didn't feel like I had that right. And I loved you, but you deserved so much more than what I could give then."

"Then?"

"Then," he whispered, eyes locked on her face.

Uncomfortable with the implication of his words, Maggie looked around the room, anywhere but at Lance. "You could have broken up with me. You didn't have to sleep with someone to end things."

"I was drunk. I was stupid. How many people make good decisions while drinking? It's not an excuse," he added as her expression turned cold. "But I was confused and scared and I didn't know what I was doing. I didn't know what to do with that depth of emotion, Maggie. You said I terrified you, well, you terrified me too."

Maggie studied Lance's chiseled features, and he waited, letting her. Her chest was compressed with ghosts from the past, and she was tired of having them haunt her. She was exhausted from carrying that heaviness around for so long. Why they hadn't worked was becoming less important to what they'd had, even if it hadn't lasted. That girl had loved that boy, and that boy had loved that girl.

"You still scare me," she finally said, offering a wobbly smile.

"Ditto," he replied softly.

They went quiet, each left alone to their thoughts. Maggie looked down, each breath of air painfully pulled from her. Her hands quivered and she clasped them together to quell it. Would she change anything, if she could go back? No. She wouldn't. And accepting that was a step forward instead of back.

Lance abruptly stood up, moved to her side of the table, and crouched beside her. He pushed her chair out so that she faced him, and looked at her with adoration. Her pulse careened sideways, off track and heading toward obliteration.

"Stop it. Stop looking at me like that. What are you doing?" she demanded, panic setting in. He reached for her hands and Maggie snatched them back. "Go away. Go. Go back to your side. Right now. People are looking."

"Maggie Smiley," Lance began.

"If you say one thing I do not want to hear, it will be bad for you. Very bad."

Lance offered his hands again, palms up, and waited with his eyebrows lifted. "The longer you delay this, the more embarrassing it's going to get for you."

Glaring at him, Maggie slapped her hands onto his. They were calloused, warm, and safe. Those hands had touched her, caressed her, written words onto her skin. Those hands had loved her as much as the man with whom they belonged.

"We've known each other for a long time," Lance said, looking into her eyes. His expression was earnest, but there was a devilish gleam in the blue eyes set on her.

"Mmm-hmm."

"Act like you like me. Otherwise it looks bad for you," he whispered out of the side of his mouth.

Maggie pasted a dreamy look on her face.

"Better." Laughter lightened his tone. "Not too much though. We want this to look authentic."

"Get on with it already," she hissed through smiling lips.

"We've been through ups and downs. Bad times. Good times. Laughter. Tears."

She yawned.

"You were my first love," he said in a low voice, the teasing glint gone from his eyes.

Maggie froze, staring at him. That was not Lance the actor. That was simply Lance.

Lance moved his knees so that his face was close to hers. "The first girl I asked out on a proper date." He smiled. "The first girl to tell me no."

"And then gave in," she said wryly.

"I was persuasive."

They shared a grin.

"Maggie Smiley." Lance squeezed her hands. "Will you please be my date for the fundraiser dinner?"

Her heartbeat tripped. The way Maggie's body responded to his words made it feel like he'd proposed to her, silly as it was. She was already going to go with him, but the fact that he went to all that trouble to ask her to be his date struck her hard, right in the heart. Lance had listened to what she'd said, and it had mattered to him.

"Please?"

"Yes."

"Thank you."

Lance grinned, and the room around them erupted in clapping as people mistakenly thought she'd agreed to a marriage proposal.

Maggie smiled, gesturing to the onlookers. "They think we're getting married."

He shrugged, getting to his feet and moving to his side of the table. "We'll probably get free wine or something. Win-win situation."

LANCE—1998

SHE HELD ON tighter.

As one year faded to the next, Maggie's love filled him, healed him, and he felt the constriction of it like a noose around his neck. Even as his heart beat harder for her, his eyes sought to always find her, even as he loved her with everything he had, a part of him resented her.

The show was doing better than anyone could have expected—two seasons wrapped up and another two contracted. The cast and crew were celebrating with a yacht party before they all went their separate ways for the two months until production picked back up in July.

Maggie's laughter floated over to him, and Lance instinctively turned her way. He went still, letting it drift along his spine. She stood across the large deck, the setting sun an accessory to her beauty. Her hair was up, the graceful lines of her neck drawing his eyes to them. Lance took in the slinky red dress she wore, swallowing hard at the way his body reacted to the mere thought of her naked.

"Stop ogling your co-star," Benton Jamison slurred, handing a cold beer to Lance.

He took it, a dim smile on his lips. "You mean my girlfriend."

Benton played Lance's dad on 'Easier Said'. Average in height, his stomach seemed to grow along with the years. Lance would bet it was all the beer he drank. His nose was wide and red, and there was a habitual flush to his face. He had balding blond hair and large black glasses.

"Better enjoy it before she comes to her senses." Benton swayed on his feet.

Lance tapped his beer to Benton's in agreement and took a drink.

The temperature was warm enough, but the more the sun went down, the cooler it got. Music played, mixing in with the sound of voices. The beers kept coming, and after a while, Lance had a buzz. He lost

Maggie in the mass of people, and it made his stomach turn at how relieved that made him. He ambled through the dark, staying where others weren't. Lance wasn't good company at the moment.

Tabitha Volden, who played Maggie's cheerleader best friend Zoe Clark on the show, stood near the restroom door. Wine in hand, black strapless dress hugging her thin frame, she smirked at him as he headed toward her. Everything about her screamed sex, from the thirst in her blue eyes to the curve of her red lips, to the way her long blond hair wildly framed her face.

"Hey, Lance," she cooed, her back against the wall and legs partially bent in front her.

"Hanging out with your friends?"

Tabitha was cast mid-season last year, her physical appeal ranking high with male viewers. Jealous of Maggie's actual talent as an actress, she was rude to her anytime the camera wasn't rolling. Tabitha was popular, but she was a flake, and she knew it. She alternated between flirting with Lance and insulting him, depending on his reception of her.

"Same as you, apparently," she retorted, pursing her lips on the rim of the stemmed glassware and tipping her head back.

"I needed to get away from everyone, too much noise," Lance muttered.

He moved to stand beside her, looking out at the dark waters surrounding them. The harder he stared at them, the dizzier he became. It was easy to feel like nothing while endless watery depths were on all sides of him.

She snorted, gesturing to the bathroom. "Great place to choose."

"Are you going to use it or just stand in front of it?"

Tabitha motioned him forward, one eyebrow lifting. She didn't move, and he had to slide past her in the cramped space to get to the restroom. With his eyes locked with hers, he did. Her breasts grazed his chest and she bit her lip, hunger dilating her eyes. She was nothing to him. She was safe. She couldn't break his heart because she'd never have it.

Lance broke their stare and entered the bathroom, ashamed that he was aroused by a woman he couldn't stand. Taking deep breaths, he splashed water on his face, and hunched over the small sink, Lance took in his image. His eyes were unfocused, skin reddened, and his dark hair was a mess. He looked like shit. He used the toilet, washed his hands, and left, hoping Tabitha would be gone when he emerged.

She was.

Lance went in search of Maggie, needing to be reassured by her presence, to be pulled back to them. It was getting more and more necessary for him to anchor himself to Maggie. Their love didn't seem to be enough anymore—or it was too much.

She stood with her back to him, facing the sea. The wind picked up, tossed her hair around. Lance barricaded her between his arms, his front to her back. He breathed in deeply, closing his eyes as he tried to form her scent, that moment, to memory. Instinctively knowing it was Lance, Maggie melted into him, nuzzling his bicep with her cheek.

"Are you having fun?"

"Define fun," Lance replied.

Maggie smiled against his arm.

"I want to stay here," she said, voice soft yet loud in his ears.

"The party ends at midnight. We'll get kicked off after that." Lance moved his hands to her waist, wrapping himself around her to keep him tethered to her. *Don't let me go, Maggie, don't let me let you go.* Lance's breaths came faster at her nearness, and he was drunk on her more than alcohol.

Maggie turned in his arms, gazing up at his face. Her eyes were bright, her breath sweet as wine as she pressed a kiss to his lips. "I want to stay with you. I don't want to go back to Iowa for the break. I want to stay with you, Lance."

Lance dropped his hands and stepped back. "What?"

The dull throb of his heartbeat grew louder, harder, heavier, until it was all he heard.

Maggie. All the time, Maggie. Waking up to her, sleeping with her in his arms. Seeing all her smiles. Laughing and talking with her during the day, being consumed by her at night. Days and days of Maggie. It sounded beautiful, and impossible. He couldn't give that to her. He was eighteen years old, she was seventeen. Too much. It was too much.

Lance's chest tightened and he put a shaking hand on his temple.

"I said I want to stay with you. We . . . talked about it before, and . . ."

Her eyebrows lowered. "Is that not what you want anymore?"

He couldn't look at her.

"Maggie," Lance began.

"Wow. Okay. I get it." Maggie moved away from him, her face blank. "I, um, I'm going . . . somewhere." She looked around them, her face dismayed at the lack of escape. They were on a yacht, miles from shore. She couldn't go anywhere. They both knew it.

"I'm going somewhere else—away from you. Don't follow me," Maggie said firmly, sweeping past him.

Lance turned and hurried after her. "Maggie!"

People looked at him and he pretended they weren't there.

"Maggie, wait!"

She disappeared around the side of the boat and he caught a glimpse of her red dress on the lower level before a door shut. Lance jumped down the steps and banged open the door, startling her, and kicked it shut behind him. A cursory glance around told him they were in the bar area, crates of beer, wine, and champagne littering the floor around them. Maggie's cheeks were blotchy, eyes red and swollen with makeup smeared around them.

Two bartenders stood frozen with alcohol in their hands. Lance glowered at them and jerked his head toward the exit. They exchanged a look, glanced at Maggie, and bolted from the room.

Sounding disgusted, Maggie muttered, "Unbelievable. You could be a rapist or a killer and they just left me here with you."

"I'm Lance Denton."

She rolled her eyes. "You are so full of yourself. As if everyone knows you. As if that makes you a good person."

"It seems to be working well enough so far. We need to talk." He crossed the room to her.

Maggie stumbled over a wadded up towel on the floor in her haste to get away from him. She turned her back on Lance, but not before he saw the devastation darkening her eyes. "Go away, Lance. I don't want to talk to you right now. I want to be left alone."

"I didn't even say anything," he cried, swinging her around to face him.

"You didn't have to. Pretty sure your face said it all." She yanked her arm away.

Maggie's face said a lot as well. It said she was hurt, and worried, and scared. And angry. She was definitely angry.

Helplessness coursed through him. Lance didn't understand how something that made him happy could also make him feel trapped.

"You can't do this anymore, can you?" Her eyes demanded the truth. "You're not made for relationships. You told me from the start—you don't want to love anyone. You want freedom, and space, and variety. Admit it, Lance. Admit that you're too scared, admit that you're a coward."

Frustrated, Lance tried to explain, knowing his words wouldn't come out right, her ensuing expression saying the same. "This is hard for me. We're young, and you want forever. You ask too much of me."

"I'm not asking for forever. I'm asking for now, and even that seems to be too much."

Sighing, he faced the closed door. There was a wall between them. It was always there, sometimes smaller than others, sometimes almost gone, but there. When he opened up to her last year, it fell away, and then it came back with a vengeance when he realized what he'd done, what he'd given her. Lance had slowly felt the wall being reconstructed, stronger and thicker than ever. Maggie had all the good parts of him, but that didn't eradicate all the faults she got along with them.

"I tried to tell you."

"You did. And you also kept telling me to give you a chance anyway."

He turned around, offering a sardonic smile. "What can I say? I'm a jerk."

"Only you're not, or you don't have to be." She swallowed, averting her sad eyes.

Numbness coated him, making the scene, her words, making it all seem surreal. Was it really happening? Were they breaking up? Why didn't he feel anything if they were?

"I feel trapped," Lance confessed. "By you, by what I feel for you."

Maggie stared at him, slowly nodding. "Relationships shouldn't be that hard. You shouldn't have to fight to want to be in them."

Lance's heart was being severed in two—one part Maggie's, the other selfishly his.

"What's changed since last month, when you wanted me to stay with you?"

"I don't know." Lance rolled his shoulders, weariness dragging them down. "This feels like a dream. A really good one, but still a dream." He rubbed his face, dropping his hands to stare at her through bleak eyes. "Dreams always end."

Her voice was sharp as she asked, "Do you want to break up?"

"I don't . . . I don't know," he said again. It felt wrong to say that. Maggie deserved a definitive answer, but Lance didn't know what he wanted. The thought of being without her made him sick, and the thought of continuing to be with her brought on undeniable panic.

"We'll take a break. I'll go back to Iowa, you'll stay here. When I come back, we can decide if we want to stay together or not. If that's what you want." Maggie's words were matter-of-fact, but her hands shook, and there was a quiver to her lower lip.

Lance nodded, reprieve burning through him.

Maggie saw it, stiffening as pain slashed her features, and then rushed from the room.

THE SUN WAS barely up when Lance decided he couldn't stand being away from her a second longer. The apartment he'd once shared with Mitch was now his, Mitch long gone from the show and his life. Lance could afford a bigger, nicer place, but he liked the smallness of it, and how it made him feel safe. It was also close to Maggie's.

Maggie spent most nights with him, and last night without her had resulted in him not sleeping and instead pacing the apartment, regretting every stupid thing he'd done or not done, said or didn't say. He couldn't lose her. Lance loved her, and whatever else he did or did not know, he knew that. Clarity was a bitch that way. It liked to come forth when it was too late.

Clothes rumpled, hair sticking up, and tired to the point that he felt drugged, Lance stumbled down the stairs to Maggie's. He knew Judith would be pissed at his early visit, but he didn't care. Shivering in the cool morning air, he fisted his hand and banged on the door.

Judith answered it, her groggy eyes flaring to angry wakefulness as they came to rest on him. Her blond hair was flat on one side and she wore a black robe. "What are you doing here so early?"

"Maggie," he croaked. "I need to see Maggie."

She pressed her lips together, looking older than her years without the camouflage of makeup.

"Judith, come on. Let me see her. I couldn't sleep last night. I need . . . I need to see her."

"You broke up with her."

"No. I don't know." Lance grabbed his hair and pulled. "We . . . a break. It was supposed to be a break, not a breakup."

Her expression said there was little difference between the two.

"Can I come in?" Lance looked around her. "Maggie," he shouted. "Maggie, I need to talk to you!"

Judith clapped a hand over his mouth and snapped, "Shut up. You're going to wake up the whole apartment building."

Lance jerked his head away from her touch. "Let me in, Judith."

"She isn't here."

"What do you mean, she isn't here? Where is she? When is she coming back?" Desperation pressed on his chest, called him a fool.

Judith sighed and opened the door. "Come in."

Fear kept him frozen in place. If Judith was being nice to him, it meant something bad.

"Come on. It's cold out." She stepped back, closing the door after him. "Want some coffee?"

Lance stared at her.

Judith looked over her shoulder as she walked toward the kitchenette and shrugged, starting a pot of coffee. The sound of percolating coffee erupted, the scent of the brew taking over.

He looked around the apartment, searching for signs of Maggie, and not surprised to find none. The only room that had any of her in it was her bedroom. He strode down the hallway, ignoring Judith as she said something to him, and flung open the door. Lance swayed, the doorframe holding him upright when his knees gave out.

"She left late last night, after the party," Judith said quietly from behind.

It didn't seem possible that her citrus scent could already be absent from the room, but it was. Lance couldn't smell her. His eyes burned as he took in the room that housed most of Maggie's things and yet seemed empty. Her clothes were gone, some of her books. Her favorite pair of earrings were missing from the dresser top on which she always left them. They were silver butterflies with her birthstone. Lance had gotten them for her on her birthday last year.

"She'll be back in Iowa by now."

Lance barely heard her.

His heart was gone, in Iowa with a hurting Maggie. As the shock wore off, purpose took over. He would go after her. He had to get to Maggie and convince her to come back, that he'd been wrong, and he didn't want or need a break. His chest hurt with each lungful of air he took, his pulse set at an impossible speed. He had to get Maggie back. Lance couldn't function without her.

He shoved past Judith, storming for the door.

"Don't go after her, Lance," Judith called after him. "Let her be for now. Lance!"

Nails dug into his wrist and he looked down, surprised to see Judith's hand on him.

"Look at me," she commanded.

His eyes lifted to hers.

"Give her time to think, and do the same."

"I don't need time to think," Lance said thickly.

Judith dropped her hand and gave him a knowing look. "You do, or you two wouldn't have decided to pause things. I know you love her and she loves you, but you're both teenagers. You have many, many years to fall in and out of love. If things are meant to work out for you and Maggie, then they will. But for now, go home, get some rest, and let Maggie do the same."

Frustration and fear hardened his jaw. "You don't like me. You've never liked me. I'm sure hearing about us taking a break was the best news you've had in months. Of course you're going to tell me to give her time. You don't want us together."

Judith shook her head, an amused look on her face. "Do you honestly think I care that much whether you're together or not? I warned you both, neither of you listened. Whatever happens is on the two of you.

And . . . I've seen how you and Maggie are with one another. Maybe I was wrong about you."

Lance laughed bitterly. "And maybe you weren't."

She'd said he was like his mother. He left the apartment and staggered toward the ocean. Lance knew it was true. No one's love had been enough for her, and yet she still kept wanting it. Never satisfied, never completely happy. She hurt the ones who loved her and she made sure they kept loving her anyway. His mother destroyed herself.

The wind was cold and welcome. Hands in the pockets of his jeans, Lance hunched his shoulders and stared into the water, wondering if she once stood where he was, wondering what she thought, who she was hurting at the time, if she loved his father. If she loved him.

He loved Maggie.

Love wasn't enough.

Love was a cruel joke.

Lance went back to the apartment Maggie helped decorate. He felt her there as he hadn't in her own room. His eyes tripped over the blue blanket she snuggled under as they watched movies. Lance knew the refrigerator had two gallons of the chocolate milk she loved. There were countless framed pictures of them around the place. He sat at the table, resting his elbows on it and holding his head. She'd already been with him all the time. Why had he freaked at the thought of her staying with him?

He took a hot shower, placing his palms to the shower wall as he hung his head. Water streamed over his face and body but all he felt was emptiness, heavy and black. Gray pajama pants on, he took the blanket from the couch and flung himself on the bed, grabbed the pillow she used, and hugged it to him. He closed his eyes and thought of Maggie, aching for her warmth, her smile.

Lance called her the next day, but she wouldn't talk to him.

He went to a friend's house and got drunk.

Five days later it was the same.

Lance wasn't eating, he wasn't sleeping. Life revolved around heartache and booze.

This was what you wanted. Now deal with it.

Two weeks went by.

Judith checked on him and he blew up at her, guaranteeing another visit would not be happening.

Half insane as he was, Lance bought a ring. It was simple and lovely, like Maggie. Silver band, heart-shaped diamond. He didn't know why he bought it. He was listlessly walking downtown when it caught the light of the sun in the jewelry store window and momentarily blinded him. He didn't know what he was going to do with it. Ridiculously enough, it made him feel closer to Maggie.

MAGGIE—2010

"IT'S WEIRD TO be back here," Lance muttered as they entered Maggie's childhood home. "And nice," he added at her look.

Maggie's mom had stopped over a few days ago and personally invited Lance to accompany Maggie to the Smiley house for a meal. Maggie thought it was sweet of her, and suspicious. Her mother only offered an innocent smile and went on her way, leaving a bemused daughter in her wake.

She led the way through the hall, the scents and sounds she associated with home present and heartwarming. It was a noisy, eclectic living space that always smelled like food of some kind and was never without racket.

"My parents are acting weird about this whole thing."

"How so?"

"I don't know. They act like . . . they like you or something."

Lance laughed. "How blasphemous of them."

"I know." She smiled. "How dare they be sensible about the whole thing?"

"Parents."

Nora and her two boys were in the kitchen, her sister slim and trim with a pink blouse and cream skirt, red hair side-parted and sleek. She looked from Lance to Maggie, and then turned to her redheaded six-year-old twins. "Nick and Nolan, say hello to Aunt Maggie and Lance."

One of the twins—horrible aunt that she was, Maggie could never remember who was who—blinked his brown eyes at Lance. "Are you Aunt Maggie's boyfriend?"

Lance glanced at Maggie. "I am definitely a boy, and her friend. She wishes I was her boyfriend."

Maggie scowled at him and he shrugged, looking unconcerned by her ire.

The other boy wiped an arm across his face, smearing chocolate on it.

"That one looks like you did on your second cheat day," Lance commented.

Maggie laughed and flicked Lance's ear.

"Ow." He clapped a hand over his ear and bumped her shoulder with his.

"Come on, boys, let's get washed up for dinner." Nora paused by Maggie. "You look nice."

Maggie blinked. "Oh. Thank you."

"Lance," she greeted.

"Nora."

Maggie frowned after her sister. "Everyone's being strange. Mom and Dad must be in the dining room. Come on."

As she was about to step into the dining room, expectant smile in place, Lance swung an arm around her waist and maneuvered her back to the hallway. "Maggie, there's something you should know."

Maggie's smile faltered when she looked at him. His expression was serious, and that worried her. "What is it?"

Lance hesitated. "It's about your sister," he said slowly.

"What about my sister?" she demanded, fear rushing up her throat.

She knew. She already knew what he was going to say. The truth was finally going to come out about her sister, and Lance, and how he came to be in Iowa, and she didn't want to know it. It was interesting that the image that popped to her mind was of Lance and Nora in each other's arms, making out, or worse, having sex. *That's* what she feared. Out of all the possible scenarios that could have flittered through her mind, only that one did.

Lance interlocked his fingers and held them to his mouth, looking at her and away. "I wasn't going to take the job."

"What?"

What did that mean? He took the job to get closer to her sister, and they ended up having a one-night stand? Where was he going with that? Why was her brain stuck on them having sex?

"Does Ken know?"

His eyebrows lowered. "Ken? Who's Ken?"

"My sister's husband," she screeched, sounding insane—the present tick under her eye supported that likelihood. "If you're going to do something like that, you should at least know who your actions are affecting."

Lance clapped a hand over her mouth. "Be quiet," he warned, looking around them. "Are you going to be quiet?"

She glared at him, tempted to bite his hand. She jerked her head in consent.

He slowly removed his hand. "Why would Kevin—"

"Ken," Maggie bit out, scowling at him.

"Whatever! Why would he need to know about any of this?"

"Why indeed?" She rolled her eyes. "I thought you agreed to come here because you wanted to help me, or even less appealing, but more likely, because you wanted me on your show. You really did it to get close to my sister? Is that it?"

As soon as the words left Maggie's mouth, she heard the fallacy in them. Lance would never do something for someone else out of the goodness of his heart, not even her. His heart wasn't that good. Everything he did, he did because he got something out of it. She should have realized that sooner.

"What the hell are you talking about?" he shouted, throwing up his hands.

"Like you don't know!"

"I don't know! I know I'm trying to tell you something and you're talking out of your ass!"

Their faces were close enough that the piercing blueness of his eyes was in full effect, breaking through all the layers around her heart to smash it. He could do that to her with one look. Right then, Maggie could kiss him, or kill him. Either would make her happy.

She stepped away, sniffing. "I do not talk out of my ass."

"Everything okay?" Maggie's mom asked as she appeared in the hallway beside Maggie, looking between the two of them.

"Yes," Maggie said at the same time Lance said, "No."

She nodded, her expression not changing. "Okay. Dinner's ready, so don't be too long. Baked chicken doesn't taste as well cold. It gets all slimy and curdled." Maggie's mom shuddered.

And then she was gone.

Lance stared after Jennifer Smiley. "It's like she has selective hearing. I thought only kids and husbands had that."

"No, mothers have it too," Maggie's mom called from the other room.

Maggie gestured to him and hissed, "What are you blathering on about anyway? Just spit it out already so I can go not enjoy dinner with my family."

Lance's jaw tightened and he spoke slowly, as though fighting for calm. "If you'd be quiet for one second, I'd explain."

Maggie crossed her arms and tapped her left foot. "Okay. I'm quiet."

"You're not quiet, because you just talked," he said through clenched teeth.

She gave him a pointed look.

"Stop . . . tapping . . . your . . . foot."

Maggie scrunched up her face at him, but went silent.

Rubbing the back of his head, he paced the short hallway, passing by the dining room each time he swung back her way. She knew everyone was watching him through the open doorway, wondering what melodramatic event had transpired between the two of them. She was sure Nora was enjoying it immensely.

Maggie growled at Lance, which, fortunately, made him stop moving.

"Nora, can you come here?" he called, eyes locked on Maggie.

Her frown deepened and she refused to look away from Lance as they waited.

"What is it?" Nora trilled, showing up exactly three minutes later, like she counted it out. And Maggie knew, because Maggie had.

"Like you haven't heard the whole conversation," she muttered.

"Don't be nasty," her older sister scolded. "And it was hard not to hear, with the two of you shouting." Nora turned to Maggie. "And no, we didn't sleep together."

Lance made a sound of disbelief. "You thought I had sex . . . with your *sister*?"

Maggie looked intently at her sister. "How did you know I was thinking that?"

Nora rolled her eyes and brushed hair from her eyes. "You're my sister. I know you. Do you really think I would do that to Ken, or to you?" She looked hurt.

"What do you mean, to me? It's not like Lance and I are dating. Why would I care what Lance does, or with whom? He's single. He can do whatever he wants, with whomever he wants. I don't care," Maggie protested. Loudly. Too loudly.

She glanced at Lance, was struck blind by the contemplative look on his face, and immediately averted her face.

"I begged Lance to work with you," Nora confessed, eyes looking everywhere but at her sister. "That's what he's trying to tell you."

Maggie's mouth went dry. "Why? As some kind of sick joke?" She looked at Lance, and it almost looked like he was apologetic. "Did you guys set this up to have a good laugh at me?"

"I didn't even want to do it," Lance said, his voice dragged down with tiredness.

"Of course not," Nora denied, staring at Maggie. "Why would you say that?"

Maggie jabbed a finger at her sister. "You make fun of me all the time. You constantly compare us, and you always come up better. You like my flaws. They make you feel better. Admit it, you wanted me to stay fat."

"That's absurd," she scoffed, but she quickly looked away.

Maggie frowned. "It is true, isn't it?"

"No. Maybe. But only a little." Nora swallowed, her face red and flustered.

"Why?"

Nora shook her head, her shiny red hair swaying around her shoulders with the movement. She didn't look like she was going to answer, but then she asked, "What am I good at?"

"What do you mean?"

Hands fisted, she snapped, "It shouldn't be a hard question. What am I good at?"

"I don't know," she said slowly, glancing at Lance.

His look said he was staying out of it.

She turned back to her sister. "You're good at exercising."

Nora glared at her. "That's my talent?"

"I'm not sure what else you do!" Frustration sharpened her words.

"Exactly! Because I don't do anything. I'm not good at anything! You have your acting career—or you did, before you decided to shun the world and live in your own dreary one."

Maggie opened her mouth, but the severe look her sister shot her way shut it back up.

"I have no talent. All I have are my good looks, my drive to stay in shape, and my children and husband. That's what my life is made up of. I love my life, I do, but it would be nice to have a talent of some kind."

She looked at Maggie. "Yes, it gave me a small amount of pleasure when you gained weight, but the pride I feel that you're getting in shape outshines any petty envy. I truly am happy that you're getting healthy." Nora's tone was sincere, as was her expression.

"And what does he have to do with it?" She jerked her head in the direction of Lance.

"I didn't ask him to help out of spite, or for whatever reason you think I did. I did it because . . ." She hesitated, looking at Lance before redirecting her gaze to Maggie. She stepped closer and lowered her voice. "Like I said before, I did it because I knew, if anyone could motivate you, it would be him. And, well, he's the guy."

Maggie swallowed as she looked into her sister's green eyes. She refused to look at Lance, but she felt him nearby, watching her. "I don't know what you mean."

Nora gave her a chastising look. "Yes. You do. He's the *guy*."

She shook her head, denying what she knew in her heart. What she'd always known, since she was a fifteen-year-old girl awed by the beauty and charisma of a sixteen-year-old boy.

Her sister wrapped her arms around her, squeezed her tight, and whispered in her ear, "I wanted you to see him again. Just once—one last time to either push him away or pull him close. You've never been as happy as you were when you two were in love. I see glimpses of it now. Do what your heart says, even if it disagrees with your head. Your head is smart, but it isn't always right."

Nora straightened, brushing hair from Maggie's forehead. The gesture was kind, as were her eyes.

Maggie jabbed a finger at her sister, voice firm as she told her, "Don't call me Bacon anymore, unless it's Turkey Bacon, which is all I'm allowed to eat."

She smiled. "You got it. Come eat soon. Like Mom said, the food's getting cold."

Her sister quietly walked from the hallway.

Maggie wiped the back of her hand across eyes that were damp, her lower lip trembling as she waited for Lance to either leave or speak. He spoke.

"When your sister called and asked me to take the job, I said no. Because I wanted to see you. Because I knew you wouldn't want to see me."

She looked at Lance's blurry image and blinked him into focus.

He watched her, dark eyes unveiled to show all the emotions he generally hid. "I don't think," he said slowly. "You are aware how much you really meant to me."

"I know you loved me as much as you knew how. You told me," she whispered hoarsely, her arms crossed as though to protect herself from her own heart.

"I did love you," Lance said in a low voice. "But you have no idea how much. I didn't even know it until it was too late. And I'm sorry about that. When—" He faltered, took a breath. "When you were hospitalized, I sat in the waiting room, crying and pacing. Begging. Praying. I knew I wouldn't get to see you. I knew it didn't make a difference if I was there or not, but I had to stay. I had to know you were okay. I didn't leave the hospital at all that night."

Maggie's eyes shot to his face, frozen by the stark pain she saw in the lines and edges of his features.

"That's all I wanted—for you to be okay. And that was how I knew how much I loved you. I couldn't be selfish with you anymore. As soon as I knew you were going to be all right, I left." Lance rubbed his eyes, revealing a sardonic smile when he dropped his hands.

Maggie splayed her fingers, palms down, and studied them.

"Judith found me in the waiting room early the next morning, told me everything was going to be okay with you. Gave me some words of advice."

"What did she say?"

"Basically, that I was toxic for you, and if I cared about you in any way, I'd never try to see or talk to you again." He shrugged, averting his gaze. "So I left." Lance took a deep breath, the stricken look on his face crushing any lingering uncertainties Maggie had about her feelings for him.

She loved him, and she didn't know if she'd ever stopped.

"I have to tell you this. I know it is years too late and it doesn't change anything—we had our time together and it's passed, but—I have to say this, at least once, okay?"

She jerked her head, swallowing hard.

"I ruined you. I ruined you, and I can't take that back," he whispered hoarsely. Eyes filled with regret, mouth a slash of self-recrimination across his face.

Lance cupped her jaw, and Maggie placed her hands over his. His thumbs lifted to her cheeks, brushed across them like they had the power to heal past misdeeds. Maggie's fingers tightened on his, pressed his palms closer, held him so that he couldn't let go, not that time.

"After it was over, I never thought I could miss someone the way I missed you. I didn't think I was capable of caring that much. When we broke up, I was shredded, but I was able to deal with it because I could at least still see you. I was still working with you.

"I did a lot of bad things after that, all to prove to myself and to anyone that was paying attention, that I didn't need you, that I'd never loved you, and that I was okay without you. It was all a lie. I ruined you, Maggie, but you ruined me too." His hands dropped from her face.

Tears burned her eyes. Maggie looked down as they made themselves known, sliding across her cheeks as proof of a love once known, and never forgotten, no matter how briefly it was theirs to hold. She nodded, her throat thick, and moved away from Lance. His words echoed through her head, all the things she'd wanted to hear at one time. He was right—they'd ruined one another.

Maggie met his eyes, saw the pain she knew was mirrored in hers. For something that occurred so long ago, it felt the same as a fresh wound.

"I'm sorry," she whispered.

"For what?" He swallowed, dropping his gaze.

"I gave up on you."

Lance laughed and shook his head. "You had to. I didn't give you a choice."

"When you love someone," she said in an uneven voice. "You don't give up on them, no matter how justified it is. I could have tried better to understand. To be there for you in some capacity, even if it was only as someone who'd once loved you."

"You hated me." The rawness of his expression told Maggie he'd never gotten over her saying that to him, and that hurt her.

"I always loved you, Lance," Maggie confessed, conviction filling and lowering her voice.

Lance took a ragged breath of air. "I always loved you too, Maggie."

I love you now, her head and heart whispered. But what she said was, "We were idiots."

A sad smile touched his lips. "We were young."

"We're not anymore."

"No. Well," he amended. "I hope we're not idiots anymore."

Then he smiled, and it was like the first time he smiled at her, over a dozen years ago, the smile her soul felt, and reciprocated. It was sweet, and hopeful, and full of insecurities and arrogance. It was Lance.

"Why did you really decide to do this, become a personal trainer?"

The smile faded and Lance looked down. "I told you."

"You did, but there's more to it, right? You did it . . ." Maggie swallowed as he met her gaze. "You did it because of me."

"Not because of you. For you. Call it penance, or a need to understand, but yeah, when I decided what I wanted to do with my life, you were in the back of my head."

Maggie reached for him and Lance crushed her to him, holding her so tightly it hurt to breathe. She didn't think about the future, or what his departure would do to her. Maggie refused to dwell on anything outside of that hug, and the way she cherished his warmth and strength, the way Lance held her back, like she was fragile and precious to him.

"Thank you," she said in a wobbly voice.

"It wasn't like I did it for free," he gently teased.

"Thank you," Maggie repeated.

Lance held her closer. "You're welcome."

"It's about time," her dad exclaimed good-naturedly from one room over. "We're starving in here!"

They pulled away, Maggie laughing as Lance smiled.

"We should eat before the food gets cold," Lance whispered.

"It's probably already cold," she whispered back.

"We should go in there before one of them comes out for us—again."

"Please do," Maggie's mom called.

It felt natural to hold hands as they entered the dining room, and when they sat down beside one another, everyone pretended like they hadn't been listening in on the entirety of their conversation, voices loud and exuberant as they talked about nonsensical matters.

With the dim lighting, blush-toned walls, candlelit meal, and happy chatter, Maggie enjoyed her family, and Lance.

LANCE—1998

IT WAS A month before she called him.

Lance was watching an episode of their show, that in itself proof that he had issues. Seeing Maggie onscreen helped, and made him miss her more. Cold pizza sat half-eaten in a box on the couch next to him. He scratched his jaw stubble, not sure when he'd last shaved, or showered.

Not getting many phone calls those days, at first the shrill sound of the ringing phone confused him. When it sank in what the noise was and that it could be Maggie on the other end, Lance dove for it, banging the receiver against his mouth.

"Hello?" he answered, his heart pounding, hands shaking.

"Hi." Her voice was soft.

Lance tightened his grip on the phone, closing his eyes. "Hi."

"How have you been?" Maggie whispered the words, but he felt the scarring of them all the way to his core. Even hearing her voice hurt.

"Not good," Lance said. A part of him, the light and energy and joy, was gone without Maggie.

He heard the sad smile in her voice as she replied, "Me either."

"What have . . ." He swallowed, throat dry. "What have you been doing?"

"Just hanging out with my family, mostly. Getting all my schoolwork finished for the year." Maggie paused. "Did you see the article on the show in TV News?"

"No. I've been . . . busy." Busy drinking, trying to forget what he was missing, moping around, obsessing over Maggie. Busy. "What did it say?"

"Oh, you know, the usual. You're charming. Tabitha is beautiful. I'm . . . not so beautiful but a truly gifted actress."

Lance's pulse tripped. Over the years, instead of getting used to the media, Maggie resented it more and more. She gave it too much authority over her as a person.

"It didn't say that."

"No." Maggie sighed. "But it was there, between the lines. It's always there."

"You're beautiful," he said brokenly, fervently, picturing her expressive eyes, porcelain skin, and fiery hair. She was uniquely beautiful, and that was better than being a copy of somebody else's beauty, like Tabitha. There were lots of blonds with blue eyes, and only one Maggie.

"Thank you. I needed to hear that. I needed to hear your voice," she added.

"Come back," he pleaded. "I am a wreck, Maggie. This was a horrible idea. Please come back. I didn't want this."

She didn't answer for a long time. "But you did, whether you want to admit it or not. You did. I'll come back in another month, and we can talk then." Her voice shook.

Anger pulsed through his veins. Lance slammed a fist against the pizza box and it toppled over to land on the floor. "This is bull shit and you know it. You're trying to punish me for having doubts."

"No," she insisted in a ragged voice. "I'm trying to give you space so you don't have those doubts anymore."

Lance didn't know what to say to that. His throat worked, but no sound came forth.

"Goodbye, Lance."

No 'I love you'. Just a goodbye and then a dial tone.

Lance called her on her eighteenth birthday. She answered, but was distant and the phone call ended up making him feel like they were more strangers than boyfriend and girlfriend. Did it really only take weeks of separation to fall out of love? Was that what was happening? And if it was, what did that say about them?

Maggie called on his nineteenth birthday, a few weeks after the first time she called. Lance didn't answer the phone. He finished styling his hair in the bathroom as her voice played from the answering machine in the living room. Lance's image was pale and hollow-eyed. It felt like they'd already broken up. He'd needed her, and she'd stayed away. Maggie broke his heart and she didn't even know.

Lance turned from the mirror, erased the message, and left.

Donovan Randolph had been Lance's friend since they were four and their dads decided to combine their solo lawyer firms into 'Denton and Randolph'. Short and stocky, Donovan had a blindingly white smile that could get him any girl and piercing green eyes set in a mocha-toned face that worked to help his boyish appeal. Lance was in wonderment of him on a routine basis.

The party was going strong when Lance got to Donovan's, the deck and pool area cramped with people. Richard Randolph's house was three levels of gray-blue siding with large windows. A glance through one of them showed people dancing and talking, most of the space taken over by teenage bodies. Lance's eardrums thrummed with bass and drums as he moved down the walkway to the back of the house and climbed the steps to his birthday celebration. Lanterns swung from the railing of the deck and lit up the night.

Donovan spotted him immediately, saying something to the girl beside him before heading for him. His green eyes wavered between humor and concern. "Happy Birthday, and for the record, you look like shit."

Lance gave him a dark smile. "Celebrating without the honored guest? Tacky." He took Donovan's beer and slammed it, wiping an arm across his mouth.

"Dude, really?" Donovan motioned to the empty cup Lance returned.

"Didn't you know that this is what happens when you accidentally fall in love?" he questioned, gesturing to his face.

"I don't want to fall in love if I'll end up looking like you."

"Most people would love to look like me."

"Yeah, well, not me. I'm good." Donovan turned as a cheer erupted. A girl was in the process of removing her bra and panties, dancing close to the edge of the pool.

"Shit. I really don't want to make her stop, but if she takes off her bra and underwear, then the next move is to jump in the pool." He looked at Lance. "My dad said no one is to use the pool—he doesn't want anyone to get hurt, adding that he is out of town and knows nothing of this party, should it get out of hand. I said what good is his profession to me if it can't even make a few tickets disappear? He didn't find that funny."

Lance grinned. "I can't imagine why."

The sound of a body hitting water followed his words, and with a groan, Donovan took off, waving his arms and yelling that the next person to get in the pool was going to get kicked out. Someone stepped forward and shoved him into the water, laughter and shouts drowning out Donovan's curses. The naked girl wrapped her arms around his neck and he quieted, allowing her to kiss him.

Lance shook his head and strode for the bar. He needed a beer.

Hands covered his eyes, and for one stunning moment, he thought it was Maggie. The perfume reached him, and then the voice, and the tiny hope died.

"Guess who."

"Tabitha." Lance heard the disappointment in his voice. He took a deep drink of the sweet and bitter beer and faced her.

Her hair was up in a high ponytail, a cutoff purple shirt showcasing her slim waist, and tight blue jeans accentuated the long limbs they covered. She shrugged. "Happy Birthday."

He nodded, finishing the beer in two long swallows. "Best birthday ever," he lied.

"I haven't seen you much since the yacht party. How are things with you and Maggie?" she questioned, leaning her back against the railing.

"Why?" he growled, getting another beer.

Tabitha's thin eyebrows lifted. "I take it things are not going well."

"Again, why?"

She looked at her fingernails. "Just making conversation. Isn't that what friends do?"

Lance swung around to put his face next to hers. He stared into her blue eyes. "We are not friends."

Her face scrunched up and she stomped to the bar. Drink in hand, Tabitha spun on her heel and glared at him.

"How did you get invited to this anyway?" he asked, watching her with hooded eyes.

Tabitha didn't answer until the beer was gone. Making a face, she got a second. "I hate the taste of beer."

"Then why are you drinking it?"

"Because I want to," she snapped, emptying the beer and going for another. "Donovan's dad knows my mom. They dated in high school or something. I was a pity invite."

"Don't you think you should slow down?"

Tabitha chugged the beer, swaying on her feet as she lowered it. "Don't you think you should catch up?"

The challenge was clear, and after a second of consideration, Lance accepted.

"My boyfriend dumped me yesterday," Tabitha slurred some time later. They were on a bench tucked away in a corner, the party alive around them.

"I don't think I have a girlfriend anymore." Lance dropped his head back and stared at the starry sky.

"How can you not know that?"

He slowly turned his head and found Tabitha staring at him.

"He cheated on me." She blinked her eyes and the momentary sadness he'd seen in them was gone. "They always cheat on me. What's wrong with me?"

"You're a bitch," Lance told her, and then went still. He hadn't meant to say that out loud.

Tabitha's scowl turned into a smile and she laughed, facing forward. "That I am."

"Ready for another?" Lance straightened on the seat and tried to stand, his legs uncooperative. "I think my legs are drunk."

Giggling, she put an arm around his waist. "I think that means it's time to stop drinking, which means you should keep drinking. Come on, birthday boy, tonight is not the night to make good decisions."

"It isn't?" Lance asked, swaying on his feet.

Tabitha didn't answer, holding him up as he tried to hold her up. They staggered toward the party, both getting another drink. Lance could barely stand, arms resting along the railing so he didn't fall on his face. Tabitha wasn't much better, her feet moving forward and back of their own accord. She laughed, and even though Lance had no idea what she was laughing at, he laughed as well.

The rest of the night became a blur of alcohol, Tabitha, and darkness.

MAGGIE—2010

AS SOON AS she stepped into the kitchen, she was awarded a stunning smile. Hair unkempt, clothed in a worn shirt and shorts, Lance couldn't have looked better if he was in a suit. Maggie swallowed thickly, feeling the smile in her heart. She was going to miss his smiles.

"Good morning, Maggie," he greeted.

"Good morning, Lance."

"You look nice."

Face reddening, Maggie nodded in thanks. Deciding to wear a legitimate outfit instead of workout clothes, she'd dressed in a pale pink sundress and kept her hair down.

"You don't," she joked weakly.

Lance laughed. "I had a late start this morning. I didn't sleep the greatest last night."

"Oh?" She strove for a casual tone, but the way she intently stared at him ruined it. "Why is that?" Had he spent the night fearing the upcoming day, like she had?

"When you date someone, and things start to go bad, you can feel the end coming. You can fight it, pretend it isn't happening. You can even delay it, for a while." Lance's smile turned sad. "Not so much with us. The end is abysmally clear. It's our last day together. What would you like to do?"

Her throat tightened and she hid her expression as she turned from where Lance sat on a barstool at the counter. Maggie slowly poured herself a mug of coffee, staring at the dark brown liquid as it flowed into the cup. Her nerves were out of sorts and emotions threatened to turn her into an incoherent mess.

"When does your flight leave?" she asked with her back to Lance.

"I have to be at the airport by six."

Maggie's eyes flew to the clock on the stove. They had less than ten hours left. She blinked as tears slammed to the surface. Taking a deep breath, she turned to face him. He'd moved to stand nearer to her, yet stayed out of reach. His blue eyes were dark, his naturally full mouth a thin line. She looked at Lance, unable to picture her life without him once more.

"This isn't goodbye," he said softly. "We can visit each other. You can come to Ohio or I can come to Iowa. We're friends now, right?"

They both knew when Lance left, it would be the second, and final, end for them. His tone said he didn't believe the words he said. Maggie's expression said the same. It would be too hard to remain friends, however distantly. Friendship with Lance would never be enough for her.

"And I'll see you next month, at the fundraiser," he continued, his voice getting thicker the more he talked. "You're my date." He offered a weak smile.

"This feels like we're breaking up all over again," she told him, trying to tease and failing. Her tone was too serious, too truthful.

"It feels twenty times worse." Lance opened his arms. "Come here."

Maggie went to him without hesitation, wrapping her arms around his torso as she tightly pressed her face against his collarbone. Lance's chin rested on her forehead, his arms banded over her back. She closed her eyes and reveled in him, wanting to hug him right into her soul.

"Thank you for forgiving me. I know I was here to help you, but you helped me too. I needed this time with you."

"I needed it too," she confessed, gripping him harder. Needed him, still needed him. Always would.

She'd let go of regret, hurt, and anger. Maggie accepted herself. None of it would have happened without Lance. Nora was right—Lance was the guy. Her sister had meant it romantically, but it was more than that. He'd opened Maggie's eyes to how he viewed her, and she'd been able to see herself in a different, better, imperfectly perfect way.

He pressed a hard kiss to her forehead and dropped his arms. "What should we do then, on our last day together?"

Maggie shrugged, desolation making her shoulders heavy. A thought came to her and she brightened, looking at Lance. "I know what we can do."

"What?" he asked warily.

"Have a horror movie marathon, starting with 'Snakes on A Plane'. That'll get you ready for your flight."

"Thanks. Thanks a lot."

Maggie held up her hands. "Just trying to help out."

"Do you even have any scary movies?"

Maggie rolled her eyes and headed for the den. "Do I have any scary movies?" she scoffed. "Wait until you see them all. Think of your collection at the age of sixteen, and then add fourteen or fifteen years to that."

"Must be impressive," he replied, following her.

"And after that, we'll make you some soap."

"Soap," Lance mused, plopping down on the couch in the den.

"Yes. Soap. The stuff that makes it so you don't smell. You wanted to make some. This is sort of your last chance."

He studied her features. "I don't like last chances. It implies an end."

"Everything has to end."

Lance sat up. Head lowered, he looked at his hands. "I don't like ends either."

Maggie put in a movie and moved to sit beside him. "It doesn't matter if you like it or not, that's just the way it is." She grabbed his arm and plopped it over her shoulders, smiling at him when he looked down at her.

"Not always," was his cryptic response.

They watched two movies, Lance with his arm around her and Maggie resting her head on his chest. Then they went to the kitchen and made flourless peanut butter cookies, standing beside each other at the counter as they ate them. It was bittersweet, and ridiculous, and Maggie mourned the upcoming hours. She laughed, and smiled, and teased, and she pretended she was happy when she was really sad.

In the basement workroom a few hours later, Maggie stared at the dozens of essential oils with Lance next to her. Maggie had changed into a stained blue shirt and purple leggings, and Lance hadn't changed out of his grubby clothes from earlier. The cool temperature faded away as she focused on his nearness to her.

"This is my favorite part," she said, glancing at him.

"What, staring at the bottles?"

"Deciding what scents to use."

He studied her face, the ghost of a smile on his face. "Why is that?"

"It's fun to try out new scents, combine different oils and see what happens."

"As long as they don't smell horrid."

"True."

Her fingers itched to touch him and Maggie spontaneously reached up and brushed hair from his forehead. Lance clapped his fingers around her wrist and slowly lowered her hand, gazing into her eyes. She opened her mouth, but words failed her. Lance looked at her in a way that made her pulse react maddeningly. Unspoken truths passed from his eyes to hers, and back again to his.

"What do you recommend?" he murmured, releasing her hand.

"Uh . . . um . . ." Maggie inhaled deeply, trying to think of a response to a question she didn't remember. Shaking her head, she grabbed two random bottles and slapped them into Lance's hand.

He read the labels, looking up with a frown on his face. "Peppermint and lemon?"

Maggie snorted. "No. That won't work. Pick one of those and I'll put the other back."

"Lemon."

"Okay. Good choice." She nodded and leaned forward, tapping her fingers along the bottle caps as she thought. "Let's be daring, shall we?" Maggie chose a bottle.

"Vanilla." He sounded skeptical.

"What's wrong with vanilla?"

"Nothing. It just . . . doesn't sound all that daring. How about . . . orange?"

"You want lemon and orange scented soap?"

Lance tucked a lock of hair behind her ear. "I do."

She shrugged and moved away to catch her breath. "All right."

Maggie grabbed equipment from a shelf and slapped it into Lance's hands. "First step—gloves, goggles, and masks."

"What the hell? I thought we were making soap, not performing some science experiment."

"Soap making *is* a science experiment. We're going to be working with lye. It can burn you, or worse, cause an explosion."

"Explosion?"

"It would be unlikely that that would happen." Maggie gathered necessary tools and set them up on the table in the middle of the room.

"Explosion?"

"It would be a minor one."

Lance grabbed her arm and firmly turned her around. "Explosion?"

Maggie looked at his troubled expression and grinned. "You wanted to be daring, right?"

"Yeah," he said faintly.

"Who knew soap making could be dangerous?"

She went to the freezer and removed a container of goat milk. Maggie then flipped a switch on the wall and a vent turned on, working to keep fresh air circulating through the area. "Over there, near the shelf, are a bunch of tubs of labeled oils. Get out the palm, coconut, olive, and palm kernel."

"You're sexy when you're bossy," Lance said from across the room, eyes trained on her.

Maggie laughed and struck a pose.

Proper gear on, all the needed ingredients and utensils in place, they went to work.

"What happens if we get burned?"

"We put vinegar on the burns."

"And what is the purpose of the lye?" he asked, stirring the pot on the stove as she measured, weighed, and added.

"It acts as a cleaning agent, attracts dirt and oil from the skin."

When the base of goat milk and lye and the combined oils were each between eighty and ninety degrees, they were mixed together. Lance stirred the components until the blend became somewhat thick, and then Maggie added crushed almonds and oatmeal to it once it was removed from heat.

"We have to work fast now. Do you have the molds picked out that you want to use?"

Lance motioned to the table. Not surprisingly, he'd chosen the alien heads.

Smile stretching her face, Maggie began to fill them. "These have to set up in the molds for one to two days, and then it takes four to six weeks for them to cure. I'll bring them to the fundraiser, if that's all right? They should be ready in time."

Lance nodded, watching her as though spellbound.

"It's just soap," she told him.

He raised his head, his eyebrows lowered. "It's not just soap. It's you, being confident, creating things. It's . . . hell . . . it's the most fun I've had in a long time. Almost as good as sex."

She laughed. "I think that nine or ten months of abstinence is messing with your head."

"I think it's the three months with you, actually. The first six months didn't seem all that bad."

Maggie went still, then hurriedly finished with the cleanup. "What time is it?"

Lance checked the watch on his wide wrist. "It's after three. I have time to shower and pack and go."

She started up the stairs, pausing as Lance's words hit her. Her pace was slower the rest of the way, sorrow adding weight to her legs. *You're fine. You've been fine all these years. You'll be fine again.* Except Maggie could no longer be satisfied with half a life, not since Lance showed her all she was excluding herself from. She couldn't not do wonderful things for fear of the not so wonderful things.

Once in the kitchen, Maggie turned to face him. "I want to co-host. Your show," she stated when a frown claimed his mouth. "I want to co-host your show."

Maggie didn't know when the thought transpired, and she didn't really remember at any point thinking that, yes, she would do the show, or even that she wanted to co-host it. But she realized she did. It was an opportunity to do something great, and she had to take it.

Pulse uneven and fast in anticipation of his reaction, she stared at Lance. They could do something wonderful together. It didn't have to be goodbye. Their end could be postponed.

Lance shook his head. "No. I'm sorry, Maggie, but no."

A frown took over her face as her hopes fell. "But . . . you wanted me on your show. Why don't you anymore?"

"Because I don't even know if there's going to *be* a show. And . . ."

Lance rubbed his face. "I don't want you to have a relapse because you can't deal with the media. I don't want you on my show anymore." He dropped his hands. "And I sure as hell don't want you as a co-host. That would be asking for problems." His tone was hard, flints of ice in his eyes.

"I'm stronger now than I was then," she insisted. "Not just my body, but my mind. You know I am."

Lance averted his face, remaining silent.

With a lump in her throat and a sick sensation swirling in her stomach, Maggie slowly nodded. "Okay. Fine. That's your decision. But tell me why, and tell me the truth."

His jaw turned to stone and Lance moved for the exit. "I have to get ready to go."

She let him go, confused and sad.

Maggie took a shower and dressed in a loose shirt and shorts, studying her image in the mirror above her dresser. She felt along her sides and midsection, turning to examine her leg muscles, flexing her arms. She liked her body. It wasn't perfect, but it was hers, and she was taking care of it. Laughing softly to herself, she turned and blanched. Lance stood inside the doorway, hair wet and black, dressed in a green shirt and dark jeans.

He watched her with throbbing intensity in his eyes. "Do you trust me?"

She tilted her head. Did she trust him? Maggie thought of where they'd started, where they'd gone, and where they presently were—all they'd been through to get them to that exact moment. She swallowed, nodding jerkily. Yes. She trusted him.

Relief lightened his eyes, took shadows from his face. He stood taller. "I have my reasons for telling you no. Can you trust me?"

"I do," she said firmly.

"Great. Now that that's taken care of . . ." He grinned like a fiend with a new plaything. "I have forty minutes. We can either have phenomenal sex or we can have . . . meaningful conversation." Lance's mouth twisted around the last words. He set the bobby pin he'd used to unlock the door yet again on a stand that housed a framed picture of Maggie with her mom and dad.

"Bobby pins and lipstick . . . I'm beginning to wonder at your extracurricular activities," she said, looking at the place he'd put the hair accessory.

He sighed. "The jig is up—I'm a robber slash drag queen. Now you know." Lance opened his arms. "Judge away."

Maggie crossed the room to him, her hand outstretched. "No judging. How about you just hold me?" she said softly.

Lance's face contorted with hurt, and then he nodded abruptly.

Situated on the bed with their arms and legs touching, and Maggie's head on Lance's shoulder, they looked at a ceiling and committed the feel of one another to memory.

"About seven years ago, one day my sister showed up here with a cat," Maggie said, Lance's shirt fisted in her hand.

"I thought she was allergic?"

"Apparently only when it comes to having them live with her." Maggie's mouth tipped down, but it quickly melted into a smile. "She thought I needed a pet to cheer me up. I was angry at first, but I took him anyway, mainly because she said if I didn't, the shelter she'd gotten him from was going to put him to sleep."

"No pressure."

"He was the ugliest, meanest cat. He was black and white and his face looked flattened, and he had half of an ear gone from previous street fighting. Anytime I went to pet him, he'd try to bite me. I named him Lance."

A low rumble of mirth traveled up his chest. "I'm flattered."

Maggie's smile faded and her eyes burned. "During the day he hid, but he used to come in my bedroom at night and sleep near my feet. Broke my heart. Lance was scared, but he still wanted love, so he'd slink into my bedroom when he thought I was asleep and wrap himself around me."

"That sounds disturbingly like me."

She laughed. "He started coming out during the day, then he'd follow me around. I'd show him pictures of you and tell him how he was such a better boy than his namesake. He'd sit on my lap and purr and bite me when I got too close." Maggie inhaled deeply. "He healed me, and I healed him. I loved that cat."

Lance's arms tightened around her. "What happened to him?"

Maggie picked at his shirt, closing her eyes. "He got outside one day when I didn't properly close the door. A car hit him. You wouldn't believe how much I cried, all for a hateful cat named Lance."

"I'm sorry, Maggie."

She moved to her elbows and looked down at a face shaded in the darkness sorrow brought. "I cried because I loved Lance and that was a good thing. Even though I ended up heartbroken, and I lost him, I was glad that I'd had him to love. That cat was more cathartic than years of counseling."

Lance flipped them so that Maggie's back was to the bed with him above her. His strong body was aligned with hers, making her yearn for him. He locked his fingers around hers and slid their arms above her head, dipping down to place a kiss upon her forehead. Lance's eyelashes teased her cheek when he pressed the side of his face to hers.

"I bought you a ring—when you went back to Iowa before we broke up," he said against her mouth.

"What?" she choked out, body taut with disbelief.

He moved his face so that their eyes were even and she could see the truth in them. "If I had been crazy enough to propose, would you have said yes? I mean—before I cheated on you with Tabitha."

"Yes," Maggie answered after a pause. "But it would have been wrong."

Lance nodded. "That's what I realized too."

"What did it look like?"

A sad smile claimed his mouth. "It had a silver band with a heart shaped diamond. Tacky, right?"

Maggie's throat tightened. "No."

"I kept it, used to stare at it for hours. It was a symbol of us to me, and I couldn't get rid of it. I eventually lost it, and yeah, I cried over that." Lance's smile faltered and the blueness of his eyes darkened. "You had a cat and I had a ring."

He kissed her, his mouth tasting like the sweet tartness of apples. Maggie let his lips tell her all she wanted to know without uttering a word. His mouth was warm and hard, soft and coaxing. They kissed like they were lovers, like a goodbye could never really keep them apart.

Words blocked her throat and Maggie kept them unsaid. She knew how she felt about Lance—he knew how he felt about her.

Maggie cupped his jaw on either side, the rough edges of it causing tingles in her fingertips. If a day could come, that allowed Maggie and Lance to either toss aside or embrace their broken, flawed love, she would take it. Every day she would take it. He ended the kiss, studying her face with flared nostrils. Eyes sparked with lust and something more, his heart pounded against her chest. Shutters fell over his dark handsomeness, hiding all he felt.

"I have to go." Lance got to his feet and started for the door.

Maggie jumped from the bed and ran, locking her arms around his waist and burying her face against his shirt. She trembled within arms that shook as they held her.

"I don't want to say goodbye. I'm not ready. I'll see you at the fundraiser." Lance swallowed and offered a half-smile when she looked at him. "It's less than a month away and the thought of going that month without seeing you makes my head hurt."

"Are you trying to say you'll miss me?" Maggie smiled, but it was laced with an ache.

"I'm trying not to say it. I'll miss you as soon as I walk out the door, Maggie," he admitted.

They hugged again, it lasting for minutes and yet over too soon. They could say words, make promises. She could say she loved him and Lance would probably say it back. Maggie could say she wanted to try again. Lance could say he'd never hurt her again. Maybe it was all true. But Maggie didn't want to claim certainties in an existence without many, so she smiled and tried not to cry as Lance walked out the door.

After he was gone, Maggie ambled around the house, unsuccessfully searching for pieces of him. She already missed him too, felt the ache where he should be. She ended up in the bedroom Lance used while there. Maggie looked at the bed, once again in its proper spot, and she smiled, though it wobbled and fell. He'd cleaned the lipstick message from the bathroom mirror, but Maggie had asked him to leave it on the basement one. Sometimes a short message was the difference between a positive and a negative outlook.

Her eyes landed on the bed and she frowned, stepping closer. An unmarked envelope lay there, and with trembling fingers, she opened it, staring at the check she'd written Lance to cover the time he'd worked with her. Her hand dropped to her side, the paper falling from it. Her heart grew, added more of Lance to it, until it was brimming with bits and piece of him, and their disjointed path that overlapped one another's. What a stupid thing to do. He needed the money.

Not that much, he seemed to whisper in her head.

LANCE—1999

THE FOLLOWING SEASON, Maggie got Tabitha fired. She told Herman either Tabitha left, or she did. Tabitha was an essential character, but Maggie *was* the show.

Lance didn't say anything as Tabitha walked off the set after doing her final scene as Zoe Clark on 'Easier Said'. She glared at him, and he stared back. Ultimately, it was his fault she was canned. If he hadn't gotten shit-faced drunk and slept with her, Maggie wouldn't have come back early the day after his birthday party to surprise him and instead receive her own unforgettable, unforgivable surprise.

Every day since the day he lost Maggie was like living in hell for Lance. Everyone on the show knew what had happened, but that wasn't what was slaying him. It was Maggie, and how he'd hurt her. Maggie looked at him like he was a stranger. Like they'd never kissed, or touched, or been together. She looked at him like she'd never seen him before, and it broke his heart. He'd thought it was broken before. He'd been wrong.

It was shattered, and it was his doing.

Herman shouted behind him, startling Lance. "Get your ass to my office, Denton!"

He turned around, but Herman was already across the room and in Maggie's face. She was pale, nodding as he went on and on about something. Lance started for them, but a hand pressed to his chest and stopped him.

"Don't," Steven Stephens urged. Steven played Maggie's father and Judith's husband on the show, and the kindness found in his character was genuine. He was the best out of all of them, Maggie excluded.

"He's yelling at her for something that isn't even her fault. I messed things up, not her. It's because of me that she's blowing her lines and not acting as well as she can."

"It is her fault if she can't be professional. What happens outside of the show, even if it involves the people on the show, stays there. She put Herman in a bad spot, giving him an ultimatum like that. If she wasn't such an integral part of the show, I think he would have let her go instead of Tabitha. Viewers are not going to be happy with the loss of Tabitha's character. Maggie will have to wow them to make up for that, and how she's performing lately isn't going to do it."

"It's hard to pretend to love someone you hate," he said dryly, referring to Derek and Cecilia's onscreen romance.

"That's a load of crap."

Lance frowned.

Steven leaned close, his green eyes sad and sympathetic. A lock of brown hair fell over his eyebrow and he shoved it back. "It's hard because she still cares. It'd be easy if she hated you." He straightened and waved. "See you tomorrow."

"See you," Lance mumbled, waiting until Maggie left to walk up to Herman.

Herman's perpetual onion and garlic smell wafted to Lance as Herman glared at him. "I said to meet me in my office!"

"You don't have an office."

"Let's pretend for a second I do!"

Lance looked balefully at the bald, perspiring man.

"You royally messed things up with that girl!"

He closed his eyes. "I know that. Everyone keeps telling me that like I don't know it."

"What you don't know, is that if your act doesn't straighten up, this show is going to tank! Do you want that? Do you want to be unemployed because you don't know how to keep your dick in your pants? Do you want everyone else to lose their jobs because of it too?"

Most days Lance wished there was a volume control on the always shouting man, and that wish was tenfold at the moment.

"I'll do better," he said through clenched teeth.

"You will." Herman nodded. "Or we'll all be looking for new jobs! Act like your job depends on how you perform from now on, because it does." He stomped away, pausing to jab a finger in Lance's direction. "Keep it in your pants! We have two seasons for sure to get through, and then I don't care what you do with it, let it loose on the world for all I care!"

Somewhat concerned about Herman's word choice and apparent views on such things, Lance slowly walked from the building. Once outside, he looked around him like he was lost. The sky was colored in gray clouds, thunder rumbling as he stood there. The door to the house opened behind him, and with a lump in his throat, Lance turned, eyes trained on Maggie.

Lance didn't know how it was possible, but she looked skinnier every season. There were hollows around her eyes and cheeks. He fisted his hands and started for her as she grappled with a box in her arms.

"Maggie," he said, his voice choked and rough.

She looked up, almost dropping the box, and then steadied it as she took the last step to reach the ground. "I'm glad I caught you."

"You are?" Hope filled the two words and he let it take over his mind, wanting so desperately to have her back. "Maggie, please. I messed up, I know that, but this can't be the end for us. Give me—give *us*—another chance. Please."

Lance didn't know when they started, but tears ran down his face, hot and unstoppable. He couldn't breathe, his chest tight, throat dry. He felt sick, and lost, and for the first time in a long time, in control. He understood loss, and grief. Lance was an instrument of his own self-destruction.

"You need help," she said in a quaking voice.

"I know," Lance whispered. "I know that."

"I came home to find my boyfriend in bed with another woman, and a slutty one at that—pretty much the one girl I hate in this whole world, actually." Maggie's voice was quiet, but as piercing as a razorblade. "Why would you ever think I would go back to you after that?"

There was no way to deny it. He did it. He was drunk and confused, yeah, but he still did it.

Maggie pushed the box toward him. "This is yours. I don't want any of it. If I find anything else, I'll let you know. You can keep it, or throw it away." She met his gaze, her normally warm eyes dark and cold. It was like looking into a void. "Please throw it all away."

Lance carefully took the box, staring down at months and months of pictures, gifts, notes. Even her Bon Jovi CD was in the box. Their love was reduced to things, and she wanted none of them.

"My love wasn't enough for you, right? No, not Lance. He always has to see what else is out there. And the thing is—I can't even be that angry with you, because I knew what you were like." She laughed, but it was sour with bitterness. "This is my fault, really."

"No." Lance dropped the box and reached for her, but Maggie yanked her arm away. "This isn't your fault. It's mine. I don't know what's wrong with me. I still—I still love you, Maggie."

"You don't love me!" Eyes wild, she pointed a shaking finger at him. "You don't know what love is. You don't love me," Maggie said in a quieter voice. "Because if you did, you wouldn't have slept with Tabitha Volden, drunk or not."

"I'm sorry," he said, his head lowered. "I'm sorry for what I did."

"Don't apologize for that," Maggie said sharply.

Lance looked up, confused. "Why not?"

"Because that isn't what hurt the most. Not that it doesn't feel like my heart has been ripped from my body, and stomped on, repeatedly, relentlessly, every second of every day, or that every time I see you I feel like I'm going to be sick, but what was worse than finding you with her . . ."

Maggie's throat moved as she swallowed. "What was worse was knowing how easily it could have been avoided, if you'd just . . . I don't know." She shrugged, dropping her eyes to where her nails dug crescent shapes into the palms of her hands. "If you'd just let us be enough. That's why you got scared, right?"

She looked up, shredding him with the grief twisting her features. "You were scared you'd want something else, something better, something more. That's you, that's Lance Denton. You want everything, and even when you have it, you want more."

They stared at one another, Lance with his guilt and Maggie with her blame, and then she walked away.

"How are we going to work like this?" he called after her as she headed for her car.

Maggie looked over her shoulder and gave him a thin smile. "I guess I'll just have to pretend you're someone else, someone better, someone more."

MAGGIE—2010

MAGGIE WAS PROUD of herself. The last twenty-four days she'd been on her own and she'd continued her healthy eating and exercising. It was said to take twenty-one days to form a habit, or break one, and she was confident of her new lifestyle. She could do it, and she could do it the right way.

She was stronger than any eating disorder or self-doubt.

Maggie could have flown, but instead chose to drive the seven-hour trip to the Berryhill Bed and Breakfast located in Agenda, Missouri—a town with under two thousand people in residence. The drive was scenic, reflective, and filled with anticipation. She could feel her heart pounding harder against her chest the closer she got. Maggie liked the smallness of Agenda, quaint shops and old structures lining the streets. Fall was approaching, leaves already showing a turn in color.

The bed and breakfast was set on a corner lot, an emerald green Victorian-style building with a pillared porch and painted windows on the lower level. Maggie parked her car in the designated guest parking behind the house, and with her rollaway luggage trailing behind her, walked to the front to stare. The air was crisp and smelled like autumn—leaves and cinnamon and apples.

"Where are you manners, Maggie? Didn't your parents teach you that staring is rude?"

Maggie slowly turned.

"Unless you're staring at me, then it's encouraged. Stare away."

Lance grinned at her from the sidewalk, clothed in jeans and a hooded black sweatshirt. They'd talked and texted, but it wasn't the same as seeing him. It was insane how fast her pulse got, and the air left her, but she couldn't draw more in, and tears stung her eyes, but she was happy. Maggie threw herself at him, and Lance's arms went around her as they stumbled to the side. The hug was warm and scented like Lance and made her heart sing.

"I brought you something," she said, grudgingly releasing her hold on him.

Lance smiled down at her. "Oh?"

"It's out of this world." Maggie moved for her suitcase, opening it and taking out the little soaps.

Laughing, he accepted the alien headed soaps. "Thank you. I was actually going to ask you about your soap making skills." He took her luggage and walked toward the house.

"What about it?" she asked.

"You said you donate a lot of the soaps you make, and you mentioned kids. Would you be interested in making some for the children's program the benefit is sponsoring?"

"I would love to do that," Maggie told him, stepping through the door of the toasty warm house. It was dark inside, country décor with dominant checkered prints flagging the area, and the smell of fruit and sugar told the tale of recently baked goods. Wood floors and furniture added to the rustic ambience.

"Say, enough to cover the uncashed check you wrote me?"

Maggie paused, facing Lance. "That's why you didn't take the money. Lance, you didn't have to do that. I would gladly make and donate soap, no payment necessary."

"Good. Then you can give me back the check. Kidding." He winked. "Let's find out where your room is and get you settled."

"If you need the money," she began.

Lance quelled her words with a look. "I don't. Things are working out better than I'd hoped. I'll be okay."

"I didn't ask you to donate your services, you know. I went into the arrangement intending to pay you."

"Oh, you will. I just haven't decided how yet."

Maggie was about to demand what he meant by that when they stepped into a kitchen and were greeted by a short, plump, gray-haired woman wearing a long brown skirt and a white blouse with a red apron over it. She wiped her flour-caked hands on the front of the garment and smiled as she approached.

"Hello, Maggie! You're the first of the guests, other than Lance here, to arrive. It's wonderful to meet you. Lance has said a lot about you. I'm Diane." Diane grabbed Maggie by the shoulders and pulled her into a warm, delicious-scented hug.

"You've been talking about me to a stranger?" Maggie loudly whispered after returning the hug and greeting to Diane.

"Stranger?" Diane laughed and took a pumpkin pie from the oven. "I'm his—well, Lance will have to tell you about that."

Maggie frowned at Lance, but he wouldn't look at her.

"Here's your key." Diane took a keyring from a hook on the wall and set it on Maggie's palm. "Room thirty-five, on the third floor. Lance can show you. There will be refreshments and snacks at four in the Leaf Room. Lance knows where that is too. See you then."

Immensely confused, Maggie quietly followed Lance up two sets of stairs. The halls on each floor were wallpapered in pink roses and stripes and lined in white trim. She didn't talk until he set her suitcase before a white door and turned to face her.

"Talk, Lance."

He rubbed the back of his neck, his expression calm even as his eyes stayed away from hers. "About what?"

"Something's going on here. Who is that woman and what do you have to do with her? You're not just a guest to her. Is there really a fundraising dinner? Because I have to say, this is the craziest place I've ever been invited to for one."

"I may not have been entirely upfront with you."

Maggie stared at Lance. "This is the part where you tell me you're insanely infatuated with me, and that you orchestrated all of this—the invitation, the training, me being here now—as a way to make me fall in love with you again, right? Next you'll announce that we're sharing a room and demand payment for your training in endless, mind-boggling, amazing sex." Funny, but that didn't sound all that bad.

"You asked your sister to recommend a personal trainer," he reminded her.

"Don't point out the flaws in my logic."

Lance's mouth lifted in a small smile. "Is that what you're hoping is going on?"

She shoved the key in the keyhole and turned her wrist. "You don't get to ask the questions here, I do."

Maggie swung open the door, stunned by the beauty within and somewhat disappointed that nothing of Lance's was in the room. The room was wrapped in cream and lace from the curtained windows to the huge four-poster bed. Sunshine streamed in through the windows, catching the crystal chandelier to create little rainbows within the teardrops.

"Wow. This looks like Cecilia's room, from the set. Prettier, of course, but similar." She stepped inside and looked at Lance.

"Yeah." He swallowed and looked at his shoes. "I picked out the room. It . . . reminded me of the show, which could be considered unsettling, I guess."

Maggie didn't speak, watching Lance, waiting.

He met her gaze and shrugged. "Diane was my therapist, the one who helped me get my head on straight. She retired a few years back and started a bed and breakfast. I don't really talk to my dad all that often, so she's kind of been my surrogate parent."

"And the dinner is here, why? And how?"

"That's all I'm telling you for now. But there really is a fundraising dinner here tonight. I'll give you time to get ready and come back in an hour?"

She nodded a numb head.

"Oh." Lance turned from the door and said, "One more thing—I'm no longer your employee. Remember what I said before? Run, or submit. You didn't run." He smiled with wicked promise, and then he was gone, leaving her breathless and shaking.

LANCE—2000

"LANCE! HOW GREAT to see you. Heads up—I got a new best friend for this season. She's replacing Tabitha. Remember Tabitha? Anyway, she's starting on the show next week. I just thought I'd let you know because I'm sure you'll want to sleep with her."

The show took its customary two-week vacation over the Christmas holidays and was back in production early January. In the months following their breakup, Maggie had turned into a viper, and he had reacted in kind.

Lance let Jackie finish prepping his hair before looking at Maggie. His eyebrows lowered. She was so thin. What the hell was she doing to herself?

"Wow. I'm back on the set all of two full minutes before you seek me out. Obviously you missed me—not that I blame you." Lance smiled, but it was dark and unfriendly. It was a lot like the smile on Maggie's face.

"I did miss you." She nodded. "Like I miss vomiting, and diarrhea, and any other horrible affliction you can think of. In fact, I feel like I could vomit right now, right here, just from standing near you."

Lance narrowed his eyes and stood up. "Good to know."

Ratings for the show were low, and everyone was feeling it. Attitudes were prickly, although that wasn't the reasoning for Maggie's treatment of Lance. She simply despised him. The remainder of the season had to have an outstanding comeback, or they were done. The chemistry between Derek and Cecilia had gone sour, and the viewers didn't like that.

Maggie tossed a magazine at him. "It didn't take you long to go back to your old ways."

He caught it, a picture of him with three women surrounding him on the front cover. He'd only had sex with one of them, unlike all three of them like the headline implied. He looked up. "It almost sounds as if you care."

"Do I care that my co-star is a whore? Not at all. Why would I care what you do? I'm not your girlfriend anymore, or your babysitter." Maggie crossed her arms and glared at him.

Lance shrugged and offered a wide, fake smile. "If you can't beat the past, might as well embrace it, right?"

"That is a wonderful motto. Sort of like saying it's hard to be a decent person, so why bother?" Her voice was sweet, but Lance knew there were spikes hidden beneath it.

"Hey." Lance grabbed her wrist when she went to walk away.

Maggie stiffened, her mouth trembling for a second before it went back to a hard line.

He frowned, surprised by that. He still felt the ache where she should be, but he couldn't imagine it being the same for her.

"What?" she snapped, trying to pull her arm from his grasp.

Lance tightened his grip. Even her wrist was bonier. "You and I have to work together if this show is going to make it another season."

"Let go of me."

He dropped his hand.

"I'll do my job," Maggie promised. "And you do yours."

Lance's voice was solemn when he said, "You got it."

An hour later they were garbed in full winter gear, clamoring around in the hills like it was zero degree Iowa weather instead of the thirty degrees it really was. The sun was high in the sky, glinting off the snow to blind him if he looked at it in the right spot. The snow was a foot deep, maybe two at the most, and supremely dull to Lance.

"What a rip off," he muttered.

Maggie heard him, glancing over her shoulder as she scaled the uneven terrain. The pink and white stocking cap looked adorable on her, her sharp-boned face glowing against the snow backdrop.

"This snow. This winter. It's a rip off, a cheap imitation," he continued, leaning down to scoop up a handful of the white powder. A light breeze blew it all away.

"Good thing none of this is real then, right?"

Lance stood, staring at her intently. "It was real."

Maggie's cheeks went red and she looked away.

"Ready, Derek and Cecilia?" Herman shouted from where he stood a few feet away. "Let's see what you got, and it better be amazing or we're all fired!"

"Way to be positive," Maggie mumbled.

Lance smiled in spite of himself.

Their eyes met, and it was like the first time they'd ever done a scene together. Lance was mesmerized as he watched Maggie turn into Cecilia, and once again, he felt himself fall a little in love with her. She was breathtaking. Whatever happened with the show, he hoped she continued to act. It would be a travesty if she didn't. Maggie was a natural.

"I haven't seen this much snow in a long time," she said, smiling at him, with her mouth but also with her eyes.

Lance swallowed thickly, feeling his heartbeat take off. "We should take advantage of it."

Maggie's smile widened and Lance used his character to love her in a way he never could. He reached for her, his fingers trailing up the back of her neck to get lost in her thick hair. Maggie's hands gripped his arms as though to push him away—she didn't. Maybe it was the warning in his eyes, or maybe she was merely being professional. Maybe she didn't want him to let her go.

"What are you doing, Derek?" she breathed against his mouth.

"Loving you, Cecilia," he murmured back.

They'd struggled through kissing scenes since the end of their relationship, but that time, there was no stiffness, no anger. There was passion, and desperation, and longing. It was Lance saying he was sorry, and telling her he loved her. It was Maggie remembering her love for him, and maybe even forgiving him, however briefly.

She tasted the same, and better. She felt the same, and even though she seemed frailer, it was better. Maggie smelled like oranges. And better. Lance kissed her in a way he hadn't before—without restraint, without fear, without doubts. Because they were over, and he could give all of himself to someone who didn't want him, messed up as it was.

It was real, and it wasn't. It was them, and it was two fictional characters. Maybe the show was all he got, the only way he could apologize. The only way he could have her. If so, he'd make the most of it. When they were boyfriend and girlfriend, Lance had always felt like they were running out of time, only he didn't know why. It was a panicked, rushed feeling, a limit on what they had. He didn't feel it anymore, because she wasn't his.

Maggie pulled away, eyes wide and filled with tears. "I love you."

She said it sadly, regrettably, but to anyone who didn't know, she said it only with her heart.

Lance felt it then, knowing in his bones that soon there would come a day when he would no longer have any part of Maggie Smiley, not even Cecilia. It made him want to cry.

"I know. And I love you."

Maggie dropped to the ground, startling Lance, and moved her arms and legs up and down.

"We have to take advantage of the snow," she reminded him when he watched her in bemusement.

"Okay. What are you doing?"

"Haven't you ever made a snow angel before?" She paused her movements, looking at him oddly.

"Maybe when I was five."

Maggie sat up, grabbed his ankle, and tugged. Lance lost his balance and landed hard on his elbow, glaring at her. She laughed and tossed up snow in his face.

"You're a bully." Lance wiped the cold substance from his cheeks and nose.

"Lie down and make a snow angel, now, before I beat you up. How's that for being a bully?" She grinned at him.

"What are you going to do, beat me up with kisses?"

"Whatever it takes."

The scene continued on like that—happy, light, loving. And as they stopped filming for the day, it was obvious they'd found something they'd lost. Everyone felt it, moods considerably better than they had been before the holiday break. Lance paused as he left the set, surprised to find Maggie waiting. She was dressed in jeans with a black jacket and matching boots. Her breaths left her in frozen air as she exhaled, eyes shifting to him and down.

"Are you . . . are you waiting for me?" He felt stupid asking it.

"Yes." She nodded, looking at him. "I wanted to ask you something."

Lance squinted his eyes. "Like a trick question?"

"No. A real one."

"Okay." He shrugged. "Go for it."

She turned her head to the side. "I just . . . I wanted to know . . ." Maggie nodded as Steven and Judith walked by, expressions curious as they gazed at the two of them. She waited until they were gone to focus on him. "What you said earlier today—*was* any of it real for you?"

"Why?" he asked brusquely. If he told her the truth, she was hurt. If he lied, she was still hurt.

"I don't know. I have to know, one way or another. Because it felt real at times—most of the time."

Lance studied her pained eyes. "I think . . . I fell in love with Cecilia, and I confused her with you. She's not real. I was in love with a character, someone that doesn't exist."

Even as he lied, he told himself it could be true. If he told himself it enough, he could believe it. Lance was desperate to believe it. And then he realized it didn't matter if he believed it or not, as long as she did. Lies could shatter hearts, but they could also mend them.

Her eyes were large and broken, something beautiful destroyed to ultimately save her. "You're lying. You didn't fall in love with Cecilia, you fell in love with me. Because she is me, and I am her. Tell yourself whatever lies you need, but don't tell them to me."

Maggie always saw through him.

"Then why did you ask me?" Lance frowned, his pulse quickening. "Do you still love me?"

She blinked and averted her face. "I did."

Lance nodded, pretending his heart wasn't stabbed by the fact that she used past tense, even as he'd expected it. "Right. That's what I meant. I fell in love with a character and you fell in love with a lie. Neither were real, so what's it matter?"

Maggie's mouth trembled. She was fighting not to cry. "It was real."

Lance lifted a hand to touch her and thought better of it. "It was real," he whispered, after a long pause.

She swept past him, stopping to repeat, "It was real."

After Maggie was gone, Lance nodded to himself. "It was real."

MAGGIE—2010

THE SOUND OF voices, music, and the clinking of dinnerware led them to the Leaf Room. The room was long and wide, seemingly endless. Across the span of it sat a table lengthy enough to house the dozen or so chairs that graced each side of it. Tin lantern lighting added a romantic flare to the atmosphere. Maggie wasn't sure why it was called the Leaf Room until she looked at the walls. The lower halves of them were plastered in what looked like real leaves in shades of yellow, red, orange, green, and brown.

"Interesting."

Lance followed her gaze. "Very."

He touched her bare back, eliciting a shiver from her, and smiled naughtily. "I find your dress far more so. It provokes countless questions. Are you wearing a bra, how does it stay up without straps? And most importantly, how does it come off?"

The dress was pale green, strapless, and fit her form in a flattering way, making her waist and tummy seem slimmer than they were. Maggie left her hair down, straightening the waves and parting it on the side.

Maggie eyed his suit. Lance looked casually polished in a charcoal gray suit with a black dress shirt. "I wonder the same about your outfit."

Lance laughed and dipped his head close to hers. "I give you permission to find out later."

Face flaming and nerves spiking, Maggie swallowed and turned her attention to those around them. As they made their social rounds, they were greeted by previous co-stars and other performers Maggie knew of, but not personally. She wasn't sad to see that Tabitha Volden was not in attendance.

Catching a glimpse of Judith, she started for her, telling Lance she'd be back in a bit. He nodded, talking sports with Steven Stephens.

"You look beautiful," Judith told her, capturing Maggie in a loose hug. The flowery perfume Maggie associated with her old friend was present, drawing her back to Virginia Beach and heartfelt conversations shared with a woman she admired.

"So do you," Maggie told her as they parted, taking in the pixie haircut, the blond locks streaked with gray. "I saw you on 'Herman's Place' a few months ago. You were phenomenal."

"Thank you." Judith offered a warm smile. "I've been offered a permanent role."

"That's wonderful! I'm so happy for you."

"I see you're here with Lance." Judith gave her a searching look. "How did that happen?"

Maggie smiled softly. "It's a long story. He's different."

"So are you," she said knowingly, giving Maggie's arm a light squeeze. "I'm going to mingle. Don't go without saying goodbye."

"Never," Maggie swore, turning to the spot she'd last seen Lance.

He stood alone near the doorway, catching her gaze on him. His face dark with hidden thoughts, he studied her as she studied him. He felt inches from her when he was truly feet. Then he winked at her and turned toward an area of the floor that was raised up higher than the rest as Diane stepped onto it.

"Hi. As you all know by now, I'm Diane Friar. If you'd take a seat, please." She waited until they were all seated.

Judith sat next to Maggie and when Maggie motioned for Lance to join her, he shook his head with a shrug and nodded to Diane. Maggie had no idea what that meant, but if he didn't want to sit by her, fine. She turned her attention to Diane.

"I want to thank you all for coming. This is quite a thing, having all of you in my home." Diane clasped her hands together and smiled. "I suppose I should start with a little background information on me and what I do. I worked as a therapist for years, mostly with children and young adults, and during that time, I saw a lot of saddening things. I wanted to reach out, to make a difference on a larger scale, but I never knew how. I set that goal aside when I retired and instead focused on running the bed and breakfast."

She gestured to where Lance stood near the wall, his expression blank as he watched her. "Lance had an idea for a televised show. He brought it to my attention and we hashed things out, trying to think of the best possible way to do what we each had in mind while somehow incorporating both of our views, goals, and inspirations."

Diane met the eyes of each of the twenty-something attendants. "The money you paid to attend is appreciated, but we don't necessarily need money to get started. What we do need are sponsors—important people with voices that can make a difference, that will be heard. And that's where you all come in." Her smile deepened. "That's my cue to step down and let Lance better explain."

Lance touched her shoulder as he stepped past Diane. He smiled his winning smile and looked at the faces set his way. His eyes landed on Maggie's, held, and passed.

"I asked you all here because I am on a quest. Originally, it was more of a selfish one. I thought a reality fitness show featuring me working with celebrities was a good idea. Don't get me wrong, it could work, and it would probably do pretty well, but I think there is something better I could be doing."

As Maggie listened to him, she tilted her head, an epiphany striking her, tightening her throat with emotion. Lance was responsible for the invitation. She swallowed and looked down to hide the tears that came to her eyes. He was the arrogant prick he'd mentioned that would be speaking. Lance had orchestrated the whole thing. That showed deviance, and ambition. Maggie was impressed.

He smiled dryly. "I was recently inspired by a friend and I want to inspire you. The reason I chose this place for the dinner is because Diane would like to donate the bed and breakfast to the program, and I wanted you all to see what you would be backing up."

Maggie stared at Lance, seeing a new side to him, a side that was always there, waiting for him to discover it.

"We all deal with physical insecurities—even me, shockingly. When do those start? What causes them?" Lance paced back and forth, the passion in his voice unable to be contained as he moved like a caged animal. "Every adult with issues didn't wake up one day and think badly of themselves. That started long ago, when their minds were sponges and soaked up everything around them. Every word, written or said, made those children into the adults they became."

Lance faced the silent room, every eye riveted to him. "I want to change that. People need to be shown, as children, that they don't have anything wrong with them. That will alter their whole outlook on life, and make them do things as adults they wouldn't otherwise even consider. If you tell a kid they can do anything, and they really believe it, they can. Simple as that."

Gesturing to Diane, he said, "Diane wanted to help kids. I wanted to help adults. Then we decided, why not help both? With the program we have in mind, we want to pair up kids with adults, have a buddy system, and let them encourage one another to better themselves—their mental and physical health foremost.

"I thought a show with multiple contestants was the way to go—it was brought to my attention, again by my friend, that that may cause conflict and feelings of ineptitude, so I would like to focus on only a few children and adults at a time. The word contestant isn't even going to be used.

"This isn't a game—this is a lifestyle. All activities are to be supervised. We want exercise programs, counseling sessions, pep talks, guest speakers, even craft time. We want this place to be a haven, a sanctuary for people, a place to learn how to make better choices, have better a self-image. I think that parts of the experience should be televised, only for promotional purposes and to get the word out. Commercials. Just enough to let people know what we're doing."

Lance paused and smiled a bright, white smile. "I think you know why I asked you all here."

"Can I sign up?" Benton Jamison called from the back of the room and soft chuckles rang out.

"I hope you will," he said. "We have a program for you, Benton."

He slapped the side of his hand to his palm as he spoke. "Constant positivity is the difference between loving yourself and thinking you're unlovable. I want to keep this short, so I'll end with this: we have power. Let's help children realize they have it too. If you'd like to hear more about the program and what Diane and I hope to do with it, don't hesitate to approach either of us. Thank you."

Maggie jumped to her feet, clapping loudly. Lance's fervency, that spark of empowerment, spoke to her, made her want to take on the world and change it. Others applauded, but none as exuberantly as her. Lance found her in the crowd, smiled, and stepped away from the small platform. He was immediately flocked by dinner guests. She longed to approach him, but didn't want to interrupt. It was his night, and he was acing it. Maggie contented herself with watching him, wonder swelling her heart.

"He's turned into an impressive man," Judith murmured from beside her.

Not for the first time, Maggie felt her eyes prick with tears. "Yes. He has."

"You're the friend he mentioned, aren't you? The one that inspired him."

She shrugged, a smile so wide it hurt her mouth, stretched across her lips. "I think so, yes."

Her old friend patted her shoulder. "He has my support."

Taking a deep breath, Maggie wiped her eyes and watched the man she loved make her fall more in love with him. The evening went by fast, most of it spent with her studying Lance from afar, but she didn't mind. Maggie liked watching him. He repeatedly found her with his eyes, smiled, and found her again.

She slipped away from the party as night lengthened, tired from the drive and yearning for rest and Lance. Maggie took a long bath in the claw foot tub, letting the scented water wrap around her, and dressed in a slinky pink nightgown, she moved for the bed. A knock sounded at the door, soft and authoritative. Wanting to run to the door, Maggie paced herself with measured steps, one hand pressed to her pounding heart.

Maggie opened the door to a disheveled but content Lance. His jacket was gone, shirt untucked with the first few buttons undone. His dark hair was hanging partially over his forehead and he pushed it back as he smiled a sweet, exhausted smile. She squeezed the door to keep her hands from him.

"Hey, I'm sorry I was a sucky date. I just . . . well, you saw. I was hoping people would be interested, but I didn't realize they would be that interested. It's—this is great. Really great." Lance dazzled her by widening his smile. "Anyway, I wanted to apologize."

"I accept your apology." Maggie crossed her arms and rested her shoulder against the doorframe, trying not to let the emotions coursing through her veins overwhelm her. "You lied to me."

"Yes." Lance paused. "Which time are you referencing?"

"There is no reality fitness show for me to co-host. That's why you told me no."

"Well, there was the outline for one, but no, there isn't, not anymore. I don't need a fitness show to impress you when I have young minds to do the work for me."

"Why didn't you just tell me?"

He looked down. "I was scared. I was nervous," Lance quietly added.

Maggie swallowed, her throat tight at the confession he usually denied. "If you're not going to need a co-host, then what do you plan on doing with me?"

Lance's eyes narrowed as he tried to figure out what she meant.

"I want to help," she said simply.

"It could be months, or even years, before anything comes of it. There is a lot to figure out yet," Lance warned, never looking away from her. The fatigue was there, but an alertness straightened his stance.

One shoulder lifted and lowered. "You'll let me know."

As he studied her, light hit his eyes and blazed across his face. Lance nodded, his mouth curved in a smile. He looked down, the smile growing as he turned his face away. "Yeah. I'll let you know."

Maggie took a deep breath, shaking from what she was about to say. "And right now, what do you plan on doing with me?"

Lance went still, carefully lifting his head. Maggie stared back, her lips parted, heart hammering against the wall of her chest. Time disappeared as they looked at one another. She wanted him to step into her room. His smile came back. Maggie wanted Lance to stay. As though knowing her thoughts, he winked at her.

"Well," he said slowly, pushing past her and entering the room. "I know I plan on spending the night with you." Lance unbuttoned his shirt. "Unless you tell me to go?"

She didn't move or speak, frozen by the heated way he looked at her.

"Are you going to tell me to go?"

"No, I'm not going to tell you to go," Maggie said, closing the door. Pulse fast, stomach knotted up, she met his darkened eyes.

"Perfect," he said in a rough voice. "That makes everything easier."

Lance took off his shirt and chucked it to the floor, his expression determined. The undershirt went next, thrown behind him with total disregard. It landed on the large rose-painted vase near the window. Then Lance strode for her, stopping inches from her and firmly gripping her face between his hands.

"I'm going back to Ohio, you're going to Iowa." It was a reminder, and a question.

Maggie dug her fingers into his shoulders and nodded. She knew. If that one night was the only night they got to share again, she wanted to take it, and treasure it, and never forget it.

"Maggie."

She frowned at his serious tone, looking into fierce blue eyes.

He stared at her, everything about Lance saying he was sincere. "It was real."

"You're not supposed to make someone cry before sex," she protested, her eyes burning at his words.

"I figured if we got the crying out of the way now, there would be less chance of it later." His full mouth lifted in a partial smile.

Maggie moved her hands to the back of his neck and pulled him to her. She closed her eyes and forgot to think, letting touch and need alone guide her. The heat of his body mixed with the scent of his skin was maddening. Maggie wanted more than his lips, more than his body, more than one night. More than was offered. Maggie wanted all of Lance.

It was sensual, his body strong and fit, eyes storm-filled, lips alternately firm and coaxing. They moved around the room in the dizzying dance of lovers, eventually ending on the bed. Clothes and inhibitions gone, Lance ended his months-long abstinence. Maggie smiled against his shoulder at the thought, then quietly laughed.

"What's so funny?" he panted, going still. "You're going to give me a complex if you keep laughing."

She laughed harder, moving in a way that made his head drop forward as a moan was pulled from him. "I'm just glad I could help you return from the solitude of celibacy."

"You're going to continue to help me tonight, many times," Lance told her, proving the truth of his words.

Later, in the dark, they lay together in the bed, miles and miles from one another's homes and yet right where they should be. Maggie's heart was broken, but it didn't hurt. It was splintered in a good way—the way that a past love could reawaken, even if only for an impermanent span of time. She'd loved Lance as a young woman, but loving him as a grown one showed her things she hadn't realized as a teenager. They never would have worked then.

They'd had to end, but endings eventually turned into beginnings.

"I love you," he whispered into her hair, an arm holding her to his side.

She went still, tears filling her eyes and spilling over to drip to his bare chest. It was hard for him to say that when they were young, but he'd said it then without hesitation, without provocation. Without Maggie saying it first. Lance wiped away her tears with his thumb.

"Crying before and after is a bad sign."

Maggie laughed shakily and kissed his collarbone. "Don't tell me goodbye, okay?"

"I won't," Lance promised, and sometime during the hours while Maggie slept the dreamless slumber of a woman at peace, he left.

LANCE—2000

LANCE DIDN'T KNOW whose house they were partying at, but Donovan had assured him he knew someone there. Not that it mattered to Lance. The basement was finished, and had white carpet—bad choice, in his opinion—with tan walls. Whoever lived there was an outdoorsman, the wall mounts of antlers, various animal heads, and fish making that clear. Lance used to want to do those kinds of things with his dad, but his dad was always too busy.

Beer in hand, he scanned the crowd of mashed bodies in the softly lit room. The furniture was pushed to the sides to allow space for dancing. Loud, fast-paced music surrounded him, pulsed in his ears like it came directly from his head. Donovan was off with his latest conquest—a daughter of one of his father's previous clients—and Lance had no clue where he'd gone.

A brunette sidled up to him, flipping her straight hair over her shoulder. She smiled at him, brown eyes shining from too much alcohol, and possibly something stronger. Her perfume was potent and made him think of vanilla, but it wasn't pleasant.

She poked his arm with a sharp fingernail. "You're Lance Denton."

"Yep." He looked at the mass of dancing bodies and sipped his beer. He wasn't in the mood for adoring fans, and as soon as he found Donovan, he was leaving.

"I'm Jessie. I watch your show all the time—well, not *your* show, but the show you're on." She waved at a friend and turned back to him. "It's so crazy you're here. Did Maggie Smiley come with you?"

Lance's hand froze near his mouth and then he emptied the can, setting it down on the mantel behind him. "We're not dating anymore."

"Oh, I know. Everyone knows. That was, you know, big news for a while." She laughed. It was a shrill sound that made a shudder crawl along his back. "I just thought that since you were both here, maybe she came with you. I can't believe you're both in my house. How weird is that? Wow. I feel special."

Jessie smiled. "You're still friends, right? I mean, you have to be, working together all the time. That would be hard. Breaking up and then having to see each other like that. How do you guys do it?" She shook her head, looking sympathetic.

He stared at her, willing her to shut up, but also wanting to know why she thought Maggie was there. "Maggie's here?"

Jessie started to answer, but a commotion pulled their attention to the middle of the room. There she was, dressed in a thin, tight black top and black jeans with purple boots, dancing with two guys. A circle formed around them, people cheering and whistling.

In one upraised hand she held a beer, the other resting on the shoulder of the guy in front of her. Her hair was pulled up, baring her slender neck. She looked wild, and crazy, and stunning. Maggie tipped her head back and laughed when the guy behind her grabbed her hips and ground against her.

His hands went into fists and Lance's skin heated up. He moved a step forward without being aware, and then forced himself to remain where he was. Lance took a deep breath, and another. She wasn't his. Maggie could do whatever the hell she wanted. He did. The tick that formed under his eye said he wasn't okay with her doing what he did.

"I guess you found her," Jessie said quietly, worriedly eyeing him. "Are you okay?"

"I need a beer."

"Oh. Sure. I'll get you one."

Lance clamped a hand on her wrist when she turned to go. "I'll get it."

Jessie's eyebrows lowered. "Yeah. Okay. Go for it. They're—"

"I know where they are." Lance let go of her and strode for the bar.

Beer was no longer going to cut it, and he switched to plain vodka. It burned his throat and warmed his chest. Lance had four shots before going in search of Donovan. His head felt foggy, but not enough to wipe Maggie from it.

He found his friend in a darkened bedroom, half-dressed and in the process of opening a condom wrapper. "I'll be out . . . soon," he told Lance. "Or not soon. But . . . eventually. Give me an hour, tops."

The girl lying on the bed beneath him giggled and pulled him to her, kissing Donovan like she wanted to suck off his face. Lance closed the door on them, restless and agitated.

A redhead stopped him on his way back to the main party, fondling him and offering drugs. He shook his head, pushing past her. Drugs weren't really his thing and right then the thought of sex made his stomach roil. He kept seeing Maggie, sandwiched between two men, and it was screwing with his head. He wanted to bash in their faces, and he wanted to grab Maggie and run.

A slow song came on and Lance looked up to see Maggie a few feet away with a different guy, their bodies close as they swayed on their feet. He snorted and shook his head, positive it was cosmic payback for him to have to witness that. The song changed and he lost sight of her. Lance took two more shots, his anger giving way to sorrow as the booze flooded his system.

The air became stifling as more bodies appeared. Needing a breather, Lance stumbled up the stairs and out the front door, gulping in the cool February night air. He went to his ass on the ground, and then he let his head fall back, banging it against a small, sharp rock. It wasn't long before he was shivering in his tee shirt and jeans. Spread-eagled on the gravel driveway, he didn't move, not caring if a car drove over him.

Lance closed his eyes and inhaled, but the sound of angry voices had him immediately springing to his feet. He recognized Maggie's voice, faint as it was. He followed the sound of it, footsteps fast as he shot through bushes and tree limbs, finding her with a tall, dark-haired guy near the backside of the house. The yard was spacious and clear, and the moon perfectly spotlighted the pair.

"I said no." Maggie tried to get around the guy, but he blocked her.

"Come on, don't be a tease," he coaxed, a hand moving for her chest.

"Don't touch me!" She slapped his hand away.

The man grabbed her wrist. "You're being a bitch right now, you know that?"

Lance's jaw hardened and he shoved the guy to the side. "Get away from her."

The guy was taller and more muscular than Lance and his pupils were dilated with a drug of some kind. "What the hell is your problem?"

"Touch her again, and I'll break your fingers," Lance vowed, moving between the two.

"You're Lance Denton, aren't you? Think you're a tough guy, huh, just because you got money?" he snarled, fingers clenching and releasing as he advanced.

"No, I'm a tough guy because if you touch her again, I'm going to break your fingers," he said slowly.

He looked around Lance. "Tell him to get lost."

"No. I want you to go." Her voice was shaky, but firm. "I made a mistake. I don't want to do this."

The guy's face darkened and he took a step closer. "Give me back the drugs and I'll go."

Lance glanced over his shoulder at Maggie, saw the guilt and shame crash over her face. He faced the guy once more. "You need to leave."

"Those drugs cost money! I want them back, or I want a piece of ass to compensate for the loss of them. You promised me a good time, and you're going to deliver."

Rage slammed through him and Lance swung, clipping the guy's chin and setting his knuckles on fire. The guy staggered back, face twisting, and Lance braced himself when he came at him. The guy was big, but he was clumsy. Knowing it was going to hurt, Lance readied himself for pain and punched him again. Something cracked in his hand as it connected with his face, and the guy fell to his knees, crumpling on the grass with a groan. Lance's hand throbbed, already swelling.

Without saying a word, Lance took Maggie by the hand and dragged her along behind him. He was angry at her—at her behavior, at her actions, at the way she was treating herself. She stayed quiet, tripping once and righting herself, until they were in the front yard.

Maggie jerked her hand from his, rubbing the flesh around it. "Thank you," she said stiffly, avoiding his eyes.

"How did you get here?" Lance stared at her pale face, not recognizing the person before him.

"How did you get here?" she shot back.

"I have a designated driver to take me home. Do you?"

Maggie laughed darkly. "You just knocked him out. Pretty sure he wouldn't have taken me home now anyway, though, so whatever."

"What are you doing to yourself?" It was a question, and a plea, and a demand.

She pressed her lips together and looked at a copse of trees nearby, her arms around her frail frame as though to hold in heat.

Lance put his face close to hers and she had no choice but to look at him. "Drugs? You're doing drugs now?"

"Like you haven't," she sneered.

"Yeah, but not often, and not anymore. And especially not from people who could hurt me." Frustrated, he gestured to her body. "And you're so damn skinny. Are you not eating, are you sick, what? What is going on with you?"

She blinked her eyes, her mouth quivering. "Haven't you read the tabloids? No one likes a fat actress."

"Are you insane?" Lance threw up his hands. "You are skin and bones," he said thickly. "There isn't an ounce of fat on you. You've never been fat. Stop doing this. Whatever you're doing, stop."

Maggie dropped her arms and glared at him. "Don't worry about me, okay? I have it under control."

"You do not have it under control," he retorted. "You barely look like you're hanging on."

"Just leave me alone," she mumbled, stumbling toward the house.

Lance went after her. "What drug did you do, Maggie?"

She spun around. "Leave me alone!" Maggie's eyes were unfocused and dark, her face warped with fury. "I want nothing to do with you! I can't stand the sight of you. I hate you. I hate you."

He fell back a step, surprised by the outburst.

"You don't hate me," he said softly.

"You kept pushing me and pushing me. You had to get to me. You couldn't leave me alone." Her eyes shone with dampness and betrayal. "I was the one girl who wanted to be left alone, the one girl who didn't need you to want them, and you just couldn't have that, could you? You needed to prove something. I hate you, Lance Denton. I hate you as much as I once loved you."

"You don't . . ." His voice faded and it hurt to pull air into his lungs. "You don't mean that. You don't hate me. Maggie . . . Maggie, you know I loved you. I know I said . . . what I said, but I did love you. I did."

"Shut up, Lance. I can't even stand to hear your voice. Do you know that? I hate everything about you." Tears streamed from eyes that stared into him and saw nothing. "That love I had for you? That was with my whole being, with all I had to give. That's how much I loved you. I was the one person who would have loved you no matter what, and you couldn't handle that. You had to prove that love is always expendable. It didn't have to be. Not with me."

His throat closed and Lance dropped his eyes to his shoes. There was no conscious decision to sabotage their relationship, but subconsciously? Yeah. It was there. He couldn't deal with emotions like that. Lance didn't know how.

Maggie moved closer to him, and with her eyes locked on his, she whispered against his mouth, "I want you to remember what my love felt like, and I want you to know that depth of emotion, that aweing, overwhelming, all-consuming way I loved you, and imagine that as hate. Take all of that love, and turn it into something bad, and there you go. You have it. Enjoy it."

"I'll take it," he breathed, his lips grazing hers.

She blinked, touching a hand to her mouth as she put space between them. "What?"

Lance shrugged, the pressure in his chest escalating, crushing him. "I'll take it, Maggie, I'll take whatever you give me, just . . . don't do this to yourself. Please."

Her face crumpled. "You never stop, do you?"

"No. I don't know how with you." Lance wrapped his arms around her and buried his face against her neck. He was shaking, holding her and yet he felt like he had none of her. "I'm sorry, Maggie. You know I'm sorry."

She was stiff in his arms. "I know, but it doesn't matter." Maggie took his hands from her and turned toward the house. "Don't talk to me anymore, Lance. Talking to you hurts me."

Maggie took two steps and collapsed.

The ambulance was there in minutes, but it felt like hours.

He didn't know how he got to the hospital—he thought he remembered telling Donovan to drop him off and go.

Lance wasn't allowed to see her, and it felt like he was unconscious right along with her.

The walls were white, piercing through his retinas and shoving nothingness into his soul.

There were chairs.

And people.

And noise. Noise surrounded him, and all he heard was silence.

He wanted to smell oranges, and bleach instead filled his nose.

Judith was there.

Maggie's dad.

Her mom.

Nora.

Lance was alone.

He wasn't told anything, eyes blinded by hot tears and still searching their faces for a sign that she was okay.

Lance stood set apart from them, scared, lost, and ignored.

And then they left to go to Maggie.

The door was closed. It would stay closed for him.

Flashes of Maggie stormed through his head.

The first smile she gave him.

The first real kiss.

Her laughter.

Her anger.

The last time she loved him.

The last real smile.

The broken look on her face when he cheated on her with Tabitha.

The sadness that never really went away when she looked at him.

How she got skinnier.

And skinnier.

And skinnier.

The pain in her eyes.

The hatred.

The last thing she said to him.

Lance was driven half-mad with the images of her, and with the fear pounding with his heart, streaming through his veins, and clamped tight to his back. It shadowed him. Hovered. Whispered in his ear. What if she wasn't okay? What if there was permanent damage? What if she didn't make it? He knew nothing. *Nothing.*

Lance paced the length of the waiting room, trembling and jumpy and sick. His heart literally ached, his arms heavy with the need to hold her. He just wanted to see her. Just once. And then he would go.

He couldn't take it anymore.

Sprinting for the room marked as hers, Lance reached for the doorknob and was stopped by a doctor. "You're not allowed to go in there, Mr. Denton."

"Why?" he rasped.

"It was the patient's orders."

He rested his hands against the door and lowered his head. She had to be okay then, if she'd been lucid enough to tell someone that. That was a good thing, even as it twisted his heart that that was what she wanted.

Lance nodded and straightened. "She's going to be okay? She must be. Right? Please tell me." His eyes pleaded with the doctor.

The brown-haired man dressed in slacks and a dress shirt inclined his head. "I cannot tell you that. You look tired. Some rest would be good for you. Why don't you go home? I'm sure someone will call you and let you know."

"I'll go, as soon as I know she's all right," Lance said in a flat voice.

The doctor eyed him, clasping his hands. "That's not possible."

Frustrated, Lance fisted his hand and brought it to the door. "Maggie! Please, Maggie, let me see you. Let me see you and I'll leave! Maggie."

The doctor grabbed his shoulder. "Step away from the door, or I'm going to call the police." He was calm, bored even.

Lance shrugged him off and moved with imbalanced, heavy steps. "I'm fine. I'm going."

He didn't go.

He couldn't.

Judith found him the next morning, hunched over in the seat in which he'd slept off and on. Lance's eyes were on fire, his mouth dry. He went to stand, but his legs were too weak. He stared at her, bleak and broken.

"She's going to be okay," she told him.

Lance's shoulders fell and he dropped his head to his hands, tears stinging his eyes.

"She's exhausted, stressed out, and not eating right. That, combined with the drugs and alcohol in her system, was too much for her body. She's stable now, but Maggie has a long way to go before she's healthy. It has been suggested that she see someone, a professional—someone that can help her."

"Thank you," he whispered as he lifted his head. Lance didn't see kindness in the gray eyes set on him, but he thought he saw empathy.

"I know you still love her, messed up as the whole situation is," Judith said, fiddling with her earlobe. "And because of that, I'm going to give you some advice."

Lance slowly stood, bracing himself for Judith's words.

"Let her live her life, Lance, and stay out of it. She won't be able to get better unless she can move on from you, and if she's around you, she won't be able to do that."

He stared at the woman. "The show's done."

Judith met his gaze. "Not officially, but yes, the show is done."

With tears on his cheeks, he nodded, knowing she was right. It was over. Maggie and Lance were done. It was all done.

"Go home. Get some rest. Take care of yourself."

"Yeah," he muttered. "Sure."

Lance turned away from Judith and walked out of the hospital, feeling like he left a part of himself—the best part—back in the building. He aimlessly treaded through the hospital parking lot in the frigid air, coatless and numb. Lance was vaguely aware of Donovan jumping out of his car and ushering Lance to it. He sat in the passenger seat, not speaking until Donovan asked him if Maggie was all right.

He nodded, his throat tightening each time he tried to swallow.

"You waited for me?" Lance stared out the windshield.

"Yeah, man, I'm your friend. Of course I waited for you." Donovan put the car in drive and left the parking lot.

With his friend beside him, Lance dropped his face to his hands and broke down, finally feeling the loss of Maggie.

MAGGIE—2010

WHEN THE DOORBELL rang three times, right after another, Maggie paused with the coffee cup to her lips. Her pulse shot up in tempo. Only one man would be impatient and arrogant enough to ring a doorbell, not once, but three times. She hadn't seen him since the night of the fundraiser over two weeks ago, and she hadn't known when she would see him again.

That night was all they'd allowed themselves to have, and Maggie had reconciled with herself that it would be enough.

She got to her feet and started for the door. She backtracked, set down the coffee mug with fingers that shook, and headed toward the front of the house once more. Fingering her hair, she tugged at her pink sweater, checked to see that no lint was on her charcoal-colored leggings, and took a deep breath before opening the door.

Lance leaned against the doorframe, but the customary grin was gone, eyes like lightning locked on her. His dark hair was swept back, black jacket and blue jeans hugging his frame. It was unbearable how much she'd missed him. Seeing him was cruel, and joyful, and cruel again.

"Hello, Maggie," he uttered in his deep voice.

Maggie shook with the need to touch him. She swallowed and stumbled away from the door. He took that as an invitation to enter the house, grazing his body against hers as he pushed past her, and leaving pinpricks of excruciating elation in his wake.

"H-hello," she croaked, lowering her eyes from his frowning face.

"I believe this belongs to you."

Maggie looked at his hand, saw the unmarked green case that held a disc. Her pulse went into a maddening beat and she felt ill.

"Take it," he enticed in a deadly voice.

She did, keeping her gaze down.

"Explain to me what this is."

"It's a disc." Maggie set it down on a nearby desk.

"Yes. I see that." Lance's voice went from sinisterly soft to loud and jovial, a potent warning sign that he was not happy. "Thanks for clarifying. I appreciate it. Now." Lance waited until she looked at him to continue. He was smiling, but it was feral. "Tell me why you sent it to me."

"It's a CD." Maggie clenched her hands to quell their shaking.

Lance shook his head before she finished speaking. "No. I didn't ask what it was. I asked why you sent it to me. Stay on track, please."

Maggie crossed her arms as she lifted her head.

A faint smile lifted half of his mouth, though his eyes remained serious. "Why did you send it?"

She opened her mouth to answer.

"Because, when I saw the mail with your name on it, I thought all kinds of wonderful, maddening, fearful things. And then as I opened the package and stared at what was inside, I thought more things. As the days went by, I thought other things. You don't want to know the things I thought. I'm sure none of them were accurate. Tell me. Tell me why you sent it," he urged quietly.

"I would if you'd ever stop talking," she grumbled.

"It was either that, or put my hands on you. You don't want that," Lance told her, moving closer.

"I-I don't?"

"No." He shook his head, the space between them falling away with each step he took.

"Why not?"

"If I put my hands on you, Maggie, I'll either strangle you, or never let you go, which . . . could also result in me strangling you. That would be bad." He tilted his head. "I think it would be bad. Right? That would be bad? Yes. That would be bad."

Annoyance set her jaw forward. "You're not making any sense and I don't know what you're asking me."

"Why did you send me the disc," he roared, his face twisted with frustration, and behind that, fear.

Maggie blinked, reaching out a hand, but Lance was already moving away.

Lance paced the span of the foyer as she watched, helpless and unsure. "Because, to me, sentimental and weak as I am, hope had me thinking it was to reach out to me, that maybe you missed me, or were giving me some kind of sign that, I don't know, that you care about me—or want more than just friendship from me, that maybe you want *me*."

He paused to glare at her. "Stupid, I know."

"Lance, wait a minute."

He resumed pacing, gesturing above his head as he talked. Lance paused by the staircase, stared up it, and then continued. "Then I thought, maybe it's been about revenge the whole time, that you've been playing me, that you never really forgave me, that you wanted to torture me some more because of the stupid, stupid things I did as a kid, but then I thought, Maggie can't be that cruel. The time I've been here was real. We both changed, matured, and got over the past—plus, we had great sex. Multiple times. I went back to thinking maybe you sent it as a way to let me know . . . something. I don't know what."

Lance stopped. His stance beseeched, questioned, and longed. She felt his need through the air that separated them.

"But that's all you sent me. A disc. No note. Nothing. I have no idea what you're doing, or why you sent it. I'm lost. I've been driving myself insane wondering, and thinking, and hoping, and—and going back to wondering." He swallowed. "We didn't give each other promises. We didn't say a single thing about the future, about the possibility of one, and I . . . I told myself I could deal with that, that I had to deal with that."

"Lance," she tried again.

"But then you sent me the CD . . . and then I went through all the crazy scenarios in my head, and then . . . then it didn't even matter anymore, because I thought, if Maggie sent that to me, then I have a reason to go to her. You cannot imagine how evilly giddy that made me. Just to see you, be near you. But damn, it'll be hard to stay away once I leave again."

"Lance!" Maggie grabbed his wrists and squeezed. "Listen to me, okay?"

He looked at her, blinking as fog lifted from his eyes. "Tell me what's going on."

"I'm trying," she said with exasperation.

"Well, quit stalling and get it over with." He scowled at her like he hadn't been monopolizing the conversation for the last ten minutes.

Maggie smiled, touching a wayward strand of hair near his temple. "Did you play it?" She clapped a hand over his mouth when it opened. "Yes or no." She gave him a pointed look before removing her hand. "Yes or no."

"No."

"Why?"

"Because I was too damn scared to, all right! I'm terrified to play that CD."

She frowned.

He sighed and ran a trembling hand through his hair. "What if it's hours and hours of you screaming how much you despise me? Or—or putting a hex on me? Or . . . I don't know . . . what if it's country music?"

Maggie laughed at the horrified look on his face. "Let me play it for you, okay?"

Lance looked unsure of the smartness of that.

Shaking her head, she went to the den and put the CD in the player, pushed the 'play' button, and then turned. Lance stood directly behind her, eyes dark with need. His eyebrows lowered as he studied her face. He put his hands on her waist and dug in his fingers, dropping his forehead to hers. Maggie held still, breaths constricted, heart hammering. He was restrained volatility, shaking with the longing she reciprocated.

"We have had a lot of firsts and lasts," he said thickly.

Maggie's face crumpled and she was glad that he couldn't see it. "We have."

"I want all of my firsts and lasts to be with you from now on, and no one else."

A small sob left her and Maggie pressed her cheek hard to his, feeling his cheekbone against hers. "I want the same."

'Always' by Bon Jovi started to play.

Lance's grip became painful and he took a shuddering breath. "That's what you sent me?"

She nodded jerkily, her throat too tight to speak.

"You just killed me," he said hoarsely.

Maggie lifted her head and looked into Lance's stricken, hopeful eyes.

"Is there a chance for us to be together again?" he asked.

"I want there to be," she told him.

"I do too. I didn't think it was possible."

She brushed silky black hair from Lance's face, gaze riveted to his. "Sometimes we get to decide our endings, our beginnings, and everything in between. I want this to be our new beginning—with Bon Jovi playing our song in the background."

Maggie laughed softly as Lance grinned and kissed her cheek.

"Always," he softly mocked.

LANCE—2013

"ARE YOU READY to do this?" Maggie asked, looking anxious as her wine-colored eyes met his. Her hair was up, showing off her sweet features, and the salmon-colored dress she wore made her skin glow. She got prettier as the years went. And Lance—Lance got more and more content.

"Yeah. Sure. How bad can it be?" he returned, swallowing thickly.

She smiled reassuringly at him and clasped his hand, her wedding band digging into his palm. He liked the feel of it, knowing there was physical proof that Maggie was his. There wasn't a chance in hell he'd ever be letting her go again. When he died, his cold, lifeless body would have to be pried away from her, because even then, he'd still be holding her. Lance supposed that was a bit morbid, but true, nonetheless.

"You're going to be amazing, Lance."

It was a warm spring day, the landscape around them cast in varying shades of green shrubbery. He never would have guessed he'd be happiest in the country in Ohio, but then, he hadn't known much when he was younger. Lance followed her gaze to the grassy turf, seeing teeth and claws as shrill sounds came from the beings before them. The sun was hidden behind clouds, cooling the air but somehow missing Lance. He swiped his free hand across his damp forehead and swallowed again.

"How do you know that?"

"Because you're an amazing guy," Maggie said.

"What if I say the wrong thing?"

"You won't."

"What if my hair looks bad?"

She laughed, tugging on a strand near his neck. Sharply sweet sensation erupted along his scalp. "Your hair never looks bad. It's very annoying, if you must know. Now stop worrying. You're going to be great, like always."

He turned to her, wanting to doubt her words. The conviction in her eyes told him not to try it. Maggie's faith in him made him feel unconquerable, like a superhero whose only role in life was to have the love of one woman, to prove again and again that he was better with her than he ever was without. It wasn't hard to do. He *was* better.

"The camera crew is ready," his wife prompted, nodding to where multiple people and gadgets waited.

"Look at them." Lance pointed to the blanket. "Uncivilized little creatures. They're vicious heathens," he whispered just as one kicked the other in the leg.

Maggie laughed, the sound twisting his insides in a welcome hurt. Any day he heard her laughter was a guaranteed good day. There were so many empty, worthless years where he would have given anything to hear it, or merely her voice—years where he would have done anything to pretend he still had her love. He didn't have to pretend anymore. He had it, he cherished it.

"They're probably going to pull my hair and bite me the whole time. What will the viewers think?"

"They'll think you're much cooler now than you were as a teenager." She stepped away and patted his arm.

"I don't think that's possible."

"This was your idea," Maggie reminded him.

"I know, and I regret it. How are we going to get through this? They're going to eat us alive." Lance shot her a panicked look. "Were they fed?"

"Yes, about ten minutes ago. You are so cute when it comes to the twins. Let's go, before they notice the film crew and want to play with them." Maggie threaded her fingers through his and tugged.

It took half a dozen steps to reach Clark and Josephine. Copper-haired and blue-eyed, the one-year-olds looked angelic but were, in actuality, tiny deviants. Nora had been less than thrilled to find out that she wouldn't be the only one in the family with twins. Then she saw Clark and Josephine, and as with all who came in contact with them, she was theirs. Lance and Maggie belonged to them from the moment they knew the twins existed.

The twins sat on a red blanket in the backyard of their Ohio country home—Josephine in a blue dress and Clark in tan pants and a blue shirt—and babbled to one another, causing Lance's heart to squeeze and release.

One look and Lance caved, a single cry and he gave them whatever they wanted. He was worthless against their charm. They were smelly, continually leaking, noise-making, fleshy blobs—and he loved them, and Maggie, with overwhelming intensity. With his little family, life was a dream he never thought he'd have.

Lance parked himself on the blanket behind Maggie, reaching for the closest Denton baby, and commenced to cover Clark in kisses. He squealed and kicked his legs, landing one of his shoed feet to Lance's groin. Lance grunted, giving Maggie an agonized look. She laughed and stroked Josephine's head of soft hair as their daughter waved her hands up and down and blew bubbles with the drool leaving her mouth.

"Are you ready?" the interviewer, Kirk Laughlin, asked, smiling at the babies.

From the way his brown eyes lit up when he looked at them, Lance could tell he was smitten. Seconds—it only took seconds. He already knew their teenage years were going to suck the sanity right out of his brain.

"Yes," Maggie said. "I think so."

She looked at Lance and he nodded.

The interviewer knelt beside them. "We'll start by going through the history of 'Easier Said' and how you two came to be where you are now, what marriage and having a set of twins is like. Then we'll talk about the success of the program the two of you co-run with Diane Friar."

Kirk looked at Maggie. "I also want to make sure we mention Smiley Soaps—your home-based soap making company. Everything you make is donated to kids in need, and I like how you incorporated workshops into the Berryhill House Project so that kids can make their own to take home. It's teaching them about responsibility, and also gives them a sense of accomplishment. It seems like a simple thing, but it means a lot, Mrs. Denton. What you're doing is commendable."

"Thank you. I enjoy doing it. Most of the time we have to prove to ourselves that we can do things on our own before we believe it," Maggie said, her eyes shining bright.

"Even with making soap," Lance murmured, staring at his wife. Damn, she was breathtaking.

"Even with soap," she quietly agreed.

Lance touched a lock of her hair to get her attention, and when she turned those large eyes on him, he winked. Maggie winked back, sending desire shooting through him like a potent injection straight to his lower region. He gave her a warning look and she smiled. He mouthed that he loved her and her smile grew, overtaking her face like the sun, blinding, ethereal.

Moving to a sitting position on the corner of the blanket, the interviewer said, "I want to talk about why you both are doing this and what your long term goals are for the program, and then we'll wrap up with some scenes of you playing with the twins. How's that sound? Should take about forty-five minutes to an hour, if everything goes smoothly."

"Let's do it," Lance said as Clark wiggled in his arms. He kissed his baby powder-scented head, leaned down to offer the same to Josephine, and then kissed his wife lastly, and firstly, and lastly.

"Tell me about the first time you two met . . ."

AUTHOR'S NOTE

WE ALL STRUGGLE with our looks—we think we should look a certain way, we think others expect us to look a certain way. It makes it hard to love ourselves, and when you can't be confident with who you are, the people around you don't as easily see that light we all have inside us. I myself have fought against my own vicious thoughts; that voice inside my head that tells me I need to eat less, be *skinny, skinny, skinny*. That nothing I ever do is good enough. That I'm ugly. That I'm worthless.

I hate that voice. That voice is a bitch.

I know it's hard to think we're beautiful when the mirror is telling us otherwise, but that's just a mirror—an insignificant, inanimate object that means *nothing* as far as our worth. Find something you like about yourself, tell yourself one thing unique that sets you apart from others. Believe that you're strong. Smash the mirrors—figuratively if not literally—and know you're more powerful than any lifeless piece of matter can ever be. You're more than anyone and anything around you. Be the voice that lifts you up. You have to protect yourself, even if it's from you. One simple sentence, if repeated often enough, can change your world: You are strong, you are beautiful, and you are loved.

And damn it, give yourself a hug, and love that imperfect body and that not so perfect face. They are yours. Own them.

ACKNOWLEDGEMENTS

SHODI MORIS WAS gracious enough to let me watch her make a batch of homemade soap, which is how I "somewhat" knew what I was talking about with the soap making scenes in Within This Frame. If you're interested in learning more about Shodi and her skills/products, check out her Facebook page and website *www.livingsecondnature.com*.

Special thanks to Amy Jibben Freese for the title suggestion of Within This Frame. It worked out brilliantly.

As always, thanks to all the people that were involved in putting this book together.

From the beta readers this round—Kathy Sheffler, Kelly Merkett, Judith Frazee, Kendra Gaither, Desiree Wallin, Megan Stietz, Tiffany Alfson, Tiffany Dodson, Jacinda Owen, Sarah Lowry, Jen Andrews, Tawnya Peltonen, Melissa Simmons, and Diana Hoenou-Smith—to Wendi Stitzer, editor extraordinaire, to Kelley C. Hanson, who took the photograph used on the cover, to Christine the formatter at Perfectly Publishable, and certainly to Kari Ayasha, who made the pretty cover—you all helped make my WIP an actual book. Thank you so much . . . and pretend that wasn't a super long sentence.

And, of course, much appreciation and love to the people who read my work: my eclectic, unique, amazing clan of Zartians.

ABOUT THE AUTHOR

LINDY ZART IS the USA Today bestselling author of Roomies. She has been writing since she was a child. Luckily for readers, her writing has improved since then. She lives in Wisconsin with her family. Lindy loves hearing from people who enjoy her work. She also has a completely healthy obsession with the following: coffee, wine, bloody marys, peanut butter, and pizza.

You can connect with Lindy at:
Google.com/+LindyZart
Twitter.com/LindyZart
Facebook.com/LindyZart
Lindyzart.com
Lindyzart@gmail.com

Listen to the playlists for Lindy's books on Spotify.com
Get an eBook autograph from Lindy at Authorgraph.com
Check out Lindy's YouTube channel.